Loose Diamonds

◇ *Loose Diamonds*

a novel by

Theodora Overton

with Barbara Morgan

FITHIAN PRESS, 2001
SANTA BARBARA, CALIFORNIA

Published by Fithian Press
A division of Daniel and Daniel, Publishers, Inc.
Post Office Box 1525
Santa Barbara, CA 93102
www.danielpublishing.com

LIBRARY OF CONGRESS CATALOGING-IN-PUBLICATION DATA
Overton, Theodora, (date)
    Loose diamonds : a novel / by Theodora Overton with Barbara Morgan.
      p. cm.
    ISBN 1-56474-355-1 (pbk. : alk. paper)
    1. Big Sur (Calif.)—Fiction. 2. Illegal arms transfers—Fiction. 3. Drug traffic—
Fiction. 4. Young women—Fiction. I. Morgan, Barbara. II. Title
    PS3565.V437 L66 2001
    813'.54—dc21   00-009926

For Lucy Dabney,
whose friendship made everything possible
and whose charm and loveliness were the inspiration
for the best parts of this tale.

*"It was a miracle of rare device; a sunny pleasure dome
with caves of ice."*

—Samuel Taylor Coleridge

Loose Diamonds

# ◊ Prologue

AS I RUMMAGED
through some old letters, a snapshot tumbled out. Its view of Spanish
iron gates through whose fretwork could be seen twisted, wind-bent cypress, brought back, in a rush of nostalgia, the excitement of a time long
gone and a place long forgotten.

Beyond the gates, up a winding graveled drive, high on a Big Sur
mountainside, surrounded by Monterey pines and cypress, was a ram-
bling early California adobe. Its setting was spectacular no matter what
the atmospheric conditions. At times the air was so cleanly clear it
seemed as if the cypress on the mountaintop could reach down and
dabble their spiny fingers in the ocean a thousand feet below. At other
times the mountaintop was totally misted, only the blurred forms of
objects showing through the veil of fog, as they do in the shrouded

11

distance of a Chinese painting. In the opaque grayness one could only imagine the ocean's existence, the sound of it muted, the memory of it dimmed. And through the overcast the people were as lost as the sea, their mental climate matching the ambient fog.

Then the wind would wipe out the fog as it roared up the mountainside, revealing the breathtaking seascape and unmasking the old adobe with its crumbling walls.

We formed our friendships as we enthusiastically raced up and down rough mountain roads in advanced-design sports cars. Driving on these byways without destination, followed by all-night partying, I became caught in a spell, fascinated by this exciting existence.

Leaving behind a life of everyday routine and sameness, of protocol and convention, I entered into an exotic and romantic one in which there were no rules. Life in this untamed milieu was lived on the edge, as on the edge of an abyss, where everything was a risk and danger lay waiting on the boundaries of the precipice.

◇ Chapter One

I HAD LIVED MY NINE-teen years confined in a life whose ordinariness and predictability were walls of gray, suffocating me. I was too unassertive to rebel against the pretensions of a family who measured all actions against "What will people say?" or "What will people think?" Nor was the time right for rebellion, for my teen years were spent in the silent fifties. Though my thoughts were continually usurped by visions of high adventure, full of risks, involved with exotic and fascinating people, it seemed impossible that anything would ever happen to me, especially in my placid West Los Angeles neighborhood.

Then I met Tom Rhodes and everything changed. I found my visions being fulfilled as I stepped into the pages of a living novel of mystery and intrigue.

During the fall semester at college my parents' best friends were giving an engagement party for their daughter, who belonged to a sorority. My mother insisted that I go to the party with the icky son of another of her friends. Dateless, as was most often my situation, I was trapped in my mother's manipulations to make me a social success.

"Alice," she intoned, "I want you to wear the dress I got you at Magnin's. It is so smart; you really will stand out."

I groaned. *Stand out.* I would rather melt into the moldings. And I would stand out for the wrong reasons—the style was more for someone from my mother's era. I would look like my mother and all her friends in their middle-class uniforms—proper, dull, beige, and ladylike. No matter how I felt, she was determined to make me into her idea of a beauty. But I was not truly pretty nor unpretty either; rather I was average—with an average face, figure, and height.

I agreed resignedly to wear the dress for there was no use arguing with my mother; hers was the only side to any argument. Besides, she was more like a grandmother; my two brothers and I were born to our parents late in life. The generation gap was more like a gulf, as though we were from different centuries.

She went on nattering about nothing. "The orange flower at the neckline will highlight your hair," she told me.

But my hair was no color in particular—hair color, I would say. No red or orange or whatever was going to highlight it. I did have the wild idea to put the flower behind my ear like Carmen or maybe Mata Hari on a spying mission, but I was too hemmed in by convention to really do it.

She droned on, "The style will give you a good line."

A line more for her age than mine. Though in the fifties and early sixties the clothes of young women tended to echo their mothers'—twenty and fifty dressed alike. Even by these standards, the dress was way too matronly for me.

Having been recruited by my mother, my date's interest in me was on the minus side of zero, especially after he took one look at the dress, which should have been on my mother instead of me. The heavy scent of Joy, which she had splashed on me, did not help either.

As we arrived at the party, the words of Chubby Checker floated above the noise of the chattering people. "Let's twist again, like we did last year. Don't cha remember when things were really hummin'...."

The polite brush-off hellos and the straight-through-me looks to someone else on the other side of the room made me very uncomfortable. I had more or less known these people in high school. I knew them and I didn't know them. Still, their treatment hurt me and I cared too much even though I didn't belong to this group. I cared so much that I had to get out of there.

The party swirled around me, eddying and bubbling, leaving me in the quiet inner eye of the excitement. Then I no longer cared, as I became the heroine of one of my fantasy adventures. Edging out of the room, I was on safari in Africa. We were encircled by a band of hostile natives dancing a war dance, undoubtedly inspired by the couples gyrating to the twist in the center of the room. A witch doctor was chanting a curse which was all mixed up with "Yeah let's twist again, twistin' time is here, aah around and round and a up and down we go again," coming from the record player.

Just as it looked as though escape was impossible, I saw a dense impenetrable growth of jungle—in reality the group of banana plants outside a sliding glass door. I stealthily maneuvered our little group out of danger—and into the patio. With their praise and gratitude ringing in my ears, I suddenly realized I was hearing a real voice beyond the patio wall—a loud "damn" followed by a couple of "hells." I opened the patio gate and walked over to the driveway next door.

A long pair of legs was sticking out from under an odd, dilapidated sports car. More epithets erupted, some of which were considered unprintable at the time. Finally in the most disgusted voice came, "That damn oil plug."

I looked down. There, a few feet in front of me was the part that had rolled away. I called to him, "Here is your oil plug."

He popped out and unfolded himself. Six feet or more of football-player build stood in front of me, wiry brown hair falling over his eyes. In spite of his grease-covered clothes, he looked exceedingly attractive.

"Where did you find it?" I gestured to the place. "Say, you're pretty sharp. How did you know what it was?"

Already overcome by his tall good looks, I became coquettish. "I'm just naturally clever."

"Say you are. I've never met a girl who knew about car parts. Are you into racing?"

"Sure," I lied, "that's my thing."

Actually, I knew quite a lot about car motors (though they bored me) because my older brother was a car nut; that was all he ever talked about.

"Hey, that's great," the tall young man said, "What are you doing here? You didn't go to that dumb party next door, did you?" Not waiting for an answer, he went on talking, saying his name was Tom Rhodes. Then I realized he was the same Tom my older brother had said was neat and was always quoting as his source of information on cars. However, they were not buddies, although I had heard they had done street racing together. Street racing, of course, was not legal.

"As soon as I get everything back together, would you like to go for a coke?"

"I'd love to." I was elated. I had made a connection with a really cool guy. He seemed oblivious of my old-ladyish dress. He was so enthusiastically involved with his crazy car, so pleased I had found his oil plug and that I knew something about motors, I don't think he really looked at me.

We went to a nearby drive-in as we listened to Wolfman Jack on Tom's car radio. Since it was Saturday night, cars were cruising through the drive-in. The carhops were living up to their name as they scooted around with their trays. But we were out of luck—there wasn't an empty parking space in sight.

Tom said, "It's too crowded and my car's making a funny noise, so I guess I better get back to work on it. I'll drop you off at your party." But he did ask me to go for a ride the next night. I was thrilled that he wanted to see me again.

The following evening after he picked me up, he started off in a roar of spinning rubber. He drove quickly through West Los Angeles, slithering in and out of long lines of cars as if he were late for an important appointment. Soon we reached the Santa Monica Mountains, which as mountains barely qualify. I had learned in geology that they are very old and had disintegrated to the point of being not much more than chaparral-covered hills. Even in the light of a weak moon, the brush looked crackingly dry. There was a hot Santa Ana wind blowing, reminding me that the suburb of Los Angeles where we lived was really a desert. With its myriad swimming pools, the oasis-like quality was a sham only made possible by the expropriation of the melting snows from the distant Sierra.

I had always been conscious of the dirt swaths lacing through the hills that run from the city to the sea. I could hardly live on the west side and not see them, as they are visible from the lowlands. I knew they were a necessity as firebreaks. Every fall since I could remember, headlines in the papers had reported a disastrous fire or two somewhere in the foothills, fanned by the hot winds of autumn, racing through the dry explosive plant growth, often burning a number of hillside houses. I was surprised when we turned off onto one of these bulldozed trails.

"Hey, is this legal?" I asked.

"Not exactly. But the chances of getting a ticket are a lot less here when I open her up."

I was astounded. Rules did not seem to bother him.

"Hold on," he said, indicating a grab bar, as he gunned the engine and rapidly shifted gears.

It was really scary and exciting as we flew through the hills, leaving behind a monsoon-like dust storm. Our conversation was sparse—not only because we did not know each other but also because the motor made so much noise we had to yell.

From the distant outskirts he drove back to where we lived, Westwood, a suburb within the boundaries of sprawling, indefinable Los Angeles, a city in search of itself. Tom stopped at a coffee house on a side street. Coffee houses were the big thing then but I had never been to one, which added to the excitement of the evening. This coffee house was called the Blue Couch, so named because of an ancient velvet couch inside. The furniture was circa old junk store—elevated to an almost antique status by the signs I had seen on some junk stores, spelling it "junque."

I was really entranced by our waitress's attire: a flowing flowered blouse over a long velvet skirt, which almost covered her purple velvet boots. Her jewelry was also very Bohemian, her fingers barely visible under a collection of heavy silver rings. Would that such things were in my wardrobe and that it would be acceptable for me to wear them, but I was in the wrong peer group for that. My clothes all conformed to regulation college style: plain collared blouses, skirts, and flats. Our wildly dressed waitress was very chatty and casual as Tom ordered espresso for us, the "in" thing to drink.

Tom Rhodes was solidly and squarely built and I noticed how oddly his large, stubby, strong-looking hands contrasted with the tiny, delicate espresso cup from which he was drinking. His unspoiled boyishness made it seem incongruous for him to be drinking what I considered to be an effete kind of coffee. Tom told me as we drank our espresso about the plans he had for a radical new car. But he was very mysterious about it.

"There are many things I can't reveal. I would be in trouble if I mentioned any names—they're all important. The negotiations are at a crucial stage."

"You mean the car is a completed design?" I asked in awe.

"Oh, I can't tell you that, yet."

He kept on talking without really saying anything. I could not follow him at all. His sentences got more elliptical but what was left out tantalized me. It was intriguing to be privy to important secrets even though I had no idea what they were. I arrived home exhilarated and ready for our next drive, which was scheduled for the following night.

Again we drove up and down the hills without direction. It was not exactly a smooth ride over the rough, lumpy roads in his hard-riding sports car. He was undisturbed by the gas fumes pouring in through the partially missing floorboards. I had to lean my head out to breathe, which was easy since his car was topless, rather like other kids' convertibles with the tops down, but Tom had no top to ever put up.

After I had gone on a few more rides with him I yelled one night over the roar of the engine, "Tom, how can you breathe with these fumes?"

He replied, inhaling deeply, "Fumes, what fumes?"

Afterwards, over coffee at the Blue Couch, Tom told me how he had acquired the car. "I was driving with a friend of mine up in the hills near where we were tonight. When we stopped to change a tire, I happened to see this really neat car. Actually, all I could see at first was a headlight sticking through a bush in a gully. I ran down to get a better look and there was this great car you've been riding in. Do you know it's one of the first designed by Lancinelli—he's a Milanese racing car designer. But it was a total wreck. I know that's hard to tell now."

It still looked pretty much like a wreck to me. The wire wheels were rusty; the paint was only a patched-up prime coat. The inside was stripped, leaving only the structure of rough metal.

"When are you going to put gauges in the holes in the dashboard?" I asked.

He looked hurt. I had spoken in a slighting way about his car, which he could only see with adoring eyes. But even though he was unable to be objective about the condition of his beloved car, he had an aura of maturity due probably to the fact that he was twenty-four. This made him more appealing to me than boys my own age.

I looked forward to our informal dates, if they could be called that; he had not yet tried to kiss me. A few times he had grabbed me by the hand or put his arm around me, like a buddy, when he wanted to show me something he had done to his prized car. But that was our only touching.

My mother did not approve of Tom at all. She felt he was too old and undirected. She wanted me to go out with someone who had a "future." If boys were older, she wanted to be sure they had those all-important degrees, which Tom, a college dropout, did not have. She tried every roadblock she could think of to stop my nightly drives with him. She usually threw studying in my face, saying I would flunk out of school and disgrace the family. To which I countered that I had already done my studying or that I did not have any to do, for I was determined to go out with Tom. I was disgusted with myself that I had not put more pressure on my family to let me go away to college. But, I thought, if I had I would not have met him.

My father did not like Tom either. He thought he was guided by road signs leading from one detour to another. "Really, though, Alice, I wonder about Tom's intellect. Does he ever inquire into anything besides a car engine?" my father asked.

"Of course he does," I answered.

"What, for example?" he asked.

"Well, I can't think of anything right now," I said. Possibly my father was right. It was difficult to talk to Tom on most subjects; either his mind drifted away or his knowledge was insufficient. But his personality and looks made up for a lot—his smile that started tentatively then ingratiatingly took over his whole face, his friendly blue eyes that turned purple in the sun. Even the essence of car grease that was always about him added to his masculinity.

After I had been going out with Tom for several weeks, he came to pick me up early on a Saturday afternoon. He seemed very agitated and in a hurry for us to leave.

"I have to go up the coast right away. Someone tried to kill my friend Pirrone and he needs my help. I'd like you to come with me, would you?"

"Sure," I replied without a thought of the danger that might be involved. "When do you think we'll be back?"

"Tell your mom not to worry. We'll be back in time tonight."

I was anxious to meet Pirrone Rivelli and see where he lived because I was very intrigued by what Tom had already told me about him on one of our nighttime drives. He was a member of a wealthy Italian family and after a few trips to California to promote his family's factories' products he had decided to settle in Northern California and become their permanent representative there. He had become involved with a group who loved to race fast, esoteric cars. Tom had worked in an auto supply store in which parts for foreign cars were sold. One day Pirrone had come to the store to get a very special part he needed and Tom had waited on him.

"It was fate," Tom told me. "Here I was selling this guy parts for his fantastic car. I was practically drooling, hearing him describe it. He asked me if I would like to come outside and see it. It was a very advanced design in racing cars. I told him about my car. Then he invited me to come to El Mirador, where he lives, and race with him."

Tom added that they had become good friends. They liked to race through the mountains together. While one drove, the other would call out the speed at which each curve should be taken. Each thought the other was a great driver, or so Tom said.

As Tom had told me, Pirrone lived near El Mirador, a tiny place on the ocean side of the coastal range, a spectacular area known as Big Sur, stretching from just north of San Simeon to just south of Carmel. My aunt lived in El Mirador. Even though we had visited her only a couple of times, this area of the central coast had left an impression that continued to haunt me—an aura of sophistication, of natural beauty, even of mystery behind its swirling fogs. Los Angeles in contrast seemed to be a parvenu city of borrowed culture and borrowed population. In the flat sunlight and dull, cloudless, smog-colored sky, everything was matter-of-fact garish, hard-edged and plastic.

Tom had shown me some snapshots he had taken at Pirrone's estate, Casa Dañada. Since Tom's car was in the center of every picture, I could only see glimpses of faded burnt-orange shutters feathered along the window openings in the mottled, ochre-colored walls, crested with tiled roofs like the rooster combs of some giant species of fowl. The early California Spanish character of the buildings intrigued me.

On most days, Tom said, races were held by Pirrone and his racing buddies on the winding narrow roads outside the property. Tom said the curves were like those of Monte Carlo. (Of course, Pirrone had been to the Grand Prix races there.) Sitting on Casa Dañada's adobe wall which followed the contours of the curving road, the drivers' friends clocked the cars as they skidded by sideways—a four wheel drift.

My excitement intensified as we raced up Highway 101, driving so fast that the cars Tom passed seemed almost as if they were parked; his speedometer registered well over a hundred most of the time. As we drove, the landscape changed gradually from seared brown to brown tinged with green, and finally to green-carpeted hills and valleys over which great crowds of live oaks congregated.

I was very curious to find out all about Casa Dañada because I was particularly attracted to mysterious-looking houses that possibly might be haunted, with spooky secrets hidden behind their walls.

I asked Tom, "What does the name 'Casa Dañada' mean?"

"Well, it is really Casa de la Dañada. It means house of the doomed soul."

"How intriguing! Why was it named that?"

"I don't know," said Tom laconically.

"You mean you never found out why?" It was incredible that anyone could be so indifferent about discovering the origins of such a strange name.

"No, I never thought about it. Names are names; as Shakespeare said, 'A rose by any other name would smell the same.'" Tom's curiosity did not go beyond finding out what was under the hood of a car.

"Oh, Tom," I said, "that doesn't apply here. This name has to mean something weird happened. Anyway that isn't the way Shakespeare wrote it. 'A rose by any other name would smell as sweet.' Don't you remember?"

"No," he said, "I could never stand English classes."

"At least you must know who the doomed soul was," I said.

"No, but since you are so curious about Dañada, I can tell you something about it. It was once part of a very large Spanish land grant. You'll see that the adobe buildings are very old. Some of them go way back to Spanish times."

"Gee, it will be exciting to see original Spanish buildings."

"Well," he said, "I don't know how original they are. They've been changed a lot through the years. The garage used to be the stables. A lookout tower the Spaniards used for sighting ships is now a guesthouse. Pirrone said the town is named for that very building. 'El Mirador' means 'watch tower' in Spanish."

"Just think what stories those walls could tell," I said.

He seemed unimpressed. "Haven't you heard, walls can't talk? Anyway, they're at least two feet thick, too thick for talking."

"Oh, Tom," I said, "just imagine what things could have happened in all those years. Why, there could even be bodies cemented into those walls if they're that thick. Poe wrote about bricking a body up in a wall. Maybe that's what happened to the doomed soul. You said the walls were crumbling. Wouldn't it be exciting if one of them crumbled to pieces and her skeleton dropped out? And what if her ghost had stayed there all that time to be near the body?"

"Alice, what's the matter with you? You have weird ideas."

"Don't you have any imagination?" I asked, disappointed.

He seemed disgusted. "Not a grisly one like yours."

From San Luis Obispo we drove to Morro Bay. The last vestiges of daylight had vanished as we continued toward Cambria and San Simeon on Highway 1—which was really only two lanes, so deserted it seemed like our own private road. The so-called highway glimmered ahead of us, reminding me of a line from my favorite poem, "The Highwayman": "The road was a ribbon of moonlight over the purple moor." This was not exactly a moor but who could tell at night?

As I put my hands up to catch the wind, I had a sudden feeling that

I was now free to do any daring thing that occurred to me. I said to Tom, "It's so bright out, it would be fun and romantic if you turned off your lights. You could be like the highwayman riding up to the old inn door."

Tom didn't see the romance in it but said it would be exciting as he switched off the headlights. (It was lucky there were no other cars on the road before he turned them back on.)

The landscape was not lit enough by the moon for me to get any sense of where we were; the only other light was from isolated houses miles apart. I knew the Big Sur coast where El Mirador was located was sparsely inhabited; still it was a surprise when Tom said, "We're here." As he said this we drove through open wrought-iron gates onto rough gravel. Tom's headlights picked up the outlines of wind-bent cypress along the side as we wound up the drive.

"I thought you said we had to go through El Mirador before we got to Pirrone's."

"We did," he said, "a few miles back."

"Why didn't I see it?" I asked.

"I guess," he said, "because it's so small and I was driving so fast. We weren't in it more than a second."

In spite of how fast Tom had driven, it was late when we arrived. As we got out of his car, I tried to place what I had seen in Tom's pictures, but everything looked different, somehow unrelated. Shimmering shapes, like castles in a fairy tale, glimmered through the pine trees, punctuated by windowpanes with a topaz glow suggesting a hidden warmth. Slivers of misty moonlight wavered through the pine branches, covering everything with a haunted, unworldly light.

We walked across a graveled courtyard strewn with pine needles, finally stepping through mission-style arches into a portico paved with tiles, across which a hollowed-out path had been worn by what must have been many thousands of footsteps. The walls of the portico provided an outdoor gallery for a haphazard collection of travel posters from the twenties, with the look of graphic paintings in tempera. There was a rather Egyptian-looking cat sitting on one of the window ledges as if guarding the gallery like a sphinx.

The living room doors opened into the portico and were somewhat ajar. Through them I could see several people, but the one who intrigued me was a handsome man lounging on a tourmaline-green velvet couch. His black hair was a little long, his sideburns earlobe length. Although he was dressed in jeans, there was nothing slovenly about him. His physique was beautifully formed but had the bearing of relaxed indolence, unmarked by the sinewy muscles of the athlete. Casual, yet somehow aristocratic, he was terribly dashing in a decadent way, his whole manner suggesting a leisurely life.

As we walked in, he said, "Hi, Tom. It's good to see you. Let us meet the lovely young thing with you." His flattery struck my foolish vanity and I began to fall under his spell.

"Pirrone," Tom said, "this is Alice." Then in a lowered voice, "I got here as fast as I could. What happened?"

"I think someone got wind of my fantastic plans and is out to stop me," Pirrone said, continuing in the same lowered voice as Tom. "I'll tell you more about them later but I've got to move a lot faster now than I had thought because of this. I want you to think about moving here after the first of the year, and that's soon because it's almost December. I need you to be on the lookout—which we'll also talk about later."

Pirrone was issuing orders that Tom was accepting without question, probably because, as I later came to realize, Pirrone was his idol. But there was something wrong here. There didn't seem to be enough concern about the attempted murder.

After this sotto voce conversation, Pirrone took me by the hand and introduced me to the other people in the room, who were slouched on couches, feet up on coffee tables. I could hear my mother saying in horror, "How uncouth," but I thought, what a neat way to be—totally relaxed and free.

Then Pirrone took center stage and in his well-pronounced English seasoned with a lyrical Italian accent, he began to tell an amusing incident about Brian, his friend, who lived at Casa Dañada.

"Brian and his cousin were in Italy driving one of those gutless two-cylinder, three wheel jobs." Pirrone used his hands as he talked, in a very Italian way, indicating the wheels. I noticed a fancy chronometer on his wrist and on his hand a heavy ring set with a large diamond. He continued with the story. "One day they were trying to find a parking place—you know how parking is in Florence. They saw a place but a large American convertible was about to back into it. His cousin thought they could beat the convertible into the space. Somehow they got that useless thing in first and yelled in Italian, 'Only the young can do this.' They felt clever as hell but after they got out they heard a crash—that big American car was parked in the same space and had flattened their car into scrap metal. The guy gave Brian his card, saying, 'Only the rich can do this.'"

Everyone roared with appreciative laughter. "I don't believe it!" exclaimed one fellow sitting on the couch near Pirrone.

"It's true," replied Pirrone. "Ask Brian when he gets back."

"Did the guy replace the car?" asked someone else.

"He offered, but Brian decided it would be easier to travel by motorcycle and took the money instead," Pirrone replied.

Wide-eyed, I marveled at the thought that someone could act with such disregard for material possessions. As Pirrone spoke, I felt that the rich Italian in the anecdote must be his counterpart, with the same kind of money with which one can live beyond convention and pay for any damage that might occur. I had entered a magic world of great fortunes, a cosmic distance from my middle-class neighborhood.

Someone asked, "Hey, Pirrone, whatever happened to that stacked blonde—Julie, I think her name was—you used to have around? She was so available."

"Yeah," another fellow said, laughing, "She went in for the big numbers. A few new ones every day."

Then Pirrone delivered an obviously clever line, "She left town suddenly. I think she got a wrong number." The group snickered. Pirrone continued, "I have a feeling she'll be back."

Everyone spoke with such self-assurance that they seemed like good actors who are able to deliver well-rehearsed lines with complete spontaneity. I felt, though, that the guests were like a Greek chorus receding into the background, echoing and applauding Pirrone's performance. As they talked I looked around. The fairly large room was both dining and living room. In the back was a pair of singular, rather sinister candelabra, each arm formed by a coiled snake constricting a candle. They were standing on a long, narrow dining table across which eight Spanish Renaissance chairs faced each other. There were some pictures of early California ranch scenes hanging near the fireplace. I could just make out the name Cervantes in the Spanish words carved on the edge of its thick mantle. "Pirrone," I asked, "what does the carving say?"

"It's from Don Quixote. 'The best climate is in bed.'"

"That fits you, Pirrone," one of the guests said, laughing. "Did you have it carved?"

Pirrone smiled as he said, "No, but I'd like to have thought of it first." I must have looked embarrassed because he said to me aside, "What it means is with no effort, one can be completely comfortable in bed."

"Oh," I exclaimed, "now I see! On cold mornings it's so nice just to stay in bed."

"Yes, that's it. But I think some of my friends had a different idea."

When all the other guests had left, Pirrone stopped the stage performance, conversing with us rather than putting on a virtuoso entertainment as before. "Tom," he asked, "where have you been keeping this attractive girl? You have been hiding her from us." Again with the not-so-subtle flattery, he tautened the line like a fisherman who, from long habit, plays the foolish fish.

"I've been working," Tom replied, with his usual talent for not directly answering a question. "But," he continued, "we rushed right up here when I heard you were in trouble. What happened?"

Pirrone seemed evasive as he answered, "Oh, some crazy idiot with itchy fingers took a shot at me. I would rather not talk about it." With that, Pirrone closed the subject, going on to a new topic. "I know you'll want to be in on the terrific plans I mentioned earlier, but I can't discuss them yet." Did the attempted murder really have anything to do with these plans, I wondered?

I could see Tom was very curious but he did not ask any questions. Instead he inquired, "How is the Fazani?"

"It's ready for you to race." Then he asked, more of himself than of us, "Where the devil is Liz?" I wondered who Liz was.

"Yes, where is Liz?" Tom echoed. I looked at Tom questioningly. He said to me, "Liz is Pirrone's wife." How like Tom. He had never told me Pirrone was married.

"Liz," Pirrone bellowed. In a few moments, we heard the flapping of sandals along the portico tiles. One of the carved doors was opened by a very tall, gaunt female who resembled one of those Giacometti figures—stretched like a rubber band to its thinnest, short of breaking. Her face was almost covered by long, straggly dark hair. I wondered how she could see. She was a real slob. I had thought that someone who lived on an estate would be well dressed and groomed.

"Pirrone, was that you calling?" the wraith asked.

"Yes, damn it. Where have you been all evening? You look horrible."

"Oh, um…umm…umm…I've been doing the laundry," she replied.

"Will you please bring us some coffee? We have guests."

"Yes, oh…oh," Liz muttered.

"Hi, Liz. This is Alice," Tom said.

"Oh, hi," Liz acknowledged. She looked at Pirrone and said, "I'd better start the coffee." Then she stumbled out, mumbling something as she closed the door.

"Is Liz in one of her moods again?" Tom questioned.

"That's no mood," Pirrone answered angrily. "She's been drinking again."

She returned in a few minutes, rattling three pottery coffee cups on a painted tray, which she set down. Then with difficulty she poured us some coffee. I still wondered how she could see. She stood there for a minute as if uncertain what to do while Pirrone glared at her. She looked at him, saying rather abruptly, "Please excuse me. I… ah… uh…must get back to the laundry."

How strange, this drudge retreating into the service regions of the house to do laundry while her charming husband entertained guests. What were these moods Pirrone and Tom spoke of? Or did Pirrone have some perverse power forcing her to slave in the middle of the night? There was something hidden here, but what?

It was getting very late and we had a long way to go, as El Mirador was several hundred miles from Westwood. It would be hard to get home before sunrise (and my mother's wrath) unless we hurried. Yet Tom and Pirrone took time to talk by the cars as we were leaving—but strangely only about cars and not the danger Pirrone was in from the attempted murder.

The stillness and the bone-biting dampness of the foggy air made me feel that we were surrounded by a void, like being in the middle of a rain cloud on a mountaintop. They continued discussing cars, which really bored me. I had learned long ago to tune out car dialogue, having heard it incessantly from my brother. Thus, on this night I only listened to the cadence of their voices in a point-counterpoint fugue of deep masculine tones.

We said a final goodnight. Pirrone reminded Tom he needed him to get back soon and said to be sure to bring Alice (me!). Soon was not soon enough for me. Pirrone had said he wanted Tom to move here, and I wondered, what about me. Mesmerized by the lifestyle at Dañada, I did not even want to leave. But moving here! Of course, no one said anything about my moving here. And how could I? The dream was evaporating as quickly as it had come.

On the way home, I remarked, "Pirrone is so interesting." (I could not tell Tom I found Pirrone to be terribly attractive and, even more, that I was attracted to him.) "But Liz is weird. How did he ever marry a girl like that? There's something wrong there."

"Oh, no, a man as busy as Pirrone couldn't be married to a woman who would demand a lot of attention. He doesn't always show it, but he really cares about her and she does look better most of the time."

I thought about Pirrone. He seemed to say just the right thing, using words as a writer does, getting the exact shade of meaning or tossing off the perfect retort, while Tom tended to be muddled and tied up inside in snarled knots. Yet, aside from cars, they appeared to have a great deal of rapport. Was there more to Tom than I had realized?

We went back to El Mirador for a New Year's Eve party at the Rivelli's. Arriving again at night, I still had no sense of the geography of the place. The party was at their beach house. It was far below the road and could only be reached by walking down a long, narrow path that was steep and terrifying. Along the way were twisted cypress trees whose mysterious, mossy fingers pointed eerily at us. I would not have been surprised if bats had flown out of them. There was a haunted, supernatural feeling about the ravine. There were all kinds of scary noises and spooky things brushing against me. I was glad Tom was there. He made me feel secure. Had I been alone, I would have screamed and run back to the car.

As we neared the house, a glow started to ooze through the mist, like watercolors spreading on an artist's wet paper. We crossed a little footbridge to a promontory overlooking the ocean and the glow suddenly became brilliant electric light, bringing us back to reality.

Walking in through an open door, we saw Pirrone. His slightly off-beat attire—a black dinner jacket over a black turtleneck sweater—gave him a certain distinction. When my eyes met his, a tingle went down my spine, making me quiver delightfully. Tom had never affected me like this. I tried hard to resist the power of Pirrone's chemistry because he was hardly available. "Tom," Pirrone was saying, "glad you made it this year." (We were very late. It was getting close to midnight.) "Did you come in reverse all the way?"

"Almost. We did have to back up." What was Tom talking about? The only backing up we did was to park.

Someone from across the room called to Pirrone. Tom and I stood there unnoticed for a few minutes. It was a mob scene. People were jammed into every corner and overflowing out the open French doors and onto the deck. There was an undercurrent of clever conversation and low-keyed amusement—so different from the parties I had been to before, with girls screaming and squealing "groovy" to everything, no matter what was said, unless it was so bad that it was "grubby" or "grungy." These people were so much more sophisticated and, of course, older. They exuded a worldliness as if they had been everywhere and done everything. They were dressed in clothes that had the look of individual designs, an understated, expensive look that they wore with casual unconcern. I was both awed and entranced by the infinitely interesting people at this party. How I would love to be in with them, doing all the exciting things they must do.

Tom looked toward an attractive girl talking to some people near the entry and called "Hi, Liz."

She came over to us. "Well, hello Tom…Alice…good to see you." She put her arms around Tom's neck and kissed him.

I was astounded that it was Liz. The transformation was so dramatic—she was like a character actress who could play the extremes in roles. Now that I could really see Liz, she was very striking. Her long, dark hair circled a clear, lustrous face, set with sea-green eyes like a maharajah's huge pearl studded with a pair of perfect emeralds. "I'm glad you could come, Alice. Where are you staying? You two can have a guest house."

"Oh…thanks, Liz." I was amazed that she could remember me from the other night and surprised by the casualness with which she suggested this arrangement for Tom and me. "But I'm staying with my aunt. She lives in El Mirador."

"That's too bad," Liz laughed, as she said, "Aren't aunts awful? Well, you two have a good time, anyhow…and Tom, you know everyone. Can you see that Alice is introduced?" Then she disappeared into the crowd.

"Hey, Tom, how have you been?" I turned to see a fellow who was holding a champagne bottle. His rugged face was friendly and full of fun, in spite of his studious-looking thick glasses.

"Fine, fine," Tom answered. "I'll be bragging if I say any more." Then he added, "Alice, I'd like you to meet Brian of the Florentine parking fame." Brian introduced me to Erica, his girlfriend, who made me think of an owl in the dark; all that stood out were her large amber eyes. I was impressed as well as surprised by the assurance with which Tom handled himself and with how much he seemed to belong among these people. Before I had thought he was diffident and would have imagined he would be out of place at a large, sophisticated party such as this.

Listening to Brian was fun. I was immediately caught up by his enthusiasm. "Has Pirrone told you about his new plans?" he asked Tom.

"He mentioned them last time I saw him. He said he had more details he couldn't discuss yet."

"It's like the adventure of a lifetime! We're going to mine gold in the Andes, but first we're going to engage in…ah…a little business— selling thousands of cigarettes in South America. They're worth twice as much there as here."

"How are you getting them there?" asked Tom.

"In the hold of a boat. Pirrone is negotiating for one right now. The real object, though, is to look over the land Pirrone wants to mine. He thought it would be fun to make a little profit on the side. It makes the trip more worthwhile."

"When are we going?" Tom was very eager.

"As soon as we can," Brian answered.

Several more people joined our group, ending the talk about the plans. I was introduced and the conversation turned briefly to me: Where was I from? How did I like El Mirador? Then the conversation drifted back to the small talk of big parties as glasses were filled all around. Tom and I slowly moved around the room, meeting one group after another. But as more wine was drunk, the introductions became sketchier and the inquiries to me were tossed off without the inquirer really listening to the reply, or the ritual was dispensed with altogether. The party grew louder but not boisterous. These people truly fitted my idea of jet-set sophistication.

I had a minute to talk alone with Tom. I asked him about some of the people I had met. He told me that Brian and Erica lived at Casa Dañada, in a guesthouse.

"Oh," I said, "they're married."

"No," Tom answered. I conveyed my shock at this revelation. "You're very naïve and middle-class," was all Tom had to say in reply. I realized I had to change my thinking a lot if I wanted to be part of this milieu.

We were soon back talking with Erica and Brian about South America. Erica interrupted, "Why's everyone leaving?" The room was practically empty and the remaining guests were heading toward the door.

"Let's find out," suggested Brian.

We walked outside to find that everyone had not left the party but had gathered on the edge of the cliff. The fog had lifted and I could see that the ocean had carved sea shapes into the face of the precipice. The all-pervading, damp air gave me a feeling of being entangled in seaweed. There was a lot of loud chatter, everyone talking at once, having by this time become quite garrulous from all the wine. Both fellows and girls were armed with empty champagne bottles, making a half-circle around Pirrone, who was standing on a large rock outcropping at the very edge of the bluff.

"Tom," I asked, "what is Pirrone doing there?"

"He is going to throw a champagne bottle over the cliff. It will spark when it slides down and breaks on the rocks." Pirrone threw one but nothing happened. The sound of disappointment came from the crowd. A voice spoke up, "Hey, it's a hoax! It doesn't spark." Pirrone threw another. There were lots of sparks followed by a crash. "Did you see the sparks? Wow! It really works! Pirrone you're a genius," someone yelled. "Pirrone…try another!"

It sparked and crashed. "Hooray!" "Midnight! Happy New Year, everyone! It's going to be a good year…." Everyone started hurling champagne bottles with wild abandon, yelling "Happy New Year!" The multitude of sparks created a Fourth of July fireworks effect and the deafening noise almost succeeded in drowning out the pounding of the surf.

Suddenly amidst all the crashing of champagne bottles, Liz screamed. She was standing next to Pirrone. Her shawl, which had been piled loosely around her shoulders, was lying on the ground, seemingly blown off.

"I felt something whiz by me like a blast of hot wind as it knocked off my shawl," she said in a terrified voice.

Pirrone picked up the gossamer shawl and stuffed it in his pocket as he said, "You must be imagining things. This is so light it probably just slid off."

Brian spoke up, "You know, I think I heard a gunshot above all the sounds of crashing bottles."

"Nonsense," Pirrone said, "but then, maybe you did somewhere in the distance. People do shoot off guns at New Year's." But that struck me as odd. We were so completely isolated from any other habitation, how could that be possible?

At this point everyone started to leave and the party seemed to be over. As we climbed back up to the road I heard a car take off in a great roar amid the squeal of burning rubber. I wondered what that was all about. It looked as though Brian might be right. Could it have been a bullet that grazed Liz's shawl, knocking it off? Was it intended for Pirrone, his would-be killer making a fast exit?

"Do you think someone tried to murder Pirrone over the South American land with the gold," I asked Tom, "and tried again tonight and missed and almost got Liz?"

"No, I don't and I can't talk about it. Pirrone is involved in a lot of things and Italians have hot tempers. But I do have to keep my eyes open to protect him. There's always danger when someone is as rich as Pirrone."

Since I had never been involved with rich people I did not know that. But that still seemed unlikely. I did not think all rich people had murderers after them.

"So if it's not the land, is there something else?"

"You ask too many questions."

Oh well, I thought, since no one seems overly concerned about it and since it's so much fun here, perhaps I shouldn't concern myself with it either.

As we got into Tom's car, Pirrone said to Tom in a lowered voice, "See you later back at the house."

I asked Tom if the party were going to be continued there and if we were the only ones invited? He did not seem to know, but he wanted to go in any case. I had come to realize that Tom was eager to do whatever Pirrone wanted.

As we drove away I thought this is the beginning of a new year, 1963. I knew things would never be the same for me again now that I'd had a glimpse of this exciting world. I also felt as though a gypsy fortuneteller had warned me of dangers that lay ahead in this new, untested time; but could any seer have known that this was the end of an era? Who could foretell that the fifties—the "blah" years—were actually ending here, even though it was well into the sixties, and that I would become embroiled in the early ramifications of the wildness that was to ensue in this decade.

I also felt as if the gypsy had cautioned me against temptations that, as irresistible as they might seem, could change my life; that if I ever found myself on the wrong road, there would be no way back. Was Casa Dañada on such a road?

All these rather weird apprehensions of possible perils to come made me feel uneasy. Content with the new life I had found, I wanted to hold it forever in a perpetually static state of ideal happiness like the end of a fairy tale.

"Tom, I just had an awful feeling that things are going to change."

He smiled a funny, whimsical smile. "You can't stop change."

I said, "I like things the way they are right now, and I wish they could stay this way forever."

We drove through the open iron gates of the driveway at Casa Dañada. El Mirador's infinite spectrum of atmospheric conditions, from deep gloom to sparkling clarity, could alter the landscape to fit its mood. On this night Casa Dañada seemed to be a Spanish citadel. I felt pulled back in time and place to some other night in Spain, long ago, almost expecting to see a Spanish knight leaving for an assignation with a Goyaesque beauty—myself, of course. I was always the center of my wild fantasies. But the sound of another car starting up fast brought me back, as it sent up a rain of gravel, its headlights like panther eyes in the dark. Then the driver, seeing us, stopped with a screeching of brakes.

"Hey," Liz yelled from the car, "we're going to the hot springs. Why don't you two come along?"

"No, thanks," replied Tom.

"Oh, let's go," I urged.

"You won't like the hot springs," Tom said.

"Oh, please," I pleaded.

"Okay," he said reluctantly. He called to Pirrone, "We've changed our minds." We got out of the car to talk. Pirrone's limousine was filled with people, leaving no room for us.

"I don't have my suit," I said.

"That's all right," Pirrone replied. "You won't need one." I did not dare to question further, but it sounded as though it would be deliciously different. "You'd better take your car," Pirrone suggested.

"I can see that," Tom agreed.

Following the limo, we drove up into the mountains on a long, winding road full of partially washed-out sections. Eventually the road deteriorated into two wheel ruts with grass growing in between. We came to a barbed wire gate. Brian jumped out of the limousine and opened the gate. We drove through a thicket of redwood trees silhouetted against a dark sky, barely backlit by a wisp of a moon. As we drove along the dirt road, the headlights of the car quick-sketched thick ferns in front of us, adding to the enchantment. What a perfect place, I thought, for spirits or vampires.

Suddenly there was a dazzle of sound and steam. The headlights turned the rising clouds of vapor into ghost-like shapes beneath which I could just make out foaming water, rushing over what looked like giant condor baths, rock formations eroded into sunken tubs ideally suited for small groups of bathers. Everyone got out of the limousine and started to undress. Liz exclaimed, "Last one in gets Pirrone!"

"Tom, what's this?" I was thrown by the actuality of the nude bathing, although I had suspected that was what it was to be after Pirrone's remark and I had been secretly thrilled by the idea.

"See, I told you, you wouldn't like it," answered Tom.

I was not so sure I did not like it. I was fascinated with the casual, unselfconscious way they were removing their clothing. It was all very erotic, even thought they seemed so unconcerned about what they were doing. I was blushing madly—it had awakened in me a libido I hardly knew I possessed. I was both shocked and titillated. I was also totally confused. I was being pulled inside myself by all the Puritan rules of my background and being pushed into unknown currents of my own sexuality by what was going on around me. As the undressing progressed, there was a great deal of caressing, fondling, and kissing going on, even women caressing women in friendly gestures. It all blurred in my mind because it was such a jolt to see something as startlingly immoral as what was happening—or so I perceived it to be. Without clothing, it was hard to tell who was who, though their genders were clearly visible. In any case, I was unsure of their identities for I had only just met these people. I did notice a tall, willowy girl with a long neck (was it Erica?) sensuously caressing the back of a guy who I was sure was not Brian. Then she gave him an endless kiss. I turned toward an even more alarming scene. Another girl lightly brushed, with both her hands, the large breasts of a voluptuous female. Holding hands or arms around each other, groups of bathers went off in pairs or threesomes to slip into the tubs. I looked away in shock as I recognized Pirrone patting the bare behinds of two girls, one with each hand, in lustful circular motions.

"Come on, Tom," called Liz.

"I have a cold," he replied, "I can't go in."

"So do I," I echoed in an automatic conditioned reaction, though the tiniest impulse tugged at me somewhere to strip off my clothes and be as abandoned as they. But, of course, it was instantly knocked aside because everything I had ever been taught told me that this nudity and lasciviousness was depraved.

"Cowards," screamed Liz, who was already in one of the pools. They were creatures of nature. In their matter-of-factness, the veneer of civilization had been dropped with their clothes. They soaked and splashed in the tubs, everyone seeming to be having a great time. There was a lot of steam churning around which, along with their splashing, obscured what they were doing. "I want to go in," I said to Tom.

"No. Absolutely, no. I won't have you exposing yourself. Let's leave."

A feminine voice, squealing in a high pitch, came from one of the pools, "Oh, let me rub your back." Then another female voice purred in a sensual way, "Ooh, that feels so good." A masculine tone confided conspiratorially, "I think Pirrone intends to ship something more important than cigarettes to South America." Another male voice spoke up, "Yeah, probably girls. What could be more important to him than girls?" With all the kidding and banter about Pirrone and girls, it did seem as if he liked girls a lot. I wondered what Liz thought of his interest?

"We're leaving," Tom called out to the water nymphs and satyrs, who, lost in their revels, could not have heard him. In a way I felt relieved that we had not gone in, having never been undressed in front of a man, not even my brothers, let alone taking part in casual undressing and caressing in a group. As much as I wanted to join the rest, I knew I could never have done it. But I was disappointed because it looked like so much fun even though it seemed shockingly sinful.

We roared off at a frightening speed on the rough dirt, stirring up a cloud of dust, but after a few turns of the road, Tom stopped just as abruptly. Looking into the dark, he put his arm around me. "If I had a lot of money in the bank I'd marry you right now," he said.

I could only say, "Oh." I had never thought of marrying him. In fact it was only recently that he had shown more than a buddy-buddy kind of interest in me. The last week he had gone as far as kissing me goodnight and holding my hand or putting his arm around me, but still more in an affectionate way than in a passionate one.

"I have a new design," he confided as if he were breaking security on a top-secret war plan.

"Tom," I said, "I would love to see it."

"I'm afraid Detroit might steal it."

"Well, I won't tell anyone."

"Someday, you'll understand," was his reply.

I wanted to scream. He was so frustrating to talk to. He never made any sense. Why did I bother to go out with such a strange person? But why did I ask myself this? If I did not go out with him I would not be going out much at all. I was not one of the popular girls. At times, though, such as at the party earlier, Tom could be absolutely perfect; then I would become filled with adulation. At that moment, he was the only man for me.

The next afternoon Tom picked me up at my aunt's and we drove to Casa Dañada. I had never been there in the daytime before. It was an awesome drive on a narrow road that slithered along the precipitous sides of the wild, insolent mountains, a thousand feet or more above the waves breaking on the rocks below. The ocean was a luminous, sparkling, deep stained-glass blue—nothing like the faded blue of the Pacific in Southern California. Every so often there were thick patches of fog in which everything disappeared—the ocean, the mountaintops, and most of the road. At those times we were isolated in our own shroud of mist, which was scary now that I knew what lay below the road—sheer, vertical drops.

We drove through the open gates of Dañada up the graveled drive to where the sprawling adobe house looked down over the vast panorama of rocky shore as if watching over the wanton sea like a dueña from another age. There were not only pines and cypress but also eucalyptus, whose leaves were dripping off the faded tile roofs like dried and pressed petals falling out of old books. The spreading decay was everywhere evident in the bright sunlight. Many of the roof tiles were cracked and the plaster was peeling off the adobe; doors sagged visibly and the paint was worn and ragged.

When we arrived everyone was standing by the Fazani, Pirrone's racing car that had been hand-built on the Adriatic Coast by an Italian race driver. Designed as an experiment in speed and auto dynamics, it was the only one of its kind. It had won second place, twice, at Côte Blanche. It stood on large racing tires, looking as if it were poised for flight. I wondered—did it ever leave the ground at high speeds? There were no license plates. When I asked Tom about it later, he explained, "Pirrone doesn't bother with them; he drives so fast that the cops hardly ever see the car, let alone the license plates."

Brian, Liz, Erica, and a girl I had never seen before were engrossed in what Pirrone was saying. We came into hearing range just as he was telling of his New Year's resolution to drive much faster. As I looked at Pirrone, my younger brother's trained falcon flicked into my mental viewfinder. Was it that sharp, sleek, chiseled look that brought up this image? Or was it his dark penetrating eyes or his aquiline nose? There was also an aspect to him that had nothing to do with hawks; he had that sensuality peculiar to northern Italian men and it was continuing to work on me, although I tried not to let myself admit it. One thing I had noticed in particular, having seen him a couple of times, was that whenever he was pleased by one of his ideas, a sarcastic half-smile would creep across his face. The smile would last as he savored whatever had delighted him; then he would return to what was happening.

I was introduced to the girl, Serena. Tom had mentioned that the Rivellis' maid's name was Serena; could she be the maid? Tom later assured me that she was. She was terribly sophisticated, unlike any maid I had ever seen before, and on such familiar terms with her employers. Her full sensuous mouth contradicted her hard, sapphire-blue eyes. She moved sinuously, reminding me again of my little brother's menagerie—this time his beautiful anaconda as it slithered across his room. She had a languid, distant look that made me feel she was completely sated from having been to all the most exotic places and done all the most exciting things.

Liz was wearing rose-colored glasses. "I love your glasses. May I try them?" I asked her. When I put them on, the landscape was red-tinged, the warm happy glow pervading everything. I did not want to take them off, ever. If the only reality is what one believes it to be, then I wanted mine to be rosy. I knew the Emerald City's wonderful magic lay in the mind, but still it could not have been green without the glasses.

Later Tom took me for a walk in the garden, showing me the prehistoric monkey-puzzle tree, which was an unusual specimen. Its branches jutted out perpendicularly from the trunk; on the very ends of the branches were bunches of spines pointing straight down. Its skeletal frame seemed to be the work of a dinosaur who had played with a rudimentary erector set, adding spikes to snare an unsuspecting pterodactyl in the same way that Pirrone's charm (or was it his rather blatant sexuality?) was trapping me, an entrapment I was powerless to stop. But as far as his reaction to me, I might as well have been his sister or his maiden aunt.

"Don't you think the shot last night was intended for Pirrone?" I asked Tom. I was beginning to believe someone really did want to murder him over the South American plans. But why?

"What shot?" He seemed annoyed with me for asking.

How frustrating it was to talk to Tom. He had to have known there was one. He was being just like his idol, Pirrone, who had said "Nonsense" to the suggestion of a gunshot.

"Are you going to South America with Pirrone?" I asked, dropping the subject that bothered him.

"It looks that way. We talked last night after I took you to your aunt's. It's fantastic. Pirrone has maps and charts and samples proving there's gold on the land he intends to buy in the Andes. But of course he wants to look it over first. We're going there after we dispose of the cigarettes."

"What about your job?" I asked.

"I'm quitting next week. After South America I won't need to worry. We'll come back with a lot of money and I'll be able to do just about anything I want. And I want you to come with me."

"Really?" I was a little surprised and quite delighted.

"Yes, and I think we should get married."

I hesitated, not quite knowing what to say. My mixed-up feelings did not let me think logically. In fact, if I had been thinking at all, I would have realized that Tom, whatever his good qualities were, was hardly ready to take on the responsibility of marriage. Still, I did know Tom's thoughts were usually preempted by cars, such as the time he completely forgot our date, only remembering the next day, then bringing me a scraggly bunch of flowers (obviously hand-picked from the backyard) as he muttered something about his transmission making a strange sound. But the adventure of going to South America…perhaps it would give him a new interest and he would lose some of his addiction to cars. As for me, my irrational emotions were all fired up by the thought that Pirrone would be on the trip. How could I be so deceitful? I was thrilled at the idea of being near Pirrone, and marrying Tom was the ticket. But I was not being calculating, thinking was no longer possible; my emotions were totally out of control. Pirrone's enticing sensuality was swamping me.

I had taken so long to answer, I guess Tom wasn't sure I had heard him. He said again, "Alice, I think we should get married."

"I'm glad you think that," I replied in the same tone as his funny proposal, accepting it as if it were an invitation to a picnic, or at most nothing more than a passport for an exciting trip—which it was, to me.

"Are you going to be here all that time before we leave?" I asked.

"Yes, and I've been thinking—do you suppose you could stay with your aunt?" His proposal must have been just one of his casual, unfocused thoughts, for he said no more about getting married and beginning a life together in El Mirador, which was just as well with me.

"Maybe, but I know my parents will forbid the whole thing. They wouldn't let me live here and they would never let me quit school."

"Talk to them about it," he said.

That would be hopeless, I knew. I said instead, "I'll see what my aunt says, since I'll be asking to live with her."

"I was hoping," he said in a low voice, "that you would want to be here with me."

"Oh, I do," I exclaimed, "I do." To be near Casa Dañada and Pirrone was my all-consuming desire.

$\Diamond$ Chapter Two

MY AUNT WAS A SPIN-
ster who had that combination of innocence and naïveté, which is
quick to conjure up sin in almost any human relationship, but I was
willing to put up with anything to live in El Mirador. However, there
was some question whether my aunt would put up with me. She finally
agreed; I expect it was because she was lonely and, being a woman, she
had a basic need to be a caregiver. Even little girls nurture their dolls.

My parents, of course, would never understand. They had big ideas
for me to finish college and marry a man with degrees. Why would I give
up everything—in their view—to live among people who were going
nowhere? Oh, well, we had never gotten along, at least since I had
grown up and learned there was another life besides their ordered,
middle-class world and my mother's social bumps.

Brashly, as soon as I got home I decided to let them in on my decision. "Mother, I'm moving to El Mirador," I announced.

"You're what?" She was already displeased, but the shock had not yet reached her emotional threshold.

"It's true; I'm going to live with Aunt Jessie," I said.

"Does Jessie know this?"

"Of course, I asked her permission," I replied.

"You asked her without asking us first?" My mother's anger was rising fast.

"Yes, and she was very happy about the idea of having company," I said smugly.

"You can't. You have to finish college." Hysteria was setting in.

"I'm quitting school. You can't keep me here forever," I said with my newly acquired arrogance and sense of independence.

"Why are you going to that God-forsaken place?" The area was known for its hedonistic inhabitants, either rich, artistic, way-out, or all three. That's what God-forsaken meant to her. It was a milieu that suited such disparate people as Henry Miller and Jack Kerouac. The rich lived on far-flung, large spreads; the rest in trailers or shacks or small old houses. The enclave of El Mirador had the same mix except none of the rich. Some of those who lived in and near El Mirador later became known as hippies. It also had just normal people who had lived there a long time in old houses. I never understood why my aunt had moved there except that she had recently inherited a nice old house from a rather free-living bachelor cousin who must have thought it would be a joke to have this prudish old lady live among people she would consider wanton.

"Because Tom's moving there," I answered my mother's question.

"Ah, that explains it. Only a bum would go there."

"Don't you dare say anything against him."

"How will you support yourself?" she asked. I already knew my parents would never contribute anything to maintain me there.

"Aunt Jessie will feed me and Tom will take me out," I replied.

She started to cry. "I can see it already. You're going to live a life of sin."

"You forgot damnation." It was hopeless. She would never understand.

"We're going to talk to your father about this."

"It won't do any good. I'm nineteen and you no longer have any control over me. Tom told me so."

My father, who tended to be more reasonable than my mother—he also rarely spoke to any of us—walked in. "What terrible catastrophe has happened now?" He was sarcastic as usual.

My mother sobbed, "Alice is leaving us."

With his characteristic detachment, my father replied, "Well, it had to happen sometime."

"You don't understand." After an end-of-the-world look my mother went on to etch in acid the grim engraving of the fallen woman I had practically become.

"Alice," my father asked, "don't you want to finish college?"

"No, I hate it. It's boring and I have no idea why I am there. You know I go to the movies instead of my classes."

"Maybe it's better if she drops out for awhile. Alice is just taking up space and wasting our money." He certainly was more reasonable (and smarter) than my mother.

Despite all my mother's tears and tantrums, I moved to El Mirador, ready for a life I had once thought would never exist outside of my fantasies.

The house that my aunt had inherited was tucked in some pine trees on the edge of the tiny place, which was really only one street—a wider place on the coast road. The few houses in town were in back of the business section on alley-like side streets, some of them not even paved. It was a shabby town in a breathtaking setting, high above the cynosure of the ever-changing Pacific. The people were so accustomed to the majestic beauty around them that they seemed to ignore it. Tom had taken me to both the restaurants in town. They were on the side of the street away from the water and neither one had any windows. On the ocean side were two gas stations and a launderette to which I had gone with my aunt the second day I was there. Miraculously, it had a picture window framing a gorgeous view. Outside of the town were only large cattle and sheep ranches or the estates of the very rich.

When I went back to Casa Dañada with Tom in the daytime, I realized it was more unkempt than it had appeared at night. The kitchen was a mess of toppling dishes and empty bottles; the living room was only slightly better, with rumpled, aged magazines scattered around and old car parts on tables, on the floor, and even in chairs. I had not seen Serena, the maid, since New Year's Day and Liz did not appear to be interested in housekeeping.

Every time I was there, which was just about every day, there were always lots of people around who seemed to have no place else to go. I wondered if they were actually invited or if they just dropped in. Although Liz acknowledged them, much of the time she seemed to be in some kind of trance. I thought she must be deep in meditation, absorbed in some kind of Eastern mysticism. Or was she trying to leave reality by losing herself in secret reveries? But why would anyone want to leave such a fantastically exciting reality as Casa Dañada?

I sensed that the feeling of decaying grandeur at Dañada enhanced Pirrone's personality, even if it did nothing for Liz. He was the lord of the manor and he never let anyone forget it. Everyone did what Pirrone wanted. Even the half-wild, uncared-for Abyssinian cats, which I noticed occasionally sitting on window ledges like sphinxes, knew he was the master. They paid no attention to anyone else, but they always obeyed Pirrone's orders.

One afternoon, soon after I had moved to El Mirador, Tom telephoned me at my aunt's. "Liz and Pirrone want you to come for dinner tonight."

"What time?" I asked.

"I'll pick you up about ten." Dinner was usually served close to midnight because life did not begin until late afternoon, everyone having stayed up until three or four in the morning either holding long discussions or racing their cars. Now I knew why Liz did her laundry in the middle of the night; for her, it was still day.

When I got off the phone my aunt remarked, "Alice, I've heard about these people. They're completely immoral and you're bound to be influenced by them."

She made me mad. I yelled, "You have a dirty mind." She started to cry, saying I was ungrateful. At that moment she was right. I hated her. She was dumpy and old. Her face had fallen into her neck and her whole body had settled around her middle. She looked like a squash. How dare she, with her wizened-up, wasted life, tell me how to live?

She moaned, "I'm going to call your mother and father and tell them what is going on."

I screamed back, "You have a filthy imagination, Aunt Jessie. Nothing is going on." She was an old prune with no style. Her name was really Jessica but no one called her that. "Jessie" had the perfect sound for a dried-up old maid. "Jessica" had too much sophistication for her. But what if she had been called Jessica, would she have lived up to the qualities the name implied? Would she have been another Auntie Mame?

She was still crying and I was still furious. "I am going to call your father tonight and tell him what a wretched little girl you are," she said hoarsely, as she lowered herself stiffly into an ugly, tapestry-covered, pseudo-French fauteuil, which was incongruous in the small, rustic, knotty pine living room.

"Don't you dare do such a thing," I answered her, taking command. "I have not done anything to deserve all this." It was then that I realized how stupid this was. We had really gotten off to a bad start. I had only been in El Mirador a week, and I was fighting with my aunt with whom I had to live if I were to remain there. I felt sorry I had blown up and apologized. Poor Aunt Jessie, an old maid with the Victorian era hanging over her, how could she ever understand Pirrone and Liz?

But my emotions were racing ahead of me to Casa Dañada; I had no room for reflections on Aunt Jessie. The thought of seeing Pirrone started a wild, animal surging in my blood, making me restless and impatient to leave at once. Eventually, after an eon, the time came for Tom to pick me up. I was filled with anticipatory joy as we drove off.

When we arrived at Casa Dañada, we walked down the steps to the edge of a cliff where a guesthouse was perched—a glass aerie with a panoramic view of the ever-changing sea moods. The house, a recent addition to Dañada, could be made into one room or divided into three by sliding panels. On one of the panels was an old map of the original ranch. On the map were quaint drawings of hills and canyons, done head-on with no perspective, as in a primitive painting. The edges were eaten away as if gnawed by a mouse, and the whole thing had the brownish, weathered look of very old age.

On this night, Liz seemed very much alive and present. In fact, she was almost too animated. She had concocted an exotic dinner built around one of her specialties, capon soaked in Pernod and garnished with baby shrimp in nasturtium petals. It was good, but definitely different. Pirrone's dark Italian eyes danced as he told us of his Renaissance ancestors who plotted revolts against the aristocratic Milanese governments. His own father had once become involved with a powerful gangster—he did not elaborate as to how or why. Pirrone had met him and always remembered the glamour of bodyguards and the aura of the gangster's power.

"You certainly have a romantic background," I remarked, still vibrating to my own private romance with this Italian god of a man.

"It's fun to talk about," he replied.

"Do you know," commented Liz, her eyes glittering with a sort of false nervous elation, "Pirrone and I were in Rome at the same time? We knew the same people and even went once to the same party, but didn't meet."

"Wow," I observed, "missing each other like that, how did you ever meet?"

"After I had been back almost a year, a friend of mine said she wanted me to go out with a man I might like. She was right because there was an immediate attraction. Pirrone and I were married shortly afterwards."

Tom said to me, "That was right after I had met Pirrone. He invited me to the wedding party. I remember a lot of dancing, Greek music, and people breaking champagne glasses against the garage wall." I could imagine Tom on the sidelines watching all the wild goings-on because he was too reserved around loud groups of people to join in abandoned merriment.

"And after that," Liz said to Tom, "you and Pirrone and I missed that curve when we tried out Rick's new car." Rick Richards was an occasional guest at Dañada—one of the casual group who drifted in and out of the place.

"At least no one was hurt," Tom said laughingly. "I don't think you and Pirrone even noticed until we hit that boulder half-way down the cliff."

"Sounds wild," I commented.

"It was," Pirrone said with a smile.

I told Liz that her dinner was delicious and that I had never tasted anything quite like it.

Pirrone turned to me and said, "Alice, if you think this is unusual, wait until we get to Peru, because in Iquitos—Peru's Atlantic port— marinated piranhas are a delicacy."

Liz seemed amazed, "Hey, its the other way around. Piranhas are supposed to be man-eating fish."

"How can Peru have an Atlantic port," I asked, "when it isn't on the Atlantic?"

"Iquitos is actually twenty-three hundred miles from the Atlantic and is near the head of the Amazon. Ocean-going freighters from Europe go up the river," Pirrone said.

Tom added, "From Lima you can drive from sea level to sixteen thousand feet in eighty-five miles."

"That would make a sensational racecourse," said Pirrone, "we could start a new racing circuit, after we've been there awhile, and invite the world's top drivers. A South American Grand Prix."

"And we could race and beat them all," Tom said with a laugh.

"Right," said Pirrone, smiling. He seemed pleased with the vision of himself in this role. Tom and Pirrone thought of themselves, without having gone through any qualifying races on a competitive racetrack, as already being top drivers and assumed that if they ever had the inclination, they could win any race they entered.

"Has Tom told you where we're going to stay?" Liz asked me.

"No," I answered.

"With a friend of mine," Pirrone said, "Varian—he stays with us whenever he's in California. He lives in Miraflores. That's a small suburb on the ocean, outside of Lima."

"The house," added Liz, "is built in an olive grove and there are some fantastic gold and blue macaws that patrol the garden."

After dinner we sat in front of the glass window wall. The view was breath catching, nothing separating us from the ocean below but a thousand feet of vertical space. In the moonlight the velvet-dark sea embroidered lacy white collars around the rocks. I could see why Liz had mentioned earlier that it was such a pretty night they had decided to have dinner in this guesthouse.

"Casa Dañada must have an interesting history," I remarked.

"Did you know," asked Pirrone, "that Dañada was an original Spanish land grant of eleven square leagues? A league is equal to three miles."

"Gosh, how large would the land grant have been by the way we measure things today?" I asked.

"Well," Pirrone said, "of course, things today are either in acres or square miles. A square league would be nine square miles."

"I can figure that," I interrupted, "eleven square leagues would be ninety-nine square miles. Wow, it must have been a really huge ranch. And as I remember from California history, I don't think there were many true Spanish land grants, were there?"

"That's right. The Mexican government made most of the grants after its war of independence from Spain.

"Liz's great-great-great-great—I hope this is the correct number of greats—grandfather was a Spaniard who settled here. Dañada was one of the largest cattle ranches in this part of California. And except for your father, Liz, it still could have been one of the biggest."

"It wasn't really his fault," Liz argued, trying to protect her father's memory.

Pirrone replied, "He didn't handle things well at all. He lost most of the land that was left. I don't know why you defend him. He was more interested in all those old cars he collected. You know, the old barns and sheds are full of them. But he didn't bother to keep them maintained. They totally fell apart from neglect while he was still alive, as I understand it. They could have been very valuable if they had been taken care of, but now they're just junk."

Later Tom told me some of the cars he amassed weren't even housed at all; they just rusted out in the weather. One might expect to see old, broken-down cars outside of some run-down shack inhabited by low-lifes, but these cars could have been kept in perfect condition.

Liz, evidently not liking all this criticism of her father, started telling about life in the early days of the ranch. "Those barns once held hay for the horses. Everyone loved to ride. Of course, that was their only means of transportation. People would say a place was a short gallop away if it were fifty or sixty miles. Even in the towns and settlements, people got on their horses just to get to another house. They were as bad as people are today with cars. They rode around on the poor creatures all day. Sometimes they even ate their meals on horseback. The animals weren't fed or watered till late at night when their owners finally got off their backs."

"Too bad they didn't have the S.P.C.A. then," I said. "That would be considered cruelty to animals today."

Pirrone said, "I am sure they never thought of that. In fact, there were so many horses just roaming wild that they were hunted down to save grass for the cattle. Thousands of cattle roamed across the hills without any range fences."

"But," said Liz, defending the early settlers, "they were very gracious people. Their homes were always open to traveling strangers. They gave the travelers meals and fresh horses to ride. The ranchers would not accept payment and even left money in their guest rooms in case their visitors needed it."

"And," said Pirrone, "the hot springs were quite popular then."

"Really?" I was surprised, remembering the shocking lasciviousness of my introduction to them.

"Yes," said Pirrone, "there were a few shanties where families would stay for several days during the summer to take advantage of the springs' curative effects."

Liz said, "Tom, you and Alice should go there now that you have recovered from your colds."

"Oh," he replied nervously, "we'll have to do that." I thought I saw Liz turn for a second to cover up a smile.

It had gotten terribly late. We said goodnight to Pirrone and Liz, who seemed content to stay where they were in the guesthouse. Climbing up to Tom's car from there, I asked, "Does Pirrone really do nothing besides racing and entertaining? What about his family's factories? Does he still represent them?"

"Thinking about the trip keeps him busy now," Tom confided. "But he really doesn't need to do anything. He once told me his investments are so extensive that only his lawyers know his real worth."

"You mean that Pirrone is so wealthy he doesn't know, himself, how much money he has?"

"That's right," Tom said as he smiled. Then abruptly, he changed the subject. "How would you like to see my new design now?"

Of course I said I would. As he took me into the living room of the main house, where I supposed he had put the design, I realized that the view was not the only reason Liz had served dinner in the guesthouse. Old newspapers were piled around in heaps, a few sweaters and pieces of clothing had been dropped on a bench and were partly spilling onto the floor, books and magazines were strewn everywhere, several pairs of shoes were scattered around, and pieces of furniture had been shoved out of their accustomed places.

Idly I picked up a small yellow Kodak film can off a messy table and absentmindedly started to unscrew the top. Tom reacted with alarm. "Don't touch that!" he ordered in an agitated way.

"Why?" I was surprised.

He seemed confused as if trying to think of a reason. "It has some film of a car I used to have. I could never replace it."

I knew what cars meant to him. If the film were exposed and ruined, it would be a tragedy for Tom. "What's it doing here?" I asked.

"Pirrone took the pictures. He's just never gotten around to having them developed." I wondered why he had not. It seemed like a simple thing to do. But I did not ask; the whole subject upset Tom terribly. I asked why everything was so disheveled.

"That woman keeps this place in a mess," Tom muttered.

"You mean Serena?" I asked.

"No. Liz," he said.

"Where is Serena?" I inquired.

"Oh, she's off taking care of something." Tom acted as though he did not want to explain further. "It's messy in here. Let's go to the library," he said.

The library wasn't too neat either but it was in better shape than the living room. Tom picked up the books that were scattered on the massive couch, a piece that could have been from the Renaissance era on which I could picture Lorenzo de Medici lounging. As we sat down Tom slipped his arm around me. The shadowy light from the chandelier of tiny electric candle flames softened the usually sharp outlines of his face, making him look boyishly innocent. It made me want to hold him tenderly.

"Alice, you're more beautiful than my Hilde was."

"You didn't tell me you used to go out with a girl named Hilde," I said.

"No, that was a car I used to have. I thought it was the most beautiful thing in the world until I met you."

I was honest enough with myself to know that I looked all right but not beautiful. But coming from him, to be compared with a prized car was the ultimate compliment; it made me feel terribly desirable.

Even though he had treated me casually for so long, I had come to realize he really cared for me. I told myself his lack of demonstrativeness was because of his shyness with girls. He felt comfortable with me, I thought, because from the beginning he had put me in a separate category from other girls—treating me more like a guy at the start.

"It's strange," he went on. "I care more about you than myself. I've never felt this way about anyone. I wouldn't do anything to hurt you, because it really means something to have someone who cares."

He had told me before that when he was little his mother had a habit of throwing out a lot of his stuff when she straightened up his room. This was very upsetting to him and translated into a lack of concern for him and a lack of interest in what he valued. I guess he had been so traumatized by this that he felt a need to be recognized. One night when we were on a hilltop overlooking the lights of Los Angeles, he said, "I want to rise above all those faceless people out there. Most of them just live and die without anyone ever knowing."

As Tom went on to tell me how much he cared for me, I began to feel a responding emotion. He kissed me and caressed me gently, arousing not wanting in me but rather tenderness. I felt confused. I was feeling a warm glow for Tom, but it was nothing like the wild, to-hell-with-anyone-or-anything-else desire I had for Pirrone. Which one was love? Or dare I call what I felt for Pirrone love? It was madness. Still, I cannot deny that there was sexuality in this closeness with Tom. But then he broke the pleasant mood, saying, "If I can't make anything of myself, I'll leave you and find some nice, dull girl and make her deliriously happy."

Why would I care how great he was? Besides, it was conceited of him to think that he was like the prince in Cinderella, with every girl in the world yearning to be the one he chose. Suddenly I remembered why we had come in there and asked about his new design.

"Design?" He seemed surprised. "Oh, did I say design? It's really too late now. Anyway, I just wanted an excuse to come up here with you."

He was back to not making any sense. Why did he need an excuse when I was sure he must have known I would have come anyway? He had been almost deceptive.

As Tom finished talking Pirrone popped into the library. "Oh, there you two are. How about a race, Tom?"

"Hey, right," Tom answered with a sudden spark of energy. "I'll race you back to Alice's aunt's."

I was thrilled that I would be in on the excitement of a midnight race. Actually, it was way past midnight.

Tom had asked me to go for a ride with him the next day but when he came to get me he was driving the Fazani. He said, "We've got to hurry. My car went over an embankment last night. Pirrone is waiting for me with a cable truck to pull it up. I am taking you to see Liz. I'll see you back at Dañada when we're finished."

"Did you race on the way back, too, last night?" I asked.

"Yeah." He sounded defensive. "The steering wheel came off."

"Tom, you're crazy. What an excuse. But are you all right?"

"I'm fine, but my car isn't. I think the front end might be demolished." How tragic for Tom—to have his beloved car damaged, even though it was already somewhat of a wreck, although not in his eyes.

When we reached Dañada after a super speedy ride, Pirrone was sitting in a truck with the motor running. He said to me, "Tom's steering wheel came off. That's a new kind of accident, don't you think?"

Then I heard Tom say to Pirrone in a whisper, "There is some of his paint on my bumper." They left with the promise that they would be back before long.

I went into the house. Liz was bringing fresh flowers in the living room. She pushed aside some of the clutter on a table and started to make a flower arrangement in a vase. I watched, entranced by her aesthetic sense. She was massing colors strikingly, sticking just the right stalk here and the right leaf there. She stood back and surveyed her artistic effort when she was through.

Then she seemed annoyed by the disarray of the room. She started to shove things into some kind of order. As she was doing this, she noticed the yellow cartridge film can I had picked up the night before. She hurriedly grabbed it as a knock came on the portico door. She quickly shoved the film can into a pocket. She seemed very disturbed. I could not tell whether it was because of the knock or the film can, but I had no chance to ask as she went over to the door, saying, "Oh, dear, who would be calling so early?" It was already after two. "Anybody we know would just walk in."

Liz opened the door and was greeted by two snobbish looking girls. (Girls? They looked so settled they could easily have been thirty.) They wore expensive but drab countryish suits. One had a fur coat tossed over her shoulders and spoke for both. "We would have called first but your phone appears to be disconnected," she said.

This sort of thing happened now and then. Liz was very negligent, rarely bothering to pay bills on time. She often let them go until the bill collectors were after her. When one called she became the English maid or German or whatever accent appealed to her at the time, not to evade payment, but rather out of embarrassment.

Liz introduced me to the callers. Then she apologized for the way she looked, explaining that she had just gotten up. They looked horrified and seemed to be trying not to stare at Liz's costume: one of Pirrone's shirts, much too large and too long, covering her cut-off jeans completely. I wondered if they thought she had nothing on under the shirt. She usually was careless in her dress but very bohemian.

The more pleasant looking caller said, "Liz, we haven't seen each other since school. We thought it would be nice to see you again. We are on our way back to the City." (To San Franciscans, there is no other city.) "We thought this would be a nice side trip. It isn't often we have the time to do something like this. We're so busy, what with the children, the League, luncheons, dinner parties, and you know all the things one has to do...."

"Yes, I am awfully busy, too," Liz exclaimed. I wondered at that statement.

"Oh, what are you doing?" the snootier one, the one with the fur coat (mink I guess) asked in a rather nasty way.

"Well...ah...I do read a lot," Liz stammered.

The other one said in a nicer tone, "Yes, you always did."

Liz did seem embarrassed about the condition of the room. She kept making little apologetic remarks about it as the callers gave darting glances out of the corners of their eyes, looking at it in apparent disbelief. It really was a shambles—a half-empty bottle of Pernod, half-filled coffee cups scattered around, a partially eaten piece of cake on a plate, a sweater partly on but mostly falling off a chair, and dust everywhere, with cobwebby lint clouds drifting lazily over the floor. Liz was ill at ease. Was she haunted by the memories of gracious living she had known as a young girl? Unlike graceful upper-class luxury, seemingly operated by an army of elves silently managing the clockworks that make the whole elegant Hollywood movie scene revolve, Liz was now committed to a slobbish life that was comfortable for her and her present entourage. But the past had intruded.

Liz said, "I wish you could meet my husband, but he's out with a friend on a cable truck."

"In a truck?" Miss Fur Coat said in startled surprise.

"He's helping Alice's boyfriend pull up his wrecked car."

Evidently, in an effort to change the subject, the pleasanter one said to Miss Fur Coat, "Why don't you tell them about the wonderful trip you took to South America."

Liz saw something in common to talk about. "Oh, I'd love to hear about it; we're going to South America."

"What airline?" they asked together.

"We're going on our own boat."

They were impressed. "Is it a sailboat or a motor cruiser?"

"We haven't bought it yet. Pirrone is looking at a keen boat—an old rumrunner."

"Oh," they said in a falling tone.

Then the less nice one said in a bitchy, malevolent way, "You'll be all set to smuggle whiskey or watches or whatever." She was being nasty rather than trying to interject some light humor. She continued, "I have been reading that it is done quite profitably by some criminal types on yacht trips to South America."

Liz looked very upset and confused by this statement. I looked out the window as Miss Fur Coat finished talking and saw a chunky, gangsterish-looking man walking through the portico. The two callers, seeing him also, gasped almost in unison.

The one who had told about the profitable smuggling said with her sardonic humor, "And there is the perfect accomplice for you." She continued that it was getting late and that they really must leave. They both said, with insincere voices, how nice it had been to see Liz and to meet me.

Liz seemed relieved when they had left. "I am glad I am not in their trap. What dull lives they must lead."

I wanted to ask Liz right away about the man we had seen but I didn't because she seemed so disturbed when her school friend had said he was the perfect accomplice. Instead, I said, "They're such snobs, it doesn't seem like they have any fun at all."

Liz said, "They're typical society hypocrites. Of the four or five people I knew who were adventurous enough to want to escape the mold only one succeeded. She's a singer in a little club in New York…she's quite good."

I knew that Liz's parents had been very much caught up in the social grind, entertaining and partying in the endless filling in of time of the wealthy and unoccupied. They had little time or interest for Liz and I imagined they were bored with each other, too. Liz, an only child, must have felt lonely and unwanted. Being shy and not pretty, she must have been hurt when she heard unkind remarks by her parents' friends, as children do. Of course, I was just imagining all this but it did seem that this must have happened to her and caused her to stray from her place in life.

Perhaps she was following somewhat the same pattern as her parents, but without any structure, in her own déclassé way, with her days spent in entertainment though casual and extemporaneous.

The encounter with her old school friends seemed to have made Liz restless. She was talking nervously, constantly changing the subject, as though unable to concentrate. She finally found something to talk about that was agreeable to her.

"Have you ever heard of Lady Jane Digby?" she asked hopefully.

Since I had not, she went on to tell me about this nineteenth-century Englishwoman who had left the confines of London society, drifting into an unconventional life with many lovers and husbands, the last a charismatic sheik named El Mezrab. I thought of Omar Sharif on an Arabian horse in *Lawrence of Arabia*. I could be in love with such a desert chieftain.

The El Mezrabs lived half the year in a semi-European style in Damascus. The members of the tribe would descend on the Damascus household, spreading themselves all over the place, watering their camels at Jane's lovely fountains, camping in her beautiful gardens and swarming all over the house, even sleeping on the stairs.

The story seemed to reinforce Liz's chosen (or, perhaps, fallen-into) situation, brightening her self-image. Pirrone did seem like a modern-day El Mezrab and Liz had that quality of giving and being gracious. She always welcomed her husband's following.

Reading about them I had become enthralled by those nineteenth-century Europeans who had first discovered the exotic, mystical Middle East—Richard Burton compiling a vast lexicon of Middle Eastern erotica and infiltrating Mecca, Gordon gallantly defending doomed Khartoum. The mysteriousness of the East with its eroticism and shadowy places fitted into my fascination with the sinister. I loved its romantic and ominous tinge and I did not associate sinister with either wrong or bad.

I wanted to ask Liz how Casa Dañada had acquired its name. I had never gotten over my curiosity but I had not known her well enough yet to ask. Since Liz was friendly and accessible this afternoon, it seemed like a good opportunity. But then I suddenly remembered the little film can. I asked about it instead.

"Oh," she said, "Pirrone took some pictures of the Fazani. I was supposed to have them developed. I forgot about it."

Her explanation seemed logical except that Tom had said the pictures were of his car. Liz must have been mixed up as to whose car had had its picture taken. But there was something strange about the way Tom had reacted over nothing more than some undeveloped film.

Liz and I wandered outside. As we passed the open library door, I was surprised to hear Pirrone talking. I did not know Tom and he were back. Then I heard a second Italian accent but rougher and cruder. I stopped and looked into the room to see who owned the coarse voice. In the gloom of the library, dimly lit with its small windows set in the thick adobe walls, a dark man melted into the shadows. I strained to see him better from our distance in the brighter light of the portico. I was certain he was the man we had seen earlier. He looked as if he had slid through a tub of Vaseline—the expression "grease ball" came to mind. His dark naval officer's cap, black turtleneck shirt, and sailors' pants made him darker yet. The whole effect was shadowy, threatening and unreal.

Pirrone said, "A schooner's too big. I would never have enough guys to sail it."

The man replied, "I can loan you some men for a crew."

As he spoke he walked into a ray of afternoon sunlight from one of the narrow windows, and I could see a gold bangle dangling from one of his ears. Immediately he turned into a pirate. Just like that he could loan Pirrone a crew—and what would he want in return? Part of the gold treasure we were going to mine in South America. Gold was always pirate booty.

"Who's that?" I asked Liz after we had passed the open door.

"A man Pirrone knows who has a fishing fleet. He has some leads on boats."

At that moment the man changed in my mind from a pirate into a big slippery fish before he became a fisherman. But he looked more like a smuggler of opium. He reminded me of some character from a very old late-night TV movie with a title like "East of Singapore." I was taken by his intriguing sinisterness. It would almost be romantic to be a fishing fleet owner's girlfriend. We could go on fishing trips together. But I was getting silly; I hated fishing. However, new and fascinating people were always turning up at Dañada.

We walked on to the driveway. Tom was there with the wreck. It didn't look very good but he said the damage was superficial. He would be able to drive it or even race it without any repairs, even though the outside was messed up.

Liz teased him about the accident. When she noticed that he seemed hurt, she said it could only have been caused by a mechanical failure because he was much too good a driver to make a mistake. He seemed to be mollified and not to have noticed the very slight irony in her voice. Liz was so kind I am sure it crept in without her knowing it.

Pirrone walked up. Again I trembled in blissful agitation, as if an electric current had been turned on by Pirrone's strong masculinity. This feeling still happened whenever I saw him, although my great overwhelming passion for him was gradually being replaced by my growing affection for Tom. I had no wild, unquenchable desire for Tom, yet what I did feel for him was infinitely easier to live with—the security of belonging to and being wanted by someone who cared deeply for me.

Pirrone suggested that we celebrate the salvaging of Tom's car at

Nepenthe, a far-out, funky restaurant in a spectacular spot on the Coast Highway. I was excited because I had been enchanted the one time I had been there a few years before. The free-form, Frank Lloyd Wright-type building fitted its thrilling setting high above the edge of the Pacific, giving it the right feeling for the Age of Aquarius. Its exuberant design created the perfect setting for a gathering place of the enlightened, free-living artists and writers of Big Sur. Adding to its aura was the name Nepenthe, a drug used by the ancient Greeks that supposedly caused one to forget sorrow. On the same magnificent site was an old adobe, which had been a honeymoon retreat for Orson Welles and Rita Hayworth.

As we sat on the veranda before leaving I was surprised to see Serena slithering up the walkway with her undulating walk. She slid in next to Pirrone.

I immediately said, "Hi Serena, did you just get back? Where have you been?"

She seemed not to hear me as she said some inaudible thing to Pirrone while gazing adoringly at him. No one else volunteered an answer for her. Soon Liz appeared carrying a plate of little cakes covered with violet petals.

Looking at them, Pirrone asked, "What in hell are these?"

"Don't you like them? They're in honor of our night."

I wondered what she meant by "our night." Serena seemed bothered by Liz's statement.

Liz went on to say, "The violets in the garden were so pretty."

"Next time, why don't you leave them there," Pirrone said in disgust.

In contrast to her cast-off clothing of the afternoon, Liz was elegantly dressed in silk printed in the grand manner of Pucci, and with her well-combed hair she could have stepped off a fashion page. Serena looked glamorous and sensual, the way I remembered her from New Year's Day.

We were waiting for Erica and Brian. Brian had been a childhood friend of Liz. His mother and father had been close friends of Liz's parents. But when his family lost their fortune, Brian started to drift through life, finally coming to rest as one of the Rivellis' hangers-on and also as a permanent houseguest. Brian had an artistic bent as well as being very erudite; neither of these talents equipped him for making a living, so the ethos at Dañada (also the free room and board) cushioned him against that.

When Brian and Erica arrived, Pirrone brought out a huge brown carton, four or five feet tall. With a flourish he announced, "Liz, I have a little present for you."

"Little," Brian said with a laugh.

Liz's eyes lit up with joy, "Why, you shouldn't have."

"Go ahead, open it," Pirrone urged.

"Is it a refrigerator?" Liz asked.

"How could I have carried it if it were?" Pirrone answered petulantly.

Liz opened the carton to find progressively smaller boxes, one inside the other. Finally she got to a tiny package wrapped in gold foil paper. She became so excited that it was difficult for her to unwrap it. At last she succeeded, disclosing a mother of pearl snail sitting on a lapis lazuli leaf surveying a ruby path across the leaf.

Breathlessly, she asked, "Is it an antique?"

"Yeah, it's an old bug. Let me pin it on you. But first I want to show you how cleverly the snail opens." He pressed something on the side of the pin, and the snail shell opened. The pin was also a tiny container.

Liz said, "That should be very handy."

I imagined she was only being gracious. What could one put in that small place—a few tiny saccharin tablets for coffee? But skinny Liz did not need those.

After Pirrone pinned it on her, she threw her arms around him. "Oh, love, it's gorgeous. How wonderful of you to think of me."

"It's nothing. Nothing's too good for you."

True. I thought, nothing is what she gets from Pirrone most of the time. Except for tonight, I had been under the impression he was more interested in his car or other things. I also noticed that Serena seemed bored by the entire performance.

"Let's go," said Pirrone.

We went to the garage and got into the cars. Serena went with the Rivellis. The Fazani started first. I liked the sound of its finely tuned engine. It was perfectly made, like a Swiss watch, except much louder. The sound of motors being gunned and of tires crunching on the gravel mixed with the gay chatter as we left Dañada.

"We'll wait for you at Nepenthe," Pirrone yelled to Tom.

"Thanks," retaliated Tom. "What do you want me to order for you while we're waiting?"

We were off and picking up speed. Soon Tom was driving at well over a hundred miles an hour. Everything became a blur of darkening land and sky. There was a thrill to the element of danger and a certain excitement to the speed itself; the only steady thing was the constant black of the pavement. There was a funny feeling that the car was eating up the broken white line.

The Fazani zoomed by us on the straightaway. We had passed it a minute before on a curve. Liz yelled something as they passed but the wind blotted out whatever it was that she said. By now it was completely dark and all I could see were the Fazani's taillights. Then we went around a curve sideways as we passed the Fazani again. I was very scared.

Tom, looking calm, told me not to worry. "I know what I'm doing. Pirrone can pass me on the straight stretches, but I can take him on the curves." But Pirrone quickly overtook us.

A car raced toward us down the deserted road. It swerved over the white line as it approached us. I was terrified. I had a vision in that millionth of a second that it was all over—my life would end right there on this mountain road. As Tom pulled hard to the right the other car grazed us ever so slightly, jolting us terribly. Only our seat belts and shoulder harnesses kept us from flying into the dashboard.

Tom swore, "That damn bastard is after me again. Last night wasn't enough. I am sure as hell not going to play chicken with him."

I was astounded. He was hit last night. That was why he went over the embankment. Why did he not tell me that? I asked Tom over the roar of the engine.

He yelled back, "You ask too many questions."

What was going on here? Who was after Tom, and why? Did it have anything to do with the secret designs for a radical new car that Tom had told me about? Was someone trying to kill him because his plans were a threat to Detroit? He had said that Detroit might try to steal them. Anyway, the other car's driver was taking a terrible chance. In a head-on collision, he could have easily been killed, too. For me, as they had for another Alice, thing were getting curiouser and curiouser.

We crossed a little bridge that arched sharply enough for the wheels of the car to leave the road momentarily as we went over the top, like a skier making a galundasprung off a mogul. A few miles further on, Tom slowed down abruptly as we saw the Fazani. It was stopped and a Highway Patrol car's lights were flashing behind it.

When Tom and I reached Nepenthe, we climbed up the winding walkway and sat down at an outside table. A short time later, Pirrone, Liz, and Serena walked in.

"Hey, Pirrone," Tom called out, "I ordered your drinks."

"Thanks," Pirrone said. "You had an unfair advantage."

Just then Brian and Erica arrived. "Did you get a ticket?" asked Brian.

"Yeah, dammit, for driving ninety-five in a fifty-five-mile zone. Actually I was going much faster. After the guy wrote it, he asked me about the Fazani. I offered to race him here. He laughed it off, but I know he was tempted." Thoughtfully Pirrone continued, "What's a ticket once in awhile? My philosophy is to enjoy life right now. Tomorrow is too late if I haven't lived today."

"Of course, you're lucky," I commented to Pirrone. "You have the means to do anything you want."

"That's true, and it's quite nice," he said.

I thought how different Liz was—for her, money had little meaning: it might as well be the blades of grass on the nearby hills. As for life, she did not seem to care whether she lived it today or tomorrow.

Pirrone was saying, "Wait until we get to Peru. After we mine the gold, we're going to build a hacienda and farm our land."

Brian broke in, "Do you know how important the hacienda is in Peru? It's an entire social system. It's really rather medieval—the people who belong to the hacienda are close to being serfs. Their lives are bound up in the hacienda from birth to death. And the funny thing is that even the few children who grow up to be intellectuals accept it without a thought because they have never known any other kind of life. This culture has hardly been written about or studied."

And here Brian, thousands of miles away, knew about such an esoteric sociological situation. How erudite he was, always reading about obscure but interesting things. Amoeba-like he surrounded all these little-known facts, assimilating them and gaining great pleasure from the osmosis. From his immense storehouse of almost unlimited knowledge, he loved extracting, and then discussing strange facets of nature or odd subjects. Yet for a person who talked a lot, Brian was surprisingly interested in and concerned about other people. He spoke from a desire to communicate with and relate to other people rather than for the pleasure of hearing his own voice.

Pirrone went along on the same line as before, indicating that power was the theme that self-interested him. "There is a bond between the peons on the place and the haciendat, as the lord of the manor is called. He is the godfather for most of the children born there. So I'll be more like the head of a big family than an employer." Pirrone's voice had an odd quality, which I had noticed before—an unearthly tone, preternatural, I thought with a cold shiver.

"But Pirrone," Erica said, "that all sounds ancestral and we'll be immigrants."

"That's true, but Varian can smooth the way for us. And he may get me a political appointment which will make me more of a citizen." Pirrone was thinking of himself, as usual. But, after all, he was financing the venture.

Brian lost interest in the subject. "I think we should have a naturalistic photograph of Dañada before we leave."

"How?" Liz was curious.

"We could pose in front of the adobe," Brian replied. "A naked Dañada portrait." Tom's eyes lit up at the thought.

"Marvelous," exclaimed Liz, "it would be like a Titian of Dañada."

"We could sell postcards." Pirrone's suggestion reminded me again of the strata of salaciousness I had begun to detect in his well-bred manner.

Until this time in my life I had read voraciously, gone to museums and movies, but for the most part lived in my imagination. But, here, sitting with me, were people who actually lived like the characters in some wild, unusual novel. I wanted to grasp the moments they created in which the dividing line between fantasy and actuality blended imperceptibly.

My thoughts were interrupted by a Highway Patrol officer approaching our table. He walked up to Pirrone.

"Hey, buddy, how about that race?"

"Sure," said Pirrone with his half-smile. "You see," he said in an aside to us as he got up to follow the Highway Patrolman out, "everything eventually goes my way. Sometime, I'll tell you about getting to people's minds."

"Love," Liz pleaded, "you promised...."

"We'll still spend the night together when I finish the race."

"I've got to see this." Brian got up as he took Erica's hand. "Come on, Alice and Liz." We all rushed down to see the start of the race as the officer turned on his siren to clear the road. Soon afterwards Liz and I crowded in with Tom and drove back at a high speed, but we were far behind. When we got to Dañada, Pirrone and the patrolman were already sitting in the living room, planning their next race. I could tell Liz was furious when she saw them but she calmed down into a weary resignation, her expression saying, "Oh, what's the use?"

Serena had gone on the race with Pirrone and was sitting next to him. He leaned over and gave her a rather loving hug, leaving his arm around her, which seemed to be an awfully friendly way to treat a maid. But, of course, she was treated as an equal.

Liz sighed and announced, "Good night, I'm going to bed." Pirrone seemed not to hear.

After the officer left I overheard Pirrone ask Serena if she had unpacked yet. She nodded. Then he said, "Run along like a good girl and put it in the library."

As Tom and I were leaving I saw her take a suitcase to the library. I wondered what she had brought back for Pirrone from wherever she had been.

The next day I happened to go into the library as Pirrone was carefully examining an empty suitcase. He looked up when he heard me come in.

"I think Serena was imagining her suitcase was badly banged up. I don't think it's wrecked enough to ask the airline for damages," he said in response to my questioning look.

But on the way back to my aunt's that night all that my mind was focused on was what was in the little yellow film can, not the contents of Serena's suitcase. I asked Tom if I could see the pictures of his old car when they were developed.

"Pictures? Oh, yes." He seemed for a minute not to know what I was talking about. Then he said, "Of course, of course, if Liz ever gets around to getting them developed."

Before, Tom had said Pirrone had never gotten around to having them done.

"Why don't you have them developed?" I suggested.

"I'm too busy."

Busy doing what, I wondered. Except, of course, working on his car or forever racing up and down the mountain roads. Liz and Tom had been so evasive about and protective of the little film can, there must be something in it that they did not want anyone to see. Had someone taken pictures of the nude bathing at the hot springs and they were afraid to have them commercially developed? Were they worried about having the film confiscated as pornography?

I asked Tom when we were going to South America. He answered in a very depressed way, "We might not go. There are complications in South America. Pirrone is now thinking of ranching in Australia."

"But," I said, "at Nepenthe he seemed very excited about his plans for living in Peru. He said nothing about Australia."

"He didn't want to upset the others because he hasn't definitely decided. But since I don't want to go if it's Australia I am sure I can influence him against it." I wondered if anyone could influence Pirrone.

"What's wrong with Australia?" I asked.

"I don't want to be a rancher," he replied, "and since I won't go, that in itself should make him have doubts, because he needs me to look after the details." How could Tom with his unfocused mind arrange details? He would keep them about as straight as Liz's living room. But I felt alarmed, afraid that I would have to leave this dreamscape and go back to college.

"Does Brian want to go to Australia?" I asked.

"He doesn't know about the new plan," he replied.

"Why don't you tell him, then the two of you could talk Pirrone out of going."

"Brian? No way. Pirrone only listens to me."

"Gee," I said, "then, I hope you can talk him into going to South America." I knew how much going to Peru meant to Tom because he had told me many times. Going to Peru had become an obsession for him—the solution to everything.

One night while we were talking, he told me that he had never found any job he really liked. He kept switching from one temporarily held job to another, driving a delivery truck, parking cars, working in an automobile parts store. But they were all stopgap things until the day he found the right situation.

I asked, "Did you expect the right job to just magically drop out of the sky like some sort of heavenly gift?"

"That's silly, but there is a lot in being in the right place at the right time. Opportunity is funny, it happens all the time unexpectedly."

"Well," I said, "I don't think El Mirador is the right place. The only jobs here are working in the gas station or being a waiter."

"Oh, but it really is the right place. After all, I wouldn't be having the chance to go to South America if I weren't here."

I realized then that he just wanted to indulge himself in his love affair with racing cars. The South American gold was the answer for him. It would eliminate his ever having to work again.

$\Diamond$ Chapter Three

I STILL WONDERED about the origins of the name, Dañada. Several times I had almost asked Liz when I was alone with her, but I had hesitated because I had a vague feeling that she was a doomed soul herself. However, my curiosity never diminished as the dulcet days floated by in a never-ending vacation.

I especially enjoyed sitting next to Tom in the Fazani, watching his intense expression as he concentrated on the tachometer while he told me about the precision with which it was necessary to shift gears. I often felt, as we slid around the hairpin curves, transported to the Grande Corniche, swirling dizzyingly at the edge of sheer drops on the Côte d'Azur. Of course, I had never been there, but I imagined it to be something like this.

I was becoming quite attached to Tom and accustomed to being with him most of the time. It was a comfortable, relaxed relationship. He was undemanding and agreeable, always seeming to be pleased with me, liking whatever I said or did. He gave me little compliments that reinforced my femininity; I began to feel both beautiful and confident. Tom also liked excitement as much as I did and he was filled with the same need for adventure. His cryptic statements, which had once annoyed me, I now enjoyed, delighting in his strange view of things. I appreciated how out of the ordinary he was and how much he belonged in the Dañada contingent—being one of them and at the same time contributing something unique of his own.

Even thought we were in the middle of a free love environment Tom never made any sexual advances toward me, which suited me just fine. While I felt closeness and affection for Tom, desire was not included. I was still consumed by lust for Pirrone.

On one of our many days spent driving around, we went along the coast toward Monterey, ending up in an area of large, newish houses hugging the water's edge near Carmel. Suddenly at the end of a cul-de-sac Tom swung into a driveway whose entrance was well hidden by dense growth.

"Tom, no one is following us. I haven't seen a Highway Patrol car all day. The sneaky way you turned in here, one would think you were trying to give someone the slip. Anyway, it looks like this driveway belongs to someone's house."

"Don't tell anyone," he said.

"Tom, please make sense. I don't see anyone to tell it to. And don't tell them what?"

"There's a fantastic house in here," he answered.

"Won't the people object to our coming in here?" I asked.

"It belongs to a friend of Pirrone's," Tom replied.

"Did he invite you to come?"

"He's away on a fishing trip."

As we wound down the long approach to the imposing fortress-like house, built of the same rocks and boulders between which it was wedged, I said to Tom, "It's such a huge estate there must at least be some servants here."

"He takes all his men with him when he goes fishing," was Tom's answer to my question.

"Do you mean all his servants are guys? Tom, is he gay?" The thought of homosexuality upset me.

"He gives those guys a chance. They have police records or dishonorable discharges or can't get jobs for one reason or another." Tom's answers were always so unsatisfactory—if one could call them answers.

I gave up trying to find out why we were there. Perhaps all he had in mind was showing me the "fantastic house" as he had said. If that was it, I might as well take a good look.

It easily could have been a hermitage; it was quite hidden and protected. Terminating a small creek was an estuary running into the ocean, partially encircling the part of the building that did not face the ocean, almost surrounding the house like a moat. I made appreciative remarks about the grounds and the many birds floating on the small lagoon, hoping that was what Tom wanted to hear, but he did not seem to react.

By the front door Tom reached under a rock, pulling out a key. He seemed to know this place well—too well. Was it used as a rendezvous for some of Pirrone's friends for their affairs as in the Jack Lemmon movie, "The Apartment"? I wondered what Tom had in mind for us?

The interior walls were made of the same rugged stone as the outside and were covered with all kinds of guns and rifles attached to them.

"Tom, what are all the firearms for?" I asked. It was so ominous-looking that I began to shiver.

"Just decoration," he answered. "He likes to display his collection. To him they're works of art," Tom added in an offhand manner, as if there were nothing unusual about having a house full of guns.

Standing on the slate floors were numerous artillery pieces. "And I suppose these are his sculptures," I remarked facetiously.

"You're right." Tom was cryptic as usual.

There was a candelabrum on a table reminiscent of the coiled snakes of Dañada. This one was a giant octopus clutching a candle in each tentacle. Definitely sinister. This fort, for that was the feeling this rock-pile gave me, could easily have held out against a small army, if the seaward windows were boarded up. The rest of the house seemed to be practically windowless. A chill of dread made me shudder. I could imagine myself imprisoned here with no one able to hear my calls for help, my cries drowned out by the surf's pounding, if my screams could ever penetrate the massive walls.

I looked over at some bookcases that were filled with what looked like sets of perfectly bound and matched books. They had to be fake, the kind interior decorators use for not very literate clients who own few books, their elegant gold, black, and red bindings merely shells hooked together in a sham facade. At the top of one of the bookcases was a row of film containers, exactly like the one that had been on Liz's living room table.

"Is he a photography nut?" I asked Tom as I visualized hundreds of little film cans hidden behind the rows of pretend books.

"I don't know," answered Tom, "why do you ask?"

"There're some little yellow film cans up there," I said as I gestured to them.

"Oh, those," was Tom's answer.

What did he mean by that? I asked him.

"They're film cans, so what?"

Why was he so anxious to drop the conversation? Was he bored with my curiosity? I decided my inquisitiveness was foolish and pointless, at least as far as getting an answer from Tom.

"Let me show you the den," Tom said, holding out his hand.

Den was right; never have I seen a room that fitted the name better. It was a real cave, with animal skin rugs on the floor and still more guns on the walls. Was this more decoration? Or were they part of an arsenal cleverly concealed as ornaments?

"Tom, he must have mob connections and this is his arms depot." Tom seemed bothered by my statement. Had I hit on a secret?

"Let's go," he said. "You don't appreciate this place."

"You can say that again. It's positively creepy."

I walked ahead, out of the house, the way we had come in. Tom lagged behind. I turned back to see what was keeping him. He had stopped in front of the bookshelves. In the gloomy shadows—he was at the other end of the long room—I saw him put something into his pocket. From my distance it looked as if it might be one of the little film cans, but I could not tell for sure. Had he taken one of them? And if he had, why?

I called to him, "What are you doing?"

"Nothing," he said.

I was more certain than ever that there was something mysterious

about the film can at Dañada, and added to these there had to be more
to it, with all the diverse excuses about them. I had to find out what was
going on. The next chance I got I would open the one at Dañada if it
was still there.

As we drove away, I thought the friend who owned this place must
be the fishing fleet owner with whom Pirrone had been talking. The
character I had seen in the Rivellis' library had offered to loan Pirrone
a crew. However, this establishment was much too grand for a mere
fishing fleet operator. Perhaps, he had a chain of fishing fleets or he
might even be a member of the Mafia—he had looked very under-
worldish. This place could easily have belonged to a gangster. When
we reached the end of the driveway, I heard what sounded like a
gunshot.

"What's that?" I screamed.

"Some car backfiring," Tom replied.

I was sure I had seen a glimpse of a heavy-set, dark-haired, Italian-
looking man in the bushes as we drove out. I told Tom. I added that it
could be the man who was trying to kill Pirrone.

He said, "You're imagining things. No one was there."

We drove into Monterey and Tom took me to dinner on the water-
front. The restaurant was in an old building which had once been a cannery. The whole area, known as Cannery Row, was undergoing a face-
lift and was being made into a posh dining and entertainment spot. The
restaurant itself was dark and elegant, but still had traces of its original
character underneath all the creative rejuvenation. It was an enchanting place.

"This is a great place for a restaurant—right on the bay. What happened to the canneries?" I asked Tom. "Did tourism push them out the
way land developers have wiped out the orange groves in Southern
California?"

"No," he said, "one day the sardines stopped coming to Monterey
Bay. Before that there had been zillions of them and then, poof, there
were none."

"Well the sardines were pretty smart to leave. They can't say poor
fish about them, can they?"

We ate, enveloped in a romantic aura in the dimly lit elegance, as
we looked out at the sparkling lights dancing lightly over the velvety-

dark bay. I forgot all about the unsettling afternoon in the arsenal. Had that been Tom's intent—to erase from my mind what must have been near-truths that I had surmised in that eerie place?

Tom was especially tender, holding my hand gently but tentatively, telling me he never wanted anything to spoil me.

"You're like a perfect rose. It's like I'm afraid to touch you for fear I will bruise a petal."

I laughed. "Tom, you're a poet. But I'm just a plain, ordinary, every-day girl."

"To me you're not. You're very special," he said with a slight look of being hurt because I didn't accept his poetic simile. But it made me feel strange that he had placed me in a glass case like a fragile art object that can only be enjoyed through a protective layer without ever being touched.

Although we returned to Dañada well after twelve o'clock, every-one had just finished dinner in the library. They were all sitting around, surrounded by the books. Dinner was not always served at the dining table. Often the meal was eaten, as it was this night, in some other place that had taken Serena's or Liz's fancy, sometimes only because the dining table had not been cleared from the meal before.

There were several clusters of people buzzing and humming in con-versation like bees, each group oblivious to the other's conversation. In spite of the party atmosphere, they acted like people who live together, each pursuing his particular interest. Erica was reading a book. Pirrone was chatting intimately with a slight, pretty girl whom I had never seen before. He seemed to be quite taken with her but she did not show the same interest. However, Pirrone always gave any new girl who appeared the same kind of flattering attention. Rick Richards and a girl named Julie, who had recently taken over a guesthouse, were locked in an en-veloping embrace in a far corner.

Julie, it seemed, was the one Pirrone's friends had talked about the night I had first met the Rivellis. She had evidently overcome her wrong number problem and had drifted back to Dañada. Julie was built for passion. She had full, curving breasts, a tiny waist, and a small but very well-rounded behind that moved in a sinuous circular motion as she walked. The capri pants she always wore hugged her round bottom and her tight crocheted tops snuggled her bosom; all her clothing seemed to sensuously caress her form. Her sexiness was not affected; it was organic.

The only one of the group who was not there was Serena—if one could call the maid one of the group. For that matter, she did not act much like a maid, nor did she do the housework a maid should do.

In another corner of the room, two bearded fellows in torn T-shirts, worn-out jeans, and sandals were singing while one of them played the guitar. When they stopped, Pirrone came over and introduced us to them. Pirrone said he had met them when they were performing in a Greek cafe in Monterey. He had invited the two musicians and their girlfriend to stay overnight. Then Pirrone went back to the girl he had been talking to before. I assumed she was the musicians' girlfriend. Tom and I sat down and started talking with the two musicians. They told us they were traveling around the country earning their way with their music.

Brian put a record on the turntable. Liz and Brian started to dance. "Let me show you a new dance," Brian said to Liz as he turned the record over.

"Keen," Liz exclaimed.

"It's called the skate," he continued. "Look…you move one arm and one foot to the side and then the other arm and foot to the other side." They practiced the skate.

Erica put down her book and joined Tom and me as we talked to the musicians. Quiet Erica was an excellent listener with the ability to empathize. She was slightly inscrutable, her wise amber eyes carefully weighing all that was perceived while revealing little about their owner.

It had taken me only a few weeks to fall into the Dañada pattern. I was a quick study for the part because this was the play in which I had always wanted to act. Yet sometimes I was not only on stage, but also down in fourth row center as if I were another person, watching the dis-jointed drama unfolding before me in a mélange of weird hypnotic colors.

In a while, Brian and Liz collapsed beside us, exhausted from their vigorous dancing. Liz was wearing the snail pin Pirrone had given her, incongruously pinned on her T-shirt. When Brian started talking, his thick glasses, like prisms, reflected the light in the room. I realized that I had never seen his eyes; then he bent his head out of the light and I could see that they were small and shrew-like. But behind those small eyes lay a busy mind.

Pirrone now had his arm around the pretty, petite girl. As they talked they looked as if they were completely absorbed with one another, unaware of anyone else in the room. Pangs of illicit jealousy hit me. Why did he sit this way with her? At least if it had been Liz, I would not have felt such searing stabs of pain. But Liz did not appear to notice. Was this part of the international life? Whatever it was, Liz went on enjoying the company of our group. But I knew she must have seen them. I silently pleaded with her to break it up. Why did she make no move? Was it this unreal, high key she was on again tonight—wound as tightly as a coil of live steel—which kept her from acting? Liz may not have appeared to be jealous, but I could see that the musicians were. They kept glancing at Pirrone and the girl in a most unhappy way.

What was the relationship between Liz and Pirrone? It hardly fitted any definition of an ideal marriage. Why was Liz often remote or withdrawn or else hyper as she was this night? However, when reachable she was gregarious and outgoing, though tense. What made her swing between depression and elation with hardly a step on the middle ground?

I could not help but compare Liz and Pirrone. Along with her disarming simplicity Liz was very gracious and aware of others in such a subtle way that they were not conscious of these qualities but were made to feel welcome and at ease. But, of course, there were those times when other people did not seem to exist for her. On the other hand, Pirrone was always "present" and in full command of himself as well as everyone else; in fact I had a fleeting feeling of a concealed craftiness. He exuded a continental worldly appeal, but his awareness seemed to be mainly of himself and the impact he made on others.

But I was sure he was unaware of the impact he made on me and my insane infatuation for him. Although I tried to hide it, I felt that no one else could miss the fires my feverish emotions lit—the blood rushing to my face when he looked my way or spoke to me, my almost total incapacity to speak or answer at these times, my lovelorn look that I could see in my mind's eye as if I were someone else looking into my eyes. I felt so guilty and so fearful that I would be found out.

Since the musicians had been talking about their travels around the country, Liz mentioned one of her experiences while traveling abroad.

As she spoke, she became even more animated, her voice jumping octaves like a soprano reaching for an even higher note than the breathtaking one before. She spoke rapidly as she said that she had once borrowed a car when she was in Europe.

"But it began to have a big problem," she continued. "I got disgusted and pushed it off a mountain."

"You what?" Brian was incredulous.

"Yeah, it's true. A family friend loaned it to me. He said it was old and he didn't particularly care what happened to it. A friend of mine from school and I were driving it in the Alps when the radiator sprang a leak. We had to stop at every little river and creek along the way. The damn thing had to be filled every ten minutes and all we had was an empty beer bottle. Finally we reached a teeny town, called Gap, in the middle of the mountains. There wasn't a bloody soul who could fix it, so we just pushed it over a cliff."

"Damn good thinking," Brian said laughing. "I would like to have done that to my motorcycle the other day."

"Liz, what did the man say who loaned it to you?" wondered Erica.

"He was a little surprised…" Liz paused, "and kind of mad. He said he hadn't meant his comments about the car to be taken so literally."

Brian said, "Really, Liz, all in all it sounds like a likely story."

"If you don't believe it ask Serena when she gets back from Peru tomorrow. She met my friend who told her the same story."

So that was where Serena had been. Why had no one ever mentioned it?

Leaving the library for the powder room for a minute, I walked past the living room. A light was on and the doors were open. I looked in to see who was in there. Julie was sitting on the sofa. She was bare-breasted and her skirt was pushed way up. Rick was on his knees with his head buried in her lap. She was urgently running her fingers through his hair, an ecstatic look on her face with her eyes closed. I was sickened by this scene. Reading about lurid lovemaking on the printed page cannot simulate the effect of a sudden living view.

When I came out of the powder room, I saw Tom in the hallway and told him that Rick was carrying on with Julie in the living room. "They were disgusting, like a couple of dogs," I whispered. "At least they could have gone down to their guest house."

Tom just laughed, "Rick probably couldn't wait."

I was disappointed that Tom, who was always so decent, was not offended.

I went back to the library and overheard one of the musicians, whose name was Hawk, saying to Pirrone in amazement, "That's heavy, man, heavy."

Then Pirrone and the musicians' girlfriend walked over to where I had just sat down next to Tom and the other musician. Their girlfriend spoke to him, "Pirrone has just asked us to stay with him a few days."

"This is really love, man." The musician was impressed. "Real community spirit. The world needs your kind of attitude, man. Then there would be peace."

Pirrone flashed his half-smile. "Peace is impossible. Man's basic nature is to fight."

The musician named Hawk had come over to join us, evidently interested in the conversation. Both musicians were aghast at Pirrone's statement.

Pirrone continued, "I asked you to stay with me because I wanted to; I don't give a damn about community spirit. This is my territory. Everyone who owns land feels that way. I know a guy who thinks he's a socialist and says no one should really own property—it should belong to everyone. But he owns his house and just let someone step on his land or build something that spoils his view and he really screams and rushes down to city hall. Let me tell you, I won't make up any phony stories about community spirit. I'm just too honest. If someone tried to take my property or even walk on it uninvited, I'd kill him if I had to."

The musicians looked as if they were ready to leave. "We thought you had love, man." They said almost together.

"I'm a very loving guy, but I'm telling you like a father." Pirrone was playing his role as the wise elder.

"If everyone thought like you," Hawk said, "we'd have wars all the time."

"That's how it's always been," Pirrone replied. "If you'll study history and anthropology as Brian has, you'll find out that men have always been willing to give up their lives to protect their territory. Without land there is no power."

"Life is only a stage in the eternal process," the second musician said.

Sensing the conversation was coming to an impasse, Pirrone suggested to the rest of us that we take a few shots with some old dueling pistols out in the garden.

We all chorused our enthusiasm, playing follow the leader with Pirrone, as usual.

As we walked down the steps, the garden did not look like the weedy, overgrown thicket that it did in the daytime. The outlines of trees and bushes were softly traced against the night sky as if by an airbrush, creating an ephemeral quality, like the setting for a movie by Fellini. Was I seeing these people through a night filter? Would they be like the garden in daylight if exposed to the spotlight of careful scrutiny?

Pirrone said, "These pistols belonged to one of my ancestors in the sixteenth century. They were used in a duel between him and the Duke of Milan."

Brian asked which one had been killed. Pirrone replied, "The Duke, of course." Like his ancestor, and unlike Liz, Pirrone seemed to be in complete control.

In loading, a rod had to be used to push lead shot and gunpowder into the pistols each time they were fired. We took turns firing at glasses of Pernod, which the guys had set aflame. Brian's aim was quite accurate, splintering the glass and sending it into shards as the lead hit. Tom and Pirrone were good too, always hitting the glasses. Hawk was definitely better on the guitar. I was a terrible shot and Liz was even worse, sparing some of the supply of glasses which she had thoughtfully brought outside.

When the musicians' girl's turn to shoot came she looked helplessly at Pirrone and said, "I've never fired a gun."

"Let me show you." Pirrone tenderly put both his arms around her, helping steady the pistol. The diamond in the ring he always wore, catching the light, shone brightly.

One of the musicians stood next to her, almost as if he were guarding her. Pirrone gave him annoyed glances. Liz must have seen them, too, for suddenly she pointed the other pistol at his back. I almost felt relieved that she was showing jealousy, even rage. But then the gun went off with a popping sound and a puff of white smoke that seemed as though it were off in the distance.

My mind went dead. Liz had murdered her husband, which, of course, he richly deserved.

Someone yelled, "That was some shot."

Pirrone's laughter came out of the darkness. "That was only a transformer blowing out." And I had thought it had been a shot from Liz's pistol!

I realized then that there was no light shining out of the house windows and none in the yard. What timing, I thought. Had Liz actually pulled the trigger and killed her husband, only I would have been a witness. The exploding transformer would have masked her shot.

Pirrone went back to the house to call the electric company to see when the power would be back on. I was sure I had heard a shot ring out from the direction in which Pirrone had gone from the garden to return to the house. No one else seemed to notice in the midst of all the target practice. Did Pirrone take a shot at something on the way to the house?

We settled down to serious target practice after some torches had been lit. We became very engrossed. Brian competed with the musicians. Liz and I were so inaccurate we decided to see who could miss the farthest.

"I think this one will take the prize," I said to Liz as I turned my back to the target and wrapped my firing arm around my body, aiming the gun without twisting my head around to see. "I have no idea where it will land."

Just then all the lights blazed on. Everyone gave a cheer and settled down to even more serious target practice now that the visibility was better. Along with the lights coming on, Pirrone appeared at just the same moment as if by magic. He had been gone for quite a while.

He went over to Tom and I heard him whisper, "That bastard tried to knock me off again. I gave him a good pistol whipping. I think that's the last of him."

Swinging around after one of my wild shots, I saw Pirrone with his arm around the girl, talking to Tom away from the group. Quietly I moved closer, hoping to catch what they were saying. I heard Pirrone say, "That's not too bad—forty-eight minutes exactly. Yes, that would work out okay."

The conversation did not seem very interesting. Race talk again; I guessed he was referring to the time it took to cover a certain distance. They were constantly clocking their cars as they raced. But I wondered what could it be if it weren't a racing time? Was it the time it took to get to the fortress-like house? What went on in that house was an enigma to me, a mystery to be solved since Tom hadn't given me straight answers about it. And what about the shot I was sure I had heard as we drove away from that house? Whom was it intended for? Or was it just to scare us? Or me, since Tom had said it was only a car backfiring? And what about the guy Pirrone pistol-whipped? Was he the one who tried to kill Pirrone just before I met him?

We returned to the library just as the grandfather clock struck three. Tom drew me into a corner and whispered, "Pirrone has just bought a boat. We're going to see it tomorrow."

"Will they need a boat to go to Australia? Can't they just fly?"

"A boat would be great for taking cruises around Australia. But I've convinced Pirrone it'd be better to go to South America."

I was delighted, but I wondered how much Tom had to do with any change in the plans. Pirrone was not the type who could be convinced by anyone.

On the way back to my aunt's I asked Tom why Serena had gone to Peru. "Oh," he said, "she had to fly there to bring back some important papers from Varian."

"Why not mail them?" I asked.

"They're too important to trust to the mail. And anyway the mail is too slow. Pirrone needs these right away, like yesterday."

And, I thought, he sends the maid. She's a most unusual maid—a courier for papers so sensitive that they had to be hand-carried as those in a diplomatic pouch are.

The next afternoon Tom took me to the El Mirador harbor, called the Cove—probably because it really was a cove. It was at the foot of a narrow canyon, with a sheer cliff on one side and a point on the other. As we walked out on the pier, the clear verdigris-green water looked only inches deep, as if one could easily reach down to touch the prickly, dark purple sea urchins, beautiful but dangerous with their poisonous spines. A sudden apprehension hit me—was Dañada, like the sea urchins, concealing hidden dangers?

Pirrone and Liz picked us up in an outboard dinghy. Threading our way through the other craft, we approached Pirrone's new boat. I was impressed with its size. "Gosh, Pirrone, it's really big." I had never been on anything larger than the small sailboats on which I had gone with family friends to Catalina. Pirrone's new purchase reminded me of the French riverboats I had seen in pictures; but there was no way to compare their size.

"It's not too bad," he said. "Seventy-five feet at the waterline."

"Why are you so astounded, Alice?" Liz asked. "The ocean liners I've been on are many times larger." But to me, it was immense and as we got closer it looked even more huge.

Brian and Erica were standing on the deck waving to us. As they helped us up, Brian said, "Welcome to the Queen Mary."

We all laughed—I, because it seemed almost big enough to be so, and Liz, probably because it was an outlandish overstatement.

Everyone's excitement vibrated kinetic energy, electrifying me more even though I was already elated. Serena was standing impassively on the other side of the deck. Pirrone went over to her and put his arm around her. They stood there facing away from us, looking out at the ocean, talking in low voices. I looked questioningly at Tom.

He said, "They have a lot to talk about. She just got back this afternoon from Peru. She probably has a bunch of messages from Varian."

We all stood around making small talk about the new boat as we waited for Pirrone, our tour leader, to show us around.

"My, the deck is flat. Everything must be below," I said.

"Yes, everything but the pilothouse over there on the forward section," Tom concurred.

I looked over at it. Square windows surrounded it on all sides.

"Did you know this was once a rumrunner?" Tom asked me.

"Oh," I said. Then I remembered that Liz had told her school friends who had dropped by that Pirrone was thinking of buying an old rum boat. This must be the same one.

Tom went on to say that it had been completely restored by the last owner. "It's really neat, almost like new."

Erica heard us. "Did I hear you say this was an old rum-running boat, Tom?" He nodded. She continued, "I imagine it must have quite a history." Tom said he knew nothing about it.

Brian spoke up. "I don't know anything about this boat's past, but I do know that El Mirador was a relay point for rumrunners during prohibition. My grandfather lived on the bluff above Fanshell Bay. The part of the bluff he was on had been undercut by waves. It was a cozy place for a rumrunner to cache his stuff. Grandpa used to tell stories about some of the things he saw. But he never got involved, even to let the authorities know. 'Live and let live,' he used to say. He strictly minded his own business and avoided trouble if he possibly could. I guess the rumrunners appreciated that trait because he often found that a bottle or two of fine old Scotch had been left in his garage. He said several times he had heard gunshots on the beach but he never found out who was firing or why. I don't imagine he tried very hard; he was definitely not very inquisitive. And besides, he was very fond of Scotch."

Pirrone walked over to where we were all gathered on the deck.

"Pirrone," Tom said, "you haven't told us how you were able to get this boat."

"I stole it." Everyone looked startled because the way he said it, it sounded as if he had really stolen it or had done something illegal to get it. He went on, "I mean I got it for a hell of a price. When I first looked at it, the guy was asking too much. It made me so mad I checked up on him and found out he was in debt up to here." Pirrone indicated his neck.

"I offered him ten thousand less than his asking price. He just laughed. I laughed, too, and walked away. The next week I brought cash and offered him twenty thousand less. He was seething with rage and told me to get the hell out. Two weeks later he still hadn't sold the boat and I offered him thirty thousand less. I think the sight of less money shook him. 'I'll sell it for twenty thousand less than I was asking.' I told him that was my offer two weeks ago and that he should have taken it. Then I took another ten thousand off the stack of money and told him next week it will be forty thousand less. It costs me to waste my time quibbling. You should have seen the guy. He was practically crying."

Pirrone laughed, delighted with himself. "He finally signed the boat over to me. It's amazing how dumb people are. I think I should devote my life to proving this principle."

There was something about Pirrone at this moment that my mind was straining to catch. The way he could force people to do his will was otherworldly, as though he were both more and less than human. The feeling that he was superhuman or even supernatural had fluttered like a moth at the back of my mind before. But if he were sometimes unreal, that probably was only natural. There was nothing real about the bewitched and bewitching life at Casa Dañada.

"What do you think of *Calypso* as a name for the boat?" Pirrone asked.

"Yes, that's a charming name," agreed Brian, " or should I say charmed. *Calypso* is the name of the sea nymph who held Odysseus in her thrall for seven years. And," he added humorously, "It fits you, Pirrone. It might be said you have nymphomania."

Tom laughed as he said, "That's a really funny switch, Pirrone a nymphomaniac!"

"That's not quite what I had in mind," Pirrone said with his half-smile.

Liz had brought a bottle of Dom Perignon to christen the boat. She broke it over the bow. "I name thee *Calypso*." (Of course, the boat had been afloat for over forty years.)

Pirrone seemed a little upset at the sight of the fine champagne disappearing into the ocean, but he took command quickly, saying, "Well, I guess it's time to show you the rest of the boat. But before we go below, I want to show you what's on top." He led the way and we all crowded into the pilothouse.

On a panel covered with dials and gauges was a large wheel, which Tom grabbed with both hands. He gazed out of the square windows, a look of distant places on his face. Being particularly attuned to wheels, he had gravitated to the ship's helm as naturally as a satellite is pulled into orbit.

Next we went below deck to the galley in single file, down a ladder, all making comments.

"Maybe we can find some old cases of rum."

"This would make a great party boat."

"We could have a wild orgy and no one could complain."

"Yeah, like those people up the road last night. They must have telescopic eyes and megaphone ears. They live at least half a mile away."

"You're right about the telescopic eyes. How could they see that Hawk and Julie had nothing on?"

"Hey, Julie, was it cold out there? Did Hawk keep you warm?"

"Julie's too hot to ever be cold."

The gathering must have turned into a wild party after Tom and I left. I knew Pirrone had some far-out friends but how could things get so out of hand? Possibly my aunt was not so far off when she talked about orgies at Dañada. Liz was just too unconcerned about what went on around her. Oh well, in any group there are always those who go too far.

As we entered the galley, I looked around. There were cupboards, known as lockers, and a long mess table at one end. A small hatchway opened into another room full of bunks. That smell peculiar to boats, of old varnish mixed with salt brine, permeated the air.

We moved on to the engine room. Tom became very excited as he inspected the twin diesel engines, saying, "I'd love to put one of these monsters in my car."

Erica laughed as she said, "Tom, you'd really be airborne with that."

Pirrone walked over to another side of the compartment and started pulling up boards from the floor (or the deck as Brian called it). "And now you will see why I bought this boat."

The removal of the boards revealed a companionway. We all followed him down another ladder and ended up in a huge compartment.

"This," announced Pirrone, "is a false-bottom boat." He pointed to the ceiling. "This compartment has a wooden ceiling and the upper cabins have wooden floors. In between the two is a layer of cement to make the false bottom feel and sound solid."

"How clever!" observed Brian, "Who would ever suspect…?"

Smuggling cigarettes! That was why their sale would be so profitable in South America. No wonder Liz looked so disturbed when her school friend made the observation about the criminal types who were engaged in smuggling everything from whiskey to watches on luxury yachts going to South America.

Pirrone's evident satisfaction with his transaction infected us all, giving the expedition an auspicious beginning. What an adventure to be on a boat like this and to be able to conceal cargo so cunningly. I was certainly being corrupted, for I was going right along, perversely stimulated by the thought of being in on a smuggling operation.

But did it make any sense for a man as wealthy as Pirrone to engage in an illegal venture? However, not much that these people did made any sense in the kind of world I came from. They took neither life nor things seriously. Fun and excitement were all that mattered to them. The element of danger involved in smuggling probably provided the thrill for their jaded appetites that no legal escapade could. I could see this easily because I, too, felt wickedly thrilled by the thought of engaging in a forbidden activity.

The lure of the sinister had always intrigued me, although I had only encountered it in literature before this time. Was it a reaction to the dull, daily-sameness of the environment I had grown up in, filled as it was with incantations for work, discipline, and order? However, it was still disturbing and slightly shocking, even scary, to think of actually being part of a smuggling scheme. But it was exciting to be no longer insulated by a safe distance and my innocence, to no longer experience ominous happenings only in a never-never land of imagination. I was being my usual ambivalent self, both eager and reluctant, horrified and delighted.

Pirrone ended my reverie with the announcement that we needed to start buying supplies with which to stock the boat right away. And he added, "I've contacted Varian. He is making arrangements for the sale of the cigarettes."

"Oh," Liz said excitedly, "we must remember to take plenty of food for Isis and Osiris."

"Who are they?" questioned Tom.

"They're the cats. I just named them. It's terrible; they've been wandering around for four years without names."

"Maybe she'll be all right soon. She has off moments like this," Pirrone whispered to Tom and me, his tone implying that her mental condition was not all that it should be.

Serena stood a few feet away with a knowing smile. She must have inside information on Liz's mental state, I thought. Liz really did seem out of it often, as if she were on drugs. But I had never seen anyone on drugs, and I only knew a slight smattering about them from the little I had read. It was foolish for me to make such a comparison because, I thought, reading about things is remote and abstract, no substitute for actual contact. Anyway, it seemed to me then that her frequent disorientation was due to an unstable emotional condition. The way Pirrone neglected her and flirted with other girls, she was certainly entitled to lose touch in order to save some sanity.

Pirrone turned to Liz with a tender expression. "You know they wouldn't be happy on the boat. Cats don't like water." Then he quickly said to Brian, "Shall we take your motorcycle?"

Brian was very enthusiastic. "What a way to see every port."

"One more suggestion," said Pirrone. "Let's eat lunch." (It was already after five in the afternoon.)

Tom, Liz, and I went ashore in the dinghy. Everyone else went in the shore launch. After we all arrived at the dock we went into the pier cafe except for Rick and Julie who were in a hurry to go someplace else. The booths only seated four people, but seven of us piled into one of them. We all talked at once with our ideas on how to proceed with the preparations for the trip until Pirrone took charge of the conversation, laying out the plans with jobs for everyone.

When we left the cafe Liz walked quickly ahead. I saw her reaching down and opening the little snail pin as she was getting in the limousine. I thought I saw her taking a pinch of something out of the pin and sniffing it up her nose, the way I imagined people did when they took snuff. I started walking very fast, ahead of the rest so that I could see exactly what Liz was doing. Pirrone came up behind me, taking my arm. A thrill raced through me at his touch.

"Alice, what's your hurry?" he asked.

I couldn't talk, not only because I could not really say why I was hurrying but also because Pirrone had an effect on me, which, while it was exciting, made me feel awkward and wordless. I looked up at him and felt my eyes lock onto his. I could not tell if he received the same signal I did but irrationally I hoped so.

He continued talking, "Slow down, we're not going to a fire. How would you like to go back with me in the Fazani? Tom can drive the rest in the limo."

"I'd love to," I said weakly as my knees nearly collapsed.

Pirrone wanted to be alone with me. How perfectly marvelous, I almost screamed to myself. I was frantic with joy. He was returning my passion—I had read all that from the glance in which our eyes met. He had communicated his love for me, I felt sure. The little island of sanity trying to stay afloat in my flooded brain told me I would be very upset if Pirrone tried to go any further. It was sweet but sad because, of course, it was hopeless; I would not really want Liz's husband. Now, though, I would have the memory of that look. I could live on dreaming how it might have been had we met without his prior involvement. How foolishly romantic I was. I had read too many novels by the Brontë sisters.

As we rode along in the Fazani, the early evening sky was fading into a faint blue, as in an old Kodacolor print, enveloping us in a haze of quiet pleasure—or was it just I who was in a daze? Pirrone made no move toward me, nor did he say anything to indicate that he reciprocated my feelings. No, he did not even look my way once. Still, I was filled with euphoria by the idea that he had asked me to go with him and that our eyes had met. But my banal spoken words were completely unrelated to my marvelously exultant thoughts as I hung onto the vague hope that he, too, was filled with yearnings for me that he was forced to hide.

"It must be fun to drive a car like this all the time," I said.

"You're right. I find, though, that I use it more for business than for pleasure. My business appointments are often quite far apart and I need fast transportation."

"Do you do anything besides representing your family's factories?" I asked.

"Yes, but it would be difficult to tell you. It's so complicated that even my lawyers have a hard time understanding it."

In this lovely mood, mesmerized by Pirrone's charm, I found the idea of smuggling cigarettes natural and acceptable. Had I realized last New Year's Eve, when Brian mentioned selling cigarettes in South America, that smuggling was involved, I would have been alarmed. I was being irresistibly drawn into the spiraling Sargasso Sea of Casa Dañada's cabal. If I had not been so dazzled by my adulation of this place and these people, I would have realized how absurd this whole adventure was. But had I realized that I would have begun to think there was more going on than was apparent.

Even then I thought there were enigmatic questions for which there were no clear answers. What was in the little yellow film cans? Especially the one at Dañada! Were the pictures on the film in that can of something over which someone was trying to murder Pirrone? But what about all those other yellow film cans back at the fortress house? What was in them? Perhaps, they all held pornographic film that someone was going to sell and make a bundle of illicit and illegal money.

Whatever, I felt as if I were in the middle of the Abbot and Costello conundrum, "Who's on first?" I didn't know what was going on or who was doing what. But I did love a mystery and I was intrigued and anxious to find out what was really happening.

◇Chapter Four

LIKE MISSIVES SENT across an unbridgeable chasm, letters came every week or so from my parents. Their pleas—why did I not consider going back to school or even getting a job?—were cries in an echo chamber that rendered them unintelligible. Their drab, practical life did not prepare them for understanding my exciting existence here.

But as the gulf widened between me and my parents, it did disturb me that I had become such a callous, ungrateful daughter. So I answered their letters with soothing replies about how nice it was living with Aunt Jessie and how lonely she would be if I weren't there. I did not mention that her house was not much more than a place for me to sleep and that I spent as little time with her as I possibly could. I wrote that I would love to get a job in El Mirador but that there was none available.

I also said that I wanted to go back to school in the fall; I was sure that would please them. Of course I had no such plans. My only plans involved going to South America.

My aunt had begun to complain about my late hours—how late she did not know. She was too sound a sleeper to ever hear me come in. But I was never back at her bedtime, somewhere around eleven. To her anything much past that was sinfully late.

"You're going to come to ruin associating with those people. Tom can't be up to any good, keeping you out till all hours," she crabbed at me one day while I was waiting for Tom to pick me up.

"Don't you dare say anything against him," I retorted.

"Your attitude has certainly changed. You didn't seem to care much about him a few weeks ago. And those people he runs around with are completely immoral. I've heard all the details—everyone here is talking about them."

"You certainly make it your business to know the nastiest-minded town-gossips," I said. "You're the type who reads every filthy novel that comes out and then after you've read all the dirty parts twice to be sure you haven't missed anything, you rant about how terrible it is."

"Alice, you're a vicious little girl."

I looked at her calculatingly. Anger made her grotesque. Her jowls sagged like a Basset hound's. The too white false teeth she bared made the yellowed whites of her eyes even yellower and her sallow skin even sallower as it hung loosely in folds like a rumpled crinkly-crepe dress. She was pathetic—unloved and powerless. She was at her worst when she was mad. When she was happy, she was rather dippy—pixilated at times—which gave her a certain attractiveness.

I suddenly felt remorseful. I should not blow up at my aunt. I should feel sorry for her. She had probably never had a date in her life.

"I'm sorry, Aunt Jessie. I shouldn't have said those things. But how can you accuse Liz and Pirrone when you don't even know them?"

"It's you, my dear, who doesn't know them very well," she said.

"You have a vivid, dirty imagination," I retorted.

"You're a very naughty little girl. I should call your father and have him come up here and wash your mouth out with soap for saying such a thing," she said.

This really infuriated me. "You're talking to me as if I were five years old. Can't you get it through your thick head that I'm a grown woman?"

Somehow that struck her as funny and she started to laugh. I guessed she really thought of me as a child. She considered she was reprimanding a bad little girl. I started to laugh, too. It was all rather ludicrous. I thought, she has been very nice to let me stay with her and she only thinks she's doing her duty by guarding my morals.

"I am sorry I got mad," I apologized. "You are right."

"Well, my dear," she said, "I am glad you're beginning to see things the way they really are."

Of course the only reason I agreed with her was because I had to stay with her no matter what she said. I could not leave the magical life of Casa Dañada, nor could I bear to be far from Pirrone.

She continued, "I am sure you will come to see how really wicked and immoral that Pirrone Rivelli is."

A knock sounded. "I think I hear your boyfriend at the door."

Who else could it be? Certainly not her boyfriend. (I was being cruel again but at least not out loud.)

On our way to Dañada, Tom and I drove along the road that passed a thousand feet or so above the Cove where Pirrone kept the boat. Tom pointed out a curl of smoke down in the harbor.

"My God," he yelled a second later, "the *Calypso* must be on fire! Do you realize where that smoke is coming from?"

I took a better look. "You're right," I screamed. It was coming from the area where the boat was moored, although at that distance it was impossible to distinguish one boat from the other. "If it isn't the *Calypso*, some other boat is on fire. We better report it right away."

"Hell, no. Stopping to phone will take too long. We've got to get down there right now and do what we can to put it out."

Tom headed for the road that wound down to the Cove, driving much faster than usual, if such a thing could be possible. As we careened toward the anchorage, the smoke grew thicker and flames belched forth as if some sea dragon lay coiled there. We could now see that the fire was definitely coming from the *Calypso*. Screeching to a halt, Tom untied the first dinghy he saw.

As we sped out, I noticed a speedboat leaving the area of the fire. It headed for the pier, passing close enough for me to see it was being driven by the same man who had been discussing boats with Pirrone the afternoon Liz's school friends had come. Was this man Joe Viscantino, the gangster I had heard about at the Rivellis'? I had caught a fragment of a conversation between a couple of people who had dropped in several nights before. They were talking about gangsters. One of them mentioned that he thought a character named Joe Viscantino belonged to the Mafia. He said he had seen him a number of times around the harbor in Monterey. The way he described him it seemed as though he were the same man I had seen in the library with Pirrone. It all went together—the house that could easily have belonged to a gangster and was owned by a man who fished and the fishing fleet owner with whom Pirrone had been talking and now the man leaving the scene of the fire (crime?). I now was sure they were all the same man. Pirrone must know, I thought to myself, that he is a gangster.

When we came aboard, we found Pirrone fighting the blaze in the pilothouse all alone. "Am I glad to see you people," he yelled. "What took you so long?"

"How long have you been here?" Tom yelled.

Good question, I thought. Did Pirrone see Joe Viscantino? Had Joe been on this boat? Was he responsible for the fire? Or maybe the man from whom Pirrone "stole" the boat set it on fire to spite him.

Tom grabbed a fire extinguisher and screamed at me to not just stand there. So I started throwing buckets of seawater blindly at the smoke, making it worse, the salt causing iridescent greens and blues like a sorcerer's brew. The smoke was so dense now the flames could not be seen.

Tom yelled at me again. "No, Alice! Get some blankets and try to smother the fire."

But the smoke was so thick I was smothered by it, unable to breathe. Yet if I were going to do anything with a blanket I had to find where the fire was burning under all that smoke. I tried to keep my eyes open, but the acrid smoke made them smart. My sight was blurred, but it made little difference because I could see nothing anyway. I could hear Tom and Pirrone coughing. They sounded so close, I felt I could touch them, but when I reached out there was no one. Eventually the extinguishers took effect and the clouds of smoke began to be cleared away.

I thought about Pirrone's remark, "What took you so long?" He was just lucky we had seen it at all. How like him to expect everyone to be ready to jump the instant he needed them and to have ESP about when that was.

"Hey, how did it start?" Tom asked.

"It burst into flames right after I started the engine. Something must be wrong with the wiring. I was going to take her out for a little spin to see how everything went."

We heard a siren and soon the Harbor Patrol came alongside the *Calypso*. Instead of a holocaust, they found three people standing beside the charred remains of the pilothouse.

"Sorry, the fire's out." Pirrone was terribly sarcastic. "You should have been here earlier for the entertainment." Then he added angrily, "Why the hell weren't you around when we needed you?"

"Yeah," I added, "we're pretty burned up."

"We had to get clearance," answered one of the men.

"Well, to hell with that. My boat was on fire. Do you wait half an hour to save a drowning man?"

"You don't have a permit to moor here. Technically, we aren't supposed to help you at all."

"Do you let a boat burn because of some fucking rules?" Pirrone was furious.

"We have to go by regulations. I have an order from the harbor master for you to leave immediately."

"That bastard doesn't have any manners. This slough is hardly good enough for my boat." Pirrone, who considered rules and regulations minor technicalities to be overlooked, was outraged. He hurled a few more disparaging remarks at the patrol before they left. After they had gone, he said, "We'll take her to Fanshell Bay. That way we'll be able to see what's going on. We can keep a better eye on her than the flunkies around here."

"She's not going anywhere," Tom said, "if we can't get the engines to run." They finally did get one going. The wiring was completely burned out on the other.

Tom said, "Even though the bay is just around the point, it's going to be tough getting her there. There isn't enough power and with only one engine, it'll be hell to steer."

"I can do it." Pirrone never lost confidence even in adversity.

I noticed how the soot etched his nose and the high Italian planes of his face, making him look like a handsome charcoal drawing.

Tom offered to pick Pirrone up at the bay, which was really only a small inlet directly on the other side of the point that sheltered the Cove. Unlike the Cove, which had a number of moorings, a general store, a cafe, and a harbormaster, the bay had nothing except a short pier in bad repair. It was home to only a couple of fishing boats.

As we drove there my thoughts went back to Joe Viscantino. I was sure he was the same man driving the speedboat leaving the spot where the *Calypso* was moored. I wondered what he was doing there. I couldn't ask Tom. Since he had taken me to what I was now confident was Joe's house, I felt there was a slight possibility Tom might be in on whatever mysterious thing was going on. Anyway, if I had asked Tom I would have gotten a nowhere answer.

Whatever the cause of the fire, Tom was depressed. "This means that wherever Pirrone decides we're going, it's going to take a lot of extra time having the boat repaired."

"I thought you convinced Pirrone to go to Peru."

"Pirrone now thinks Australia might be better," Tom replied.

"Why?"

"That's top secret," he said.

"So Pirrone's not planning to ranch there?"

"I didn't say that. Anyway, the last thing I ever want to do is ranching, so I'm not going," Tom said with great disgust.

"But Pirrone was also talking about farming the land in Peru after the gold was all out. What were you going to do then? Now are you planning to leave here right away?" I was becoming quite alarmed. I certainly didn't want him to leave ever, because if he did I would have to, too. I needed to find out my fate.

In answer to my question, he replied, "No. I'll have to help with the repairs."

Tom was a loyal friend. I doubt that Pirrone would have done the same for him. But then Pirrone never depended on anyone. His leadership or magnetism or whatever it was made it unnecessary; people became his satellites, often his slaves.

"Won't Pirrone have enough help with Brian and everyone else?"

He answered, "Yes, but Pirrone relies on my advice." Tom was still convinced he could advise Pirrone. But really how could he? He had trouble directing himself. And did Pirrone, who was so certain of himself, want advice?

Tom must have guessed my thoughts. "I know it's hard for you to understand why Pirrone needs an advisor. But even men in his position need a friend they can trust to discuss plans with and get advice from."

As we approached the bay, a blood-orange sun was fast disappearing. Soon, heliotrope clouds feathered out over the sky, which had turned cyclamen, spreading a lavender glow over us, creating a mood of quiet detachment. We saw the *Calypso* limp around the point, a purple intruder in the setting sun's changing spectrum of colors.

Tom gave a cheer. Unlike Pirrone, he had worried she would never make it. Pirrone dropped anchor and came to the pier in the outboard.

"How's the scorched nymph?" Tom asked.

"She's been ravished!" They broke out in knowing laughter.

"How do you suppose the fire started?" asked Tom when he had stopped laughing.

"On the way here I found some burned rags behind the control panel. They must have been covered with gasoline. When I started the engine, sparks from the ignition wires must have ignited them. You know what I'd do to that guy who sold me the boat if he had anything to do with this."

"I'd help," offered Tom.

"Pirrone, maybe that horrible Joe Viscantino started it. I think I saw him whiz by when we were coming out to help put out the fire. You know him don't you?"

Pirrone just laughed. "That's ridiculous, I would have seen him."

He did not answer my question as to whether or not he knew Joe. I had thought I might trap him with my statement into admitting that Joe Viscantino was the fishing fleet owner I had seen at Dañada. There was no doubt in my mind that the man I saw coming from the spot where the *Calypso* was moored was the same man as the one I had seen that afternoon at Dañada. I also thought it strange that Pirrone did not question me about how I knew who Joe was or what he looked like. Pirrone was hiding something.

I thought about Pirrone's business trips, about which he was so vague. Was Joe working out some secret deal with him to smuggle disassembled cars to avoid the duty in Australia? I decided Joe must have known about the false bottom in the boat and sought out Pirrone. Joe might even be planning to cache drugs in the cargo, thus getting Pirrone to do illicit smuggling for him unwittingly. No wonder he had to keep his name a secret. Joe had probably sworn Pirrone to secrecy. But, I thought, Pirrone is not aware of the full extent of Joe's plans. I was still crazy about Pirrone so naturally I was excusing him from complicity in any criminal activity.

Probably the day Joe came to the house, Pirrone had to tell Liz that he was just a fisherman because he had been sworn to secrecy.

Pirrone went back to his tirade about the fire. "Damn those idiots in the harbor department. They'd be finished if they had to think for themselves."

"That's probably why they have to work for somebody else. They aren't smart enough to make it on their own," said Tom—which was ironic, since Tom had yet to do anything on his own.

As we drove back to the Cove to get Pirrone's car, a heavy downpour started. "Wouldn't you know," Pirrone complained, "the rain would start after the fire. Must be Murphy's Law or something."

At dinner Pirrone turned the day's misfortune into an amusing story. He ended by saying, "After those fools, I'm glad we're leaving here for Australia."

Then it had been definitely decided. Poor Tom. He looked very downhearted as Pirrone continued, "I'm looking into some land in the outback. The ranch is about a hundred and sixty square miles—much bigger than the original size of Dañada. Of course, it will be tough the first year, getting started with raising sheep. But after things are going well, we can leave the ranch with a foreman and go to Sydney, Japan…anywhere."

"It sounds marvelous," purred Serena, who was sitting next to him. The idea that she was the maid was absurd, although she had cooked the dinner, which was quite good.

"I think I'll vacation every year on a South Sea island," Brian said with a hungry look, "to sample the island girls."

"Hey," Erica admonished.

"Sorry, baby, I couldn't help myself for a minute," Brian replied.

"Oh, Pirrone," exclaimed Liz, "remember the funny goat I had that chewed those big holes in the Fazani's seats? We could have hundreds of goats." Everyone laughed but Pirrone. He obviously couldn't see the humor in it.

"For God's sake, Liz, forget the goats. I'll get you a horse."

Tom said nothing all through dinner and it was difficult for me to join in the enthusiasm because I knew how disappointed he was and also, if he did not go, I certainly wouldn't be going. I felt suddenly like an outsider hearing the plans for a wonderful party to which I was not invited.

◇Chapter Five

THE RAIN THAT STARTED
after the fire quickly became torrential, coming down in solid walls of water, causing huge sections of the steep hills to break off and crash down, blocking the highway. The graveled drive winding down from Dañada was like the sluiceway of a placer mine—a trough of running water filled with rocks.

The rain did not stop for four days. (It seemed more like the biblical forty.) I could not get to my aunt's, although I phoned her daily. She was very upset that I was sleeping at Dañada, but she had to accept the inevitability of it.

I had to sleep on a couch in the library, for as large as the main house was, all the rooms were occupied. Erica, Brian, Julie, and Rick had all taken over guest rooms, as it was too hard to get to the guesthouses. Tom, who usually stayed in rooms next to the garage, had moved to a guest room, too. Serena had her usual suite (not a maid's room, which would seem more proper for a maid).

The main pastime, racing, was impossible; no one could even drive anywhere. Because of all the water, the house was practically floating, confining us within its walls. It was as though we were on an ocean liner. And as I had heard one did on shipboard, we looked forward to the nightly movies, silent films from a collection that had belonged to Liz's father. Being so out of date, they were funny and inspired us to think up slapstick parodies. Pirrone thought of a couple of good titles— "The Sound of Engines" and "Three at the Hot Springs"—and we entertained ourselves with stories to match.

My infatuation with Pirrone had begun to wear itself out from the sheer impossibility of it and also the realization that the only person he really cared for was himself. I felt very close to Tom; I enjoyed being able to spend so much time with him even though it was only because a mud barrier prevented him from going out to the garage to commune with his car, which he seemed to think impatiently awaited his loving touch.

With the flood, thought about the forthcoming adventure was temporarily replaced by more immediate concerns such as when the power would be back on and when it would ever stop raining. We were always rushing to put pans under each new place the roof had started to leak. We talked about everything except Australia as we idled away the days. Pirrone, although interested in Brian's discourses, seemed to prefer to bask in Tom's adulation, for Pirrone, always the star, needed an audience. Between Tom and Brian there were few paths of communication. How could there be? Brian, his head crammed with information, loved to discuss things, while Tom, with mostly non-verbal ideas, had little to say.

One afternoon Tom and I were sitting in the living room when Brian came in, eager to share his latest discovery. "Hi, I've just been reading a selection by Richard Burton called 'A Day Among the Fans.' It's very interesting. The location is Africa."

"No, kidding," Tom replied. "Has he made a movie there, too? I guess if you can't get away from the fans you might as well write about them."

"You've got the actor Burton mixed up with the author Burton. The

Fans are an African tribe." Then Brian asked, "Haven't you ever read *A Thousand and One Nights?*"

"I've never read that many nights in my whole life."

Brian tried to straighten things out. "The Richard Burton I'm talking about explored the Middle East and compiled the stories he heard there into *A Thousand and One Nights*. He even managed to get into a harem once."

"Really?" asked Tom. "I didn't know that. Oh, I remember, I read one of his books about Cortez in Mexico."

"That's Richard Halliburton!" Brian was exasperated.

"I give up," said Tom, laughing.

Liz spent most of her days lost on her private planet. Sometimes she came to earth to read, managing between chapters to throw a few meals together. She always seemed to have her snail brooch pinned onto whatever she was wearing, even old sweat shirts or T-shirts; it didn't seem to matter how incongruous it looked. I wondered again what it contained, since I had glimpsed her taking a pinch of something out of it several times when she must have thought she was out of sight of everyone.

From somewhere in the house Serena would appear occasionally, usually just before dinner. I reassessed my impressions of her. Her cold, blue eyes were definitely out of place with the way I perceived her. She was, for me, the embodiment of the Middle Eastern voluptuaries about which I had read. I could almost feel the hot desert winds swirling around her. There was nothing about the idealistic purity of romance about her. She looked as if she indulged in pleasure whenever and wherever it came to her, not actively seeking but indolently accepting it almost impersonally, as though her life were lived in the senses without any higher emotional or mental activity.

Tall, willowy Erica, the artist, could often be seen sketching. With her wide, soft eyes and long, sleek neck, she reminded me of a giraffe. In other ways, too, she was like one, serenely oblivious to all the disturbances beneath her—detached and yet observant from her treetop level.

I thought I was getting over my infatuation with Pirrone but I was wrong. Being near him every day during the rain merely renewed and intensified my desire for him. One afternoon, I was walking out of the living room just as he was walking in. He brushed up against me lightly as we went in opposite directions through the double doorway. The erotic feelings that coursed through me almost sent me sailing to the ceiling on a tide of exquisite sensations.

"Excuse me. I'm sorry, Alice. I didn't mean to bump into you," he said as he walked into the room.

I could say nothing, not even, "That's all right." I wanted to say *if you only knew how wonderful that was.* In my wild imagination I could feel him grabbing me and holding me in his arms as he kissed me madly. But, of course, if the encounter had excited him, he could hardly have done anything about it with Liz and Brian in the room.

That night Pirrone, Liz and I were sitting in the living room. While Liz read, I watched Pirrone cleaning his guns. He was taking gun-cleaning compound from a little yellow film can, ending that mystery for certain. Or did it? Was he using that as a decoy to throw me off what was in the other little cans like it?

He picked up one of his guns and looked down the barrel at me. "Alice, girls have been shot for less than what you are doing to Tom."

Baffled, I cowered at the gun pointing at me, which I hoped was really unloaded. He continued, "Why are you so distant with Tom? Wouldn't you be more comfortable in that big bed in his room?"

Very embarrassed, I stalled with, "What do you mean?" But sitting under Pirrone's hard gaze, I decided I was a coward, hiding behind outdated morals, afraid to commit myself—I, who was so sure about what I wanted out of life: not to waste a minute on dreary dullness, to have the most fun possible. Why would I not go all the way to the greatest fun of all? What held me back? I knew, of course. Pirrone was keeping me from Tom. Even before the encounter that afternoon, the attraction to Pirrone had revived itself with a bang. I had begun to tremble every time I saw him. Exciting shivers tingled down my spine when he came into a room unexpectedly.

I clung to the fantasy that he shared my feelings, even though I never had another sign from him since the day he asked me to ride back with him from the pier and our eyes had met for one mesmerizing moment. I told myself he could not express himself because he was honorable to his wife. But how ridiculous I was in fooling myself; I had seen him flirting with lots of girls and even more, acting in a cozy, intimate way with them. And then there was Serena. He most certainly was more than casual with her. But I still went on with my fantasy, telling myself that was just a superficial display of masculine ego, not the real thing he felt for me and had to hide. But even though Pirrone might be harboring a secret love for me, I had become so fond of Liz I could not let myself speculate too far about her marvelous husband.

My mind returned to Tom. But first I had the unlikely idea that because Tom was such a good friend, Pirrone was hiding his true feelings and playing the advocate as John Alden had for Miles Standish. But was Tom physically attracted to me? Although he said he wanted me, he never pushed. Was I an intellectual rather than an emotional love for him? He had deified me into an untouchable prize of rare perfection, which, of course I was not. His comparison of me with a perfect rose that he was afraid to spoil had left me with the uncomfortable feeling of having been placed out of reach like a museum piece.

Pirrone never stopped staring at me as these thoughts darted around in my head. I squirmed again in embarrassment as I repeated, "What did you mean by that?"

He replied, "Alice, stop playing games. You're being unfair to Tom."

I started to say that I didn't understand what he meant when Tom walked in. I stopped in mid-sentence and looked at him in surprise.

"What's happening? Why did you stop talking? Was it about me?"

No situation was beyond Pirrone's aplomb. "Yes. We were talking about you and distances."

"Whatever the distance I can handle it."

We laughed and Tom was pleased, thinking he had made a clever remark.

Erica came in from the kitchen. "Liz, I'm ready," she announced.

"Ready for what?" Pirrone asked, chuckling.

They left and soon after, Serena wandered in and sat on Pirrone's lap, putting her arm around his shoulder. He seemed pleased, ardent I thought, as she walked her fingers up the back of his neck and giggled, "What have you been doing all day?" He laughed lightly as she kissed him. She added, "And what are you going to be doing tomorrow?" He laughed softly again. Then he kissed her back—a long passionate kiss. Startled, I looked on in disbelief as if I were watching a movie—the only place in my experience that things like this happened. Jealousy grabbed at me, making my heart race. I was devastated. This was more than a casual flirtation. I could see the look of desire in Pirrone's eyes as he gazed at Serena. I was in a daze. I heard Brian's voice from somewhere, sounding as if he were a great distance away in a dense fog. I looked up. He was standing in the entrance to the living room. I was so distraught, nothing seemed real—everyone in the room appeared to be in a thick haze.

Brian said, "Where's Erica?" Pirrone told him she was in the kitchen with Liz. Brian went to the kitchen but came right back. "They've locked the kitchen door."

"I didn't know they felt that way about each other," Pirrone joked.

Serena got up to pour everyone a little Pernod, the usual, but unusual, aperitif of the Dañada household. When she passed me a glass, my inner fury made me want to hit her. At that moment I hated her intensely. As we sat sipping our drinks, the jealousy burning in me made me want to jilt Pirrone (as if he cared!) and rush to bed with Tom. All I could think of was to hurt Pirrone.

Just as Erica came to say dinner was ready, a phone call came for Pirrone. I would have liked to have heard what was said on the other end, for Pirrone exclaimed, "Oh, hell! Joe, that's disastrous. I'll be down as soon as I can get out of here. But who knows when that will be?" Joe Viscantino, of course. Who else could Joe be?

During the conversation I noticed a startled look on Erica's face. What did she know about Joe? At the first chance I would have to sound her out.

Even though I was still in shock over the goings on between Pirrone and Serena I tried to join in the dinner table small talk. But to add to my unhappiness I could not eat the roast venison, thinking about how it had come to be. Pirrone had shot a poor, sweet, innocent doe that had inadvertently ventured onto the veranda, slipping and sliding on the slick paving stones in the pouring rain.

The final course, the pièce de résistance of the evening, which must have been what Liz and Erica had been concocting behind closed doors, was brought in by the two of them as they laughed and giggled. It looked like a mudslide on a platter (how appropriate for the situation we were in), an appearance that must have been achieved by dumping a lot of melted chocolate on a cake. They started to sing "Happy Birthday" to

Brian. Then everybody joined in, mostly off-key and some with their own off-beat versions. I think only Liz and Erica had known it was his birthday.

Pirrone took a magnum of Dom Perignon out of the wine cooler of champagne bottles Erica and Liz had brought in. "It looks like a muddy birthday sliding by," Pirrone said indicating the cake as he opened the bottle.

"Yeah, I'm sliding—twenty-five—a quarter of a century. Five more years and I'll be middle-aged. I've got to hurry and get some more living in."

We spent the rest of the evening with suggestions for Brian, which, if followed, would give him a most bizarre life. During our barrage of often-hilarious ideas for Brian, Erica picked up a sketching pad and started to draw an amusing birthday portrait of him, becoming quite engrossed in her work. When everyone started to wander off she was still busily drawing.

Brian tried to drag her away, saying in a low whisper, "Come on, babe, let's go to bed, I feel horny as hell."

"Wait a few minutes while I finish this sketch for your birthday."

"I can't wait. Julie wouldn't keep me waiting," Brian said, annoyed.

Erica flared up with rage, so unlike her unflappable self. "That slut! Don't you ever touch her."

It began to sound like Julie was being passed around like a second helping of cake, ready and willing to be eaten. She walked as though she were making love with those clothes clinging in a perpetual embrace around her sexy curves. Just yesterday she had come up to Tom from behind, putting her arms around him while she bit his ear. He seemed to enjoy it, as he reached back and pinched her rear. I had seen her loving up to Pirrone, too.

As Tom walked me to my couch in the library, I asked him, "What does everyone see in that Julie? She acts like a bitch and she's shaggy enough with that messy hair to be one."

"She's got a big heart."

"You mean a big ass and no mind."

"Alice, what's gotten into you? You shouldn't use such crude language."

"What do you expect? I hear a lot worse around here."

Tom put his arm around me, kissed me and told me I was a funny little girl. But he also seemed concerned as he said, "Alice, I've been worrying about you on that couch. Aren't you cold sleeping there?"

My earlier resolve to jilt Pirrone by going to bed with Tom had evaporated. I was back to my resistance to anything physical with Tom. Maybe it was only I who prevented anything from happening between us. The idea that he had placed me on a pedestal could possibly have been mostly my invention.

I coyly answered Tom's question about my being cold while sleeping. "Oh, I'm fine. I have a quilt and a couple of sweaters plus my knee socks to keep me warm."

"Well, that isn't exactly what I meant. I've thought of a way that you won't need all those socks and sweaters."

"I don't really mind. I'm practically dressed when I get up. It makes things very simple."

"Yeah, too simple." He walked away in disgust.

The next afternoon there was a break in the storm. The pewter sky hung sullenly over hills newly clothed in velvety, emerald green shadowed by the dark gray above. With a hint of crushed pine needles on its breath, the clear clean air was as refreshing as a long drink from a mountain spring, energizing and reviving us.

I had not been up long (one must remember that at Dañada the day did not start till afternoon) when I bumped into Serena, who was just leaving, dressed as though she were going to catch the next plane for New York. She looked more like the lady of the house than Liz ever had.

I had a hard time talking to her, hating her so much, but I exclaimed, "You're going somewhere?"

"Yes," she said.

"How can you? There isn't any way out of here."

"I'm just going down the road a little way for a job interview."

With whom? Joe Viscantino? Did he have his headquarters or a hideout in that dilapidated house hidden by a grove of redwoods in the next canyon? That place always seemed very creepy when I strained to get a glimpse of it from the highway. I did not want to let her know I knew about Joe, so I did not ask that question. But I probably should have asked her what kind of a job; she certainly couldn't be applying for a position as a maid.

"Why?" I inquired very nastily.

"I want something to do until we go to Australia and it would be nice to have some spending money."

"Oh," I said because I couldn't, at the moment, think of anything else to say.

"Of course, Pirrone doesn't want me to get a job. He says I have enough here—a place to live and the use of any of the cars."

"What difference does it make to him whether or not you work?"

"I live in his house, and it would hurt his pride if I get a job." The house was really Liz's. But I guessed Pirrone with his vast wealth considered himself its master.

"So what? You aren't married to him," I said.

"No, but I am part of his household and to Pirrone it's the same." She went on to explain, "It's the Italian temperament."

This whole job thing was obviously a contrived cover-up; she had to be somehow involved in the secret plans. New developments in the Joe Viscantino smuggling case, as I now considered it to be, were coming too fast and the suspense was driving me nuts—on top of everything else! I had to be able to discuss the clues and their implications with someone; as a detective, I needed an assistant.

After Serena left I looked for Erica as the one most likely not to be involved in the illegal smuggling. I finally found her in a bathroom trying to pull the knots out of her hair—she said the clearing weather had inspired her to comb it. I had located her by the ouches coming through the closed door as she yanked on the snarls.

In my agitation, I gauchely blurted out, "What do you know about Joe Viscantino?"

"Joe who?"

"Erica, you don't have to cover up for me. I already know about him."

It turned out upon further conversation that she really knew nothing and had never heard of Joe. But she was curious. I told her of all the evidence I had gathered, if one could call it evidence—it was really only suspicions formed from various things that did not add up.

Erica reflected, "You know, I've seen some unusual things, too. I saw Pirrone talking to a gangsterish fellow on the pier who might have been he, now that you have described him, and one time when Serena came back after being gone I overheard Pirrone ask her what Joe had to say. I didn't think about these things at the time, but...."

It seemed that Serena must be an accomplice. Did Liz know all this?

"Erica, we have to find out what's happening. Smuggling cigarettes is probably not so bad, but drugs, that's really awful. You're here all the time; you can watch for clues."

Actually if I had thought about it we were like those children's stories detectives, the Hardy Boys. As detectives we would be more like defectives in our sleuthing—we were just two silly girls with no expertise. But at the time I was very serious because the idea of dealing in something as illegal as drugs scared me and was beyond any of the adjustments I had already made in my moral makeup.

Erica pondered, "Do you suppose our destination was changed to Australia because it's near those places in the Far East where Pirrone could pick up a large shipment of heroin?"

I had not considered this. I had wondered, though, about Pirrone's desire to ranch in the outback; he was not the pioneering type.

The break in the storm did not last long. Late that afternoon it returned with a steady downpour that depressed everyone. The witty chit-chat disappeared, as did a few of our group, retreating to their rooms or elsewhere in secret corners of the sprawling house.

That night I had not been asleep for long when Liz came into the library.

"Oh, I'm sorry, I hope I didn't awaken you. I need a book. I just had the most awful dream."

"That's too bad," I said.

"Yeah, I was standing in the Roman Forum—all white marble, just as it was two thousand years ago. Suddenly great swarms of Romans in white togas rushed at me from all sides. I tried to run, but I couldn't move. I couldn't scream; my voice wouldn't work. I saw Pirrone and Serena in the crowd, laughing derisively at me. Then Serena smiled that cold smile of hers. They closed in on me just as I woke up screaming, 'Togas, get the togas.'"

"What do you think the dream meant?" I asked.

"I guess it's all the people. I don't mean you, Alice. It's just that sometimes I think I'll go out of my mind if I don't get away from here—like for a month."

"That long? It would be so boring. What would you do?"

Liz sighed, "It would be wonderful to do nothing." As she said this she took a little yellow film can from a desk drawer and poured out a few pills and popped them into her mouth.

I guess I looked startled because she said, "Oh, these are just sleeping pills." I stared at the can. She said, "This is a handy pill box." What a strange place to keep sleeping pills—and in the same kind of container as gun cleaning compound. What else was kept in these cans that seemed to proliferate everywhere?

I said, "Aren't you ever worried about getting it mixed up with the one Pirrone keeps his gun-cleaning compound in?"

She laughed, but said nothing. Then I told her how beautiful I thought her snail pin was, suggesting she could keep a few pills in it.

She said, "A good idea, but not sleeping pills. I wear it a lot, but not to bed."

I had not been clever with my strategy to find out what she did keep in the brooch because she did not offer any explanation. She picked out a book, saying, "This should keep me occupied. I love a mystery story."

"Won't you bother Pirrone if you read?"

"He's not there."

I asked no more. Because of the preview of the night before, I now was sure that Pirrone was more than just a "screen" lover. No wonder Liz had dreamed about Pirrone and Serena laughing at her. It had never really occurred to me that the fulfillment of lust and disregard for marriage vows went along with their unconventional ways. I had to have been really naïve and stupid not to realize this in the very beginning. But how could Pirrone be so callous and cruel to his wife? But ambivalent as I was, I still hated Serena for being the one who had him. If he were going to be unfaithful, why couldn't it have been with me? Here I was feeling awful for Liz and still desperately wanting Pirrone.

And I was, it seemed, more destroyed by this than she was. Why did she allow her husband to sleep with another woman? And in her own house! Was she only interested in his wealth? But material possessions seemed to mean little to her. Was his faithlessness the reason for the variability of her moods, which I had halfway attributed to drugs? Although, if there were some magic drug in the little cans, she could be hooked on it. She had ample reason for taking it.

In all my mixed-up emotions I was also unhappy for Liz for I was strongly attracted to her. I really liked her, no matter how peculiarly she acted at times. She was kind and thoughtful but also very vulnerable. I felt like crying for her, but even more for myself; and strangely I did not feel guilty for coveting her husband.

I was so disturbed that I had a hard time going back to sleep. I was only half-asleep when I heard a strange moaning sound. I thought at first it was one of the cats. But then I realized it did not seem at all cat-like. It was like nothing I had ever heard before. It sounded almost human but not quite. There was something high-pitched and unearthly about it. It also had a desperately miserable ring to it.

Then as I was falling back asleep, I saw a ghostly shadow on the library wall opposite me. I could have been dreaming during the first throes of trying to get back to sleep but I don't think I was really asleep when I saw it.

The next day Liz was wandering around with a vacant look in her eyes, muttering unintelligible gibberish, oblivious to everyone. I said "Hi" to her but she stared straight ahead, walking past me still muttering.

I was so unhappy and confused by all that had happened I thought I would get a book to take my mind off my woes. I went into the library for one. Erica was there alone, painting. I asked how it was going. "Fine," she said amiably.

She seemed so open and receptive; I thought I should be able to talk to her easily. "You're lucky you can paint," I said. "It really is boring with nothing to do. I can't find anyone to talk to. I tried to talk to Liz but she is totally out of it. She didn't see me or hear me. I think she is as haunted as this house."

"Why did you say that?" Erica asked.

"Well, last night as I lay in bed, first I heard weird moaning, then I saw the shadow of a ghost, and now today Liz is acting more strangely than ever."

"I'll have to agree with you," Erica replied. "She is behaving more peculiarly than I have seen her before. I wonder if the curse of Dañada has fallen on her? I always thought it was a lot of hokum but now I am beginning to believe it."

"What is the curse?" I questioned eagerly. I had suspected that Liz might be a doomed soul, a counterpart of the original one for whom the house was named. Perhaps now I would find out all about it.

"You do know about the legend of Dañada?" she asked.

"No," I replied, "but I have been terribly curious about the name Dañada." She seemed surprised that I didn't know. I went on to say that I was even more curious when Liz avoided opening a door. "When I asked her about it, she acted as though she hadn't heard me. The door had to have been to a bedroom because it was in that wing of the original adobe. I sneaked back later to peek in the room but it was locked."

Erica said, "That was probably the room of Don Ignacio's bride. He is the one who had the house built."

"She must have been the doomed soul!"

"Yes, that's the way the legend goes."

"Oh, tell me about it, please." I could hardly contain myself in my impatience to hear the whole story.

Erica started to tell me. "It seems a wife had been chosen for Don Ignacio when she was just a little girl in Spain. She was sent to California to marry him while she was still very young. That was the custom then. Don Ignacio was, of course, much older than she."

I am glad, I thought, that I did not live then. It would have been awful to have one's parents pick out one's husband. If mine could do that, I would get some miserable creep, for sure.

Erica was saying essentially the same thing: that this girl took a dislike to her new husband from the start. "However," she said, "they had a son soon after they were married—like nine months and two days later, I would imagine."

Yuck. The thought of this young girl having to submit to sex with an old man she couldn't stand was too wretched even to imagine.

Erica continued with the story. "The father idolized the son and neglected his bride, who couldn't bear the sight of her husband anyway. She was lonely for her friends and family back in Spain. Few people ever came to visit her on this huge, isolated ranch in the new world. She became more peculiar all the time. Then several years after her first child, another son was born. This one was misshapen and deformed. The gossip was that the devil had been her lover and that this was his child."

I laughed in a rather, for me, sardonic way. "I guess even the devil would have been an improvement over her old, creepy husband. I wonder what I would do, if I were propositioned by the devil?"

"Oh, Alice, you are ridiculous and Gothic, I might add. Where do you get these dark ideas?"

"I don't know," I replied, "but sinister things really intrigue me. However, I'm stopping you and I want to hear all of the legend."

"There isn't much more to tell. The baby lived only a few months. The mother went into mourning for this child and took to her room. She never left it again. A few years later she died. It was said she had gone completely crazy."

"That's a gruesome story." I shuddered at the horror of it all. But I was also enthralled by it, for nothing attracted me more than the dark underside of life. "I suspected something terrible because of the meaning of the name, Casa de la Dañada; but I never imagined anything quite like that. But you haven't told me what the curse of Dañada is." I was determined to find out everything.

"Oh, I was getting to that. They say the devil wanted his son to carry on his evil work here on earth. But when the baby died, he was so furious, he cast a spell on the mother, causing her to go mad. He also put a curse on the house. It would fall, so the legend goes, on every female descendant who remained in the house after she was grown. So Liz fits right in: she was born here and now she is the mistress of the house. She does act crazy a lot of the time. But, of course, the legend is just a weird story with no basis in fact, as far as I know."

"Yes," I said. "But still, legends don't just grow out of nothing. Something strange must have happened that caused it to start. There had to be some reason why this place was named the house of the doomed soul—or is it the *damned* soul."

"You're right about that. The first bride of Don Ignacio did go mad, they say, and I believe that part. Also, she could have easily had a malformed son. That's not unusual."

"That's true," I said, "and in those olden days if a baby weren't all right, there was nothing they could do."

"Anyway," Erica continued, "the house is supposed to be haunted by Don Ignacio's first wife. On stormy nights, they say, one can hear her soul mourning for her dead child."

"I heard it last night," I cried.

Erica laughed. "It was probably just the wind blowing the rain through the pines. It can sound very mournful. I have heard it."

I said no more. What I had heard was not just the wind in the pines. I am sure it came from the locked room, which had to have been the young bride's bedroom, and I had seen the shadow of her ghost. Erica might not have believed in the legend but I did.

The next day the storm cleared up completely. The freshly scrubbed landscape was filled with clear, shiny color. The greenest of greens were emerging everywhere in vigorous renewal. We, too, were newly invigorated by the magnificent day.

In high spirits we all breakfasted in Liz and Pirrone's bedroom. Coffee and toast were served at the foot of their huge bed with its tall headboard painted in a fading pastoral scene, chipped and fragmented in places but still retaining the elegance of eighteenth-century France. Voluptuous court ladies, some nude, some half-dressed, some garbed as shepherdesses, all gamboled on the grass, keeping company with a couple of nude male forms with the animal legs of Pan and several men in tight britches and colored stockings wearing fitted waistcoats with lace frills at the collars and cuffs. Crowning it all, a pair of cherubs kissed above a soft sea-green sky.

Pirrone, propped against all the pillows, was wearing a T-shirt. There was an earthy, sexy appeal about him with his day-old beard and uncombed hair. Liz, still half asleep, was blinking her eyelids and mumbling about having slept with her contact lenses in and now being unable to extract one of them. Serena sat in a wide armchair with Brian while Erica made room for Tom and me on a chaise longue.

Tom eyed a copy of *Roaring Road* magazine lying on a small table. He picked it up and started to read. "Listen to this! 'For Sale: driving lights with the candlepower of airplane landing lights!'"

"The way you fly over the bridge, those are for you," Pirrone said, laughing. Then he wondered, "What shall we do to celebrate the clearing of the highway?"

"Let's go to the eye doctor," suggested Liz who was still trying to remove the lens.

Erica said, "I think I'll paint. The colors outside are marvelous today."

"How about a short race?" Tom offered.

Pirrone did not seem to react to Tom's question. He had the look of someone who could no longer resist telling a sensational piece of news. Then he announced, "Varian called last night." The monkey-house chattering stopped abruptly as Pirrone continued, "A fantastically rich vein of gold has just been discovered near the land I'm thinking of buying."

Tom's excitement transmitted itself to me in shock waves of electrical force.

Pirrone went on, "Ranching in Australia might be fairly lucrative, but I can't let a new gold discovery get away."

Was the gold the only thing that made Pirrone change his plans? Or had he and Joe found that whatever they were going to smuggle would bring more profit in South America because of Varian?

Pirrone got out of bed and dressed very unconcernedly in front of the group. "Let's go down to the boat. Why don't you come along, Serena. Liz is staying home to clean up the house."

Pirrone looked lovingly at Serena, making me jealous again. But Liz did not seem to notice.

We all piled into the limousine. The car seemed to glide on a cloud over the rough, storm-damaged road, and I heard no engine noise. The interior, resplendent with vicuna upholstery and rosewood paneling, did not go with the jeans and tennis shoes we were wearing.

Winding down the narrow road through the upper part of the canyon leading to the bay we played hide and seek with the vast reach of Chinese-roof-tile-blue sea below. Every time we came back around a curve, the incredible view of bright ocean was a sudden surprise.

As we were riding along, Serena asked Pirrone, "What kind of party are you giving Liz for her birthday?"

"Something small," he replied.

"Let's give her a big party," suggested Serena, "with live music and lots of guests."

"Why?" He was astonished. "She doesn't need a party like that."

"It would be fun and a good excuse to do it," answered Serena, teasingly.

"Maybe," Pirrone said with a sardonic smile.

As we drove, I mused about things at Dañada. I knew it took a great deal of money to finance this seemingly simple lifestyle. The twelve-cylinder Fazani needed to be completely tuned every couple of weeks. Even though Liz often looked as if she might be a welfare recipient, she wore expensive designer clothes—their run-down condition was the result of her throwing them on the floor and walking on them, which was easier than hanging them up and taking care of them. Although meals were thrown together haphazardly, to feed such a gang of people, great quantities of food were delivered regularly from Carmel's most expensive gourmet market. Liz also went in for delicacies such as Beluga caviar and French double-roasted coffee shipped weekly from a little delicatessen in New York.

When we reached the bay, big-eyed, black-rimmed holes stared at us from the fire-scarred remains of the pilot cabin on the *Calypso*, around which hovered a family of pelicans. With their long scissor beaks on their funny crooked necks, they looked like a humorous caricature of a chorus of gardeners with pruning shears.

Brian noticed them, too. He said, "Those pelicans must be a good omen. They are as large as albatrosses. Unless someone is as foolish as the Ancient Mariner and kills one, I'm sure they will prove to be lucky for us."

I hoped he was right. We certainly needed a good omen—with all the ominous things crowding in. The unanswered questions kept haunting me: what was really in all those cartridge film cans, which kept disappearing and reappearing in different guises? Was Joe Viscantino involved in smuggling some undisclosed illicit cargo on our boat?

I pondered all this while we were standing on the pier waiting to be ferried out to the boat. I noticed that Pirrone and Serena had walked a few steps away from the rest of us. They were talking in low voices in an intimate way. They had their arms twisted around each other as they held hands.

A stray breeze blew the end of a low whisper my way. Serena was saying, "He should be more careful. One of these times someone is going to get suspicious."

◇ Chapter Six

TOM AND PIRRONE started going on long business trips. This was a new development, although Pirrone had gone away by himself for short periods, to take care of his family's business I assumed. Since they were very uncommunicative, like army officers on a secret mission, I thought these trips should have a secret code name, such as "Operation Wild Goose," which seemed appropriate since I was certain the business trips had to do with the smuggling. Once, when I asked Tom about one of the trips, he replied, "It was fun. We were caught in a snowstorm."

"In Los Angeles?" I exclaimed.

"No, Arizona," he said, "in the mountains around Flagstaff."

"What were you doing there? I thought you had business in Southern California."

"We went for coffee at an Indian trading post I wanted Pirrone to see."

Because Tom liked nothing better than driving, his explanation sounded possible. On these jaunts were they minoring in business and majoring in fun? What was really disconcerting was that Serena often went along, Liz even waving gaily goodbye. As if she were in a pride, sharing her lion with another lioness, Liz seemed unbothered by Serena's relationship with Pirrone. But it bothered me. I still wanted him as much as ever. My enthrallment with him had corrupted me. As fond as I was of Liz, I would have been ready to hurt her if it meant I could be with her husband.

After Tom returned from a trip with Pirrone and Serena, I asked him, "Don't you think Pirrone is horrible to Liz, openly consorting with Serena?"

"Of course not," Tom said. "Liz understands. She knows Italian men need more than one woman. After all, she is the wife and has a permanent position. She knows his girlfriends are only a passing interest. One might say it is the Italian way."

"I think the American way is better. At least when a man cheats on his wife, she usually doesn't know about it and no one is hurt. It seems a lot less damaging to keep these things secret."

"That's dishonest," Tom said. "Pirrone is completely open about everything. That's much more decent. And besides, it's a lot less trouble. Can you imagine how impossible it would be to hide anything around here?"

I thought maybe Tom was right. Perhaps there were fewer problems this way, and as in a French movie, a ménage à trois did seem like a sophisticated way to live. Without completely changing my personal attitude, I bent my code of ethics to make an exception for this triangular arrangement because it was part of the Casa Dañada life I had so enthusiastically embraced. And even if Pirrone had a harem, he was such a marvelously fascinating man, how could any woman give him up? I knew I wouldn't have been able to, if I had had him. Like the queen's gardeners, I was busily painting the red roses white.

My aunt still ranted on about my friends' characters and their sins. I did not bother to argue or listen; for what she could not see was that they had found the ideal way to live—in a happy state of anarchy. But while I thought they had found the answer, I was not ready to break through my early conditioning that was restraining me from traveling the whole road myself, at least with Tom. If it had been Pirrone, I think I would have done anything he wanted.

One evening I walked out to the garden with Tom to watch the sunset. It was spectacular, as sunsets often were in El Mirador. Tom put his arm around me and hugged me to him as he asked me, "Alice, what are you holding out for? Why are you so worried?" He smoothed my hair back and said gently, "After it happens, you're going to wonder what all the fuss was about."

"But, Tom, don't you want to wait?" I said as I pulled away from him slightly. "Don't you want things to be right? I don't want to sneak around, or even worse, end up having to get married."

"You certainly wouldn't have to sneak around here. I can't wait much longer. Don't you want to sleep with me?"

"No," I replied, as I pulled away from him abruptly, "not under these circumstances." I started to walk back to the house.

"Wait a minute," he called after me. "Don't you know you're missing out and you're making me miss out, too?"

I stopped and turned around. "If you want me so much, why don't you want to get married?" Since his first vague proposal, he had never mentioned marriage again. I know I was not only being stupid and bourgeois, I was really being perverse, for as I had known all along, I did not want to marry Tom. But I was fond of him and liked his companionship; besides I could not reject him and expect to remain at Dañada.

Tom was miserable, "I do want to marry you, but it's out of the question now. At least we could have these months together."

Months, I thought, is almost like saying never. But I didn't care. Although I enjoyed being with Tom, I could not imagine him as a husband, even if I were madly in love with him. I did not think my father had been too far wrong when he said soon after I had met Tom, "He's just a bum. He'll spend his whole life driving from one highway exit to the next."

Tom, himself, had said to me one day when we were in the Fazani, "When I'm driving on the freeway, I hate to ever take an off-ramp. I just want to keep going."

That night, as I often did, I lay awake in my innocent bed, in heart-pounding excitement as the most vivid Cinerama images and sensations crowded in on me of unbelievable thrills, skin-to-skin with Pirrone. What duality, these wild diversions of my secret self as opposed to the pure, uptight front I presented to Tom. I was living emotionally all that I had heard or read or that my fired-up feelings could conjure, thus avoiding the risk of commitment, holding my precious morals above the water-line as far as Tom was concerned. But my defenses were so weakened that even though it was really Pirrone I wanted I was almost ready to have sex with Tom because it was clear that Pirrone was totally uninterested in me. I might as well partake of the fruits in that gorgeous garden of delights as everyone else here did. Tom was the only person who could take me there.

Life continued unchanged at Casa Dañada, though Pirrone's frequent absences left us with little direction. Like butterflies caught in a glass box, everyone flitted about purposelessly filling in time—Erica painting, Brian taking pictures and fiddling with his cameras, Liz and I reading. Without Pirrone, the fun seemed to be missing; there were no big things going on—no projects, no big plans, and no races to cheer. Although nothing was being done to prepare for the trip, the South American adventure was an ever-present topic of conversation—wild fantasies of the things we would do when we had the ancient gold the Incas had first discovered.

One day, after I had spent weeks—it seemed like years—in a routine of doing nothing, Tom called me at my aunt's and told me to be ready to leave right away because Brian was going to take his portrait of Dañada. When I asked if I could wear a bikini, Tom told me no one was wearing anything.

"Tom, I just can't do that."

"You wanted to go to the hot springs. What's the difference?"

"This is different. It's a funny idea, but to really do it...."

"Don't worry. Alice, everyone will be dressed the same way."

I laughed as I said, "Or undressed." Anyway it would be fun to have something different to do.

On the way to the picture taking, I thought of the fable about the contest between the wind and the sun to find out which was stronger. The sun had won because its warm rays had made a man take his coat off, while the wind had blown and blown to no avail.

The force of the Dañada enclave was no less strong on me than the sun had been on the man in the fable. Emerging from the chrysalis of my inhibitions, I was preparing to shed all my clothes and break free. I felt a little giddy as we drove along, the sun beating down, seeming to say as it beamed its rays directly at me, "Go ahead, Alice, you'll be much more comfortable without all those hot clothes. And think of the lovely tan you'll get. No strap marks or anything, one lovely shade of bronze all over."

When we reached Dañada, I expected to find everyone draped in front of the house in different poses, but the only thing there was Brian's camera sitting on its tripod.

Liz called from a window, "Tom! Alice! Hurry and change. We're almost ready. You can use a guest room."

"Who needs it? We can change right here," Tom replied.

I thought of the many murals I had seen in reproductions and in museums and wondered how a portrait of Dañada, blown up, would look on the portico wall. By the time I had got down to my bikini, which I had worn under my clothes just in case, Tom had taken off his shirt and was very slowly untying his shoes. For all his talk he seemed a little reluctant.

Liz yelled from the house, "Oh, I forgot—your props are on the bench by the living room door. We're going to make it a Roman bacchanal."

She walked out the door. I could see only her head above a framed section of a Botticelli painting she was carrying in front of her. The reproduction showed only the part with Venus, unclothed, emerging from her seashell. Liz was a nude behind a nude.

Tom was surprised. "Liz, is that the real you?"

"No, it's just a frame of reference."

"Do you have a picture for me?" Tom asked. He seemed relieved.

"No, but would you like a bolt of chiffon?"

He laughed off her suggestion. "That would be better for Alice."

"Liz," I exclaimed, "I like your costume."

She seemed pleased. "I just happened to see it on the wall at the last minute."

How odd that Tom, who had been so opposed to disrobing before, was prepared to carry out the photograph explicitly and that I, who had been intrigued but reticent, was also going to comply, while Liz who was as unconcerned about nakedness as an aborigine, was so imaginative with the painting.

Brian ran into the courtyard. "Hey, everybody!" he called. "Wait! I only have indoor film. I'll have to go into town to buy some outdoor film."

"Oh," said Liz, "that will take too long. Let's go to the hot springs instead. You can take the pictures some other day." When Liz was in one of her high moods, she was impatient and restless, unlike those periods when time seemed suspended for her while she drifted though a timeless void.

"Tom," I exclaimed, "that'll be great and we're all set."

"I'm going to work on my car," he replied.

I was terribly disappointed. Would I ever get to experience one of those wild encounters at the baths? "But what about the hot springs?" I asked again.

"I'd rather work on my car. You can go if you want."

"No, I'll stay with you."

"Let's go, Tom and Alice," Liz said as she walked back out of the house wrapped in a large beach towel.

"Thanks, Liz, but I have to work on my car."

"Do you have a cold again?" she chided. He did not reply.

After they left I asked Tom, "Where is Pirrone? Why wasn't he here to be in the picture?"

"He's much too busy with more important things." I wondered if the more important things were meeting with underworld contacts, whatever or whoever they might be?

We walked to the garage, which had been the stables in earlier times. Moldy, mildewed saddles hung on the walls along with pictures of racing cars. A workbench, strewn with car parts, lined one wall above the grease-stained dirt floor. An oilcan rested on a saddle stirrup, rubber tubing hung from a saddle horn, and monkey wrenches dangled from the same nails as rusty bridles. Tom sat on one end of the workbench and looked at his car with a rapt expression.

"Tom, what are you thinking about?"

"Car bodies and shapes," he replied.

He had confessed to me once that sometimes he did not listen when people spoke because he was lost in a world of geometrical designs and that even at night he would dream of complicated objects with countless angles and vanishing points.

"What are you going to work on on your car?" I asked.

"I'm going to put on a new hood ornament."

"Why did you get a new hood ornament?" I did not dare to say that I thought his car was more in need of floorboards.

"It'll do until I get a new fender."

I did not see how a new hood ornament could take the place of a fender, but such was his logic.

"Oh, I can't get started until I go get the tools in the room," Tom announced. "I'll be back in a minute."

Anyone else would have said "my tools in my room," but he had this annoying habit of not using personal pronouns. He had once told me about the way his mother would throw out his prized possessions when she straightened his room. Tom had in his early years come to believe that nothing belonged to him, except for his car, and perhaps that was why he was so attached to it.

After I had been watching Tom tinkering with his car engine for a while, Pirrone drove in, having returned from wherever he had been. "Do you two want to come with me to Monterey to look for a birthday present for Liz?"

Since the picture taking had fallen through and watching Tom was a bore, this seemed like it could be the "something different to do." On the way they might drop a hint about why they were always away on long drives. I needed clues to the mystery. Erica and I had been watchfully waiting but nothing had turned up since our talk.

"I'd love to," I answered Pirrone.

Tom said, "Okay," and we drove away in the Fazani. The day was crisply clear as we drove along the coast, a breeze ruffling the treetops that pushed their heads out of the deep ravines and gently undulating the sharp young greens of spring that played in sprightly profusion up and down the hills.

The ride was fun, the sparkling weather infecting us with its gaiety. On reaching Monterey we stopped at an English car dealer's, where we spent over an hour inspecting the models. Pirrone decided to try out a specially built limousine that was there on consignment. It was upholstered in matched water buffalo hides and was complete with a bar and a back seat that folded into a deep, downy bed. It was being sacrificed for seventy-five thousand, having been made for a financier who had changed his mind. I could not imagine Pirrone really buying it for Liz, since he had just bought his own limousine a short time ago. He could be planning, though, to ship it to South America with contraband hidden in the gas tank, the tires, or some other secret place.

We test-drove the limousine, going out to the marina to get some boat lines and winches. Pirrone suddenly had the idea that it would be easier to buy a new boat rather than to fix the *Calypso*.

We were looking at a large motor cruiser, when Pirrone saw a schooner in the next slip and exclaimed, "There's the perfect ship for our trip." But rather than appraising the boat, I noticed that his eyes were following a very pretty girl with pale, shining blonde hair walking around the deck with a large white German shepherd.

He said, "Come on, let's see if it's for sale."

As we walked over he called up to the girl. She replied, "It isn't for sale, but would you like to come aboard? Schooners are rather a rarity."

Pirrone became absolutely enchanting as he told her he needed a large boat for a South American cruise because his own needed extensive repairs. He was casting such a romantic spell I could understand the girl's enthrallment, for again I was ready to drop into Pirrone's net if he had wanted me.

Soon—I did not know exactly how he arranged it, I was in such a trance—the girl, Kristen, was coming with us. Pirrone had invited her to Casa Dañada for dinner. She could not have been over eighteen; very young to me who had already turned twenty. As we returned the limousine to the dealer, Pirrone told her he had thought of buying it for his wife's birthday, but that she did not deserve it. On the way home, he never broke the intensely romantic mood he had created, making me envious as he tightened his hold over Kristen who was now completely his, even though she had been promised nothing and was being taken to have dinner with his wife.

At Dañada, Brian, Erica, and Liz were sitting in the living room. Pirrone introduced Kristen, and then demanded, "Liz, would you please fix dinner."

"Sure, baby," she replied pleasantly.

Liz's cheerful acceptance of her husband's extra girls caused me to think they were necessary because of the smuggling—merely red herrings to throw nosey people off the track.

Liz poured Erica and me a glass of wine while we helped her in the kitchen, but she also kept refilling her glass from the cooking wine as well and soon became very animated. She was gesturing with a carving knife as she made devastating remarks about Pirrone and his women. She cut a smiling face of Pirrone in one slice of bread and a frowning one in the other. They were such funny caricatures that we burst out laughing. She made the faces into a sandwich, which she entitled "The Two Faces of Pirrone." Then she cut the sandwich into unequal thirds, giving Erica and me the pieces with the most of the faces and taking for herself what was left of Pirrone. And, I thought, that is all she ever gets. One wife and one full-time mistress were not enough for this contemporary son of Dionysus.

Brian called from the living room, "Hey, Pirrone's getting hungry!"

Liz giggled. "Little does he know, Pirrone's all gone," she said as she ate the last bite of the sandwich.

We stumbled into the living room, laughing hysterically as we tried to compose ourselves. Liz carried the platter of hamburgers, Erica and I, the various accoutrements such as mustard and ketchup. As we sat down, Liz, Erica, and I kept snickering amongst ourselves as we watched Pirrone's facial expressions.

"The hamburgers are delicious, Mrs. Rivelli." Kristen was deferential, as if speaking to a much older person.

Erica, who was sitting next to me, asked me under her breath, "Does she think Liz is Pirrone's mother?" I had never thought before about the protocol of what to call a new boyfriend's wife.

Brian, who seemed to find Kristen attractive, asked her, "Will you be in El Mirador long?"

"Oh, my, I hope so. It's so lovely here and Pirrone is going to show me some of the exciting places to go."

Erica whispered to me, "What exciting places? The Wagon Wheel Cafe or the launderette?"

"I'm going to look for a job," continued Kristen. "Pirrone has asked me to stay with him till I find one."

Erica nudged me. "What is this? Pirrone's unemployment hostel?"

Tom hardly said a word all during dinner. He just gave me longing looks, barely eating anything; this was unusual for Tom, who was normally a voracious eater. Later, he asked me to go for a walk with him. He was very sweet and loving as he told me how he wished I could go along on some of the trips with him and what a good time we could have. (Of course, I would have gone, had he ever asked me, but perhaps, he was referring to future trips.)

"You don't know how much I miss you when I'm away. I'll be so happy when we're on our way to South America and we can be together all the time."

He was very gentle and tender as he held both my hands and kissed me softly on the neck, next my cheeks, and then delicately on the mouth, barely touching my lips, but enough to be quite thrilling. We held those lightly brushing kisses for many seconds and they really moved me. I became filled with extreme desire for him, heightened by the fact that I had decided I would sleep with him at the first opportunity now that I had begun to talk myself out of my lust for Pirrone.

We were kissing in the garden near the library when the quiet softness of the night was pierced by Pirrone's angry voice, coming from the house. "God dammit! You embarrassed me, giggling at Kristen. She is our guest."

"I'm tired," Liz's voice yelled back in outrage, "of always having to entertain your girlfriends."

"You can't complain," Pirrone's voice was hard, cold and controlled. "I give you one night a week to be alone with me." So that was what was meant by "our night," the term Pirrone used the evening he gave Liz the snail pin.

"How would you feel," Liz cried, "if I had an affair?"

"I won't tolerate an unfaithful wife."

"I might leave you," she screamed.

"You better not." He must have grabbed her because I heard scuffling. "If we weren't leaving soon I'd have you committed."

Tom grabbed me and started to propel me away. But I protested. I wanted to stay to hear everything.

"What's the matter with you?" Tom asked. "You certainly don't want to listen in on a private quarrel, do you?"

I had no rebuttal. He was right; it was not the thing to do. But in their anger, they might reveal some secret about the smuggling. Was that the real reason Tom wanted to get me away from there? As Tom led me toward the garage, I could still hear Pirrone as he yelled, "Stop stuffing those pills in your mouth like candy. That's your answer to every problem—take a pill or a dozen."

No wonder she took pills—tranquilizers, probably. Who could blame her? It now seemed that Liz might be a victim rather than a co-conspirator. She was probably going along with the smuggling against her will, forced to entertain Pirrone's girlfriends, and when no longer of any use, she would be discarded in a mental institution. Perhaps she was really crazy. A sane person would have left him long ago. Or was she blindly and compulsively attracted to Pirrone? I knew what that was like.

"Tom, you don't think she's crazy?"

"Let's not talk about it. Some other time."

As we approached the garage he held my hand tightly, leading me into his room, its bookshelves filled with car parts and models set out as if they were on exhibit in an art show. The only books were automobile catalogs and manuals.

I began to feel scared. Noticing I was nervous, Tom told me, "There's nothing to be afraid of. I love you."

Not only was I nervous, I also trembled because I had only just changed my moral code. But all the wonderful things I liked about Tom filled my emotions—his mystical blue eyes, the blue extending inward as if through layers of stained glass, his big protective shoulders.... Now I would be really close to him and experience what everyone else at Dañada took for granted.

We stood inside his room, by the door, which he had carefully locked. Tom enclosed my body as he moved his big hands over it in an all-encompassing caress. We kissed eagerly, open-mouthed. The meeting and mingling of our tongues was a sensual experience that grew more arousing as the rhythm and intensity of the exploration continued. We soon collapsed in an awkward huddle on his bed. He turned me off my back, pulling up my turtleneck as he expertly unhooked my bra. He seemed to know just how to do it. That surprised me. He must have had a lot of experience to be so proficient. I had not thought this before because he had always been so reticent with me in terms of sexual affection. He reached around and cupped both my breasts in his hands. It felt good as they hardened and the tips stood up in his fingers. A surge of glowing warmth flowed through me as all my nerve endings joined in producing the most pleasurable sensations.

As those lovely feelings started to immerse my whole being, a loud knock jolted us and Pirrone's voice coming through the door ordered, "Wake up, Tom!"

Tom sagged. "Hell! Damn!" Nevertheless he pulled my sweater back down, got up and opened the door.

Seeing me, Pirrone said heartlessly, "Sorry, Alice, some other time. I need Tom now. We've got to go to Los Angeles this minute." Then, turning to Tom, he added, "We have to pick up a shipment at the harbor first thing in the morning or we'll lose it. Alice, we'll take you back to your aunt's."

I was faint from having my emotional state abruptly interrupted and at the same time I was charged with adrenalin by my rage at Pirrone for his callousness.

A couple of days later Erica came to pick me up at my aunt's. Very excited, she rushed me out of the house and we got into Tom's car, which she had borrowed. "I found an M-14 in the trunk of the Fazani!" she told me. "I woke up early this morning and couldn't get back to sleep so I took a walk. When I passed the Fazani I noticed the trunk was ajar, and so naturally I looked in."

"So," I exclaimed, "Pirrone is planning an arms shipment to South America! Of course, they're going to put them in the bottom of the boat and cover them with cigarette cartons."

"You're right on. It must have come from South America. I looked in the trunk because I thought it might be a good chance to look for a clue. Boy, did I find one! I first saw an empty crate marked P. RIVELLI HANDLE WITH CARE and it came from South America. I lifted it up, and underneath there was the gun."

"How did you know it was an M-14?"

"I recognized it right away. I've seen them before."

"It must be a sample of the guns some revolutionary group wants," I surmised. Alarming fears started crowding into my mind. "Erica, this is different from smuggling cigarettes. There's something evil about shipping guns. Although when I first heard that cigarettes were going to be smuggled, I was upset. Do you suppose I'll get used to this, too?"

"Oh, Alice, you do adjust your principles to fit—just like stretch pants. I've never thought any kind of smuggling was right. I'm only going along with it because of Brian."

"What does he think?" I asked.

"He likes the easy life and it's the only way he knows to get it." Erica was very honest up to a point. But I suppose that being a woman, she could not afford the luxury of being completely truthful with the man she loved. In this masculine world, it seemed to me that men could be open with women because they were in control—numero uno—but a woman had to carry on her little deceptions unless she was to become a mindless automaton, always seconding a man.

I said, "Guys always think they're right and that they're the only ones with the answers."

"Yeah, they've got fragile egos, I guess. We have to go along with them or they'll find someone else who will."

Then I remembered the little aluminum film canisters. I had not seen any since the night Liz had taken some pills from one of them. No pictures of Tom's car had appeared either. I asked, "I wonder what has happened to the yellow film cans?"

"I have no idea. Do you still think they're somehow connected to all this?"

"Well, everyone got so upset whenever I started to open one or ask about them," I answered.

"Oh, I think you just imagined that."

"I don't think so. I think there is something strange about them. And I think they have all disappeared because they were worried I would find out what was in them."

As we drove back to Dañada, I became exhilarated by the gorgeous day and the marvelous view—the scintillating blue ocean at the foot of the cloud-reaching mountains. Often these mountains had their tops in the clouds and their bottoms sunk in thick low-lying fog, but today their rugged sculpture was sharply outlined from sea to sky.

A motorcycle whipped by us. The girl riding behind the guy had a familiar look, though it was hard to tell who she was underneath the large leather jacket and the scarf tied babushka-style under her chin.

Then it came to me. "Serena!" I exclaimed. "She was the one riding with that guy on the motorcycle."

"I thought she had gone away for a few days to visit a friend. Pirrone would kill her if he knew she was with another man," Erica said.

"I thought his mistresses were only passing fancies. How could he be that jealous of her?"

"He obviously feels differently about her—very possessive. Haven't you noticed?"

Perhaps, I thought he considered Liz and Serena to be his property, and as he had told the two itinerant musicians, he would shoot anyone who tried to take or even touch his property. That might be the reason he showed no interest in me—because he thought of me as belonging to his best friend. Or was I just feeding my vanity because I failed to turn him on? I knew he had little respect for other people's belongings.

When we got back, Pirrone and Kristen were standing in the driveway by her little MG, which she had picked up in Monterey the day after she had come to Dañada. Pirrone was saying goodbye to her.

"Kristen, where are you going?" I asked.

She started to stammer something, but Pirrone broke in, "She'll only be away for a few days." He spoke with a finality that closed the subject. Pirrone did not seem to want me to know where she was going. Was he sending her on a smuggling errand?

Pirrone put his arm around Kristen lovingly while giving her a long, sexy kiss. "Be careful," he cautioned. "Remember what I told you." Pirrone has promised her something, I thought to myself. He wants to be sure she'll come back. I knew that he was very attracted to her.

On the way to Liz's birthday party, I asked Tom, "What did you do while you were away?"

"Wait till you see what I got Liz for her birthday," he said, ignoring my question.

Even though I really wanted to quiz him about the midnight drive to Los Angeles, which had to have something to do with the gunrunning, I knew he was not going to tell me anything. Instead, I mused, "I wonder how those girlfriends of Pirrone feel, going out with a married man who also has a mistress. After he drops them...."

He interrupted, "They have wonderful memories of him—it's a talent he has developed with years of practice."

"Tom, how can you believe that?" My indignation was more for show. I yearned for one of those memories.

Tom answered me, "It's true. Besides, with a wife who's crazy, can you blame him?"

"You told me once that he really cared for Liz."

"He does. But he's convinced that she isn't all right and he wants to help her. You've seen how moody and unpredictable she is…the odd statements she makes. Just last week she ran out of the house at four in the morning and I heard her scream, 'Not again! Not again!'"

"So?"

"She yelled that because Pirrone had only brought a girl home to stay who had no place to go. That wasn't very gracious of her."

"Poor stray girl," I said sarcastically.

"Liz should be happy to make Pirrone happy."

Something had been left out of Tom's mental make-up—the ability to judge and select. Blotter-like, he had unquestioningly absorbed Pirrone's attitudes and lack of ethics.

Speed-hungry Tom zoomed past a car and in the blur of an instant I saw an unmistakable profile—the fishing fleet owner who I was convinced was Joe Viscantino.

At Dañada, a loud rock group was spewing out music, the resounding vibrations filling every space with throbbing sound. This was the first time I had ever heard live music like this, obviously avant-garde.

People were everywhere—in the living room, in the library, and scattered throughout the garden. Some were dressed in evening clothes, some looked as if they had been hired for a costume production by Central Casting, and a few people were in jeans and sandals. A small knot of weirdos was huddled in a dark corner. They were quiet and withdrawn, detached in their individual trances, seemingly mesmerized by the rock beat. I would not have known what was going on if Tom had not told me; this was the first time I had ever seen anyone smoking pot.

I really only saw these guests in my peripheral vision, as I was concentrating on finding the likeness of Joe Viscantino to paste onto the image of his features that was filling my consciousness. I was like my younger brother and his stamp collection, looking for the proper stamp, disregarding all the others, in order to place it in the right stamp album square already imprinted with its copy.

In the living room, where people sat talking, presents for Liz were piled on a table. A number of guests were dancing, each in his own abandoned way. Three girls kept bringing hors d'oeuvres to Pirrone, who gave each girl, in turn, his complete interest. Brian and some other people were talking with Pirrone. We sat down next to them as Brian was saying that as soon as they got to South America the first place he was going to visit was Macchu Picchu.

"It's the lost city of the Incas," he said. "No one knows how, why, or when it was built. Some people think it could have been a fortress or a summer capitol for the Inca rulers. There's even an idea that it was a retreat for young virgins who were dedicated to the sun."

When Pirrone heard that, he said, "I wouldn't have wasted those virgins on the sun." Everyone laughed. Then he added, "I like women so much, that if I were one, I'd be a lesbian."

Tom changed the direction of the conversation. "I have a great idea which I told Pirrone about yesterday. I want to attach a camera to one of the fenders of the Fazani. That way we could get the sensation of mountain road racing on film. It would be really something when we're going over a hundred and seventy."

"That would be terrific," Brian said, "but you might get a ticket for speeding when you show your film." The group laughed again.

Tom always felt encouraged to go on talking when what he said entertained people. He continued with a funny idea about painting his face with different colors of grease paint, then shocking people by rising up out of manholes on sidewalks in San Francisco. In his phrasing and wording, Tom had consciously or unconsciously adopted Pirrone's storytelling style.

Tom got up to refill his glass and I moved over to another couch and sat down. I began talking to some people whom I had never met before, but my mind was only half there as my eyes searched for a glimpse of Joe Viscantino. After a few minutes of aimless—and inattentive on my part—conversation with the girl sitting next to me, I was brought to instant attention when one of the fellows in the group confidentially said to another one, "Did you hear what happened to Joe's last shipment?"

"Yeah," the other one said, "but there's more where that came from."

Here was a clue, but what did it mean? They certainly must be referring to Joe Viscantino. I had just determined that he was not at the party, not only because I had not seen him, but also because I realized that Pirrone would not want to be seen with him openly as that would be incriminating. However, Joe and Pirrone could quite possibly have had a secret meeting near the property. Pirrone could have easily slipped away from the party for a few minutes without anyone noticing. It seemed as though more and more people were involved in Pirrone's smuggling plot. I felt I had to stick with these fellows for the rest of the party, for they might drop another hint, which could explain the first clue.

Suddenly, there was a loud clattering of iron wheels across the tiles outside the living room. Heads turned toward the doorway as Tom pushed in an antique Spanish picnic cart on top of which was a large object covered by a tapestry. Like a covey of ducks lifting off the water, a flutter of ideas arose as to what lay beneath the tapestry.

"It's a cage with a parrot for the boat."

"No, there's an albatross in the cage."

"I think it's a lifetime supply of chocolates for Liz's birthday."

"You're all wrong," someone called out. "It's a statue of Pirrone in bed."

Pirrone strode over to meet Tom and the cart with the air of someone about to make a momentous announcement. Pushing off the tapestry, he said, "One of nature's wonders from Peru—giant fighting piranhas!"

A collective gasp arose from the crowd, quickly followed by comments of surprise and excitement. The fish were horrifying, their jaws gaping open with jagged pointed teeth protruding from the outer edges. There was a lone fish in each of the two side-by-side tanks. Pirrone said with great relish, as he reached for a net to place one of the fish in the aquarium with the other, "I always thought it would be great sport to watch hungry piranhas go after each other."

Unable to watch such a vicious battle, I turned away and walked toward the French doors leading to the garden. I had heard all about how piranhas attack like lightning and can even slice a finger or toe, bone and all, from a man as easily as a gang saw ripping through a log, or strip the flesh off another fish, leaving only a skeleton. What a terrible idea of sport: this dramatic display of violence that Pirrone could produce and control at will.

I was walking through the doorway when I heard Pirrone say, "a couple of days ago Tom and I went to Los Angeles in the middle of the night to get these."

Why did Tom have to go with Pirrone on such a silly errand? I had thought at least the early morning race to Los Angeles was for something vital for the South American expedition. To have been dumped for a couple of piranhas was too much. The only urgency must have been to extricate the piranhas, which are illegal in this country, before anyone discovered what was in the shipment. Or were the piranhas there to cover up the gun?

Outside the moon cast a pallor over the yard, making the various couples intertwined in the shadows resemble marble statues. Feeling uncomfortable about being alone in the romantic hush of this place, I decided to go back to the light and sound of the veranda and to trailing my two unintentional informants.

As I started to leave I saw a profile backlit by moonlight. It was Tom. I was walking toward him when he bent down to give a long, lingering kiss to an upturned face.

Stricken, I turned back to the house, trying to tell myself that it must have been someone else, even though I knew it could only be he. How could he even think of kissing another girl? Maybe it was not a kiss at all; but no, that, too, had been unmistakable. Dazed, I stumbled onto the veranda and then drifted back into the living room. Some guests were seated and some were standing in knots of three and four, drinks in hand, talking noisily. Several people spoke to me but I didn't really hear what they said, although I answered them in a sort of involuntary way. It seemed as if it weren't actually I speaking but someone else as I listened to my voice floating in space. I looked over at the fish. One was gone. I shuddered as the shocking thought of what had happened to the other fish snapped me out of my trance.

Pirrone stood up and announced, "It's time to open the presents." Then he walked out onto the terrace and repeated the announcement. Guests straggled in, Tom among them, with a pleased look on his face.

As she opened each package, Liz exclaimed with surprise and delight, thanking the donor with an appropriate comment. When she opened Tom's present—a huge stuffed iguana—I was as startled as she was. But Liz, ever gracious, said, "What a clever idea. I can put it on a gate post to scare the bill collectors away!" She saved Pirrone's gift for the last—a case of Pernod, his favorite drink, and a red rose. I wondered about the sincerity of the offering.

Since the people I had been eavesdropping on were nowhere in sight, I went with Tom to look at the ocean from the glass-aerie guesthouse. The sky was filled with fuzzy clouds, like patches of snow. The moon, veiled by layers of gauzy mist, had a hazy golden halo encircling it. We walked in silence. I could only think of Tom kissing that girl. Who was she? I wanted to ask, but the words would not come.

Finally I said, "Tom, you're suddenly so different."

"What do you mean?"

"I saw you kissing a girl," I blurted out.

"Oh, no. Where?"

"In the garden."

"Oh, she lost her beads. I helped her find them and then I fastened them around her neck."

"Do you still want me to go to South America with you?" I cried. "You could go with that girl and have a wonderful time."

"Alice," he implored, "it's you I want. I love you. I was just helping that girl."

He was so sincere. Perhaps I had imagined more than I had seen. He put his arm around me and kissed me so tenderly that all my doubts were dispelled. I felt so close to him that I was able to bring up the subject that had been dominating my mind for the past day. "I know about the gunrunning," I said in a confidential manner.

"The what?" exclaimed Tom. "How much have you had to drink?"

"You're acting awfully innocent for someone who drove to Los Angeles," I accused, "to pick up an M-14."

He laughed. "Pirrone bought that to keep surfers off the boat."

"Is he planning to kill them?"

"Of course not. He just wants to scare them. After all, if they're trespassing...."

I did not believe Tom. He was covering up for Pirrone and that story about the surfers was just too dumb.

A frantic tooting of horns in the driveway and loud calls of "A race!" ended the conversation. Tom grabbed my hand and we dashed off to join the crowd.

<h1>◇Chapter Seven</h1>

WE WERE BREAKFASTING listlessly in an enervating saloon-like atmosphere, stale with last night's party smoke and old alcohol fumes from drink glasses, which were still around. Almost any other kind of air would have been more invigorating. The collective lethargy produced only sporadic conversation. I gazed vacantly around the room at the party decorations, which looked much stranger than they had the night before and definitely droopier. A couple of blankets were in disarray on a couch and the down cushions looked as if they had spent a bruising night. It seemed that more than one person must have lain there. I asked, almost to myself, "Who could have slept there?"

Liz, who was sitting next to me, answered, "Pirrone and the spirit."

"The spirit?" I was surprised.

"She was here last night," Liz said. "Do you remember her? The one in the floor-length gauze?"

"I think so. Was she the ethereal one?"

"Yeah, I guess. But that isn't why I call her the spirit. It's because she seems to appear and disappear out of nowhere. And after she's gone, it's as though she's never been here."

Liz's description confirmed my suspicions about something supernatural about Pirrone. He actually consorted with a spirit. Whether Pirrone's conquests were supernatural or not, Liz never lost her sense of humor, even though her husband's public flaunting of his unfaithfulness had to be humiliating. Liz was a tragic figure without a trace of tragedy.

Tom got up and came over to tell me he was going to Monterey to buy a winch. What a funny hour to leave. It was well after four in the afternoon. By the time he got there it would be after closing time. What dealers in boat hardware did business at night? There must be an ulterior motive for this errand. I had not seen Pirrone all day and no one said anything about his whereabouts. Was he with Joe Viscantino and was Tom going to meet them?

I hoped Tom was only a dupe in the gunrunning. But he did go on all those extended business trips. What could they be for if not to work out the details of the gunrunning? I thought as decent as Tom was, his idolization of Pirrone had corrupted him. As far as I could tell, Pirrone's evil essence tainted everyone it touched. I had been affected, too. I still could not stop desiring him insanely. There was no rational reason for me to continue with this unrequited lust. It had to be the result of his preternatural influence.

What if it turned out that Pirrone was a smuggler of real contraband and that Tom was involved? And what if Liz were involved, too? Would this enchanted life be snatched away from me like a cherished and irreplaceable jewel? There was only one Casa Dañada. In a whole lifetime I would never find another.

As for Liz, her husband spoke of having her locked up in a mental institution, but she was already in a cage on her own estate, with Pirrone hardly the kindly keeper, forcing her to be a servant to his mistresses. He ignored her, except when he was giving her orders. In reality, she was the maid and Serena the head wife of the harem.

The next day Kristen returned, two days too late for the party.

Pirrone greeted her with enthusiasm. They immediately went off together. I thought bitterly, he can hardly wait to get her into bed.

Later on I saw her walking toward the library swinging a carry-on suitcase as lightly as if it were filled with cotton balls. It had to have been empty or nearly empty.

"Kristen," I said jokingly, "it looks like you're off on another trip."

She laughed. Then she sort of sputtered, "I think I got it banged up. Pirrone is going to check to see if I can collect for damages from the airline."

"Oh, you flew somewhere?" I was surprised.

"Yeah," she said without elaboration as she walked away.

I remembered Pirrone checking Serena's suitcase for damage. This was an odd coincidence. I laughed to myself as I thought, Pirrone is the self-appointed baggage inspector for Dañada.

Late that night, long after two in the morning, I sat alone in the living room filled with romantic thoughts, waiting for Tom to get back from an errand for Pirrone. When he arrived I asked what they had been doing.

Tom said, yawning, "I'm too tired to talk." Then he collapsed on the couch next to me and instantly fell asleep. I felt like turning up the stereo as loud as it would go. What right did he have to leave me alone for a couple of days and then fall asleep immediately upon his return? It certainly did not help my self-confidence. Feeling angry and hurt, insignificant and unattractive, I sat there and stared at him. What kind of boyfriend was he? He was either asleep or away. And what made matters worse, a little later when Pirrone came into the room, Tom woke up and was instantly alert.

They started talking about the difficulties they'd encountered getting parts, as Pirrone mapped out an assignment for Tom the next day. The lateness of the hour combined with the boring content of their conversation made me very drowsy. I lay down on the couch, soon falling asleep. I dreamed a mixed-up dream about dozens of statues of Tom kissing long lines of marble girls in the garden. Then the statues started laughing. Their laughter had a hollow sound as though it were being echoed back and forth in some huge empty hall. Then all the Toms said in chorus, "I was only fastening her necklace."

I don't know how long I had lain there, dreaming, when I was awakened by Tom kissing me. Even in my sleepy state I noticed he was quite nervous.

"What's the matter?" I asked.

"Every time I get close to you I get scared," Tom said.

"You do?" I laughed.

"I want you, but I'm afraid to hurt you. You're the only really good thing in my life," he said.

"Well, then, why do you act the way you do sometimes?"

"Maybe it's the uncertainty of the trip," he answered. To my knowledge the only uncertainty was the smuggling. Was the uneasiness to which he was referring his conscience?

"Why are you afraid of me? I'm just a girl," I said.

"You're different from the rest."

"From the rest!" I was upset. "Whom else have you been going out with? Is that what you do on those wretched business trips?"

"I still want you to go to South America with me," he replied, evasively.

"Well," I proclaimed, "I'm going to go out with other guys." Which was a big bluff. What other guys did I have to go out with?

"Maybe you should," he said in a flat monotone.

His changed attitude frightened me. "Oh, Tom, if you won't go out with anyone else, I won't either."

"Alice, I'm suddenly not in the mood."

What caused him to make this totally out-of-context comment? He had not given any indication that he had been in the mood for romance, unless awakening me with a kiss could be called that. But it was usually hard to decipher what was behind Tom's abrupt conversations. However his last statement made me react emotionally, causing me to read my own semantics into it. I started to cry.

"What did I say? What have I done? I don't understand at all," I said.

He put his arm around me comfortingly. "It isn't you. It isn't your fault. It's me. There are some things I'm not sure of yet."

Seeing that I was so dejected by this last statement, he tried to comfort me more. Soon I forgot my disconsolateness in the warmth of his embrace. Our kisses were long and pleasant. I was overcome with erotic feeling for him as I welcomed his tentative caresses over my clothes. He managed to unhook my bra with the same expertise as before. Then he slipped his hands under my blouse and caressed my breasts. But his caresses became much stronger and soon he was kneading my breasts like bread dough, making them hurt. He became much rougher and more awkward than he had been the night we were interrupted by Pirrone. The tempo and pressure of his handling of me increased until he became a throbbing, unstoppable animal. He pulled my pants down. The thick callouses of his hands on my delicate places were as abrasive as sandpaper. I was becoming more tense and rigid as this whole proceeding became more and more unpleasant.

I pleaded weakly, "Please, Tom, let's not, now."

He seemed not to hear me. He fumbled, trying to penetrate me and I stiffened myself involuntarily. Then he seemed unable to wait a second longer and accomplished it in one giant shove. I cried out in pain, which he mistook for ecstasy. Then it was all over.

"I'm glad it was good for you," he said as he became relaxed and gentle, holding me softly.

I could not answer. How could he have been so insensitive? I thought, here I am wondering if this is what rape is like while Tom is thinking it had been good for me. It had been horrible. It was as if an incubus had consorted with me in a nightmare. He had been like a demon in his wild lust—a brutish caveman, not a tender lover. He had destroyed me. This couldn't be what sex was really like, I thought. Was it only because in my fear and lack of real desire I had pulled back and been uncooperative?

I started to sob uncontrollably. As I cried, Tom patted me. "I didn't realize you were so emotional," he said. "I know it can be a marvelous emotional experience for a woman."

Again he totally misread my feelings. I dissolved into tears completely and could not stop crying. Soon Tom left, saying he would be late if he did not get started. Late for what at this already extremely late hour, I wondered? But in my dejection, I did not give the thought much attention.

"I'm sorry to leave you like this," he said as he kissed me lightly on the forehead.

I should have asked him to take me back to my aunt's first, but I was so broken up, I could not move or talk.

I lay there sobbing for a long time. Finally I pulled myself together enough to get up. I walked down the portico to an unoccupied guest room. I began thinking about Tom's quick departure. Why did he leave so suddenly? He should have stayed with me. I felt very rejected. He had used me and then deserted me. Trying to get the whole miserable experience out of my mind, I became preoccupied with an examination of the room. The central piece was a canopied bed with narrow spindled posts; a velvet coverlet matched the tasseled and scalloped Spanish-tile-colored canopy. Deeply recessed bottle-glass windows glowed under a coffered ceiling. In front of the shuttered windows stood a pair of urns filled with lemon leaves that should have been thrown out ages ago. A massive old oak cupboard with a carved pediment filled one corner. A faded forest-green dado banded the yellow-ochre walls.

The room had a Renaissance look that triggered something in my memory that I could not quite place. The idea kept pushing against the fringes of my mind but I could not bring it into focus. Dismissing it, I started to undress, when suddenly I recalled a print I had seen of Carpaccio's painting of the legend of Saint Ursula. This room was like my remembrance of the painting. Could the interior designer have been an admirer of Carpaccio?

I climbed into the four-hundred-year-old bed. At least it seemed as if it were that age—the mattress was newer. I soon faded into a dream of Saint Ursula. Pirrone became the pagan king of the legend and I became Saint Ursula. When I refused his proposal of marriage, in a rage over my rejection, he began to slay my retinue of eleven thousand virgins. The massacre was interrupted by a voice. I climbed up through the layers of sleep from that distant time and place to the insistent present. Opening my eyes with great effort, I saw Pirrone standing above me with a roll of papers in his hand which I, still half dreaming, mistook for a club. "Don't! Don't!" I screamed.

"Don't worry." He laughed. "We don't have time."

But I would have had time for him, anytime. "Oh, Pirrone," I said, still trying to shake my dream, "I thought you were a king."

"Well," he said in a flattered tone, "are you always so visionary when you wake up?"

By this time my brain had cleared. "I didn't know where I was for a moment." I don't know how long I had slept, but daylight filled the room and I could see Pirrone clearly.

He smiled as he said, "I didn't know where you were either, but you left the door ajar and I saw you here in bed. I'm sorry to awaken you, but you women have to leave right away."

"Why?" I asked.

"You have to go shopping. We need a lot of things for the boat. If we don't get it fixed soon, we'll never be able to leave. All the guys are down there working now." As rich as he was I wondered why he just didn't hire some marine repair company to fix the boat. But then it occurred to me why he couldn't do that. They might discover that it had a false bottom.

On the way to Monterey to do the shopping, I noticed how indolently self-assured Serena was, half withdrawn into some mysterious interior, as though she were the sultan's favorite kadine, while Liz was open and enthusiastic like a small child. I could see why Serena intrigued Pirrone. There was a hint about her of an elusive voluptuousness that could slip away at any moment with that cold look from her eyes. It was like some marvelous, mysterious phenomenon that appeared and disappeared, but ever lured the searcher on in the hope of finding its secret. But poor, undemanding Liz had no such aura. She was just Pirrone's ready slave, putting up with anything.

It occurred to me as we rode along that, after last night, I was more a part of this group, as if I had gone through the rites of initiation and could now become a member in full standing. But had they all gone through such an initiation as I had? I thought not. Thinking that made me feel even more unfulfilled and disillusioned. It had been a messy, ungainly event. What I had been holding out against and then pushing for turned out to be a ghastly, miserable experience. When Tom had said he did not want to hurt me, he had meant emotionally, but he had succeeded in hurting me physically as well. However, I finally decided it wasn't his fault; it was because the situation had been all wrong. If we had spent a romantic evening with lots of loving feelings, kisses, and caresses, Tom would have been, I felt sure, a thoughtful, considerate lover. Then I would have found out what everyone was so excited about.

My mind went back to my dream in which I was still a virgin in the person of Saint Ursula, wishfully thinking that Pirrone wanted me so much that he was enraged by my rejection of him. There was no question that I wanted to forget that last night had ever happened.

When we got back with all our purchases, I said I would rather not go down to the boat—that I wanted to stay behind because I had not slept well. I knew everyone at Dañada would have been surprised if they found out that last night was the first time Tom had made love to me (a misnomer if there ever was one). I did not want to face Tom down at the boat with the others and have to act as though nothing unusual had happened. I wanted to be able to see him alone; but first I wanted to straighten out my thoughts and feelings. I wanted Tom to be sweet to me so I could get over the terrible trauma of the night before. I felt empty and drained. I knew I should be with Tom to try again right away so I could wipe out that terrible first time experience. But more than anything I wanted to experience what everyone seemed to think was so great.

Now that the group had gone down to the boat and I had the house all to myself, I felt I could keep my mind from riveting onto the misery of the night before by doing some sleuthing. Searching for clues might be engrossing enough to push all these disturbing thoughts aside.

With no one there, a stillness fell upon Dañada as though it had been long uninhabited. In the hush, I decided the library would be a good place to start. This old adobe room with its small, deeply recessed windows was, like the other rooms, dark even in the brightest of noons. But now in the late day, there were deep shadows interspersed with a few patches of dull light from the windows, which, because of the contrast, were very glaring. Everything was either too dark or too light and my eyes could not adjust to both conditions at the same time.

I opened the center drawer of the desk in Pirrone's massive, antique Italian table desk. Groping among the papers, my hand struck a metal tube. Pulling it out, I saw that it was one of those little yellow Kodak film cans. Unscrewing it clumsily, I spilled some of the white powder it contained.

Could this be gun-cleaning compound? But if it were why would it be hidden in papers in a desk? Heroin! It had to be heroin. I felt sick. This must be what they are going to smuggle. Or cocaine. I thought, they're going to bring cocaine back from South America in the boat.

The sound of footsteps outside the door startled me. Terrified, I shoved the drawer shut and was just bending to dust the white powder off the rug as the door opened. I straightened up, shaking with alarm, like a burglar who is caught stealing. I was really surprised to see Liz, because I had thought she had gone to the boat, too. It was probably because of the feeling that had come over me of being in a vacant house. I wondered why she had stayed behind.

Walking toward me, she said, "How can you see? Let's turn on a lamp."

She did not appear to notice how awkward I felt as I clutched the can in my fist so tightly my knuckles turned white. At the same time I tried to rub the powder into the rug with my foot. Possibly she was aware of my discomfiture but thought it better not to let me know she knew.

Trying to get onto a subject, any subject, to cover up my nervousness, I noticed that her T-shirt looked odd, as if it were embossed with trapunto around the neck. "Liz, your T-shirt looks so unusual. What are those bumpy things around the neck?"

"Oh, it's the necklace I was wearing the night of the party. It was under my dresser and I couldn't find the case. I have to wear it until the darn case shows up. What if Serena decided to clean house and swept out my diamonds?"

What about a drawer if not its case? A diamond necklace would be hard to sweep away without noticing. And when did Serena ever clean house? How could anyone believe the myth that she was the maid? Since she lived permanently at Dañada, was that an invention for appearance's sake? But who around here cared for such proprieties?

As we sat down, I managed to slip my tightly closed hand under a pillow and push the can down the back of the couch. I was not starting out very smoothly on my first spying mission.

"The necklace was beautiful on you at your birthday party." I was nervously groping for something to say.

"Thank you; would you like to try it on? It belonged to my grandmother."

Unfastening the clasp, she pulled the heavy strand from under her T-shirt. I was dazzled. Large pear-shaped diamonds—yellowish and very clear, a thousand lights glittering beneath the surface—dripped from a wreath of diamond leaves.

I stood up and put on the sparkling stones in front of a golden oval mirror. I felt as if I had robbed the Tower of London. I noticed in the mirror, as I was admiring the necklace, that Liz had opened the snail brooch which she was wearing pinned to the hip of her jeans. She took a pinch of something and sniffed it up one side of her nose while keeping the other side closed with one finger. I turned around and asked, "What are you doing?"

"Oh, that's medicine for my nose. This nasty, damp climate gives me a lot of trouble with my sinuses. My little snail is a handy place to keep it. Would you like to see the rest of my jewelry?"

I said I would, as I reflected to myself that I had never heard of anyone using powder for sinus trouble. People always used nose drops, I thought. But, I guessed, anything is possible in medicine—new cures were being developed all the time.

We went to Liz's bedroom. From an ornate box she took out a bracelet of deep, clear green emeralds, like serene forest pools, contrasting with the cold fire of their intricate diamond setting. Other bracelets and rings tumbled out in profusion. I had never dreamed of real people owning such jewelry—only Indian potentates. How incongruous, for Liz was really a slob. She showed me other diamonds, emeralds, and sapphires, some of which were unset and some uncut, and a few gold rings and bracelets.

"They're all magnificent," I said.

"Thank you," she replied modestly as she lovingly put them haphazardly back in the big jewelry box, "I knew you'd like them. They never lose their beauty however they're treated." I could understand her deep attachment to them. These brilliant jewels with their eternal luster she could securely possess; they could never turn against her.

Picking up a small, loose diamond she had dropped, she handed it to me. "Here, take this as a keepsake. I've loved spending this time with you." Then she surprised me with, "I never wanted to get married—to anyone. But Pirrone insisted."

I wondered why he had wanted a wife? He really did not have much use for her. He liked to have lots of women and had no trouble getting them. Perhaps, he was in love with her estate, Casa Dañada. But with his vast wealth he could have bought anything he wanted. Or was he really a reincarnation of the devil, who had driven the first mistress of Dañada mad, working his evil magic by driving Liz crazy too?

Liz suggested we take a walk to the lookout since the day was lovely. The fog having lifted, the outlines of the dramatic coast could be seen in sharp relief. We followed a path through darkly lit arches of ancient wind-bent cypress trees, coming out by the rocky glacis of the embankment on top of which stood the lookout, almost as if it were a watchtower from a medieval kingdom. It was square and its wooden exterior was weather-beaten in the extreme. The actual lookout itself was above a larger base composed of a couple of rooms where Brian and Erica were staying. I had never been there. Liz asked if I would like to climb to the top to see the view.

"Oh, yes," I said eagerly. I was always interested in seeing more of this fascinating establishment.

After climbing up many, many steps on the outside we got to the entrance to the tower. Inside was a winding stairwell, not unlike, in its design and crumbling condition, the interiors of tenement buildings I had seen in movies, except that there were no floors with apartments or landings—the steps just kept going up without a resting place.

Winded after our long climb up the steep stairs, we ended up in a space at the top, which seemed to be used as a storeroom. It was filled with scattered junk—broken-down, dust laden furniture, old rolled-up rugs, tattered, faded draperies folded up in one corner, and everywhere groups of beat-up boxes filled with stuff. I wondered who was custodian of the stuff.

Liz gestured toward a ladder on one side. A little mischievous grin turned up the corners of her mouth as she crinkled her nose. "I'm sorry to tell you this," she said, still breathing hard, "but we have to make one last climb to see the view. But it's worth it. It's really fabulous from there."

We went up the ladder and Liz, ahead of me, pushed open the trap door in the ceiling. We came out on a flat roof with a railing around it, similar to the widow's walks on top of old New England seacoast houses.

My eyes were momentarily blinded by the vibrant landscape radiating out around us, the late afternoon sun glinting off the distant silvery-blue horizon. With a feeling of detached omnipotence, like a lord surveying his domain from the top of the castle keep, I gazed at the expanse of turreted mountains that guarded the astonishing panorama.

Liz spotted a spider at the corner of his spoke-like web. "Look he's under his umbrella. With all those channels, it looks just like my mind." She paused, saying, half to herself, "We're all caught in a web here, a tangled web."

"The web is a fantastic creation, isn't it?" I said.

"Look, he's spinning another thread," Liz pointed out. "Let's see what happens if we drop him from the ledge and hold his thread."

The spider dropped part way down the tower. As Liz swung him back and forth, she was wistful. "Imagine being able to swing free from all your entanglements."

"But," I said, "it isn't free. It must always go on spinning." I couldn't help thinking how Liz herself was like Arachne, who, having been turned into nothing more than a spider, was the captive of the web she had to forever spin.

Coming back down, I bumped into a solid stack of new, square-cornered cartons sitting next to the ladder. They were completely unlike the half-smashed, half-collapsed boxes of odds and ends scattered around the rest of the space. I quickly scrutinized them. They had no markings on them.

"Oh," I blurted out, "are those boxes of provisions for the trip?"

"No, they're for the cats."

"The cats?"

"Yes," she replied. "It's cat food. There was a sale at the market."

What a strange storage place. The climb was too long and difficult. I suspected that was not the real content of the boxes; I decided to get back there and check them out as soon as possible.

Oh dear, I also had to get the film can from under the sofa pillows and back into the desk drawer before anyone missed it. But first I would have to take a little of the powder for a sample to find out for sure what it was.

As we were walking back from the lookout, Brian called to us, "Liz! Alice! We're leaving in a week!"

"Keen!" exclaimed Liz. "Now, I can say goodbye to this place forever."

Pirrone came up behind Brian. "You women can start buying the cigarettes right away."

"Which brand shall we take?" Liz asked. "I'll have to watch all the television commercials to find the best."

"Don't be ridiculous," replied Pirrone. "We'll take the best deal. Who cares what brand? Anyway, do you think they would advertise the brand that is best for smuggling?"

I asked Pirrone where Tom was.

"He's still working on the boat. He'll be back later." Brian walked off to the lookout, and Pirrone informed Liz he wanted to talk to her alone. That left me with the opportunity to go to the library to recover the little film can. Had Pirrone discovered that it was missing? Was that why he had to talk to Liz alone? I took a long, round-about route, trying to look as if I were not going to the library and that I was not in a hurry wherever I was going.

When I reached down between the seat cushion and the back of the couch, the can was no longer there. I frantically started pulling all the cushions off the couch in case it had slipped into some crevice. In the midst of all this, Pirrone walked in.

"What's the matter? Have you lost something? Can I help you?"

"No, thank you," I gulped. "I thought I lost my glasses when I was in here earlier. But I just remembered I left them at home."

"I didn't know you wore glasses."

"No, they were dark glasses," I replied, getting out of that one. Or did I? For Pirrone must have been the one who found the can—or had Liz slipped back there to retrieve it, realizing what I was doing when I pushed it behind the cushion?

Tom came in at dinnertime. He greeted me more tenderly than usual, even though the entire Dañada contingent was there ready to eat. But he also appeared to be as embarrassed as I, as we both tried to avoid each other's glances throughout dinner, talking casually to anyone but each other. I sensed he wanted to be alone with me, too, or rather to be intimate. I really wanted to try again under better circumstances. I wanted to experience something wonderful instead of pain.

But as we were finishing dinner, Pirrone said, "Tom, you've got to get back to the boat to test that engine again. I don't want it to freeze up."

What a shitty situation, I thought, using language in my mind that I had never as much as formed in mental words before. Why did Tom have to go? Why not Pirrone? Why was Tom always docilely following Pirrone's orders? But Pirrone was the captain on land as well as sea. He only gave orders; he never took them.

After Tom left, everyone lingered over coffee and cognac. I sat there dully, too, immersed in my frustration. Pirrone was telling about his latest deal in which he again demonstrated his ability to take advantage of other people. But he soon lost the interest of the rest of the group who drifted away from the table. Only Erica and I remained and my attention was not there. Pirrone continued talking; I heard little except that he said he had a feeling he was immortal—and no wonder, I thought, because he's some kind of underworld devil. Then he made the statement that with money one can do anything.

My interest piqued, I countered with the obvious, "You can't buy real friends."

"No, but you can come damn close," he answered, "and I could do something better. I could buy your soul." He spoke with an evil gleam in his eyes.

"Just like Dr. Faustus. That would make you the devil."

"Not exactly," he said, smiling as if he did not mean it. Which only reinforced my feeling that he was an agent from the preternatural world.

He went on, "Take you for instance, Alice. If I wanted to, I could make you so dependent on me you would no longer have control over yourself."

"There's no way you could get complete control over me," I said. But he really already had because of my insane infatuation.

"Ah, but there is. I could satisfy your every material whim, give you so much luxury and pleasure that you couldn't give it up. To keep it, you would have to depend on me." Or, I thought, you could try to get me hooked on drugs, as you probably have done to Liz.

"I'm not that crazy about luxury in the first place," I said.

"If I presented it slowly and attractively you would be caught without realizing how much I had changed you," he said.

"Honestly, Pirrone," Erica said, "sometimes I think you're depraved."

"Sometimes?" he said, very pleased with himself. Having capped the conversation with a good exit line, he got up and left the room.

I reflected that perhaps he was already working his evil magic on my soul; after all, I was involved in a venture that I knew was basically illegal. Had Pirrone been working on Tom, too?

After Pirrone left, I was able to talk to Erica alone to tell her of my discoveries. We both agreed that we should find out right away what was in the boxes in the lookout before they, too, disappeared. Because I had already been caught in a compromising situation, it seemed wiser for Erica to do the investigating. Anyway, it would be easy for her since she lived in the lookout.

Later that night, Pirrone was sitting in the living room with yet another girl, Nancy. Liz seemed to have disappeared completely. Soon Kristen came in. She threw her arms around Pirrone and kissed him on the mouth. Nancy looked quite shocked. Pirrone sounded vexed as he said, "Oh, Kristen, don't be such a good sister."

"Sister! I thought we had a date tonight," Kristen said.

"That was this afternoon," Pirrone replied. Then he went to work immediately to erase Nancy's doubts. I had seen him weave his magic spell so often it was like a rerun of the late-night movie. Could Kristen have had similar feelings as she sat impassively, a spectator, too?

Pirrone had not yet been able, as far as I could tell, to make an impression on Nancy, when a telephone call came for him and he had to leave. Pirrone took Kristen aside, saying to her, "I want you to watch Nancy and not let her get away. Why don't you take her to the library and talk with her?"

Kristen and Nancy went out, presumably to the library. But only a moment later, Nancy opened the living room door, asking breathlessly, "How do I get out of here?"

Erica started to answer when Kristen, coming from behind grabbed Nancy and said, "We haven't finished what we were talking about."

"I'm finished," Nancy replied. Kristen, being stronger, pulled frail Nancy away from the doorway and started leading her in the direction of the library.

"We've got to see this," Erica exclaimed. We went out to the portico and started to walk toward the library. Kristen was leaning against the library door, through which we heard loud shouts. Then the shouting stopped. Erica nudged me. She pointed to an open window farther down the library wall, through which Nancy was emerging. Almost falling on her head, she landed in a scraggly shrub growing out of a large terra cotta pot. Extricating herself from the branches of the comatose plant, she jumped out and ran in the direction of the driveway.

Kristen, unaware of all this, was still leaning against the door. Soon she seemed to become alarmed at the quietness of the library and opened the door. Seeing that Nancy had gone, Kristen shrieked, "She's gotten away! I've got to find her before Pirrone gets back."

On this moonless night it was quite dark outside. We watched as Kristen went into the library. Grabbing the first thing she saw, a candle, Kristen lit it and rushed out calling, "Nancy...." A few minutes later, we could see a flicker moving around and could hear Kristen calling, "Nancy...Nannccy...where are you? Don't go away. Pirrone needs you." She searched outside for a long time, but Nancy had escaped. "Oh, dear," Kristen moaned as she came back inside, "What will Pirrone do when he finds I let Nancy get away?"

"Yes, what will Pirrone do? There are only six women left in the house," answered Erica. (Julie was still floating around, although she left for days at a time. Rick had departed, leaving her behind, I guessed, as a thank-you present for Pirrone. Perhaps, she was the perfect houseguest's gift for Pirrone, who seemed to enjoy her sexy behavior toward him.)

As Kristen had feared, Pirrone was miffed. "I went to a lot of trouble to get that girl to come up here." Kristen was dejected about being in his disfavor. Pirrone continued, "You know how important all you girls are to me." Kristen seemed even more upset.

Pirrone had once said he would like to have been a sultan with a seraglio. Actually he had a small harem but, instead of eunuchs, he had girlfriends guarding other girlfriends to keep them from running away. However, most of his women were not permanent, passing through Casa Dañada for a few nights, but also often returning for a night or two. Some, like Kristen and Julie, left for a few days or a week but always came back to stay.

A sinister shadow fell across my mind. Were Pirrone's revolving girls important to him for more than sex? Were they collecting something that was to be smuggled on the boat? He always seemed to be very concerned when they left, giving them advice, telling them to remember everything he had told them. I could see why some of them kept coming back. I knew how he affected me. Every time those dark Italian eyes met mine, a warm, marvelous excitement flowed through every nerve and cell in my body. More than once I had seen him give a girl an envelope when she left. Did they contain packets of heroin or cocaine that they were supposed to deliver? I probably just had too vivid an imagination. Pirrone was very domineering, always ordering everyone to do as he directed. It would be natural for him to tell his bedmates what to do. The envelopes probably contained a present of money.

Restlessly waiting for Tom to get back, it occurred to me that while some people were thought of as dipsomaniacs, Tom with his addiction to this boat could be called a Calypsomaniac. Finally, very late that night, after I thought he would never get back, Tom arrived. He kissed me sweetly, almost dutifully as though we had been married for ten years. Where was his passion? Where was mine? Although I had been waiting all that long day to be alone with him, relief rather than desire was a better word for how I felt.

Tom took my hand and led me to the same room in which I had dreamed of Pirrone the night before. Perfunctorily and covertly, I undressed. Nervously, I got into bed still wearing my slip. It was warm and pleasant lying under the covers next to Tom as he told me about his problems with the ship's engines. Then he expressed his affection for me and kissed my hair as he smoothed it. He still had his T-shirt on. How Victorian we were, approaching each other half-clothed.

Our lovemaking was tentative and inexpert, certainly on my part, and far from satisfying. There was something missing. Afterwards Tom fell instantly asleep but I had to awaken him to take me to my aunt's. I would have a hard time explaining last night's absence; tonight's would be impossible.

◊ Chapter Eight

IT WAS AFTER SIX AND already light when Tom dropped me off. My aunt, the early riser, was already up. I had been gone not only most of this night but also the entire night before. I had called her and told her that Tom was having trouble with his car, the only excuse I could think of. But she did not believe my story. Every night before I had gotten back around three or four, but being one of those unwakable sleepers she had not realized how late I was. When she had gotten up early in the morning I was always in my bed.

She immediately accused me of the truth, which I hotly denied, screaming at the top of my range to cover up the lie but also because she made it sound as if I had committed some vile, contemptible crime, a crime she probably never had the chance to turn down.

"You're a cheap, trashy little girl. Only the town tramps stay out all night. Don't you have any morals at all?"

"You're a self-righteous old biddy," I yelled back. I was equally outraged by her stupid, outmoded standards. "The time of day has nothing to do with morals," I added.

"Oh, yes it does," she said in a superior tone. "Only sinful things go on when all decent people are asleep in their own beds."

"What is this own bed business? Does that mean I was in someone else's bed?" I said.

"What else could you be doing at that time of night?" she asked.

"Ha, what you're referring to is morning, isn't it? Early morning, right?"

"That's night to respectable people," she said indignantly. "The people who are not asleep then are doing dirty, immoral things," she proclaimed in a hell-and-brimstone preacher's voice.

"The sin of fornication," I said caustically. "You sound just like a Bible-belt revivalist. You're narrow-minded and stupid. The nasty things that go on in that tiny brain of yours are unbelievable."

The cold look in her eyes pierced me like ice-splinters. She raised her arm and slashed her hand across my face. "You're a little slut," she said in her most arrogant voice. "Get out of here and don't you dare come back and bring your shame into my decent, respectable house."

I thought, maliciously, her house of good repute; it would have been to her credit had she been capable of maintaining it's antonym, a house of ill repute. She would at least have been more human.

I stalked out of the living room and into my bedroom. I started jamming clothes into two suitcases. I thought about myself as I grabbed my clothing. Aunt Jessie pictured me as practically a whore but I was still the same Alice, almost as innocent as if I had never gone to bed with a man, though I did feel strange—different and yet not different. I guess I felt as though nothing had happened to me erotically although I had been physically initiated. I felt changed only because I thought I should feel changed, as if I had been metamorphosed from a girl into a woman of experience—but what an unsatisfactory experience.

Carrying my suitcases, I stamped by Aunt Jessie and out the front door. She did not say a word, not even goodbye or good riddance. I walked the two blocks to the Wagon Wheel Cafe. I went in, sat down at

the counter, and ordered a cup of coffee. The only other person in the
cafe at this early hour—it was just barely seven—was a man having
breakfast at the counter. He started talking to me. It was a relief to talk
with someone who was friendly, after my aunt's diatribes. He offered to
drive me up the road as he was going that direction. I arrived in a cattle
truck to take up residence at Dañada.

I was quickly pursued by letters of remorse from Aunt Jessie. She
was sorry, she wrote, that she had thrown me out. Whatever I had done,
she would forgive me, and I could have a chance to start over. How does
one, I thought, start over being a virgin?

More persistent than Aunt Jessie's letters were the threats from my
parents who had found out that I had moved to Dañada. My mother
wrote that if I didn't leave there immediately, she would notify the authorities. What authorities, I wondered? And what law had I broken?
But that was my mother's way—to always threaten action from a higher
body. Evoking the fear of punishment from an outside force had always
worked before because I had been submissive. But she had the new me
to reckon with: her methods were no longer effective.

Her next effort was one she had used before, too. I knew it was a
phony; she had tried it too many times. She wrote that she had heard
that Pirrone was no good and that she was having him investigated. I
knew the investigation would go no further than the paper on which
she had written me. I also knew that in a short time I would get a letter
reporting the terrible facts the investigation had unearthed. The facts
would only be hinted at in veiled innuendos because her powers of invention were not up to being explicit.

I settled down into a quasi-marriage with Tom but unfortunately I
was still obsessed with Pirrone. Perhaps, I told myself, it's just his gal-
vanic personality—he has that effect on every woman he meets. There
was certainly plenty evidence of it with all the revolving girls floating
around.

Tom turned out to be gentle, considerate, and kind as a lover, yet he
never stirred me to reach the great, wonderful culmination I had expected. But I grew used to his warmth and companionship at night. I
missed him when he was away with Pirrone or just away on business for
Pirrone. Often in our lovemaking I would become very aroused thinking
of Pirrone, but I would stop myself from the ultimate dishonesty of

completely changing Tom into a fantasy Pirrone. It was as if I were try-ing to recapture my virginity in my passionlessness. Often my mind would wander, latching onto such things as Joe Viscantino and the smuggling, or I would wonder why the preparations for the expedition were going so slowly. The original idea a while ago that we were "leav-ing in a week" had long ago evaporated as the week grew into weeks and more weeks.

I was very fond of Tom, but my feelings did not include desire. But perhaps it was an easier way to live. An argument Tom had once used in trying to induce me to sleep with him came back to me—"After it's all over, you'll wonder what all the fuss was about." That described lovemaking with Tom perfectly.

Now that I was living at Casa Dañada, I continued my sleuthing full-time, but nothing turned up. I looked everywhere but could find no little film cans at all   not even ones with sleeping pills. They had com-pletely disappeared. I asked Tom again about the pictures of his car.

"Oh," he said, "those. They didn't come out. The film was ruined. Did you open the can, by any chance?"

"No, of course not. The only one I ever saw opened had gun-clean-ing compound in it. You remember that night," I said.

"Not really. But if you say so," he said.

Now that everyone, I was sure, was wary of me, I would never be able to get hold of one of those film cans to find out what was in them. I felt positive that the one I had discovered in the desk drawer and had slipped behind the sofa cushion had heroin or cocaine in it or else it wouldn't have disappeared.

One morning when Tom had been away for a couple of days on a business trip, Pirrone came in and awakened me, saying, "You women have to go shopping right away. We found a vehicle for hauling the cigarettes. It was among the old cars at the top of the hill."

Liz came to the doorway and added, "Hurry, Alice. Erica and Serena are waiting for us."

Waiting for me in the driveway, Liz, Erica and Serena were standing next to a rickety contraption that looked as if it had been dug up from a scrap heap, not just from a collection of old cars. It had once been a small bus. The sea air had helped in its deterioration. Its non-descript, blotchy color might have been called tan, or perhaps rust, for that was its predominant hue, actual real rust. As for its shape and design—well it must have been one of the first buses ever made.

"Liz," I questioned, "are you sure this thing runs?"

"Yeah, I guess. Pirrone told me Tom has been working on it off and on for some time. You know how he loves working on cars. It was a challenge for him to get the damn thing running. Let's hope it doesn't quit on us."

Since Liz had never driven a bus before, she insisted on driving. It rattled and creaked, making me think that with each curve in the road it would fall apart. Somehow the whole effect was made worse by Liz, who drove on the wrong side of the road half the time. Now I knew why she never went anyplace alone; everyone was afraid to let her loose behind the wheel.

With Liz driving and considering the condition of the bus, I felt happy to be alive when we reached our destination, a small town, if one could call it that, not far from El Mirador. It was really only a collection of a few stores.

"Where shall we go first?" Erica asked.

"Let's go to the shopping center," Liz replied.

"That's a shopping center?" Serena commented. "When those two buildings were built 'shopping center' wasn't even in the language."

Serena and Erica went to the drugstore, Liz and I to the market. In the market, we went to separate checkout counters (there were only two).

"How many cases of cigarettes can you sell me?" I asked.

"What?" the clerk asked as though he had not heard me correctly.

"How many cases of cigarettes can you sell me?" I repeated.

"Cases?"

"Yes, cases," I said.

"You must have the habit bad!"

"Yes, it's terrible! I smoke cartons a day."

"Just a minute, please, young lady. I'll have to check on this."

When he came back, he said, "There's another lady who wants to buy cases of cigarettes, too. Strange.... We'll only be able to sell you five cases."

"That's fine," I said.

"Five different brands!"

"Oh, well I smoke so much, I never know what I'm smoking, anyway."

After I had paid for the cigarettes, he offered to take them out to my car. "Which one is it?" he asked.

"Thanks, it's the…oh…ah…sort of tan bus."

"Bus!" he was surprised.

As he was getting the cartons together, I heard him tell the other clerk, "She smokes cartons a day…so much she doesn't know what she's smoking…and drives a bus. If you ask me she's the biggest case leaving the store."

Serena and Erica had done much better than I and had been not only to the drugstore but also to the bar and gas station. They returned with four men who started loading the bus with their purchases.

One of the fellows said, "Your girls must be having a really big party."

Liz, who had also done better than I, getting nine cases out of the market, answered, "Yeah, a pirate party, all in costume!"

As we drove away, Liz laughed, "It looks as if we 'cased' this shopping center."

We went to the other market, the cafe, the inn, the other gas station, and all the cigarette machines. At every place, people were amazed at the amount of cigarettes we bought. "Are you buying for an army?" "Are you planning to open a cigarette stand?" "Is this for some sort of research?"

The drive back was even more frightening than the beginning of our excursion because Liz could not see out of any of the rear windows. The cigarettes, which had not been stacked too neatly, slid around every which way. On each curve that we skidded around Erica, Serena, and I had to shove back boxes, cartons, and loose packages that kept spilling over on us.

As we drove through Dañada's gates with the day's haul, we heard gunshots. Liz said that Pirrone must be target practicing. Looking in the direction of the sound, I saw Pirrone at the top of the lookout.

When he stopped firing, he came down, the M-14 slung over his shoulder.

"What were you shooting at?" Liz asked.

"There were some skin-divers trying to get on the boat."

"But, baby, they were probably just curious. You might have hit one."

It seemed to me that he was much too far away to be shooting near the boat, but he said, "That's the idea. Next time they'll think twice about their curiosity about my boat."

He had just vindicated Tom's explanation of the purpose of the gun. Or had Pirrone really been shooting at someone hovering around the tower—someone who might be trying to get what was in the unmarked cartons? Either way, he had just shot holes in Erica's and my gunrunning theory.

I still thought this was all just a cover-up for what his real target had been. But then if he were really trying to keep people off the *Calypso*, probably whatever else they were going to smuggle besides cigarettes was already on board the boat.

Looking at the disarray of cigarettes, he asked, "What did you do? Roll the bus over a couple of times?"

We laughed. "Almost," Erica answered.

"We'll unload these cigarettes later," Pirrone said. "Serena, I want to show you something." He pinched her, making her squeal.

Show her something! What an excuse. She had been away all day. He wanted to do more than show her something. I still had not been able to get over my obsession with Pirrone. My passion for him caused me endless suffering. He, without knowing it, was keeping me from fulfillment with Tom. Had I never known Pirrone, perhaps I would have found with Tom the ultimate happiness that was my feminine due. Sometimes I would be sitting in the same room as Pirrone and would start wondering how it would feel to have him, undressed, pressing against my bare skin. I would quickly try to stop myself from going any further with this fantasy, fighting to push the obscene images out of my consciousness; but the picture would keep sneaking erotically back into the center of my feelings.

A distinguished looking man wearing a business suit walked into the driveway. "Oh," Liz said, "please excuse me." She walked over to meet him. She greeted him and they talked for a minute, but they were too far away for me to hear what they were saying. Then they walked toward the house and went inside. I wondered what that was all about. The man had a very aristocratic air. He did not look like the type who would be involved in smuggling. Perhaps, he was an old family friend.

Once again, it had been decided that we would be leaving in a week, yet life went on as usual. Everyone was excited about going, but no one seemed to have shifted gears. A week might as well have been a month. Would this deadline, like the last one, pass without notice?

The afternoon dragged on. Erica and Brian decided to spend the rest of the day at the beach. Tom had still not gotten back and Liz, having acquired a headache during the talk with the man in the business suit, had gone to bed.

There was nothing for me to do so I took a sunbath in the bright afternoon light. On the terrace I took everything off but my shorts. I wouldn't have dared to do so if I had not been alone. However, Liz, Erica, and Serena thought nothing of going topless.

Soon I grew so hot and enervated from the sun I decided to go inside. As I entered the dimness of the living room, it took my eyes a second to adjust. I saw a fuzzy tangle of bare arms and legs, and at least three heads. One was definitely Serena and another had shiny blond hair. I backed out instantly, not wanting to believe what I had seen. But I had seen a lot anyway. Serena was kissing Kristen. Pirrone was on top of Kristen, kissing her breasts and fondling Serena's. Most horrifying of all, Serena was "touching herself down there," an activity my mother had always explicitly forbidden. Lurking in the background, I thought I saw another head above a long, lean stretch of thigh, but I could not really make out who it was or if it were just my imagination.

I was being rudely awakened from what was left of the once beautiful dream. The looking-glass house was no longer what it had seemed. Its reflections were being distorted into fun-house grotesqueries. This place in which anything was accepted and practiced was in another solar system from the secure adolescent one I had left behind, in which a certain pattern of behavior was expected and deviations were not tolerated.

Had Tom traveled the same route as I to discover this otherworldliness? He had changed. Although he was more assertive with me at night, he gave no other hint in our sleeping together. But his once boyish appeal had been replaced by a new sophistication. Where before he had been reticent in group gatherings, he now entertained his listeners with anecdotes from his recent journeys. Mostly they involved new methods he and Pirrone had devised to speed down crowded highways—such as driving in the passing and turn lanes dividing the two sides of the road—and in cities, driving through empty left-hand turnouts.

What with communal sex, perversion, and smuggling, I knew I should leave before I, too, could no longer distinguish between right and wrong. But how could I desert the South American idyll and go back to the constrained middle-class environment of correct behavior and dull routine? I still had a little of my moral code intact; I would be on guard against further inroads.

Disturbed by that pornographic living room scene, I ran away from the house as if chased by demons. I did not stop until I reached the bluff. I sat down on a granite outcropping surrounded by intensely blue wild morning glories, rather like being on an island as Odysseus had been. I wondered what would happen to our odyssey. Now that I had heard the siren's song, like the unwary sailor passing by, I was held in a spell. But the wild undercurrents, exposing the treacherous shoals beneath, had filled me with anxiety that I might be shipwrecked before even setting sail.

Alice, oh, Alice, I asked myself, what are you doing? What are you looking for? Excitement? Do you know any more? Did you ever really know? There are complications you had not thought of. But listen, voice, I told myself, it's still fun here. Pirrone may be some kind of sexual superman or even a supernatural man but he's always entertaining. Liz makes her funny remarks and we talk about the books we have read and I'm going to Peru with all the fun people here.

I went on trying to tell myself Pirrone was not really evil and dangerous, just without any sense of right or wrong, animal-innocent like the cat who presents his master with the lovely, lifeless hummingbird it has just instinctively pounced upon.

But then there was the smuggling. Did I want to go on a boat that might have narcotics hidden on it? Erica had already decided not to go if we discovered any drugs. But all we had discovered was a frayed rope of circumstances in which some of the twists had already been broken. The unmarked cartons in the lookout might have revealed the secret, but when Erica went to investigate, they were no longer there. I had already found out while shopping for provisions that they could not possibly have contained cat food. In the market cases of pet food were stacked in an aisle where a clerk was replenishing a shelf. The brand names were clearly printed on the top and on the sides. I asked the man if the cases were always marked like that.

He answered, "Of course. How else would anybody know what was in them?"

Somehow I had to find out if drugs were being smuggled. If I could go to the boat with Erica or even by myself when no one was there I felt I could make such a thorough search that I would discover the cache that Pirrone was worried the skin-divers would find. At night when Pirrone and the rest of the gang were occupied would be ideal.

Sitting in the living room after dinner, I could not stand the suspense any longer. I had to get down to the boat right away. But how? Tom was asleep in a chair, exhausted from his day's work repairing the boat. I could certainly leave without any protests from him. He would not even miss me. But I had to have a reason to give the others. Having to go to El Mirador to get cigarettes would never do; there were enough here to keep everyone supplied for the next twenty years. I could not complain about being ill and needing medicine; I looked and felt too healthy. I finally announced I was going to the drugstore to get some aspirin and other necessities for our trip.

But Liz, of all people, gave me trouble. "What's the hurry? Get them when we go shopping for supplies. And anyway, it's too late. The drugstore will be closed. This is not the City."

I could not think of any urgent reason for protesting, so that ended it. But it hardly stopped my insistent urge to find out. As I lay in bed that night, sleep was impossible; I was one taut nerve, like a violin string ready to vibrate at the slightest touch. I could not close my eyes or even lie in bed any longer as the irrational energy created by my obsession seethed through me. I stealthily slid out from under the covers, even though I doubted that anything would have awakened Tom; he slept like a bear in winter hibernation. I could have jumped up and down and rung bells without arousing him. Still, I was not about to test this theory; I automatically operated on the belief that if I breathed the wrong way he would stir.

I took each step in slow motion. Sometimes when I heard a

floorboard creak, I paused in mid-air as in a stopped-action movie dissolve. It took me an agony of hour-long minutes to get across the room and more sixty-minute seconds to take Tom's keys out of his pants pocket without rattling them. Exaggerated to a heart-stopping pitch, night sounds were thundering in my ears, some of which I am sure I had never ever heard before. My senses were needle-sharp, picking up the tiniest vibrations; probably my ears were inventing new ones. Reaching the bedroom door, I turned the knob as slowly and silently as possible, closing it the same way behind me. Tom and I had moved from the garage to a guest room so that I was now out in the portico.

Making my way to the courtyard, a loud "hoo-hoo" startled me until I realized it was only an owl. I took a few more steps before I heard the leaves rustle in the nearby bushes. Frightened, I flattened myself against the wall, the shadow of the roof concealing me from the moonlight. A stray breeze caught the hem of my nightgown, fluttering it out in the eerie brightness of the moon. I shivered as I realized that was all I had on. In my concern over disturbing Tom, I had completely forgotten to dress. My whole being had been concentrated in one effort: to get out of the room as quietly as possible. I could not turn back now; I would have to go as I was.

The rustling in the leaves made me feel as if somebody or something was following me. The bottom of my nightgown flying out like a white flag in the night air must have made me very visible. In the quietness of the late hour, I could hear breathing, the way one can hear surf a mile away when the night is still. Of course, the breathing had to be quite close but how close I could not tell. It did not seem to get any closer or any farther away, either. Whoever or whatever was following me must have stopped each time I did, waiting for me to move. Then I thought I must have been hearing the reflection of my own breath. Calmed a little by this idea I went on. I speculated that the leaves I had heard moving were blown by the same breeze that had caught the edge of my gown.

I continued, but after a few steps the rustling started again. Did I feel another whip of wind or was it just a chill of inner terror? I had to go on; the only thing to do was to try not to listen. Then I suddenly had the feeling of being in the grip of a huge vise and that I could not take another step or even move a muscle. A shadow fell across me, scaring me more than I had ever been scared in my whole life. From sheer fright, I started running faster than I knew how to run. I reached Tom's car in one wild whoosh. The adrenalin pouring into my veins had shot me along the pathway like a rocket.

After that heart-in-mouth experience, I shook like an aspen leaf in the high Sierra wind as I frantically tried to get the key into the ignition lock, finally jamming it in. The motor started with its usual roar, which sounded ten times as loud as it did under ordinary circumstances. I prayed that it had not awakened anyone. Somehow I made it out of the driveway without Tom or Pirrone running out to stop me. But I was scared all the way to the bay by thoughts of who or what had been tracking me earlier. I also worried that I might have aroused the whole house when I drove off. What if it were discovered that I was missing along with Tom's car before I had time to do my work and get back? Surely, they would follow in hot pursuit. Still, I drove on relentlessly, with no thought of giving up.

I parked the car on the pier, looking for shadows into which to slide. The moon had gone down which, though scarier, was better. If anyone could have seen me, I must have been rather scary looking myself—a ghost in a white nightgown, billowed out by the sea air. And I did have the uncomfortable feeling of eyes watching me from somewhere. But if someone had been following me back at Dañada I did not think that person had followed me here. I certainly had not heard or seen a car driving behind me. Then I began to get scared all over again, thinking that my follower had phoned or somehow alerted someone here that I was coming. But that was crazy; how could he have known where I was going? Even so, I envisioned a Mafia hit man after me.

As I untied a dinghy at the pier I saw a faint brightness in the water near the *Calypso*. It was a dead cormorant, its white underfeathers picking up light uncannily. I shuddered. Had Pirrone shot it when he was trying to scare surfers? I wondered if, like the Ancient Mariner, he had doomed our voyage.

Boarding the boat made me even jumpier. The deck was dark and shadowy. Now I was terrified that the Mafia hit man would jump out from behind the pilothouse and kill me. I ran into the pilothouse for protection. No one was there. I began to feel safer.

There were all kinds of new noises—wet noises such as the water slapping against the boat as it moved up and down on the swells, so different from the dry, crackly night sounds on land. They were soothing sounds that eased my nervousness. The creaking of the *Calypso* as she pulled against her moorings engulfed me, making me feel like an integral part of the lines as they were yanked back and forth by the rising and falling of the sea surface.

Lulled into a sense of security by the mesmerizing quality of the night on the ocean, I systematically started to go through everything in the pilothouse. Finding nothing, I moved down to the galley, searching the same way. Then I went on to the lockers and compartments, feeling more than seeing, as I had no flashlight and dared not light the ship's lanterns. Slowly, though, my eyes were able to distinguish things more and more in the diminished light. I still had found nothing as I approached the hatchway to the compartment under the false bottom.

A gradual awareness had been creeping over me that among all the creaks and groans of the boat there was the faint swishing movement of someone following, but keeping hidden. This apprehension grabbed me by the throat like a giant hand, constricting my vocal cords and paralyzing my whole body. I really wanted to run as fast as I could to get out of there and back to Tom's car, but I was unable to move.

After I stood motionless for a while and all that I could hear was the sound of water washing the boat, my resolve returned. I continued, but I was much more tense than I had been in the beginning. There was no place else to search but the hold. I pushed back the concealed trap-door hatch cover and went down the ladder. It was absolutely black in there. It was hopeless; I would never be able to find anything. If I had the highly developed senses of the blind, I might have been able to grope in the nothingness.

As I started to climb back up the ladder, the hatch cover slid shut and snapped. My earlier fright was nothing compared to this new horror. There had been someone watching me; now I was his prisoner. The show was over; I probably would be bumped off by one of Joe Viscantino's henchmen. Oh, why was I so nosey? Why had I not forgotten the whole expedition and left Dañada with its decadence and danger, its exciting but unreal people?

The attenuated minutes stretched on and on and on but no one came to finish me off. I collapsed onto the boards laid over the bilge. As

I waited and waited in mounting agitation, my pounding heartbeats seemed to resound off the sides of the compartment, even reverberating back and forth between the ribs of the exposed structure on the inside of the hull.

Eventually I lapsed into sleep in spite of my tension, this harrowing night having finally drained every last drop of my energy. When I woke up I felt very cold and wet. I touched my nightgown; it was soaked. Was it perspiration or seawater? Was the boat leaking? Was it sinking? I tasted the fabric; it had a nasty salty taste. I had never noticed bilge water washing over the boards before. The *Calypso* was sinking. They were going to do away with both the evidence and the sleuth. There was an inch of water sloshing around me. I felt in front and in back of me; everywhere I put my hands there was water. I shivered not only from the cold water, which had soaked through me but also from mounting alarm. The boat was sinking for sure.

Panic took over and possessed me. All I could think of was that my life would end here in the secret compartment. No one would ever find my body. Even if divers went down to search the sunken boat, they would not know there was a hidden hold.

I started to cry. Forlornly, I gave myself up to crying as a lost child does. The crying was therapeutic. I began to feel better. With my will revived, I decided I couldn't just give up and drown without trying to save myself. What could I do? I groped for the ladder; at the top I would at least be able to survive longer. In my hurry up the ladder I bumped my head on the hatch cover. It hurt so much I let out a scream. The scream gave me renewed release. I screamed again and again. I though about it: my captor might come down to see what was going on. I would rather see my killer face to face than drown all alone. I screamed again, even louder.

No one came. I clung to the ladder. Unbearable anxiety engulfed me as I waited for the water to cover me; I almost prayed for it to hurry up and end my misery. Then I heard footsteps, many footsteps, an army of footsteps, it seemed. I yelled and pounded and pounded and yelled some more. After an eon of time the hatch cover slid open. Instead of a gangster there was Tom's face almost bumping into mine as he stuck his head down the opening.

"You crazy idiot, what are you doing here?" he asked.

"Oh, am I glad to see you. I thought no one would ever come and I would sink with the boat."

"The boat's not sinking," Tom said, as though he thought I was even crazier.

"But there's water in the hold."

"Oh, that's normal sometimes. The bilge pump doesn't work when the generator's turned off. But you didn't answer my question. What are you doing here in your nightgown?"

I gathered up the edges of my wobbly mind and started, like Scheherazade, to tell a story to save my life. "I dreamed someone was cutting the lines of the *Calypso* and I had visions of her drifting out to sea or worse than that, drifting into shore and crashing on the rocks. I guess I was half asleep when I got up and rushed down here in your car."

I saw Pirrone's face peering over Tom's shoulder. He was disgusted. "What a lot of b.s. You can do better than that. Try again. Who were you meeting here? Tom, she's not a very clever cheater. Except for the 'corpus delicti,' I would say we caught you almost in the act. What was your reason for locking yourself in the hold?"

I lowered my head, saying nothing. As terrible an accusation as that was, it was better than the truth. Then I noticed that Pirrone looked very uncomfortable. He and Tom were exchanging suspicious looks as though they were wondering if I had discovered anything. Then I wondered if Pirrone, linked as I thought he was to the devil, had some sort of supernatural antennae, which had let him know where I was and what I was doing.

He said, "Don't you ever come on this boat alone again. That's an order."

"Why?" I asked innocently.

"It's dangerous. You might fall overboard and drown or something."

That was a silly reason. Pirrone knew I was a very good swimmer. I was certain, now, that I was on the right trail, even though I had found out nothing yet.

◇ Chapter Nine

LATER THAT DAY I
tried to patch things up with Tom. I thought I should try flattery—that
was always a winner. I walked up behind him and gave him a kiss on the
back of the neck. "Hi, TNT," I said.

"What do you mean by that?"

"Just that you're dynamite and T'n'T also stands for tall 'n' terrific."

"Come on, you can't get around me by sweet-talking."

I had to do better than that. I guessed it was all right with me if
Pirrone wanted to think I had had an assignation, but I didn't want Tom
to think that. Of course, I did not want either of them to think I was
spying. I told him I had felt restless. When I could not get back to sleep,
I decided to go for a drive in the moonlight, going out on the pier to be
closer to the water, then thinking it would be nice to be on the boat.
But he did not buy that version either.

But I had found out one thing for sure: they did not want me prying around the boat. And there certainly was someone who had trapped me in the hold. I doubted that the hatch cover had slid closed by itself when the *Calypso* rolled in a swell.

The plans went ahead as though this incident had never happened. No one said any more about it, for which I was glad because I felt very foolish. But as silly as my behavior had been, at least I had learned that something mysterious was going on, especially since no one talked about or kidded me about my nighttime excursion.

Towards evening, several days later, Liz, Brian, Pirrone, and I were in the living room, having a glass of Pernod, when the phone rang. Pirrone answered and then he said to the caller, "Wait a minute, I'm going to another room."

I decided that the caller must have something to do with the smuggling. If it had been one of his girls, he would not have left the room; he was completely open about them, never bothering to hide anything. I felt it was important for me to eavesdrop. I wondered how I could get out of the living room without being obvious. "I think I'll go take a shower and change my clothes. I look grubby," I announced.

"You look fine, what's your hurry?" Liz said.

"I feel sticky," I said, walking out of the room. I headed for the library, where I thought Pirrone must have gone. A window was slightly open. I pressed myself against the wall next to it.

I could hear Pirrone's voice, but I could not tell what he was talking about; his words were too noncommittal—such as "I don't know" or "Maybe" or "I'll see if I can." I was almost ready to give up when I heard him say, "That was not the way to stop her—trapping her in the secret compartment. I've ordered her not to go to the boat alone. But she keeps sticking her nose in everything. She is very suspicious. She's really a pain in the ass, but Tom wants her to be with him." There was a long pause while he listened to the caller, after which Pirrone answered loudly, "No, you can't! You'll have to find a better way."

I was shaking badly but I quickly moved away from the wall after Pirrone hung up. I could not let him know I had been listening. I started to walk as naturally as I could down the portico to the guest room Tom and I now shared. I reflected that this was the first real confirmation I'd had that they realized what I was doing and that now I knew positively something highly illegal was being smuggled. And someone had planned to do away with me that night on the boat. My life was in danger, no matter what Pirrone said. Or was I safe, because the devil—dba Pirrone Rivelli—would keep anything from happening to me for the sake of his friend Tom? Tom was my only real protection. As long as he cared about me, I was out of harm's way. A thought came to me: virtue may not be exciting but it is certainly safer than my slightly illicit behavior amidst the highly illicit machinations going on here. This should have been my cue to leave and go home to my parents, but I was too emotionally involved with this place and these people to make that decision. I wanted to hang onto the dream even if it was becoming more of a terrifying nightmare.

The preparations for the trip went ahead in the usual disorderly fashion, somewhat taking my mind off my peril. It was generally felt that we had only a short time before we would be leaving. Deadlines regularly came and went but the time for our departure was somehow inexorably moving closer. We had to get the boat provisioned. Every time we took supplies down to the bay, we slipped cartons of cigarettes under the groceries and sundries. Pirrone did not want us going out to the boat with the cigarettes blatantly exposed. Although it was not illegal to buy or possess great quantities of cigarettes, or to fill the *Calypso* with them, he felt that because we were going to Peru, someone might get the idea that we were eventually planning to sell them there and alert the authorities in Peru. But I was sure the real reason was that he wanted no one checking up on anything on the boat for fear they might discover the…whatever it was.

The boat was tied up at the pier, making it easily accessible for our preparations for the long sail. One afternoon Liz, Erica, and I had gone aboard to stock it with provisions. While Liz and Erica were putting cigarettes in the secret compartment, I was busily stowing peanut butter and jelly and such oddities as Indian preserved peaches and pickled octopus in the galley. I heard Pirrone's voice coming through the hatchway, "I think this pier is definitely in bad shape."

Then a voice I had never heard before said, "You don't think it could take a loaded truck?"

Pirrone answered, "No, and it would be dangerous to unload on shore and bring it out by dinghy. And it would take too many trips to do it."

Curious, I crawled up the ladder and peeked out, expecting to see an underworld character. I was surprised to see the state assemblyman for the district that included El Mirador. His face was unmistakable—so honest and earnest. I saw it every day in town as we shopped, plastered on walls and phone poles, because he was up for reelection. I felt as though I knew him. It sounded as if they were talking about the cargo that was to be smuggled, but it must have been some generality—such as the problem of getting materials out to repair the end of the pier.

On the other hand, perhaps their conversations was not so benign after all. I remembered reading in an article some time ago in a popular California magazine that this assemblyman had Mafia connections. Of course. He must be involved. And if what was being smuggled was heavy, it was probably guns, after all. I strained to hear more, but they had turned and were walking down the gangway on to the pier.

Tom had been gone almost a week, after telling me the day after my imprisonment on the *Calypso* that he would be back the next day. Driving back to Dañada with Liz and Pirrone (Erica had gone ahead with Brian), I brooded about Tom, which was perverse of me because often when I was with Tom, my mind was filled with images of Pirrone. I was scared, too, because I felt Tom was my only protection against anyone who might be trying to kill me. I wondered if he had deserted me because he really believed I had gone to the boat to meet a guy. My battered pride would not let me ask where he was. I hoped no one could detect my underlying despair.

Back at the house, I drifted into the living room. Liz was there hanging black cloth from the wrought-iron drapery rods. I asked her what in the world she was doing.

"I'm going to do some *tour jetés* on the edge of the cliff. If I don't come back, Dañada can mourn for me. Who else would?"

I felt like saying I would join her and we could leap off in a double suicide. But the thought of dying intentionally, when the other night I had been in actual danger of dying unintentionally (on my part), had a cathartic effect on me. It suddenly felt good to be alive. After all, I had done nothing criminal. It was not worth giving up one's life over just looking around a boat at night.

"Liz," I said, "what kind of joke is this? That would be dangerous."

"It's no joke. I've got to break free from here before I go mad. I think

I'll entitle the ballet 'The Fallen and the Damned,'" she replied as she draped another piece of black cloth over her shoulder.

"You can't be serious," I said with a forced laugh. "This is macabre. Anyway, Halloween's a long way off."

"Oh, no, I'm dead serious—oh, what a terrible pun!" As she finished speaking we both noticed the smell of burning meat. We raced to the kitchen and found that the roasting leg of lamb had turned into a charred and shrunken remnant of its former succulence.

"Damn!" Liz was despondent. "This ruins all my plans. I wanted my last meal to be memorable. I feel awful. Please excuse me; I have to lie down."

Stunned by Liz's death wish, I wandered back into the living room. Absently I picked up a book from the coffee table. A color print fell out as I opened the book. I reached down to pick up the photograph. I became ill as the images etched themselves on my brain. There on the eighteenth-century painted bed were Pirrone and a girl, her face obscured by his head. But there was no obscurity about what they were doing. The worst thing of all was Liz lying next to them, with a strange expression on her face that I could not interpret—sick pleasure? Or was it despair? Yes, despair. An unwilling voyeur. No wonder she wanted to kill herself. But how like Liz to plan a dramatic death, falling from a ballet leap to the rocks below, like the mad dancer in the old movie "Specter of the Rose," who finished his ballet with a *grand jeté* through a skyscraper window.

Erica walked in but I hardly noticed her for I was in a state of shock. Furtively, I slipped the picture back into the book. Somehow sharing it would have made it more distasteful.

"Erica," Brian called from the entrance to the living room, "guess who just came to see Pirrone?" He looked very excited as he said, "Two FBI agents."

Erica gasped, "FBI agents!"

This disclosure blotted out the horrifyingly obscene snapshot. "Why do they want to talk to him?" I asked.

Brian did not know but conjectured, "They might want him to gather information about fugitives in South America."

Erica raised her eyebrows. Naturally she was thinking the same thing as I. They had somehow found out about Joe Viscantino and the smuggling. This seemed to me to be further confirmation of really illegal smuggling. Maybe the FBI had enough evidence to arrest Pirrone on the spot and take him off in handcuffs to jail! But as I was thinking that, Pirrone walked into the living room acting very nonchalant.

"Were they really FBI men?" Brian asked.

"Remember that gold bar I showed you? They wanted to see it, so I gave it to them."

Brian remarked, "You were smart to do that before they took it away, since it's illegal to own them."

"That wasn't the way it was, man. I found it for them."

How like Pirrone to cover up so well. He had the makings of a master criminal. Maybe instead of Joe Viscantino controlling Pirrone, as I had assumed since the conversation I had overheard, it was the other way around. Was it gold that was going to be smuggled? Erica and I had never thought about that. Had the boxes in the lookout contained gold bars? I felt relieved. The idea of narcotics had frightened me, but smuggling gold would be an adventure just as the cigarettes were. Perhaps they were planning to drop it off in Mexico when we reached Acapulco. Because I had questioned Liz about the cartons, they probably felt it necessary to move them immediately. Erica and I would have to search the boat and be careful to do it in such a way that we would not get trapped as I had been.

Brian asked, "Pirrone, you never did tell me where you found it."

"Well, it wasn't I who found it. The mechanic who was working on the boat's engines saw something behind the steel plates and pulled a gold bar out that was stashed there. Since he knew about it I thought I had better call the FBI." Putting on a good show, as he always did, he must have looked very surprised, telling the mechanic he was going straight to the authorities. The workings of Pirrone's mind were intricate. With such a brain he could be making another fortune legitimately. But, I thought, in spite of all his money, with his evil mind this was more fun. "I told them," Pirrone continued, smiling his half-smile, "that someone must have put it in the back of my car. I didn't want them to search the boat and find all those cigarettes." And, I thought, all the rest of the gold.

But even as dumb and naive as I was, I decided the FBI agents must be even dumber if they believed Pirrone's story. That was the flimsiest excuse I had ever heard—that someone would just put anything as valuable as a gold bar in the back of his car.

"Maybe you should have bought them off with a few cases," suggested Tom, who had just walked in.

Tom! He had surfaced just when I had almost despaired of ever seeing him again, vaguely thinking he had disappeared at the hands of one of the gangsters (I now thought of them in large plurals). This whole thing had so many twists and turns it seemed as though many sinister types must be in on it. Tom was like a playful porpoise in a game of underwater tag, momentarily surfacing for air only to return to his hiding place under the sea. And I was like the child who has been left out of all the fun while Tom and Pirrone were constant playmates. If they had not both been men, they would have been perfect for each other. I felt as if Pirrone had stolen Tom away from me.

Tom seemed embarrassed to see me. Did he wish I were not there? I felt as if my presence were inconveniencing him. I also noticed a day-old growth of beard, which was rare for clean-cut Tom.

Suddenly Pirrone exclaimed, "What in hell are those black things over the windows? Who's expecting an air raid? Has war been declared?"

I explained that it was for Liz's ballet. Pirrone gave his look of "See what I mean? Liz is really insane."

"Who were the men I saw leaving?" Tom asked Pirrone.

"FBI."

Tom seemed impressed, "We're getting important, aren't we?"

Pirrone was amused, but then asked more seriously, "Have you finished everything?"

"No." Tom turned to me and said, "Alice, I'll be back later this evening."

I felt weak. He was being casual, as if he hardly knew me. Was he still mad at me?

When he returned a few hours later, he seemed preoccupied rather than angry. The smuggling must have been of more concern to him than I was.

I asked, "What were you and Pirrone doing on the boat?" This was a bluff, of course; I had no idea where he had gone.

"He wasn't there. He wanted me to check the engines."

My bold stab at his whereabouts had hit right on the mark. So I tried another stab. "Where did you hide the rest of the stuff?" I asked accusingly.

"What?"

"Whatever you're smuggling."

"You know as well as I do where the cigarettes are hidden," he answered.

"I mean the gold or the drugs."

"Alice, you've been reading too many of Liz's books. What makes you think there is gold or drugs on the boat?"

"I've been checking up on Pirrone."

He burst out laughing and put his arm around me. "You silly girl," he laughed again, "I thought I detected something funny in your attitude lately. It's the way you look at Pirrone as if you're searching for something."

"I don't have to look anymore," I retorted. "We've already found the clues."

"We?" Tom was concerned. "Who else is in on this?"

"I meant I." I could not let him know about Erica. Already I had said too much. Tom could pass me off as a "silly girl," but if he thought there were two of us and that we were seriously spying, he might tell Pirrone; then we would be through and in even more danger from the underworld.

"Alice, do you think I'd get involved with drugs? You must know that's ridiculous."

"Well, what have you been involved in, then?" I cried. "I never see you anymore. You're like a stranger. Something's going on. I know it is, and it's bothering you, too. I can tell. You're secretive and cold toward me." He seemed disturbed as I rattled on in self-pity, "I know why you're treating me like this. It's because of what you think happened the night I went down to the boat, isn't it?" He didn't answer. Then I really started crying as I sobbed out, "Well, you're all wrong; nothing happened. But you'll never believe me; I know it. You don't love me anymore, and you're planning to discard me. I'll be just like Liz."

Tom smiled slightly as he said, "You'll never be like Liz." As usual, he was evading the issue, receding into his shell like a giant clam.

"Oh," I moaned, "I'd rather talk to a wall. It would be more satisfying. At least walls are not supposed to talk." Tom was silent (just like a wall). Neither of us spoke for a long time. I sat, sniffling and wiping my tears but he did nothing to comfort me. "Can't you say anything?" I asked finally.

I was interrupted by the phone ringing. Tom answered it. "Yes, I do, you know I do," he said in a sort of covered-up intimate way, as if he were trying to hide the fact that he was talking to a girl with whom he was romantically involved. I felt like pounding him on the head. Was he deceiving me with another girl? As I listened to his guarded phone conversation of three-word sentences, his tone changed to a more conspiratorial one. Maybe he wasn't talking to a girl after all. However, he wasn't communicating much to his caller, whoever it was, at least nothing that I could figure out. But as little as he said, he said more to her or him than he had said to me all night; and I had thought I was his…oh, dear, what was I?

When he hung up he was extremely agitated, "I have to go on a…ah…a…away for a short time on business."

"At eleven o'clock at night?"

"It's a last-minute contact. I can't help it."

"Why don't you take me along? We're sailing in a few days, anyway."

"Is it that soon? Alice, I can't. I can't take you. Someday I'll be able to tell you all about it."

"So, there is something wrong going on!"

"It isn't what you think it is," he replied, as if my prying had gone too far. "I have to leave. I'll tell you on the boat."

I stood there for a moment, shocked by the way he had bolted out the door, and then I yelled, "I might not be there!" But he had already disappeared from the courtyard.

Between Tom's behavior, the mysterious smuggling, the threats to my life scaring me to death, and the shocking, sickening aberrations of Pirrone and Liz, I was so muddled I hardly knew what to do. Who had taken that obscene picture? Another girl? Brian? I was caught in a moral jungle where there were no rules, no taboos. Even animals had better instincts. Did these people have no sense of evil? Uncontrolled primitive passion might be natural, maybe even healthy, but this was unnatural and twisted. They were like the devil's children; or, as I had half come to believe, was Pirrone the devil himself, satanically hypnotizing these sweet girls who joined him in plural couplings? Charming, lovely

Liz must be, I thought, some kind of victim; or was she truly crazy, driven out of her mind by her husband's perversions?

My impulse was to run away from this house of horrors and return to my clean, simple childhood. But, for better or worse (and it definitely seemed like worse, much worse), I was still mesmerized, and I really still wanted to go on the trip. I was not yet ready for a separation.

No one had ever suggested that I witness perverted couplings. I had just stumbled on them accidentally. I was disgusted with Pirrone and I now knew I would never fall into his pit. And I wanted to be with Tom on the boat where he could not be disappearing all the time. We would have happy nights together.

The next day I became further disillusioned about what had once seemed to me to be an idyllic existence. I bumped into Liz outside the front door as she was talking with the same man who had come to see her the afternoon after we had gotten back from our first cigarette-buying excursion. She introduced me to him, saying he had been a friend of her mother and father.

He said to Liz, "Your mother had really exquisite jewelry. I always admired it."

"Yes." Liz said, "I did, too. I am lucky to have it. I've never worn the bracelet, even though it is the most magnificent piece of all the things Mother left me. It is much better for someone to have it who will enjoy wearing it." Liz did not sound too sincere. I had the feeling she didn't mean what she was saying, that she was very unhappy about giving up even an unworn piece of her collection.

"I'll bring my wife over tomorrow. She remembers the bracelet, too. I am sure she will want it when she sees it again." He said goodbye to us and expressed his pleasure at meeting me.

Liz turned to me as he walked away and said, "Let's go in and have a drink. I really need one." She seemed terribly upset but I could see she was not going to offer an explanation. Possibly over a drink she will, I thought. But she never did.

The next time I was alone with Erica, I told her about Liz's conversation with the friend of her parents, and I told her how upset Liz had seemed by it.

"Poor Liz," Erica said. "She had to sell her lovely jewelry to finance this trip."

"Why?" I asked. "Pirrone's wealthy. Why does Liz have to chip in?"

"Pirrone's not wealthy," Erica told me.

"What about all those family factories?"

"Nonsense," she answered. "All lies. When he married Liz, Pirrone was just a car-racing bum."

No wonder Pirrone had been in such a hurry to marry Liz. And now his expensive tastes must have depleted Liz's immediately available funds, forcing her to sell her beautiful baubles. Now I understood why he wanted to have her committed—to gain control of her remaining estate. An expedition that had to be financed by the sale of her beloved heirlooms seemed tawdry. I hoped the Andean gold would be plentiful enough that her forfeited jewelry could be replaced, perhaps with jewels from some impoverished prince's family treasure.

Now more than ever I was determined to find out what the secret cargo was. I thought of the old derelict house, hidden in a grove of red-wood trees in the next canyon. I was sure something was going on there, if only because it would be a clever hiding place for any bulky cargo such as arms for some South American revolutionaries. It was only a short walk away and I felt that I had to go immediately for there was little time left.

Rather than take the road, when I got to the canyon I slipped into the redwood trees. The quietly uplifting stillness in the grove made the smuggling seem remote. The shafts of sunlight piercing the vaulted spaces between pillars of redwood trunks made me feel sanctified. A deer glided noiselessly through the ferns that carpeted the cathedral floor as a furry squirrel scurried by, a bouncy, wavy line in abstract ani-mation.

I was transfixed, until I heard a car going down the driveway leading from the house to the road. I thought I had better get inside while who-ever had been there was gone. The house, which was literally wedged between the trees, looked even more abandoned than it had from the few glimpses I had gotten from the road. The boards and battens on the outside were split and curling away from the framework. A few of the windows were broken and the door sagged. It was a place for goblins and witches. My curiosity overcame my terror at going into such a creepy place. I tried the door but it did not open, although the hardware looked rusty and aged. I walked around to the back. There was a casement window in which the lower panes were completely missing. I pushed on the spindly partitions that had held the glass. They gave away as in a breakaway movie-set window designed for fight or flight. I thought, if I have to make a hasty exit, this will be my way out. I slipped through the thick dust into a damp, dark unfurnished room. I had tried to come in silently, in case anyone was there, but the floor creaked loudly, announcing my arrival.

As my anxiety intensified, I prayed with all my being that no one was there. I felt as though my heart would burst the bands of my ribs as it strained against them.

I was afraid to make another move. As I stood motionless I heard all kinds of weird and scary noises—among them an eerie, groaning sound as though some giant were in pain. Probably a tree blowing against the house, I told myself, trying to be rational. Then I heard footsteps on the roof, followed by more footsteps, treading quickly and lightly. The ultimate terror: I realized, as my flesh flash-froze into sheet ice, that it had to be the Mafia killers who had been after me on the boat. I was sure they were going to slip down the outside wall and come in through the window I had pushed out.

I was an odd mixture of quivering, scared rabbit and stolid stone statue as I moved as noiselessly as I could over to the darkest part of the room and pressed myself against the wall. I heard a rustle outside the window. I looked in that direction and saw a raccoon peering in, like a burglar with a mask across his eyes. Another one sneaked up by his side. I saw then that it was getting late; it was almost dark outside. I knew I had better hurry as fast as I could with my investigation and get back to Dañada.

I heard someone knocking at the front door, an insistent, rapid knock. Someone had to be in the house, someone the knocker had come to see. I waited for the knock to be answered as the ice again spread through all my cells. But it was not answered. Then it stopped for a couple of minutes. When it started again it came to me that it was a woodpecker, drilling away on the roof shingles. My relief was short-lived, though, because I realized that if someone were there he would know the knocker was only a woodpecker. With this thought, the apprehension that I was not alone returned.

The branches continued to thrash around in the March wind, and what was undoubtedly a gate cried in anguish, as it kept slamming shut and then creaking open. My finding logical reasons for the noises did little to calm me. As I moved through the room, I could feel spiders crawling on me. I brushed at them. My hands became covered with spider webs. I tried to flick them off but they clung to me, making me squirm. I walked through several deeply shadowed rooms full of tattered, old furniture that oozed stuffing through the worn and split coverings.

I thought again about all the noises and their probable causes, but it did not dispel the feeling that there definitely was someone in this house and that I should get out of there as fast as possible. But then I noticed that the slanting beam of early dusk light from a small window reflected off something new and shiny. It was a lock that had been newly inserted under a falling-off, shabby black doorknob, raw wood showing around the edges of the lock where the hole had been drilled. Here was the first evidence of something unusual in this ramshackle place. I tried the door. It was unlocked; I guess they weren't expecting me, the indefatigable sleuth! The door opened on creaky hinges. There were stairs leading down. I groped down them, nearly falling several times, not only because it was so dark but also because the treads were split and broken, my feet catching in the cracks. Just trying not to make a misstep absorbed me so much I had no room left for fear. But I did reflect on how crazy I was, going down into another dark hole, driven by the insistent urge to get to the bottom of the mystery. Bottom was the right word, I seemed to have a faculty for plunging there in my search: the hold of the boat and now this cellar.

When I reached the floor at the end of the steps, my hand found a switch on the wall. I flicked it on. A bare bulb glowed faintly at the end of a dangling wire. As the awareness of what the light exposed came over me, I trembled and my heart raced in a frigid surge. All my disquieting forebodings about gunrunning were realized in this dark basement arsenal.

There were crates and boxes stacked everywhere. I walked over to one and examined the top of it. It had six round depressions at the edges, two on either side and one at each end. In the depressions, which were rectangular but close to being square, were rusted catches somewhat like trunk latches. On the box "30 Cal Ball Cartridges" was printed, and underneath that the muzzle velocity was stated with a number, and under that was printed "Remington Arms Union Cartridge Co. Inc." I tried to lift the box but it was far too heavy for me.

Nearby were stacked long boxes. One was open. I could see guns covered in plastic. I ripped open the plastic on one of them, perhaps wanting to prove to myself that I was hallucinating, that this was not real. The gun felt as if it were coated in Vaseline. It was all too real. As I wiped the thick greasy stuff off my hand onto my sleeve, I realized my hands were cold and clammy.

I thought I had better leave before I got trapped in there, too. But as I turned to go, the light went out. I heard heavy footsteps starting down the stairs. A strong flashlight beam glared directly into my eyes, practically blinding me. I was unable to see who was holding it. I was caught. There was no place to run to, no place to hide. My terror was so great I was paralyzed; my legs felt as if they were made of thousands of pounds of immovable cement. I could not scream, either; my voice seemed as if it were tied in my throat by chains. Yet, paradoxically, each cell of my frozen being felt as if it would burst. I could see myself exploding into a myriad of icy fragments. Then as the flashlight bearer came close to me, I saw something coming toward my head fast. I heard a sharp crack. I was swallowed up by a violent, crushing pain. That was the last I remembered.

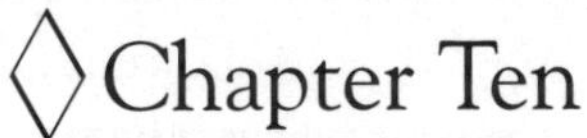# Chapter Ten

CONSCIOUSNESS
gradually intruded on me, bringing with it increasingly excruciating
pain. I felt as if an enormous sandbag were pushing my head into the
ground. For quite a long time (or so it seemed) I must have slipped back
and forth between a terrible awareness of my frightfully aching head and
a numb kind of passing out.

In my more or less conscious states I began to notice little bits of my
situation. I was lying on a mat on the floor. I seemed to be closely surrounded by stone walls. From a clerestory window high above me, light
came into the little room at an angle, making a square of light on the
cupboard doors lining the opposite wall. It must have been some kind of
small storeroom or large closet.

As I became more alert, it came over me where I was: the stone fortress-house to which Tom had taken me in my early days at Dañada. I could feel more than hear the pounding of the surf outside. The reverberations from the waves crashing against the sea wall made my head feel as if it would split apart. I must have passed out again—for how long I had no idea.

I drifted back awake with the feel of rough hands on my head as they tied something around it. I opened my eyes but could see nothing. Then a man lifted me up—it had to be a man, a strong one, by the easy way he slung my limp body over his shoulder. He reeked of garlic. The smell nauseated me. I was too dazed and dulled by pain and physical misery to be fully cognizant of my peril, but I reacted at a barely conscious level by trying to kick him and push myself away. However, I was powerless. I realized why—my hands were fastened together and my arms were wrapped by something holding them against my body. My legs and ankles were tied together, too. I tried to scream but nothing came out. I think it was the pounding in my head that would not let me yell.

Terror finally seized me like a giant claw tearing into my heart as I was being carried. I could tell we were out of the house as I heard a car's motor idling nearby. The shadow of my impending doom was forming in my mind like a sudden dark thundercloud. I was dumped like a sack of trash on a hard surface, which I knew had to be the floor of the trunk of the waiting car. I heard the loud sound of metal slammed against metal as the lock snapped above me.

Extreme panic such as I had never known before seeped through my stupor and suffering. There was no way out of a locked rear compartment of a car. I knew now I was being taken someplace to be disposed of in an underworld fashion—probably in a watery grave weighted down with blocks of cement.

My fear was so great I could no longer feel any pain—it had been usurped by something far worse: the sure knowledge that my life would be ended soon. In my terror, time had lost all relevance, so I had no idea how long I had been driven before the car turned onto a very rough road, nor did I even notice when it started to get bumpy. But when the jolting of the car got much worse, I was aware that we were no longer on a road, just rough dirt. Seconds later the car ground to an abrupt stop. I heard the steel trunk top being opened. I was yanked out like a fifty-pound bag of dog food (except that I was a lot heavier than that).

I felt myself being thrown and then I felt myself falling, but my fall ended almost immediately as I made a quick but hard landing on something rocky. Luckily the thrower had not thrown me far enough. However, I was not out of danger for I started to slide, and being bound and blindfolded I had no way of stopping myself and I had no idea of where I was or what I was sliding toward.

I slid slowly at first, then faster and faster, over a jagged surface that I could feel was ripping and tearing not only my clothes but my skin as well. It was all happening so quickly that I had little sensation except for the horror that death could come at any second. In all my life my heart had never pounded like this; it felt as if it would break through my chest and that I would split apart, my two halves flying in different directions. Finally I slammed into something that felt like cement. After that I don't remember feeling anything; I guess my nerves were anesthetized by the impact, unable to relay any pain signals. Or maybe I was completely knocked out.

Eventually (again I knew not how long) it slowly filtered through my haziness that every now and then water was washing over me; it was cold and refreshing. Like a tonic, it brought me to my senses. I tried to pull my hands apart. The rope was loose; it fell off as I pushed my hands away from each other. It must have been cut or broken on the rocks that I could now see on the precipice above me. I managed to sit up. The blindfold must have been torn off as I was sliding. I looked around. I was on a tiny strip of sand. Every so often the trailing edge of an especially large wave washed over my legs. I tugged on the rope binding my legs and ankles; it would not give.

The waves were not only coming in closer all the time but they also seemed to be getting bigger. Again, panic filled every nerve in my body as I thought, good God, the tide is coming in. The waves would soon be breaking against the bluff. I had little time to get out of there before the tiny spot of sand disappeared as the ocean reclaimed it. But I had had so many shocks and had been subjected to so many lethal threats that I had reached a state of resignation.

I sat there dumbly and numbly waiting to drown. My hand, moving idly in the sand, found a broken abalone shell, which probably had been discarded from some sea otter's lunch. But it gave me new hope. I was able to cut through the cord binding my legs and ankles with its sharp edge. I could now walk, but where? The face of the cliff was un-climbable. Swimming out was impossible, too: the ocean in front of me was littered with rock formations that the waves were crashing over, and farther out the sea seemed to be breaking on some kind of reef. And even if I could have swum out through the rock-strewn surf, where would I have swum? The whole coast was virtually impregnable except for the Cove and Fanshell bay, and I had no idea where they were since I had no idea where I was.

As the water crept higher, the sun sank lower, a molten ball of fire just above the horizon. Soon it would be dark but even before that, I thought, I'll be swallowed up by the sea. I glanced up to the top of the precipice. Way up at the top I saw a young couple, arms around each other, gazing out toward the fast-sinking sun. Hope excited me into action. I screamed as loudly as I could, amazed to hear my voice, which I had been unable to summon earlier. I kept on screaming but the ocean's roar must have obliterated any sound because they did not look down. My elation at seeing them began to fade. They'll never look my way, I thought; they're too involved with each other and the sunset. I kept on trying, though. I started jumping up and down and waving my arms wildly. At last they saw me. The fellow seemed to realize my plight. He yelled something I could not hear. Then he left. Soon he came back and let down a long line. When the end reached me, he made motions to tie it around my waist and loop it over my shoulder. I held onto the line as he pulled, and I walked up the scarp the way I had seen mountain climbers scaling heights in movies.

The girl asked as I landed at the top, "Are you all right? You look very battered. It's really dangerous to walk alone. If you slip and fall, there is nobody to go for help."

"Yeah," the fellow agreed, "it was a lucky thing I had this nylon cord in the back of my car. It's very strong. It has braided steel wire in the center. It's for pull cords for some thirty-foot-long draperies I'm hanging in the museum. They are very heavy and have to have extra strong drapery cord. Anything else would break the first time they were pulled. You're fortunate. The stuff I usually have would never have worked."

The girl told me by way of explanation that he was a drapery in-staller. Then she asked me where I lived.

"About five miles north of El Mirador," I said. I had no idea where we were. When I saw the amazed expressions on their faces, I added, "I really am into marathon walking. Ten miles or more is nothing to me."

"Well, we can at least take you to El Mirador," the fellow said. "Can you call home and get someone to pick you up? In your condition I wouldn't recommend any more walking, even though ten miles is nothing to you."

I assured them that I could. Whatever they suggested was all right with me; I was so extremely grateful to have been saved. As I got into their car, I began to feel pain in every sore inch of my body. My head throbbed, making it hard for me to respond to their questions, which they were only asking to make conversation.

They left me at the public telephone next to the gas station. As I dialed the Dañada number with the dime the fellow had thoughtfully given me, I wondered what on earth I could concoct as a story. I did not dare announce that I had been trying to track down the mysterious, secret cargo. Yet my condition—my body and face bruised and swollen, cut and scraped, my clothes torn and blood stained—needed an explanation. I decided I would say I had taken a long walk and fallen down a steep incline, which was the handiest excuse since it was what my rescuers had assumed had happened.

As I waited for my call to be answered it struck me that I did not know how long I had been gone. Had it been one day or two? I had lost all track of time because I had passed out so often and with no idea for how long. As I was trying to figure this out, Brian said, "Hello."

I said, trying to sound matter-of-fact, "Would you mind coming to pick me up? I'm in El Mirador."

"What the hell are you doing there? And how did you get there? Erica was looking for you and wondered where you were." If I had been gone for over twenty-four hours, I thought, Erica wouldn't have been the only one who wondered where I was. Everything must have happened this one terrible day.

"I went for a walk," I answered him.

"That's a long way for a walk. I can see why you're not walking back. We'll come and get you as soon as we can."

While I waited for them to come I thought about it seeming as though it were starting to get dark outside the old house. However it could have been a lot earlier than it looked since the house was in a deep ravine densely filled with huge old redwood trees; the little sun that filtered through would have been blocked out in the early afternoon. Thus, the attempted disposal of me must have taken place late the same afternoon.

Erica was shocked when she saw me. "That must have been some fall. You look very bedraggled. Are you all right?" I tried to laugh, but it did not come out that way. Everything hurt so much I ended up crying.

Erica was alarmed by this. "You know, you really look more as if you were beaten up and thrown off the ledge rather than having fallen." I gasped when she said this. Erica looked startled. She must have suspected she had inadvertently come close to the truth. But I could not let her know with Brian there.

Between sobs, I said it really had been a much worse fall than I had described on the phone and that I was emotionally broken up because I had thought no one would ever find me and that I would be drowned by the advancing breakers as they hit the cliff. All of which was true.

Over the next several days I never had a chance to be alone with Erica to tell her about the ammo and gun depot and the true version of my disastrous adventure. She did not show any anxiousness, although I thought she suspected there was more to it than I had disclosed the night she and Brian had picked me up. But as the days went on, the busy activities for the trip pushed the whole episode into a back corner of my mind, where its enormity dwindled into something unreal like a half-remembered bad dream.

But at night in bed, it became more than real. I would wake up tormented by the feel of rough hands jerking me up and flinging me into an abyss. My body would twitch in a miserable restlessness, alternately hot and cold, continually moist and sticky. Then I would fall back asleep again as scenes from my abduction were replayed with ferocious intensity, only twisted and mixed up and infinitely more alarming than I remembered them when I was awake. These dreams were intermingled with even more horrifying ones filled with monsters and demons. At times both kinds of dreams would blend together in a terrifying montage. I thought I must be really going crazy.

In the mornings I began to think that nothing had really happened to me, that I had dreamed or imagined most of it or all of it. Yet my head was still sore and I was covered with bruises and scratches. Had I just walked down the road and fallen off the edge? Could the concussion from the fall and the short coma, which I must have been in, have made me imagine that I had been in the old house and had been kidnapped from it? Or perhaps the ghost of the first bride of Dañada had haunted me, causing me to have hallucinations....

Finally one day, Erica and I were alone at Dañada, everyone else having gone off on various errands. "Well," she said, "when you were out walking did you slip or were you pushed?"

"Oh," I said in an attempt at humor, "I thought you would never ask." Erica laughed slightly—a phony, polite little laugh. I started to explain, "I found a cache of guns and ammunition in the old derelict house down the road."

She was surprised. "Are you sure?"

"Yes, well, no, I'm not sure anymore. I am beginning to wonder. I don't know whether or not I really saw all that—no, that's not what I mean. What I want to say is that I don't think it has any connection with Pirrone or us. I think I accidentally discovered a Mafia arms depot—they tried to kill me by throwing me over the cliff."

"What?" Erica was alarmed though incredulous. She looked at me as if I were out of my mind (which in truth I was beginning to think I was). "Alice, I think you are hallucinating again. You always seem to be imagining that someone is after you to do you in."

I wondered why Erica didn't want to believe me, but then I hardly believed myself anymore. It began to seem like some long-forgotten nightmare that I vaguely remembered having had but could no longer recall.

I said, resignedly, "Maybe you're right, Erica." But a half-formed thought was gathering in the back of my mind: when I was abducted, that is if I really had been, did they in some way brainwash me so that I would doubt that I had found their arsenal?

Preparations for our expedition were going ahead at a slow pace. But still the trip was getting inexorably closer, like a time bomb, already set ticking away until D-day—departure day—whenever that might be. In spite of our ineptness, things had gone too far; too many commitments had been made, including, of course, the secret smuggling arrangements, whatever they were, for anything to stop our voyage.

We made our sallies to the boat with the results of our helter-skelter shopping, stowing the articles without order or system. It was almost dusk when Pirrone and I got back from an errand. All the gang except Tom were in the courtyard undressed, getting into a pose for Brian's naturalistic portrait of Dañada.

Liz yelled for Pirrone and me to get out of our clothes for the fare-well picture—the Roman bacchanal—that had been planned once before. Brian, with a garland of leaves on his head and a beach towel draped toga-style across one shoulder, was focusing his camera on its tripod before coming to get in the group.

Pirrone was flinging off his clothing while telling me to hurry. I was sort of numb, not making a move. Pirrone grabbed the zipper at the back of my turtleneck sweater and the one at the back of my pants with his other hand, exciting me to the toes as he unzipped them both. With all that stimulating help, I was suddenly caught up in the spirit of the picture taking.

I quickly undressed. Pirrone grabbed my hand as thrill after thrill raced through me. He took a bunch of grapes off a table of props for the bacchanal and lay down on an outdoor chaise that was in the center of the group, pulling me down with him, my heart beating away some-where in my head. A strange mixture of uncomfortable embarrassment and sexual excitement made me see the rest of the people in a haze (which was made hazier by the fact that it was getting dark). I had dreamed a few times of being ashamed when I realized I was in a crowd of people and had no clothes on. I always woke up at that point. It was time for me to wake up, but evidently not yet, because I could vaguely see bare bodies everywhere with wreaths on heads. I could also see that everyone was drinking out of wine glasses. It never dawned on me how Brian was going to take the picture with so little light unless it was going to be a flash photo. Possibly he had already taken it and I had not noticed.

Pirrone reached over and grabbed Serena by the thigh, pulling her down, too. Just then Tom, whom I had completely forgotten about, appeared in the courtyard. He grabbed Brian's towel toga off him and flung it over me as he brutally yanked me off the lounge.

Everyone was yelling at Tom, "Spoilsport," "You old wet towel," and all kinds of epithets far worse than those.

As Tom dragged me off, the last thing I heard was someone saying,

"Let's go sulphur pooling," and someone else answering, "That's too much trouble, we're all set for a great orgy right here."

And that's what happened, for during the next few days I heard snips and bits about it. The Roman bacchanal turned into a drunken affair with everyone having sex with everyone else. It was as if all the rules of social and sexual behavior, rules I had been trained to accept as true and good, were suddenly turned upside down. And had it not been for Tom, I would have been there, and been part of it. I wondered what was wrong with me because I had suddenly been so pliable and willing to join in the bacchanal—I who felt so sure Pirrone would never get me in his pit.

After Tom marched me into our room and made me dress, I tried to say it was not my fault, that I had been dragged into it.

"I suppose someone tied your hands and feet before undressing you and putting you on the lounge with Pirrone."

"Practically," I said weakly.

Tom gave me the coldest, most disgusted look I have ever seen. After that neither of us said anything the rest of the night. I knew Pirrone was his idol only up to a point. Tom was basically straight-laced and prudish; he could not accept behavior outside his moral code for himself or someone he was involved with—namely me.

The next day, the only words he spoke to me were a few short orders in a bitter tone. He took me to the boat with him where he worked on the engines. Then he took me back to Dañada, where he dumped me off. As he left, he muttered something about being late, as cryptically as the White Rabbit. But lately he hardly spoke to me anyway. The reason for his trips was never discussed or disclosed. The most I could ever get him to say was that they were necessary because of very important business. I was planning to travel thousands of miles to another hemisphere with him, and unless he should change drastically en route, there was no hope of communication.

But worse than traveling with someone I couldn't talk with was the prospect of being on a ship carrying illegal cargo. All I had were clues as to what that cargo might possibly be—but no confirmation. It could be guns and ammunition (dangerous even if they hadn't been illegal). But I wasn't even sure that I had really seen them; or if I had, it could be that I had stumbled into someone else's scenario that had nothing to do with our expedition.

It did seem logical that whoever had the arsenal would not want anyone to know about it, whatever was planned for it. And if they were unscrupulous—and people with such a cache would almost have to be unscrupulous—they would think nothing of killing the discoverer of their secret. It had never occurred to me before (how dumb I was) but now I wondered if they thought they had definitely disposed of me and that my body had been washed out to sea. What if the killer saw me again? Would he recognize me? I thought with mounting dread, I had better disguise myself. But how?

Then it came to me: nothing changes a girl's identity more than her hair. I would become a blonde. The ads always proclaimed that blondes have more fun. I could use a little fun, the way things had been going lately. I was definitely not having a good time anymore. The next morning early—ten-thirty (I had hardly slept all night)—I borrowed the limousine without asking; at this unreal hour, no one was up to ask. I drove to the drugstore to buy the stuff to turn myself into a dazzling blonde.

As I was driving, a plan began to formulate itself amidst my speculations. Assuming the guns were indeed related to our venture, the person who really knew what was going on had to be the mastermind, Pirrone. Somehow I would have to get him to talk. How could I do that? I had always heard that the way to reach a man was through his stomach, but Pirrone's appetite was mainly for girls. How could I be one of them (as I had secretly longed to be before I discovered I could only have been one among many—an orgy mate for a quasi-devil)? I would have to make myself so sexy and alluring Pirrone would not be able to resist me. I had once wanted him so much; now I only wanted to use him. I would drop him before things got out of hand. That should damage his ego. No girl had ever turned him down before as far as I knew (except for Nancy, who had gotten away before he had a chance to enmesh her with his evil charm). Thinking about the girls he had brought to Dañada, I could find no pattern; they were all different. Perhaps the quality that appealed to him was not discernable to the female eye. I would have to be as seductive as I possibly could and hope that would entrance him.

At the drugstore I bought the longest, thickest false eyelashes they had plus some really outrageous eye shadow. I chose a bottle of perfume that was guaranteed to drive men mad. I could hardly wait to try out my sexy new image. I stopped a mile out of town and attached the eyelashes and applied the eye shadow, using the rear view mirror. Not being able to see too well through the dense brushes over my eyes, I almost had several collisions. Maybe I had gotten them too low on my eyelids. At least by trying them first, I would learn the pitfalls of wearing them.

After putting the limousine in the garage, I rushed into the bathroom to bleach my hair. I followed the easy step-by-step directions, which were anything but easy. I got the stuff in my eyes. It hurt so much, I thought for a couple of minutes I would go blind, but I managed to wash it out. My eyes were flaming red but at least I could see. When I finally finished the messy procedure, my hair looked and felt like yellow straw—coarse, dry, and lifeless. It was not alluringly soft and silky, as the blurb on the box had indicated it would be. I did look different, though—a straw-haired scarecrow. Even if it wouldn't serve to make me look glamorous, it might save my life—my would-be killer would never recognize me.

I was exhausted from the hair-coloring operation and from having gotten up at such an unaccustomed early hour. I lay down on the bed. (We had moved back to the garage so Tom could be near his car). I dozed fitfully for a while. After I was finally fully awake, I lay there for a long time trying to summon the energy to get up. Staring at the sheer draperies over the windows inspired me. I would whip up a see-through blouse using one of the curtains. A poncho affair, basted together under the arms with a hole, deeply cut in the middle for the neck, would be the simplest and quickest to make. Tight black pants would be a slinky conclusion for my kiss-and-tell outfit. (I hoped that after a kiss, I could get Pirrone to tell me what I needed to know.)

Excited by my idea, I jumped off the bed. I took down one of the curtains. They were all in separate panels bunched together, ready-made rather than custom made, good enough for a garage apartment, I guessed. I rearranged the others on the rod to cover the gap so that it was impossible to see that one had been removed. All this motivation filled me with energy so I quickly completed my creation.

I dressed and reapplied the eyelashes, this time a little more expertly so I could see better. I had removed them before doing my hair—a good thing for otherwise they would have been bleached when I got the junk in my eyes. I didn't think straw-colored lashes would have enticed anyone. By the time I had put the eye shadow on and liberally doused myself with the Odalisque perfume, I was quivering in tremulous anticipation of my projected conquest. My new reflection in the mirror, with those wickedly sexy eyes, excited me erotically. I thought, I can't miss, if I do that to myself, Pirrone will be wildly turned on.

I rushed down to the living room, which, thank heavens, was unoccupied. Taking off my sweater, I arranged the folds of my gauzy drapery concoction and started practicing seductive poses and erotic sighs.

Liz wandered in. Mistaking my posturing, she asked, "Why are you writhing around? Do you need some calamine lotion? You must have been near some poison oak. It is maddening when it happens to you, isn't it? Gee, I guess it kept you awake all night. Your eyes look like two black holes. I'll bring you some sleeping pills when I come back."

Either she was being myopic or my make-up was a total failure. But, I thought, she's not a man; of course it wouldn't seem alluring to her, so I should not be upset by her reaction. I proceeded with my preparations. I arranged myself into what I was sure was a very distracting position, but now I could hardly breathe. The air had become heavy and suffocating with the scent of the Odalisque perfume, which was really awful. Maybe I had overdone it. I had liberally saturated every pulse point and then splashed it all over myself as extra insurance.

With all my concentration I tried willing Pirrone to walk in, now that I was really ready. And the power of my will worked. Unfortunately, that was the only thing I was able to achieve, for he took no notice of me. All he was concerned with was airing out the room.

"It smells like someone broke a dozen bottles of some god-awful after-shave lotion." What an insult to my expensive perfume, I thought, even though I had to agree that it was pretty dreadful. "I've got to open the windows," he continued.

I rushed over to Pirrone as he was opening a window. "Let me help you," I cooed as I rubbed up against him.

"Get out of my way and open your own window."

I decided my tactics were all wrong and that I should be aloof and cool, but terribly attractive. I sat down in the farthest corner of the room and strived for a Marilyn Monroe look with half-open mouth and half-closed eyes. Pirrone finally looked over at me. "Alice, are you sick? You don't look well and for God's sake take off that fright wig."

The planned seduction had not gone well. I should have known I was not his type, whatever that was. But here was the opening for another tack.

"I don't feel good. I need something, something strong."

"How about a drink?"

"That's not strong enough."

"Alice, what have you been on lately?"

"Oh, dear, I have a hard time getting it."

"I didn't realize. What are you going to do on the trip? Or are you on one already?"

I acted distraught. "My contact will only accept gold or guns."

"Whatever you're on, it's certainly making you crazy."

"Pirrone, you had one gold bar. Do you have any others?"

"What are you, some kind of gold digger? Poor Tom, does he know?"

"Please don't tell him. I was just having a little fun."

"Don't worry, he probably wouldn't believe me. I hardly can myself. Why don't you wash all that crap off your face, and while you're at it soak your head in cold water. It might clear your brain."

Mata Hari's memory was secure. I was certainly an inept spy; whatever I tried failed. I didn't think the CIA would be recruiting me.

Later that night after we had already sat down to eat, Pirrone walked in with another new girl. He did not bother to introduce us individually. He just announced her name. She did not look outstanding, but she must have had something I did not. Even Brian seemed to find her attractive. Did she have any connection with the smuggling? Or was Pirrone just storing up on girls, so he would not get too hungry on the voyage?

The mystery was still a mystery. It was frustrating never to be able to trip up Pirrone, or Tom, who had to know a lot. Pirrone was far too clever; I would never find out anything from him. But maybe Pirrone was right when he accused me of being on some kind of trip. Was I losing my grip on reality? Had I lived in this illusory place so long that I had imagined the guns and gold and dreamed up the idea of drugs? But I had confirmation, in the phone conversation I had overheard, that someone actually did try to "bump me off" on the boat (or do something to me).

I remembered Erica saying she had seen things; or did I dream that, too? She evidently did not believe the account of the kidnapping from the derelict house and the attempt to kill me. Something in all this must be real. I felt I had to hear her say she was there and heard the conversation about the FBI and the gold bar. After dinner I practically forced Erica out of the living room, pulling her by the arm to the driveway.

"What's the matter?" she gasped.

"Erica, tell me all these suspicious things we've been checking actually happened."

She was no help. "Except for the gun I found, which turned out to be exactly what it was—just a gun, you saw them all."

"But Erica, we did hear about the FBI and the gold bar together, didn't we?"

"That's true, but then there could be a logical explanation. Pirrone could have planted it on the boat because he planned to play some kind of joke on us, like telling us 'We don't need to go to Peru, I've discovered gold on board,' then he could have us searching for more gold bars, which of course we would never find. It would keep us occupied on a long, boring trip, like some kind of wild Easter egg hunt with no eggs."

"Then you're saying I'm crazy."

"Don't be silly, Alice. But we've never found anything, really, have we? Have you actually ever seen Joe Viscantino? You may just be imagining he's the man you've seen. Who knows what Joe Viscantino looks like? Has anyone ever seen even his picture? I'm not saying that something funny isn't going on and I'm not going to give up being on the lookout. If we find something really bad, I'm not going. Even if we discover it en route, at the first port I'll leave. But it's beginning to look as if you might have dreamed up the whole thing."

Evidently she had completely discounted my abduction and the ammo dump I had discovered. I said, "There you go again. You really do think I'm losing my reason."

"No, of course not. I'm just saying it's easy to build a case out of things that seem odd or that you have no explanation for."

It was clear to me now that I must be in some paranoid state that everyone was too kind to mention. I could conceive of them saying behind my back, "Poor thing, she's really out of it." Tom and sanity, I said to myself, please come back to me soon. A brisk sea voyage—that could be a doctor's orders to get the cobwebs out of my mind. How lucky that we were leaving in two days.

The following afternoon I thought I would go for a short walk. Maybe I would meet Tom on the road. Surely he would be arriving any minute, for we were leaving the next day. As I was walking by a stand of pine trees that covered a gradual slope, I heard a car coming fast, but it was too quiet for Tom's racing vehicle. I looked behind me to see a big black sedan coming closer. I stepped off the edge of the paving and some intuition caused me to run toward the trees. The car swerved off the road as panic crumpled me like tissue paper, my heart racing like a sewing machine with a stuck foot pedal. I felt I could not breathe but fortunately my legs, which seemed to have become independent of my body, kept going. The sedan went off the road far enough to barely brush my loose jacket ever so slightly but enough to knock me down.

It scared me so much, I felt my heart give one giant burst, and then it seemed to stop completely. I am dead, I thought, it's only a matter of seconds before I will die now that my heart has stopped. I felt myself rolling down the hill. I thought about the car swerving back onto the road at the same speed it had been traveling; it had not slowed down even a fraction when it grazed me, even though it was off the road and practically in the trees. I realized that it was because I had reached the perimeter of the trees that I was not hit head-on.

I did nothing to stop myself, so I kept rolling down the fairly gentle slope on a route that somehow missed the tree trunks. My good old heart must have been still ticking away even though I could no longer feel it. Though terrified, I was thinking clearly. I felt I should roll a little farther down the hill. It was easy to do because the wet, muddy soil was soft. I wanted to get as far out of sight as I could if the driver came back to finish off the job.

Then, I thought, how do I know it was a killer after me—namely the one who kidnapped me from the old house? Perhaps it was only a car that had skidded on the wet paving. Yet if that were the case would not the driver have stopped? Or could he have been one of the hit-and-run types? Or maybe he didn't even see me, and since he barely hit me, thought he had scraped a tree. No, I decided, I am convinced it was not an accident. It had to be the same killer as the one who had tried to get rid of me before. But I had become so muddled in the last few days, I wasn't absolutely certain that I had been abducted and flung off a cliff.

Caution was the best idea for me to follow; I was not about to take any more chances. I was more or less hidden in the deep shadows of the trees. I decided to wait until it was almost dark to climb up the hill. I hoped the killer felt that he had really done away with me this time. I was glad we were sailing the next day. On the boat I would be safe from the Mafia or whoever was after me.

As the daylight began to fade I left the protective trees and quickly ran back to Dañada. When Pirrone saw me coming up the drive, he looked surprised. "What happened to you? Did you go for a mud bath?"

"I took a walk. I slipped in a muddy spot and fell." I tried to be unconcerned about it.

"Another fall?" he said quizzically. "Are you all right?"

"I think so. I'll have to take a shower to find out." Had Pirrone been surprised only because of my condition? Or was he surprised to see me still alive?

By late that night Tom still had not returned, even though we were sailing at nine the next morning. I was too tired and numb from all the shocks, anguish, and anxiety that I had been subjected to during the past week to think much about his not being there yet, or even to think about anything. Like an automaton I was mechanically helping with the last-minute packing.

I gave no thought to the fact that I was planning to leave without calling my aunt. The little she had heard about the trip when I last saw her had enraged her.

"Those unsavory people are probably leaving because they are afraid if they don't they'll be run right out of El Mirador."

"Oh, Aunt Jessie," I said, "this isn't colonial America."

"Well, at least I know you have better sense than to go with them." So how could I tell her that I was actually going?

If I had phoned my parents, in their apprehension over my taking such an unconventional form of travel and with such unsuitable traveling companions, they would have driven up instantly and physically dragged me back home like a naughty puppy that has run away. I decided to write them a letter and mail it from the first port and ask them, also, to let Aunt Jessie know.

I had avoided Erica since the day she had insinuated the whole mysterious mess was in my imagination. Besides that she had cast my morality into question because she had said, "In you, Alice, inhibitions masquerade as character." Was I really that superficial? I must have become neurotic to have my feelings hurt. I tried to forget that I had ever suspected something clandestine—anyway, I had never really found out anything definite. Maybe Erica was right. Maybe I had imagined everything. Was I haunted by the ghost of Dañada?

During the completely chaotic packing, Pirrone kept screaming orders at Liz, orders that to be carried out, would have required ten hands. I could not understand his agitation. He was seething with an inner rage and was venting it on Liz, the only one at whom he could really lash out.

He picked up a suitcase that had just been packed to take it to the limousine. Because it weighed so little he opened it, thinking there was some mistake. Finding it was inhabited only by a stuffed iguana (Tom's birthday present), he yelled, "Liz, what in hell is this for?"

She came over to see what was wrong. "I thought we could hide gold in it when we come back."

"Why didn't you pack something with it?"

"I didn't have anything that would go with an iguana."

Pirrone gave her a quizzical look. "Well, try." He looked as if he wanted to hit her as he said again, "Just try, will you please, to find something…anything…to put in here with the iguana."

After we had gone on with the packing for a while (more or less quietly, all of us lost in our own private thoughts), I realized it had been at least fifteen or twenty minutes since I had seen Pirrone. Had he taken a short sabbatical to be with one of his girls? As I started to ask Erica where he was, there was a faint explosion, something like a distant gun being fired. At the same time all the lights went out. Evidently a transformer had blown out.

Liz laughed, "This is a good time for a break. Not that we have any choice. Does anyone know where the candles are?"

Everyone scurried around in the dark looking, or rather feeling, but in any case trying to find candles. I groped my way to the dining table to light the candles in the candelabra of coiled snakes, but all the candles were gone. No one else found any candles either. Pirrone seemed to have disappeared along with the candles and the light. Evidently he had left us in the dark in more ways than one.

I wondered why the lights had gone out when there was no storm. From what I had recently learned, transformers go out when water gets in them but there was no wind to blow the rain into the transformer, nor had there been any rain. When this had happened the night of our target practice with the old pistols, it had also been very clear. Was there a connection between the two events? There was something strange about this but I could not imagine what.

There was nothing we could do in the dark. We sat around making stupid jokes, laughing at the dumbest things in a slaphappy way as tired people do.

Erica laughed as she said rather seriously, "We better not forget our passports. What if we went all that way and couldn't get into South America? Hey, Alice, you just got yours, let's see what you look like."

"Luckily it's too dark. I look like the devil."

"What do you mean, Alice? Did you sprout horns for your passport portrait?"

Everyone laughed uncontrollably. I sputtered out while still laughing, "That would be very apropos here. One more devil would hardly be noticed."

After about forty minutes the lights came back on.

"I'm almost sorry to see," Erica said with a laugh.

"Sorry to see who, me?" Brian asked facetiously. We all laughed, still silly from fatigue.

Erica answered him, "No, just plain see anything. We were having so much fun. Now we have to go back to packing, ugh."

"I agree," said Liz. "Packing is a real drag."

After an hour or so Pirrone came back. He seemed to be in a much worse mood than before. Did his absence have anything to do with the lights going out? And if so what was he doing that he did not want anyone to see? Was it to cover some maneuver, one that had not gone well by the look on his face?

By the time we were through—about four-thirty in the morning—Tom had still not gotten back. No one seemed to know why. Everything was getting more and more peculiar. The only reason I could think of for his failure to return was that he had been caught with drugs or gold or guns or whatever was being smuggled, thus spoiling the plans. Was that why Pirrone was so mad? Of course, I had never been able to determine for sure that anything was being smuggled besides the cigarettes.

We unwound with a glass of Pernod before finding a bed and sleep. Brian and Erica looked as if they were already asleep. Pirrone, his anger somewhat dissipated, said, "Soon you will see what it is to have the power to do exactly as you please. Wealth and power are synonymous in South America."

"It seems to me," Liz said, "that you have already had everyone and everything."

I had never heard her publicly rebuff Pirrone. She seemed to have acquired a strikingly new attitude and personality. Was this the true Liz emerging from under a camouflage net of meek submissiveness? Had the secret plans made it necessary for her to play the shuffling role of a resigned captive? Or had Dañada been a psychic prison whose walls she was now leaving, a free person?

But how could I know if this were the real Liz? Does the real anyone exist, I wondered? We all live in a secret inner world, veiled and partly hidden even from ourselves. Was Liz's interior space a foreboding one of anxieties—as black as the color she had revealingly once wanted to paint her living room? In any case, she seemed to have added a new dimension: that of facing reality.

With Tom not back, when I lay down I could not get to sleep. I was extremely anxious about him but too exhausted to worry. My thoughts were like insects caught in amber and as in those fossilized remains, my thinking processes were frozen at the point of their most furious activity, finally reduced to numbness after the previous few days spent in various degrees of anguish, anxiety and alarm over all that I had been subjected to (probably because of my own stupid nosiness).

This night I should have been exhilarated because I had come to the apex of my drive to live in a fun-filled, unhumdrum way. But instead a sharp uneasiness was attacking me. Had Tom not gotten over his pique at finding me posed with Pirrone for the bacchanal? I lay in bed pleading to myself, "Please don't leave me, Tom. You'll never find me within fifty feet of Pirrone again (a little hard to avoid on a boat that was only seventy-five feet at the waterline), and I'll always be dressed."

The next thing I knew Erica was shaking me, saying, "Wake up.

Wake up. Hurry, we're late." I wondered why it mattered when we left. Maybe it had to do with the tides or some kind of clearance.

I quickly got dressed in my sailing outfit of tennis shoes, jeans, turtleneck, and nylon pullover parka. I looked around the room to see if I had forgotten anything, glancing outside into the garden for a last look. In the thick early morning fog I could distinguish some birds perched on the stone garden wall; for them it was just another day. Then through the murky haze I saw something else: beyond the low wall an alarming tableau was taking place. Pirrone seemed to be counting out something he was handing to a stocky man. As he turned to go, I could see his profile through the dimness. It was Joe Viscantino. Pirrone must have been paying for the heroin to be smuggled on the boat.

But wait a minute, I thought, heroin is smuggled into this country, not out. It could have been amphetamines to be taken to Mexico for reshipment here. But that was wrong, too, for I had read that amphetamines are legally shipped to Mexico in large quantities. They do not become illegal until they are sent back here for resale without prescriptions (and for lots more money than when they are legally sold). The only logical thing I could think of was that Joe was selling Pirrone drugs so that he could keep Liz supplied on the trip. I did not imagine what I had seen. I would have to talk to Erica, who still doubted that I had ever seen Joe Viscantino or that I had any idea what he looked like. I had another thought—that Pirrone was making arrangements for the disposal of the gold in Mexico, if indeed gold was already stashed in the secret compartment. I must have been the really crazy one. I was leaving without ever having found out what was really going on!

After I gathered my things together, I walked outside. Pirrone was standing there as though nothing unusual had happened. I asked him about Tom. He said we had to leave immediately. "If Tom isn't back by the time we're ready to sail, he can meet us in Los Angeles. He told me before he left to go down there that he might not get back in time."

"What is he doing there?"

"I can't say. You're coming with us, aren't you?"

"Yes, but it's just that I wanted Tom to be with us, too."

"Oh, he will be," Pirrone said. Pirrone seemed to be very happy: was his problem of the night before solved by the meeting with Joe this morning?

Soon we were joined by Brian, Erica, and Serena. I was surprised to see Serena, for I had understood she was not going with us to Peru. Brian handed Erica a letter addressed to him, to her, and to me. Erica opened it and read aloud,

Dear Conspirators:

Alas, Serena is leaving to do some weekendish type thing. I must stay to look after things. I suspected this, damn.

Anyway, the upshot of all this is—I can't leave with you. It's always more fun with more of us against the mal-contin-gent. [Did she mean male-contingent or was the connotation the bad-contingent?] I would love to be with you for the "maiden voyage."

See you in Los Angeles, and take care.

Liz

Was she meeting us there to bring contraband aboard? And if she did, then I might be leaving the boat just as Tom was boarding. Was it really planned that Tom would meet us in Los Angeles? And if so, what was his mission—a fresh supply of girls for Pirrone's long sea voyage?

"I guess Liz doesn't know you're going, Serena," Erica remarked. Serena did not answer.

"Who told Liz she had to stay home to take care of things?" Brian was indignant.

"It's just an excuse," Pirrone explained. "It was too early for her to get up. She thought it would be easier to take an afternoon flight tomor-row and meet us in L.A."

That was obviously a fabrication. Had he finally had her commit-ted? Or was she making last-minute arrangements to remedy a flaw in the plans that had caused Pirrone to be so agitated the night before?

We picked up our belongings and piled into the limousine. I said to myself, I hope Tom gets here before we finally sail, but that did seem unlikely.

◇Chapter Eleven

WE SAILED WITHOUT
Tom. I did not want to go without him, but Pirrone assured me he would
be meeting us in Los Angeles. Anyway, it was too late for me to turn
back. The start of our voyage was uneventful. The weather was good
and it was pleasant to be out on the ocean with its timeless peace. We
were making the knots that Pirrone had hoped we would.

By the end of the day we had reached the Channel Islands, a small
chain off the coast. From the windward side we approached El Fuego,
one of the group whose cliffs had been swept clean of vegetation by
roaring winds funneled through the channel. Along the water line the
ocean had carved many caves undercutting the perpendicular cliffs, as if
sea animals had notched out homes for themselves. As we cruised near
the shore we could hear sea lions barking. Many layers of water-depos-

ited salt caused the cave entrances to glow with rich colors, as if the water creatures had decorated them with magic paint brushes.

After motoring around the southern end, we anchored in a protected inlet where grassy, green hills rose gradually from the ocean. Brian told us that Fuego meant fire in Spanish and that the Spaniards had given this name to the island because in summer, from a distance, the golden, parched grass, undulated by the wind, gave the place an appearance of being on fire.

Looking at this island, untouched by man's machines, I could imagine how the mainland of California must have looked hundreds of years ago. A light breeze, redolent of sage and salt air, had begun to pick up. A few stars, like candle flames, lit their way into the darkening sky. The only sound was the slap, slap of ocean ripples as they softly hit the boat and splashed back into the sea.

Serena prepared a dinner of rock bass soup from some fish Brian had caught while trolling. By this time the sky was showered with sparks as though from a celestial forge, and the earth in its rotation seemed to be gently rocking our boat on the black water, as though it were softly pushing us in a patio swing on a cool summer evening.

After dinner Pirrone and Brian were examining some sea charts when Brian exclaimed, marking a spot on the map, "Look at this! We're in 'Ensenada de las Contrabandistas,' which translated means Smugglers Cove. What a coincidence! And I remember reading about the history of this very same place."

Pirrone was interested while Serena was completely unimpressed. Her passion for Pirrone had definitely diminished. She now appeared to be afraid of him. She shrank from him and kept moving to be out of his reach. Even hate seemed to smolder in her eyes, a strong emotion for languid Serena. Somehow I had the feeling she had not come along of her free will and really did not want to be involved in the project. But I could understand how she still intrigued Pirrone—that Near-Eastern quality of mystery that kept her always aloof and veiled from him, a quality that made it impossible for him to possess her no matter how hard he tried.

I turned my attention back to Brian's conversation. "Because the Mexican government placed one hundred percent duties on what was brought in, the ships would drop off the most valuable part of their cargos at El Fuego and then proceed to the custom house. After they declared their stuff, they would sail back here, pick up what they had left, and begin trading along the coast. El Fuego became known as Smuggler's Paradise."

"They did the smart thing," Pirrone remarked. "It wouldn't have been bad to command a Spanish smuggling galleon for a big profit."

"Did the Spanish have galleons then?" I inquired.

Brian, the authority on practically everything, said, "No, and Spaniards weren't even here at that time."

Ignoring that fact, we began to pretend we were on an old Spanish smuggling ship, addressing each other in the little Spanish we knew, except for Brian who spoke it well and kept correcting us. Pirrone's Spanish was quite funny with his accent and his use of mostly Italian words. We made up a sea chanty in Spanish and had a marvelous time singing it at the top of our voices.

Just before we went to bed, I got Erica on deck alone and told her what I had seen in the early morning before we left. (With the urgency of the information, I overcame my pique from Erica's gentle jabs at the state of my reason and not so gentle ones at my moral fiber.) She thought it plausible that Joe Viscantino was making a delivery to Pirrone and she found a basis for an explanation.

"A few days ago, I walked in on Liz just as she was popping a handful of pills into her mouth. I asked her if she were ill. 'Oh, no,' she said, 'just something for my nerves and a diet pill.' Can you imagine Liz on diet pills? She's only about two inches wide. If she had only said 'something for my nerves,' I would not have thought anything of it."

"Erica, if she thinks she needs diet pills, she must have that terrible problem some people have when no matter how thin they are, they think they're too heavy."

"No, that's not the answer. I really think she's been on something rather strong—you know, her lethargy, then suddenly that artificial kind of elation. I think it's possible Pirrone got her hooked so that he could further subjugate her. You know, drugs can induce states that are similar to psychotic ones. He could have decided to work on a case about her mental state by pointing out her incoherence and odd behavior at times, when in reality, it could have been due to her drugged condition. That's why I think you may very well have seen those underworld characters you thought you did and even that they tried to kill you because of your nosiness. They could have been Pirrone's 'connections,' and with this kind of connection, Pirrone could have gotten involved with smuggling drugs on the *Calypso*."

"We've got to search the boat," I said. "We must find where the drugs are hidden." At sea I felt I could continue looking for contraband safe from gangsters and killers.

Erica answered me, "You mean if there really are drugs on board. We're just guessing, you know."

"I'm sure of it now. There have been too many things that all add up."

"How do you plan to search the boat?" Erica asked.

"I've been thinking about that. Pirrone said he is not going to bother with night watches while we're anchored in this deserted place. After everyone is asleep, you and I can get up and search in the hold and while we're at it we ought to search for gold in the engine room where the mechanic found the gold bar."

"Okay," Erica said rather dubiously. "I hope we don't get caught."

"No chance," I said, with a newfound confidence. "Everyone will be asleep. We ought to wait long enough to be sure, though."

Lying on my bunk, trying to stay awake while waiting for the sounds of deep sleep coming from my bunk-mates in the cabin, the strange coincidence of the transformers blowing out twice in perfect weather kept going through my mind. Then it came to me. Someone had to have caused them to go out because, as I had realized earlier, they usually blow out during storms when water gets into them.

The first time was a test. That night when Pirrone had said to Tom forty-eight minutes was okay I had thought he was referring to a racing time but now I realized that was the time it took the electric company to fix it. I did know that in the city when a transformer went out the electric company got it repaired quickly because the electricity came back on in a short time. In that out-of-the-way place, even though this happened when there weren't all the emergencies of a storm, it would take much longer.

I decided that the second time was planned for the actual cover-up for moving a large bulky cargo. It all fell into place. They had to get the gold out of Dañada and even more importantly loaded in the hold of the boat without anyone being able to see them. I was sure I was right. I just could not get all the mechanics of it together exactly.

In the stillness of the engine room, the gentle slapping of the water against the boat, like love taps from an amorous whale, was the only sound, as we pierced the darkness with tiny stiletto beams from our pen-lights. Erica had thoughtfully brought a wrench from the garage, and as I held the light she started to unbolt the steel plates on the deck around the engines.

"This is terrific," she exclaimed, "these bolts are really loose. It's a cinch to get them out."

"Someone must have just taken them out," I said with enthusiasm because I thought we were onto something. "They probably wanted to leave the bolts loose so they could get them out in a hurry the next time when they took the gold out."

After unbolting several plates, we could reach in with our flashlights and illuminate the whole area underneath, but it was empty.

"That's weird," I said. "Could they have had it in here and decided to move it someplace else just before we sailed?"

"Possibly," Erica said, "or they may be planning to hide something here later, like something we might be picking up in Mexico."

"But Erica, they must have the gold on board someplace. I'm sure of it because of the transformer caper I told you about a few minutes ago. Let's go down and search the secret compartment. The gold and drugs may both be there."

"That's too scary to do at night."

"We certainly can't do it in the daytime," I replied. "Come on, let's do it right now while we can." Erica reluctantly agreed to go with me.

After we had been fruitlessly (or I might say goldlessly) opening boxes that just contained cartons of cigarettes, I moved one of the boxes and thought I glimpsed the corner of a wooden crate under the next layer of boxes. I had my hands on the box underneath the one I had just opened, planning to move it aside when a strong light beamed in through the open hatch. Terrified, I tried to close the top of the box of cigarette cartons, which was still open. My hands shook violently. My mind was racing out of control, like a car with a stuck throttle. How could I be so stupid as to get caught snooping again? Had I really seen the wooden crate? If I had, did it contain gold? This time I would be killed for sure. Tom wasn't there to protect me and Pirrone was utterly ruthless. He wouldn't want me around with my knowledge of his guilt. Yet, what harm could come to me on the open sea? To what authorities could I report my find? And his buddy, Tom, would be very upset if Pirrone did away with me. At least I thought he would be.

"What are you doing here?" Pirrone demanded.

"What are *you* doing here?" Erica demanded back, coolly throwing suspicion on him instead. Erica can be calm and casual, I thought; she does not know about my discovery—if in fact, I had actually made one.

Pirrone answered Erica, "I ran out of cigarettes."

"That's funny," I said, "so did we." Pirrone's sheepish answer had soothed me and I was able to reply in an off-hand manner.

But Pirrone also seemed very distraught. "Since you're up, you two can help me. We have to leave right now."

"For where?" Erica inquired. "It's the middle of the night."

"We're behind schedule. Tom just called on the ship-to-shore radio. He is going to meet us in Ensenada instead of Los Angeles. We'll have to travel by night, too, to get there in time."

"Tom," I screamed. "Is he all right? And why Ensenada instead of Los Angeles?"

"We have some business to take care of in Ensenada. Now let's get to work." I could tell Pirrone would never explain any further.

We helped Pirrone lift anchor and then I went to bed, alternately happy about seeing Tom and apprehensive about the change to Ensenada from Los Angeles. Would Liz be in Ensenada, too?

As I pondered this problem, Pirrone's voice floated into my ear in a soft whisper, "Alice, if you're not asleep, could you get up and help me for a minute? The sea is rather rough. I think we'd better secure the anchor; it could slide overboard."

I jumped up and followed him out. After we had finished, Pirrone put his arm around me. "Thanks, Alice, you're a sweet girl."

Looking into his eyes, the old thrill raced through me. He held me tighter and kissed me in the most sensual, urgent way I had ever been kissed. All the wild excitement that I had felt when I had first known him returned as he deftly caressed me—my breasts, my behind, there was hardly a place he missed, his caresses were everywhere. He even gently bit my toes and caressed my bare feet after he had nudged me down onto the deck. He quickly reached the most wonderful places, places that I was hardly aware of with Tom, turning me into one mad emotion of hungry desire.

I became not only pliant, but eagerly, actively, oh, so actively involved, right there on the deck under the cold scrutiny of those unbelievable, sea-oriented stars. My tongue sought his as my body strained to press against him. I was powerless to stop as my excitement built to an almost unbearable intensity. I was possessed by a lust I had never known. The waves lapping the boat seemed to wash over us and unite us in a flowing, watery oneness. My entire existence since I had first met Pirrone had been building toward this sweet consummation in becoming a part of him. A spasm of joy struck me as I floated outside myself to join those brilliant watching stars.

His sureness and familiarity with my body had been amazing. But in my emotional state, I did not realize that, of course, I was like all girls. To him any girl was every girl. His experience with women had been infinite.

"That's what you've always needed, Alice, a good fucking by a real man." What was he implying about Tom, his trusted friend and companion? Pirrone could be really cruel. Then he pulled on his pants and left me.

I had been used by Pirrone when no one else was available, Serena having so obviously spurned him. I felt dirty and cheap. I was ashamed and exhilarated; I was sick but I had never felt better. How faithless to good, sweet Tom. What a miserable thing I was. I had held Tom off interminably and finally when I did sleep with him I might as well have been asleep, I was so unawakened and unresponsive. Yet one touch from Pirrone and I turned into liquid fire, returning pressure for pressure with an abandon I did not know I possessed.

Pirrone had not been gentle like Tom, but his rough handling had aroused me erotically in a way Tom's tenderness never had. (Although when Tom had been rough with me that first night, all it had aroused in me was pain. After that he was always gentle.) In spite of the remorse in the tiny area of rationality left in my brain, I was filled with a deep peacefulness as I wandered off to bed to fall into a dreamless sleep.

The next day Brian, Erica, and I sat on the deck enjoying the sun and sea air. Once in awhile a coastwise freighter, reduced by distance to the size of a child's toy boat, would pass along the horizon, briefly breaking our sense of detachment. Like bathers' heads in a steam bath, land protuberances would occasionally break through the fog, which clung to the shore. Civilization's only sound was that of the boat's engines.

Despite the relaxed pleasure of sailing, I was filled with disquieting portents as I tried to blot out the night before with its wonder of womanhood fulfilled, then callously betrayed. My emotions were all mixed up. It was not so much that I hated myself as that I violently hated Pirrone. Why did he cause me to discover myself in such a loveless way? He made me no better than a whore. What kind of person was I, that I had not only enjoyed the encounter but also reveled in it? Or was it not my fault at all? Was Pirrone a devil who could take even the best and the purest (although I was hardly that) and turn them to his will? Was he sent here to test us all? If so, I had failed miserably. I was so undone, I was sure now that Pirrone was the incarnation of an evil spirit.

"I wonder what we are going to be doing five years from now—will we still be pawns pushed around in Pirrone's plans?" Brian was depressed and he was more or less confirming some of my terrible thoughts about Pirrone. Brian continued, "You know, these weren't the first plans he ever had. Before Peru, it was Guatemala."

"Why did you come, then?" I had thoughts of his being lured on, powerlessly, by this evil tester of human weaknesses.

"It seemed for real this time. He bought the boat…he had maps."

"You're talking as if we aren't going to South America," I said. Visions of this whole adventure being a mirage were taking shape, further disturbing my already unstable state.

Brian was morose, "I really believed in it. But now I don't know. When I talked to Pirrone a little while ago, he looked like he wanted to kill someone."

Erica said lightly, "Oh, he's threatened that many times before. The latest one is Rick Richards."

"Why?"

"He's Serena's new lover. You remember him—he was Julie's roommate for awhile at Dañada."

"So that's why she's so cold to Pirrone!" I exclaimed. "Do you think she was with Rick all those days she was supposedly looking for a job?"

"Probably," Erica replied. "Serena begged Pirrone to leave Rick alone. That's why she's here. Pirrone told her she would have to give Rick up and go to Peru if she wanted him to live. Pirrone's protecting her from further mistakes."

"Ha," I said sarcastically. "Pirrone the great protector."

Brian asked Erica, "Who told you this?"

"Serena," she replied.

Pirrone's solution to problems seemed to be murder. I felt he might carry it out should his threats fail. Or perhaps he did have supernatural powers and could throw a curse on someone, which would cause his downfall. I shivered as the sinister implications came over me. Perhaps I had saved my life by being so compliant the night before. I must get away from him, and the whole Dañada clique. But until I could I would have to be careful not to cross him and to do whatever he wanted.

I noticed again how Serena was trying to avoid any contact with Pirrone. She came from the pilothouse, followed by him. He tried to put his arm around her but she pushed it away as she recoiled from him, giving him an extremely hostile look. This was quite understandable from what Erica had said.

Later in the day I was lying on the bow, working on my tan. Serena came over and lay down beside me. She was very friendly, which she had never been before. She offered to rub suntan oil on my back. In a lowered voice, as she rubbed on the oil, she warned me to be careful. She said Pirrone used everyone for his own ends and that I would probably be next with Tom away. (She was a little late, I thought. He has already used me. But this was very alarming information.)

"Do you think he'll kill me?" I blurted out rather loudly. I was suddenly very scared. Serena knew him well; she must have felt he was capable of murder or of having one of his underworld contacts do it for him. I realized now that I should stop my sleuthing if I valued my life.

"Sh, sh, speak more quietly. There's no telling what he might do if you get in his way. He's completely unscrupulous."

"Oh, my God, I have felt for a long time that he was dangerous but I always felt that Tom would protect me. Now he isn't here. What's he doing in Ensenada? Do you know?"

"Don't count on Tom," Serena said. "He's there making arrangements for a shipment of heroin we're picking up in Ensenada and bringing back to the U.S."

I felt as if my entire insides had turned suddenly cold. I had a sick, empty feeling. Everything was falling apart for me. I had suspected Tom was involved in some highly illegal venture for some time. But actually knowing it was indescribably worse.

"This is terrible, Serena, we're all in danger—if not from Tom and Pirrone, then from the authorities."

She laughed when I mentioned authorities, as though they were as inconsequential as paper tigers. "The one to be afraid of, as I said, is Pirrone. He'll stop at nothing. We have to play it cool. You can't let him know that you know anything. Don't tell anyone else what I've told you—at least for now. I think I have a plan and I'm going to need your help."

"Do you think there is anything besides the cigarettes on the boat now?" If she knew about the heroin she must know about everything else. I continued, "Pirrone was always worried about Erica or me going out on the boat alone. Or anyone, for that matter, boarding it when he or Tom was not there."

"I don't know," she answered. "Other than the cigarettes, I really don't know." Of course, I thought, Pirrone would not let anyone know all the details. Only he, the mastermind, would know the whole scheme. The others would have been told only what they needed to know to do their part in the caper.

"I need to talk to you about this some more, but here comes Pirrone. Say something unimportant—thank me for putting the suntan oil on your back or it was interesting hearing about life in Australia."

"Serena," Pirrone cooed, "come here. I want to show you something." She suddenly became her old self, stretching her hand sinuously for him to help her up. She walked off with him, fitting her body to his as he put his arm around her.

It was clear that she was being compliant only because she planned to thwart him in some way later on when the time was right. I wondered if she suspected, as I did, that he was the devil's representative who had come back to take up where the original legendary Casa Dañada devil had left off?

I thought, I've certainly gotten myself in the soup. No one forced me to remain at Dañada. I was so attracted to the people and the lifestyle that in spite of knowing there was something very illegal about this venture (even though I had never been able to discover what it was), I never really wanted to leave. Now that I was in this mess, I had to do what I could to extricate myself.

I was even more scared of being caught by the Feds or the narcs or whoever went after drug smugglers than I was of Pirrone. He would not dare kill me. I couldn't imagine he would want to contend with a murder on his hands when he was trying to get away with smuggling drugs. Besides, murder was certainly a much more serious offense than being caught with drugs. As for myself, I did not want to spend even a day in prison.

To save myself from that, I decided that I had to be instrumental in helping the authorities; then I would be safe from prosecution. I would have to continue my search for other contraband as well as expose the heroin shipment when we docked in Los Angeles.

I was, of course, very frightened. I felt threatened by the underworld, the one of demons, for who knew what a devil alias Pirrone might do? But the underworld of gangsters was haunting me, too, for I was sure that the person who had tried to kill me by throwing me over the cliff had to have been a Mafia hit man, and all because I had nosed my way into their territory when I found the ammo dump (if indeed that actually happened). And then, also, Pirrone had to have some connection with the Mafia. What a terrible predicament! But I had no choice. My only way out was to continue my sleuthing.

That night I lay on my bunk unable to sleep. The thought of the heroin shipment we were about to pick up distressed me terribly. As I tried to concentrate on working out the details of my plan, all kinds of pieces of the puzzle jumbled in my mind. I thought about Pirrone's girls peddling heroin. Did some of them never come back because they had been caught? But then, wouldn't they have "squealed" on him? On the other hand, maybe he was able to extract extreme loyalty from them by bewitching them.

Then I thought about seeing Pirrone on several occasions examining the suitcases girls had brought back—for damage he had said, so that he could help them collect from the airlines. I almost shouted to myself as the real reason came to me. They must have brought back something hidden in the linings of the suitcases. It had to have been either heroin or cocaine, which he would then store in the little yellow Kodak film cans (that is until I got too nosey). I wondered where it was kept afterwards. How terribly sordid. I was completely shocked by my deduction. Hating myself for not having figured this out sooner, I got very hot and uncomfortable. I had to get up; I could no longer lie there perspiring in my sleeping bag.

I looked at the luminous dial on my travel clock. It was three-twenty. I decided to sneak down to the secret compartment again to try to find out what was in the wooden crate that I thought I had seen and to see if there were more crates like it. I remembered this was Brian's watch. Even if he should see me, I didn't think he would stop me because he wasn't involved judging from the way he had talked as we'd sat on the deck the previous morning.

When I had gotten the hatch cover open, I turned on my penlight and proceeded down cautiously. I went directly to the spot where I thought I had seen the corner of a crate. I quickly pushed the cases of cigarettes aside. There below me were the exact same kind of ammunition boxes I had seen in the cellar-arsenal in the derelict house—the round depressions with the thumbscrews, and the inscriptions: "30 Cal Ball Cartridges" and the muzzle velocity. As I frantically pushed aside cardboard cartons, I uncovered more ammunition boxes and then I came to the long rifle crates, also exactly like the ones I had seen before—guns for revolutionaries in South America, as I had once suspected. A boat was the only way to get something as heavy and bulky as munitions to Peru.

This confirmed everything. I seethed with rage. It meant that Pirrone was the one who had tried to have me killed. I started to shiver, and my whole body shook with convulsions. But had he only meant to scare me so much that I would stop snooping? That was still a frightening thought. If he had only intended to scare me, he had come awfully close to having me killed. Had he arranged to have Joe Viscantino do the scaring? The Mafia doesn't play games; they play for keeps. If he had given Joe the order to do something about my spying, then he should have known that death was planned for me. To someone like that murder was the only way.

I quickly pushed everything back in place. I had to get out of there immediately. If I were found in the hold again, the game would be up for sure. I could not let anyone know what I knew. I felt certain this knowledge would save me from prosecution when I exposed it to the authorities along with what I could tell them about the heroin. When I got back to my bunk, I could not stop shivering and shaking. I also could not sleep. As I lay there I thought of the transformer going out. The cover it provided was not for moving the gold but for transferring the guns from the old house to the boat.

The next morning when I went up on deck, Brian announced, "We are now in Mexican waters."

I looked out to sea but could see nothing different from the day before. "How can you tell?" I asked. "The ocean looks the same to me."

Brian laughed. "That's what navigating is for. Did you expect to see a sign saying, 'You are now entering Mexico,' just like a road sign outside a town?"

"Well," I said defensively, "it could at least look more tropical." I had expected some marked change. I had visualized a distillation of all the oceans I had ever seen in pictures—the Caribbean, the South Sea Islands, and all such places—pristine, emerald-green water through which one could see brilliantly colored fish swimming deep below. Not only was the water a disappointment but the land that could be seen didn't look lush and gorgeously verdant with tropical vegetation. It was in no way as interesting as the shoreline around El Mirador. We were close to land but I could see only low, barren, desert hills.

However, since the day before there had been a perceptible change in the weather. It was warmer. As I stood there basking in the sun, Serena walked up and took my arm, saying, "This sunshine is too good to be wasted. How about lying out on the stern deck with me and soaking some of it up?"

"Yeah," I said, "this is a heck of a lot better than foggy old Dañada. We really should take advantage of it." Serena had more than sunbathing on her mind. I was desperate to find out all she knew about what was going on.

Spreading coconut oil on her back, I asked, "What was that business about all you girls bringing back suitcases to Pirrone to examine for damage?" I wanted her to confirm what I had deduced.

Serena's explanation validated all my suspicions. They were all couriers bringing back cocaine from South America in the false-bottomed suitcases. (It seemed Pirrone was addicted to bottoms, false or not.)

Serena went on to tell exactly how they operated. "We traveled with different passports each time and new identities. But things have gotten a lot tighter. The customs officials are examining luggage much more closely, lately. We try to look different each time. But the last time I got the same customs inspector I had had only a few weeks back. He thought he had seen me before. I calmly assured him it was my first trip to South America, but I was plenty nervous inside. I decided I never wanted to go again. It's nerve-wracking enough to try to be casual when you know your suitcase is lined with coke. But when they start getting nosey, it's too much. It's a wonder none of us was ever caught. They are beginning to catch quite a few 'mules' these days, I gather."

"What about all those girls who were only at Dañada a night or two?" I asked, "What happened to them?" I had visions of them in prison, having been caught on their first trip.

"Oh, they didn't measure up or Pirrone felt he couldn't trust them. He picks his girls very carefully. They're young and extra good-looking." (I had noticed that.) "That kind can pull it off better than some dog of a woman. We all flirt with the inspectors who are, after all, only men."

"You talk as if there are a lot more than the regulars at Dañada."

"There are more. Pirrone has an apartment in San Francisco. Some stay there. The rest of us usually stop over there on our way back to Dañada." Is that where Tom and Pirrone went on all those business trips? I did not ask, because it was obvious, adding to my distress over this whole revelation.

"Does he have sex with all of them?" And does Tom, also, I wondered as I became more depressed and disillusioned.

Serena answered my question, "Naturally he does. You know how Pirrone is." She did not say anything about Tom. Was she trying to spare me?

"How does he get all these girls to do it?"

"It's simple for him. You must have noticed how women are attracted to him, even though you, yourself, have not been affected." (Little did she know about that.) "Once he has gone to bed with a girl, she'll do anything for him. I know," Serena continued. "I have been with him for more than a year. But it's all over. He has no power over me now. Anyway, Pirrone thinks things have gotten too hot to smuggle coke that way anymore. He's going to be able to bring an awful lot back on the boat."

I asked her if there had been cocaine in the little cartridge film cans. "Natch," she said. "They thought no one would ever open film cans and risk exposing film. That is, not until you got so inquisitive. They had to give it up then. Pirrone said you were a big pain because your curiosity kept fouling things up. He said, 'Some day that damn girl is going to get her nose broken if she doesn't keep it out of other people's business.'"

"What about Liz? Does she know all this?"

"Sure, she needs the coke. She's so insecure she got herself hooked on it, plus other things like amphetamines. No wonder. With looks like hers who wouldn't be insecure? I guess it was easy with all the stuff floating around. I think it's quite obvious she's on drugs. People who take coke are pencil thin because they never eat. Didn't you ever notice she eats practically nothing? She also shows other symptoms."

"Oh, poor Liz. I suspected it." I was sure it suited Pirrone just fine to keep her on the stuff. But I wondered if it were insecurity that caused her addiction. I think Serena just didn't like her so she would say bad things about her. I think it was more that she was sensitive and vulnerable but also that she had a certain amount of daring—always ready to try anything.

"Have you any idea where she is now?" I asked, "Will she be with Tom in Ensenada?"

"I don't really know." Serena seemed as uninterested in Liz as ever.

"Are we going to take the heroin to Los Angeles?" I asked with growing alarm.

"Close to L.A. We are going to meet a fishing yacht somewhere near Catalina Island," she said. The reality of everything was getting much worse. I was now very ill. I was in the middle of the worst crime I could possibly imagine. I sat up, shivering in the hot sun.

"What's the matter," Serena asked, "are you cold?"

"Freezing," I said as I trembled like a badly frightened dog. I was completely undone. Even though I had suspected a lot of what she told me, the effect of her revelations on me was devastating. Serena picked up my sailing jacket and put it over my shoulders.

Pirrone walked over to us. "You two girls are getting awfully cozy. What's going on?"

Serena laughed. "We're just two sun-worshippers enjoying the balmy air."

"It looks as though it's not warm enough for you, Alice. You look cold, and ill, too, I might add."

Trying to hide my true condition, I spoke up, "I think I'm coming down with a cold or the flu or something."

"That's too bad," Pirrone said, without a speck of sympathy. I thought, he probably hopes I'll get pneumonia and conveniently die or at least be out of commission for a while.

He walked away but not far enough for us to continue talking. "I'll ask Erica to help us with lunch since you don't feel so hot," Serena said. As I lay there shivering, I laughed slightly at the double meaning of her term "hot." I also realized that her intonation when she said this was meant to convey to me that it would be a good chance to talk when we were in the galley cooking. Pirrone would be topside navigating, well out of hearing range.

Serena got up and moved languorously over to Pirrone's side. He pulled her against him and bit her neck. He told her in a low, intimate voice to go below with him. She went along meekly, but she also slithered along in her usual sensual way, undulating her body in the sexiest movements. She was doing her bit to keep Pirrone from suspecting what she really felt or was planning.

The day of our first conversation, when Serena had said she needed to speak to me some more, she had said she thought she had a plan. I realized the reason she was suddenly so friendly was only because she needed me in some way to help her with the plan.

Erica came over from wherever she had been and lay down beside me. "What's going on between you and Serena? You've gotten awfully chummy."

"Pirrone said the same thing. But I can tell you the situation is really bad—worse than we suspected." Since Pirrone was busily enjoying Serena's charms at this moment, I felt secure in telling Erica what I had learned. She was as horrified as I was and very afraid. She was also remorseful for ever doubting me and my clues. I added, "Serena wants us to help her with lunch. She has something more to tell us."

"I hope she has figured out how to get out of this mess," Erica said in a desperately wishful way. "I don't think I've ever been this scared in my life. Somehow the whole idea of guns and drugs seemed remote till now—sort of like a scary story that gives one goosebumps but isn't really threatening. Now our lives are in real danger."

"I don't think yours is," I said. "You have never been caught trying to uncover the plot, but I have. I'm the one in danger."

"Oh, Alice, I really truly apologize for thinking you were imagining things. You were so right. I never quite believed it, even after you saw Pirrone making the transaction the morning we sailed."

"It's getting near lunchtime," I said. "I don't feel much like cooking or eating for that matter but I think we had better go down to the galley and hear what Serena has to say."

Looking pink and bleary-eyed, Serena came into the galley after we had been there a few minutes. "What are we going to do now, Serena?" I asked.

"Fix peanut butter and jelly sandwiches—lots of them. The sea air makes guys very hungry."

"That's not what I mean," I remonstrated.

"I know. We can't do anything here," she said in a very low voice. "We'll have to wait for an opportunity to slip off the boat. I am hoping we can get away in Ensenada."

A streak of silliness came over me, as it often did when I was nervous or frightened. I started to giggle. "Liz the whiz, will she whiz all the way down to old Mexico to join the fun?" Serena ignored my outburst, but Erica asked where Liz was. Serena shrugged her shoulders, saying she didn't know.

Regaining my composure, I said with impending apprehension, "We should be in Ensenada soon. How do we get off the boat?"

"Be ready to grab whatever opening you can to slip away," Serena said. "We'll have to be on our own and figure it out for ourselves."

I thought about Tom. I never wanted to see him again. I was glad I would be getting off the boat just as he was boarding. He had gotten me involved in this with his lies and evasiveness. He was as much a criminal as Pirrone. Then I wondered about Brian. I asked if he were involved.

"I certainly don't think so," Erica said. "He's never done anything even slightly suspicious." I thought she must be right, especially in view of the conversation on the deck after the plans had been changed to go to Ensenada first instead of Los Angeles.

"You can handle whatever you want to do about Brian," Serena said to Erica.

"What do we do when we get off the boat?" I asked.

"We can all meet at Hussong's. That's a busy place, full of U.S. tourists. From there we can figure out a way to get back across the border—maybe with tourists going back," Serena explained.

"There is something that has always bothered me," I said, "Is Pirrone mixed up with Joe Viscantino?"

Serena was surprised. "How did you know about him?" she asked.

"I just guessed," I answered. He had seemed so obvious to me from the very beginning. Perhaps I was more clever than I had thought.

Serena finally answered my question about Joe rather reluctantly. "I don't know, it's possible. Pirrone has underworld connections, you know. In fact I think someone has been after both Tom and Pirrone, trying to scare them by almost killing them because Pirrone has been cutting into their cocaine business." So that explained the gunshots that they had dismissed as nonsense and the attempts on Pirrone's life that he had admitted but brushed off, not wanting to talk about them, pretending they were not too serious. It also could have been the reason for the car that had tried to run Tom off the road the night we had gone to Nepenthe.

We had been making the sandwiches as we talked and had a huge stack of them finished when Brian called down, "All hands on deck."

"We must be in Ensenada," I yelled excitedly as we rushed up, leaving the sandwiches behind. I looked out toward shore, but I could see no town or buildings—just low hills covered with scrubby patches of brush.

There was a cove with still water and a small, sandy beach. I gazed down at the green-blue water. It had somehow a much warmer look than the ocean near El Mirador. As I stared at the endless blueness below us, the constant back-and-forth movement of the water and the hotness of the sun lulled me into a pleasant spell of tropical lassitude. But my moment of languor quickly passed, for everyone was yelling. Then, as I raised my head, I saw the cause of all the excitement—a decrepit little fishing boat was chugging toward us through the ground swells.

"We're taking on fresh supplies," Pirrone announced. "I'll need all your help to get everything on board."

"You don't mean here?" Serena asked in surprise. "We're going to get them when we dock in Ensenada, aren't we?"

"We're not going there, it would waste too much time. This way we won't have to dock. Tom has arranged to have the stuff brought out to us in a boat. There it is coming toward us."

◇Chapter Twelve

SERENA'S PLANS FOR our escape washed away on the shore swells that the little fishing boat was plowing through. It was now perfectly clear what was happening. The heroin would be stashed in with the provisions, hidden in some clever way. This isolated little fishing cove, far from any probing authorities, was a much safer place to take on contraband than a harbor like Ensenada. But how could we slip off on a tiny boat meeting us out in the ocean? And if we could, where would we be? A remote fishing hamlet where no one spoke English. How fiendishly ingenious Pirrone was. I felt as if I had sunk to the bottom of the sea, weighted down by huge chunks of lead. It was hopeless. I was stuck on this boat in the middle of a horrendous crime, with no possible way to save myself.

The fishing boat pulled alongside and one of the two Mexican

219

fishermen threw up a line, which Pirrone secured. The men passed up dozens of crates of tropical fruit, also boxes of big red tomatoes, their stems with serrated, furry, dark green leaves still attached, tortillas, steaks, huge spiny California lobsters, and whole fish with their pop eyes and rigid fins. It was like market day in a Mexican village square.

I asked about Tom. Pirrone answered, "He couldn't make it down here. We'll have to head back to L.A. to pick him up."

"But," I said, "I thought he arranged for all these supplies. How could he have done that if he is still in Los Angeles?"

"Oh, he arranged it by phone when he found he couldn't make it to Ensenada."

"Where is Liz?" I asked.

"She's with Tom," Pirrone replied. I persisted, trying to find out more with further queries. "You're really a bore with all your dumb questions about details." I thought, not too irrelevantly, the devil is in the details and Pirrone is that devil. But I should have known he would not tell me anything.

Pirrone took charge of all the boxes and had Brian carry them down to the galley. After that, he told Brian, Erica, and me to stay on deck and enjoy the view of the coastline. He said he would put the food away with Serena's help. Of course, he did not want us helping him. He had to extract the hidden packages of heroin. Erica and I exchanged helpless looks. In what unfindable place would he hide them?

On deck, Erica and I engaged in a despondent conversation. Erica had already filled Brian in briefly about what was happening. Now she went on to finish the details of the caper, that is, as much of it as she knew. Brian was bitter. He had not suspected anything until we had to travel by night to get to Ensenada in a hurry. Even then he did not suspect things were much more sinister than the cigarette smuggling. He had certainly been naïve not to suspect anything amiss before.

"We've all been had," Brian said with acrimony. "He has only used us as a crew for his foul mission."

"That's Pirrone's only purpose with anyone—to use them," Erica said with an I've-always-known-it air. "He is the worst conniver and criminal I've ever met."

Brain raised his eyebrows. "What other criminals have you known, my pet?" he asked.

"I didn't mean it that way. You know what I meant, silly. Brian, you sounded serious. What's the matter with you?" Erica seemed perturbed.

"It's the whole sordid mess we're in. I guess I've lost my perspective. Probably in six months we'll all laugh about it."

Lost his perspective! I was the one who had done that. I could hardly think past this very minute. I was absorbed in my speculations as to where Pirrone and Serena could be hiding the heroin. I was so engrossed with this that I was not joining the conversation with Brian and Erica. I had to get Serena alone to find out where they had put it. I decided I would offer my help with dinner. (Serena had been the cook ever since we sailed; she had an undeniable talent for it, which I did not.)

When I next saw Serena it was close to dinnertime. "I'll help you with the cooking tonight, if you'd like," I said rather too eagerly.

Pirrone overheard me. "Now Alice, cooking is definitely not your forte—I've tasted your sandwiches. Anyone who makes such dry, inedible ones should not attempt anything further. I have a better idea; you can help Brian straighten out these lines."

Rats, I thought, Pirrone knows exactly why I suggested helping Serena. How would I be able to ask Serena in private where they had cached the junk? Maybe I could corner her in the head.

Erica spoke up, "Serena, I'll help you." She had picked up my lead. She would follow through for me and find out everything from Serena.

Pirrone butted in, "Serena doesn't need your help, Erica. She's quite capable of doing everything by herself. You can be more useful on deck." Pirrone was not going to let any of us question Serena. She must be, I thought the possessor of some very important information—namely the whereabouts of the heroin.

After we had eaten dinner, I did manage to get into the head with Serena. "Where did you put it?" I whispered.

"Frankly, I have no idea. We stowed everything in the lockers except for the fruit, and I never saw anything suspicious—no plastic bags or anything. Pirrone never said a word about it and, of course, I dared not ask or he would have been suspicious. All I can figure out is that he's planning to go back to the galley when no one is there, it must be hidden in something. I would guess he's planning to sneak the stuff up to his cabin and hide it there."

That night I embarked on another perilous search. The night before when I was snooping around, I had not known how great the danger was, but now it was totally evident. Nevertheless, I had to find the heroin and throw it overboard. I knew about the crime and human misery that was caused by heroin. I guess I felt the least I could do, as penance for getting into this seamy situation would be to get rid of the drugs, thus saving hundreds of people from wrecking their lives, and of course, save my own. My life would be ruined if I got caught by the authorities in the company of all that heroin.

I tried to think of where Pirrone could have hidden it. Then there was the question of how much of it there was. I thought that it didn't take much to cost a lot. I wondered if an amount that he could hide in a fairly small area would be worth enough to make the side trip worthwhile? As Serena had said, the most likely place was in his stateroom, where he could guard it while he slept. Could the shipment be small enough to fit under his mattress? He probably could layer a lot under there. Or maybe he could have stashed it in places all over his cabin? I would just have to look everywhere—but how?

I thought of my encounter with Pirrone the night he found out we had to change our first port of call. I would snoop around while he was sleeping. If he woke up, I would use the cover-up of coming there to seduce him. I'd had sex with him once for no reason. I would do it again, if I had to. After all, I had sunk to being a whore; I might as well use my new profession for a good reason.

After everyone was asleep, I started on another of my nightly prowls. I silently slid into Pirrone's stateroom as I opened the door. I had become adept at being cat-like with all the practice I was getting sneaking around at night. Pirrone's cabin also served as an office in the daytime (or whatever one calls an office on a boat), and I was very familiar with the layout, having been there a number of times. The bed folded into a couch. There was a built-in desk and a chair but not much else except for a small locker for clothes.

I felt my way around in the dark, knowing quite clearly the location of everything. Pirrone was sleeping very soundly, especially for someone who should have been filled with guilt. However, I was sure he had no conscience and that the evil he was doing did not trouble him in the least. I poked my hand into every opening and slid it along every surface, searching for the heroin packed in what I did not know. Serena had said plastic and I had read that smugglers packed it in black plastic bags. So I kept feeling for plastic packages under and in everything.

I had worked my way around to the desk and was pulling out the top drawer when it made a scraping sound. Pirrone coughed. I froze. I was scared but I had rehearsed my excuse for being there so many times in my mind that I was sure I could pull it off perfectly. Pirrone moved to another position in bed but his breathing was loud and regular, as a person's is when sleeping soundly. I sifted through the assorted things common to desks: paper clips, pencils, pens, rubber bands, opened envelopes with the contents stuffed back in, but no plastic bags. I opened another desk drawer, which stuck and made a popping noise when I pulled it out. I was sure that would awaken Pirrone, but he merely turned on his back and started snoring loudly. The drawer was empty.

I opened another drawer that slid easily, but it, too, was empty. I was planning to move over to the locker but first I felt carefully on the top of the desk. At the very back I found a small, tightly rolled plastic package that felt as if it had powder in it when I squeezed it. I picked it up, but in doing so, I knocked an ashtray on the floor. Pirrone woke up, saw me and yelled sleepily and angrily, "What the devil are you doing here?" (Funny he should say "devil," I nervously thought.)

"I just thought you might like to love me, again," I stammered.

"Hell, no. I don't want to fuck you. Get out of here. I choose who and when I want to fuck. No damn girl is going to tell me when to get it up."

I had never heard such crude language in my life. He is showing his true criminal colors, I thought. He was vulgar as well as lewd. I hated him enough in that moment to kill him. I got out of there as fast as I could and ran to my bunk. I lay there for a while. Then in the darkness I felt a shadow over my face. I opened my eyes and saw hands with the fingers curving in as if to strangle me, coming toward my throat. I may have only dreamed it in one of those light dreams that are the transition between being awake and asleep. I screamed and the hands instantly disappeared into the shadows. It did seem that I must have dreamed it. But I wasn't sure. I thought the whole thing was some indication of my mental state. I had awakened Erica with my scream. I told her I was just having a nightmare. I thought of the children's riddle: why did the boy take oats to bed with him? Answer: to feed his night *mares*. I was revert-ing back to being a little child. How safe and secure that would be.

After that I was wide awake. I was so jumpy and apprehensive, sleep was impossible. I was much too restless to lie in my bunk; I got up to start my search again. Even with all my anxiety—or because of it—I was drawn irresistibly to finding the heroin and disposing of it. The secret compartment might have the answer to the whereabouts of the heroin. Pirrone could have hidden it there—except for the sample I think I found on the desk. Of course, it also might be under his mattress or in his locker. I quietly went down into the hold, carrying my little flashlight.

I had been so driven to continue my search, I had not thought about someone else going down there. I was startled out of my concen-tration by the light from another flashlight. I snapped mine off and tried to slink away but there was no place in which to hide. The flashlight came relentlessly toward me with Pirrone's walk behind it. My blood seemed to coagulate into thick glue, clogging my veins. I felt a terrible pain in my ribs as my heart went into a mad rampage at a zillion beats a minute. The glue in my veins spread to my muscles and I became para-lyzed. I realized that I had gone to the hold too soon. I had arrived at the hiding place before the heroin had been hidden. Pirrone had come to stash the contraband at the same time I had come to look for it.

The flashlight was now inches away from my face. Then I heard a whoosh as the flashlight rose up in the air and came down with a crack-ing sound on my head. I don't remember feeling any pain. The next thing I remember was Erica shaking me. Once again, my head was terri-bly sore and ached. I reached my hand up and felt a large bump that was very painful to touch. The air seemed stuffy and still. I was still in the secret compartment.

Erica was talking to me. She said, "I woke up and you weren't in your bunk. I thought it was awfully early for you to be up. It's just barely getting light. I looked all over for you. I finally realized you had to be here because there was no place left to look. What in the world hap-pened to you?"

After I told her, we both decided my life was very much in danger. I had said to her that I thought Pirrone had not expected to find me there and the only expedient thing he could do at the moment was to knock me out with the only weapon at hand—his flashlight (which I knew was a big heavy one). I also said I thought maybe he would come back before anyone else was up and dump me overboard. Then he could get the idea going among everyone that I must have gotten up in the night and fallen overboard.

"I'll tell Brian," Erica said. "He's the only one here who could protect you; certainly Serena and I couldn't. He'll have to stay close to you like a personal bodyguard. You'll have to move your sleeping bag between us. Maybe we can crowd into a corner together."

"God, I hope I'm not here tonight. I'm definitely planning to jump ship in Los Angeles."

"But what if we don't dock there?" Erica asked.

"We have to—to pick up Tom and Liz."

"What if they're on the yacht meeting us in the Catalina channel? Then we would have no reason to dock in L.A." Straight-thinking Erica was as logical as ever.

"I never thought about that. What in hell am I going to do? I'm trapped here with a killer. Sooner or later Pirrone is going to kill me." A frenzy of fear and confusion, swirling together, assaulted me, making me feel as if some terrible demon had attacked me and was about to consume me. My mind tore at possible ways to save myself. I would have to somehow prevent the *Calypso* from meeting the other boat. Then Pirrone would have to make a landfall in Los Angeles.

The terror-prompted adrenalin pouring through me fired my brain into high gear. My mind raced like a computer, sorting through possible ways to stop the *Calypso* from making her fateful rendezvous. I would throw the anchor overboard with Brian's help, to slow the boat down. But that would be noticed right away and the anchor would be hauled up pronto. I would fool with the engines to foul them up. But I knew nothing about ship's engines—I had only a superficial knowledge of car motors. Besides I might do something to make them explode and blow up not only the boat but also myself and everyone else. However, more probably, any dumb thing I did could be quickly repaired. And as with the anchor, Pirrone would know who the perpetrator had been, only increasing my jeopardy. I would be wiped out by him for sure.

Then amidst all the welter of non-workable ideas, the perfect solution came to me. I had heard that even a small piece of metal placed near a compass could throw it off. A compass being magnetic, I knew the metal would have to be iron or steel. My older brother had told me once about a ship a friend of his, who was in the Coast Guard, was on. Somehow, somebody had left a knife next to the compass, which no one had noticed. They cruised for a whole day with it that way and had gotten completely lost until it was discovered. The compass on the *Calypso* was in a kind of dashboard. The compass itself was surrounded by drip slots that were fairly narrow and I imagined fairly deep. I could slip something in there while no one was looking. With the compass being inaccurate, Pirrone would set the wrong course to make connections with the other boat. All I needed was to sneak a small knife out of the galley. I wondered if a bobby pin would do it—or a whole handful of bobby pins—if I couldn't get hold of a knife.

Elated about my new plan, I could now relax. It was still early in the morning. I would go back to bed. I dragged my sleeping bag over to where Brian and Erica slept. Erica was already in bed asleep but Brian was not there. I guessed it was still his watch. How lucky it was that Erica had found me before Pirrone's watch, when I am sure he would have disposed of me overboard. I fell asleep happy because I would now be able to thwart Pirrone. But I wasn't thinking about what Pirrone might do to me before I could get my plan into effect. I might not live to achieve that moment. I had put the thought out of my mind, as well as what he would do once he discovered who the perpetrator was.

Later that morning, after I got up, I could see that Pirrone was furious but perplexed about what to do about me. I was sure then that by escaping from the hold, I had ruined his plan to throw me overboard. He had probably thought he could do it on his watch. He never let me out of his sight; even when I went to the head, he managed to be just behind me, waiting right outside the door. No matter where I went he seemed to be always nearby, but thankfully Brian was also hovering around me. Pirrone kept tracking me with his murderous eyes.

Of course, searching for heroin was now completely impossible. Nor could I get near the compass. We plowed on relentlessly through the rough water, as I grew more uneasy, wondering how I would ever be able to follow through with my plan. If I could only get out from under Pirrone's surveillance, it would take me just a second to slip a knife down into one of the compass slots. But first I had to try to get a knife.

Serena said she really needed my help fixing lunch, as she was beat. Pirrone assented, but also said he would go with us, because he was very hungry and needed to nibble on something while waiting for lunch. I sliced him some cheese with a small paring knife, which I then managed to slip into my pocket without his noticing. While he was nibbling on the cheese and Serena and I were putting together the sandwiches (I was really only laying out the bread slices and washing the lettuce, since no one was impressed with my sandwich-making capabilities), I kept trying to figure out when and how I was going to accomplish the deed. I didn't want to be either too early or too late with my manipulation. If I were too early, Pirrone might notice that the landmarks weren't right, since we could see land most of the time. If I were too late, then we might make the rendezvous in the channel before I could have effectively changed the course.

I needed to have some idea how close we were, but it would be too obvious if I asked. During lunch, Erica unknowingly came to my aid. "Pirrone," she asked, "exactly where are we now? Are we near L.A. yet? How will Tom and Liz know where we're docking so they can be there to meet us?"

Pirrone seemed disturbed by her second question. I scrutinized him to see his reaction, since his answer to the first question was vital to me. He responded, "We're off Balboa, if you know where that is." It didn't matter whether Erica knew, I did; and that was all I needed to know. We were approaching the channel and I needed somehow to get to the compass.

Erica answered Pirrone. "Balboa is south of L.A. and not far from it so we should be there soon. But where do you plan to land? The place is so big there must be a number of places you could dock in the harbor. Or are they meeting us at Marina del Rey instead of San Pedro?"

He just said, "You're right," then proceeded to give orders. "As soon as we have finished eating, I want you girls to do the dishes and then clean up the galley. It's filthy and needs a thorough scrubbing, top to bottom." I thought, he wants to keep us down here while he meets the other boat. But first things first. I had to get to the compass before we finished eating.

I immediately excused myself to go to the head, hoping Pirrone would not think of a pretext to follow. The minute I was out of the galley I sprinted to the pilothouse and dropped the knife into a slot. Since no one was there, the autopilot was on. I had just barely gotten back on deck when Pirrone appeared.

He said, "I thought you had to go to the head."

Thinking quickly, I replied, "I really needed to get up on deck. I was feeling rather queasy. I thought I might upchuck. I didn't want to spoil anyone's appetite by saying that. I think I'll just stay here, till I feel better."

With that, Brian appeared, saying that he had finished lunch and needed some air. Was I ever thankful to see him. I had been petrified that Pirrone might take advantage of our being there alone and quickly dispose of me overboard.

I had worried about Pirrone recognizing landmarks (though I don't think he would have, because he was not familiar with the area) but luckily fog had crept in along the horizon and the coastline had disappeared in the mist.

Brian said he thought we must be very close to the Catalina channel. Pirrone said, "You're right," as he took charge of the navigation. I started to go below. He said, "Just a minute, where are you going?"

I said, "I'm going below to help the others."

"I thought you said you didn't feel too good."

"Oh, I'm much better now. I'll be all right."

Then he said he needed me to hold the charts for him. I said, "Why don't you have Serena do it? Serena is a better cook than I, but I'm a whiz at clean-up."

"Serena is good at cleaning. Anyway, I'm the captain and I'm ordering you to stay here." (I had never seen Serena, in her capacity as the maid, ever doing any cleaning! But, of course, he didn't want me out of his sight.)

After an hour or so, with my help holding the chart for him, he evidently decided we had arrived at the right spot, because he slowed down the engines to bare power and headed into the sea to keep us even. I had no understanding of cruising charts but I prayed that we were in the wrong spot. If placing the knife beside the compass had really thrown it off, then we had to be in the wrong place.

Pirrone checked his watch and rechecked our position and seemed satisfied that everything was okay.

Then he told me to come with him. "We're going to the galley to check on the cleaning to see if those girls are doing a good job."

I said, "I'm starting to feel woozy again. I think I'll stay up here."

"No," he said, "you're coming with me. That's an order. I'm appointing you my aide and you have to stay with me at all times." We went out on deck and he asked Brian to come, too. Little did he know that Brian would have come anyway; I might be Pirrone's personal aide now, but Brian was my personal bodyguard. Thus there was a guard guarding an aide but the last thing the aide wanted to do was any aiding.

When we got down to the galley Pirrone announced that we were meeting another boat to give them some pineapples and mangoes, which were needed for a market in Avalon, the town on Catalina Island. So that's where the heroin is hidden, I said to myself, marveling at his cleverness. He had left the heroin right where it was when we took the supplies on board. The crates of fruit had not been put away as the other food had but were piled in a corner of the galley. Probably the top boxes were clean in case we decided to partake of the luscious things.

But as for his story about meeting a boat with produce for a market, I wondered whom he thought he was fooling. Since Serena knew about the heroin transfer in the channel, he had to have been her informant although she never said. Did he think she had kept the secret to herself? He must have suspected I knew about it because of all my prying, and if I knew then I would have told Erica and Brian…or maybe he thought all I knew about was the guns. Perhaps he wasn't smart enough to figure out that we all knew that heroin had been hidden someplace in the provisions from Mexico. Or maybe he was. Maybe he thought now that the stuff was being moved to another boat, he wouldn't have to worry about it anymore.

Pirrone ordered Brian to start carrying the crates up on deck. Pirrone followed him up the companionway and stood at the top watching Brian but also keeping an eye on us. He was keeping track of the crates in both places. Soon all the boxes were on deck. Pirrone looked at his watch, the stainless steel chronometer that he always wore. I thought he seemed somewhat anxious. I guessed my plan was really working, because there were no boats in sight. However, I couldn't be sure—the boat could be late and if it were a really fast speedboat it would only show up shortly before it reached us, and I was sure it would have to be such a boat.

Pirrone kept checking his watch as the minutes slid into a half-hour and finally an hour. He got more and more perturbed. He was jumpy and nasty. I wondered if he had a gun on him. I became quite alarmed as I began to think, when he finally realizes the boat is not going to show up he might become angry enough to shoot someone—me, for example— and if he ever discovers that I was the one who put the knife in the compass slot then it is curtains for me for sure.

After two hours he was in a really horrid mood. He had been trying to reach someone on the ship-to-shore but without success. Brian spoke up, "You know, Pirrone, there should be lots of boats in the channel, coming and going. I haven't seen one since we got here."

This really scared me. I had not told Brian—or anyone else—what I had done to the compass, but now that something was wrong with our course setting, Pirrone would probably realize what I had done. But Pirrone seemed unconcerned. It dawned on me that of course he hadn't really planned to meet the other boat in the busy channel because it would have been too obvious. He had just said that to throw us off. So even though we had to be in the wrong place, it didn't worry him because he didn't expect to see anyone else there except his connection when it showed up.

It's possible that we weren't even off Balboa when he had said we were. We could have been much further south. What was lucky for me was that the land mass was still shrouded in fog, and even luckier that the fog bank remained along the horizon. If either of them had been able to identify any landmarks at this time they would probably have realized right away that something was wrong. On a clear day Catalina can be seen from the beach areas around Los Angeles and so I would imagine out on the water one would be able to see not only the coast but the island as well.

Finally as the sun got lower in the sky, Pirrone decided we had better head for Catalina and a calm mooring out of the rough water and wait for morning to find out what had happened to the other boat.

They both seemed to be worried, as it took a lot longer than they had thought it would to get near the island. When we finally sighted land, Brian realized something was wrong because it did not seem to be Catalina.

Brian asked, "Did you recheck our position? That is definitely not Catalina." Even I could tell that, having been to Catalina several times. What we were approaching looked like a barren table mountain, not at all like hilly Catalina.

Pirrone answered him, "I didn't need to; I was sure it was right."

"Obviously, it wasn't," Brian observed.

They pored over the charts and after awhile Brian said, "You know what I think, your navigation stinks. This has got to be San Clemente Island."

Pirrone said, "Man, that's impossible."

"No, I'm positive. And that's a really bad mistake you've made, because San Clemente is a U.S. Navy island and it's strictly off-limits. No one is allowed to moor there."

Pirrone refused to believe he could have been wrong. Undoubtedly he had never been to Catalina and had no plans to go there because it was not on our itinerary. I guessed he never bothered to find out what the island looked like. He rechecked his navigation. He was sure it was right. He said, "It's impossible. San Clemente is way out beyond Catalina and further south."

Brian said, "We could have drifted a lot while we were waiting for the boat to meet us."

Pirrone said that was ridiculous, there had to be some other reason for the error in our position. He was getting more furious all the time as he checked everything again and again. He finally decided there was something wrong with the compass. He examined it carefully. He then slipped it out and discovered the paring knife. He was livid with rage. "Who the hell put this knife in here?"

No one, of course answered his question. But under the circumstances he quickly took control of the situation with first things first and corrected our position, setting a course for Catalina. I was cowering, wondering how I would get out of this one when he figured out I had to have been the perpetrator.

Brian seemed to have sensed, probably by looking at me, that I had dropped the knife in on purpose and that it was no accident. I guess he felt he had better come to my rescue and cover for me right away before things got out of hand and before an explanation was too late. He spoke up, "You know, Pirrone, I might have been the one, and if I was, I can't tell you how awful I feel about it. I was peeling an apple while I was on the wheel. I must have set the knife down to eat the apple. Now that I think about it I don't remember taking the knife back to the galley. It probably slipped into one of those slots."

Pirrone seemed to accept his explanation even though he was as mad at him as a March hare. (I have no idea how mad a March hare got or even why a March hare got mad, but people seem to think that's being very mad and crazy, too. Pirrone was terribly, terribly mad, insanely furious.) I didn't know how I would ever be able to thank Brian enough for saving me and for being so tuned in as to realize what I had done.

I think the reason Pirrone never questioned that Brian's carelessness was the cause of the erring compass was that it never entered his head that someone he considered a dumb girl would have ever thought of such a smart maneuver. I guess he had never heard that it is impossible to make anything foolproof because fools are so ingenious.

◇Chapter Thirteen

THE ATMOSPHERE ON board the boat was gloomy and fearful. Pirrone was still livid over Brian's negligence with the knife. It was a miracle that he had accepted Brian's version of how it happened to be next to the compass. If he had suspected I had put it there deliberately he would have been so enraged he would have done away with me in a hurry. As it was, Pirrone was taking his anger out on everyone. We were all shaking in our tennis shoes, afraid of what turn his insane madness would take. I was the most fearful of all because before this setback for Pirrone my life was already in danger from him.

Our course was set for Avalon as the nearest place for a safe anchorage. It had gotten quite dark as we sped along, cutting through the inky-black, choppy water under the vast, endless expanse of night sky, gleaming with a zillion silver stars. But the beauty was lost on this terror-stricken crew—or at least it was on me as I wondered how I would ever get the mission I had created for myself accomplished and how I would ever get away with it without losing my life in the process. So far I had been able to prevent the drug transaction, but when we got to Avalon Pirrone would probably be able to straighten things out and get the heroin to his connection. What could I do to stop it?

After awhile everyone was very hungry even though we were tense and upset, so Serena fixed dinner. Usually during a meal there was a lot of gay banter but that night not even a ripple of enthusiasm appeared. Pirrone was not talking; whatever his plans were, he was not confiding in anyone. His silence extended to the rest of us, who were like robots programmed to eat. No one, of course, wanted to venture any opinions on any aspect of what was happening or going to happen.

Serena had hurriedly thrown together some sandwiches, using the pickled octopus we had brought aboard when we were provisioning the *Calypso*. How she ever thought of that seems inconceivable, unless it was symbolic of the entanglement we were in, for who knew what terrible fate awaited us, trapped here with Pirrone in his murderous rage.

We were barely able to eat the sandwiches, even as hungry as we were. They tasted like plastic and might as well have been made out of old tires. As we sat munching on the dreadful fare, no one was up to making caustic aspersions about how awful it was, each lost in unhappy thoughts, wondering what was going to happen next.

Out of the sullen silence, Brian's voice, never quiet for long, boomed out, "Serena, I know what's wrong, you used the tentacles and threw out the octopus!"

We all burst out into hysterical laughter, tears rolling down our faces. This served to break the tension and for the rest of the evening we made stupid, ridiculous remarks about the tentacles, breaking out into sporadic laughter.

Even though our nervous gaiety had temporarily allayed our fears, it was getting scarier and scarier being there with a crazed captain. No one wanted to go to Peru now. Serena never had; she was only there to save her lover, Rick. Erica and I didn't want to go on a dope and gun smuggling ship, and neither did Brian now that he knew the inside story—namely what was inside the boat. We were running low on diesel and would have to refuel in Avalon. Could we all jump ship there? How could I dispose of the heroin before Pirrone could get it delivered? Maybe I could get up in the night and shove the crates that were sitting on the deck overboard. But I was too tired to think about it.

Late that night we tied up to a mooring in Avalon Harbor. Before going below Erica accosted Pirrone and asked him when and where we were going to pick up Tom and Liz. "Since you're so smart, you figure it out," he answered her.

Everyone was exhausted from the emotional trauma of the last few hours, so we went to bed without any further talk. I fell quickly asleep; my thoughts about pushing the heroin-laden boxes overboard evaporated in a numb, troubled slumber from which I did not awaken until morning.

Early the next day Tom reached Pirrone on the ship-to-shore. Whatever the message was, Pirrone wasn't telling us. Brian located a place to refuel and we headed for it. Serena, Erica, and I huddled out of Pirrone's sight and decided we would have to get off the boat there; we had no idea how we would do it, or how we would be able to leave the island without getting caught by Pirrone's henchmen, but the most important thing was to make our getaway.

On the way to the fuel dock, Pirrone announced that we were heading back to El Mirador to pick up Tom and Liz. Collectively we chorused, "What are they doing there?" Pirrone chose not to answer us. He just started giving orders. He told the three of us to go below and tidy up everything and for Brian to stay on deck to help with the refueling. We hesitated, trying to linger on deck as we gazed out at the shore and the little town clustered on the lowland at the center of the bay with its houses and hotels marching up the hillside.

Erica spoke up, "We'll go down after you refuel. We'd like to see what Avalon is like from the water. And maybe we could go ashore for a short while and look around."

Pirrone said, "We have no time for fooling around. We need to get back as fast as we can." With that he turned and walked very quickly to the pilothouse.

Erica called after him, "What's the hurry?" But her question was lost in the wind.

We stood there on deck not making a move. I was flabbergasted that Liz was still at Dañada and that Tom had returned there. What were they doing there? What was going on? I conveyed my concerns to the others, who were asking themselves the same questions. We couldn't figure out any reason for it. But obviously something had gone wrong with the plans, more than just my ruining the rendezvous with the boat in the channel or wherever it was supposed to have taken place. Did Tom even know? Had Pirrone told him about that fiasco?

As we were pondering all this, Pirrone yelled at us that we had not followed his order to go below and clean up everything. We said we didn't want to.

He said in a truly scary way, "You're not following my orders. That's mutiny and the penalty is death. If you don't do as I say you'll find out."

Needless to say, we scurried down the companionway in a flash. All our lives were in danger from this madman. There was no thought now of trying to jump ship in Avalon.

After the refueling was over and we had pulled away from the fuel dock, Pirrone ordered me up on deck because he wanted his aide nearby. I wondered why? He ordered Brian to take the crates of pineapples and mangoes below so they wouldn't spoil out in the sun. Did he really still think that none of us knew there was heroin hidden in the crates? Did he really think we believed his cockamamie story about the market in Avalon? And we were in Avalon Bay. Wouldn't he know that we would have thought it strange not to have them taken off the boat and delivered to the market?

He must have read my mind, because as I was standing near him, he said to me, "We didn't have time to arrange to have the fruit taken off the boat for the market, so I guess everyone can feast on it when we get back to Dañada." I supposed he planned to extract the heroin before then. I would just somehow have to beat him to it. But how?

Just to make conversation and keep things from being any more awkward than they were, I pointed out the Wrigley Mansion overlooking Avalon from on high. I lightly said, "That beautiful place was built with chewing gum."

Being Italian, I guess he had never heard of Wrigley, for he said, "You're even sillier than I thought." Just as well, I said to myself, that he discounts my intelligence. That will make my drug busting easier. This way he won't think I'm capable of figuring out what's going on.

Leaving the bay, we passed the lovely round tower-like building on Casino Point. As we rounded the breakwater at the end of the point a burst of sadness and nostalgia caught me for a moment as I wished I could have revisited this charming island with its lovely serpentine, palm-lined walk around the harbor. I had had fun there a few times in the past, seeing all the fascinating fish on rides on the glass-bottom boat, among other pleasures.

As we reached the open water and headed north, leaving the oak-studded hills of Catalina behind, I tried to fathom what would happen next on our trip back to Dañada with our satanic captain. It was a beautiful day with none of the previous day's land-based fog and haze. We cruised up the coast, which was in sharp relief. The air was crisp and refreshing, which helped to invigorate me, giving me new resolve as my mind busily plotted what my next moves would be. Did I dare risk a try at disposing of the heroin? Pirrone still did not seem to suspect that we had any idea of what was in the containers of fruit, because he wasn't keeping an eye on them.

I somehow had to talk with Erica if I were ever going to accomplish my risky venture. As lunchtime approached, I announced to Pirrone that I was going down to the galley to help make sandwiches, as Serena did not feel too well. Amazingly, he didn't object. Possibly it was because he seemed to be very preoccupied. I thought it was incredible that he didn't suspect that we knew there was heroin hidden in the crates of pineapples and mangoes, especially since he knew how snoopy I was.

Down in the galley, standing next to the tropical fruit, which was back in its original corner, I asked Serena, "Why do you suppose Pirrone is not worried about the stash in these crates? He must know that we know."

"I don't know why," she said in a tone of voice meaning there would be no reason for him to think that we knew.

"But didn't he tell you," I asked, "that we were picking up heroin in Ensenada and delivering it in the Catalina channel?"

"No, he doesn't know that I found out about it."

"Well, then, how did you find out?"

"I can't tell you that. I swore I would never say who gave me the info." Was it Joe Viscantino? Earlier she did admit she knew him and that Pirrone took orders from him but kept trying to switch the roles so that he, Pirrone, would be in control. It was Joe who was trying to keep Pirrone in line with the attempted murders.

"Pirrone'll probably make me stay with him after lunch. While you're doing the dishes, do you think you and Erica could look for it in the fruit? We've got to find it and get it out."

"Why?" Serena asked. "You'd only bring Pirrone's wrath down on you." She seemed uninterested in doing away with the heroin. I would have to get Erica to help me. Serena continued, "Pirrone has to bring it back to Joe Viscantino. If he doesn't have it Joe will kill him this time for sure. Joe's already paid him for it."

"So what?" I said. "Pirrone would deserve it. You don't care if he dies, do you, Serena?"

"No, not really, but Joe could go after me, too, because I have been so close to Pirrone."

"By the by," I asked, "how do you know all this?"

"I have my ways of finding out things. I can tell you that Joe is furious that Pirrone missed the meeting in the channel."

With that Serena said that Erica and I should finish the lunch; she wasn't feeling too well and was going to lie down. In fact she said she didn't feel like eating either. Maybe Pirrone knew she was ill and that was why he did not object to my helping.

Well, that did give me the opportunity to talk to Erica alone. I asked her, "Do you think you can try to find the stuff if I have to go with Pirrone?"

"Sure," she said breezily, as if it were no big deal. I marveled that she could be so calm in the face of danger.

After lunch, as I thought he might, Pirrone ordered me to come with him. I guess he wanted to watch me if I weren't otherwise occupied such as helping in the galley. I am sure he did not want me prying into things such as the boxes of fruit. It was not fun being with him. He was in a foul mood. However, I followed all his orders so as not to incur his anger.

As we approached the Santa Barbara Channel, Brian pointed out Point Mugu, a naval facility, on the mainland on our starboard and Anacapa Island on our port side. I was learning nautical terms; I now knew port from starboard. Pirrone was heading up the coast in the most direct way he could without going too far out to sea. I was sure that since he was in such a hurry to get back to El Mirador, there would be no thought of finding a safe anchorage for the night. We would just race through the night with the engines at full throttle. During that time would be my last chance to get rid of the heroin. I wondered if Pirrone would take all the night watches, thus thwarting me completely.

I also wondered how Erica was doing with her search through the crates? I finally decided I couldn't stand the suspense any longer. I would just have to find out if she had been able to find it. If she hadn't, I could give her some clues such as looking in between the wooden boards in the bottom. Pirrone was so inclined to secret bottoms maybe the ones in the containers were false, too. I said I had to go to the head. He said, "Okay, but make it quick. I want you back here in a hurry."

I went to the galley instead. Erica was systematically going through the crates, keeping everything looking as though it had not been disturbed. She had discovered that, as I had suspected, there were double bottoms in them and they were lined with plastic bags filled with powder.

She said, "For God's sake don't let Pirrone come down here. Do anything you can to keep him up on deck. But where will I put them?"

I thought quickly, deciding that under our mattresses was the safest place. She said, "You know this is all going to take time. Do you think you could get Brian down here to help?"

"No," I said, "Pirrone might really wonder what was going on, if Brian were down here. I'll just have to keep Pirrone occupied somehow. However, he doesn't have any interest in cooking or kitchens so I don't think you have to worry about his coming here."

With that I rushed back up on deck, trying to think up ways to keep Pirrone busy there. Could I spot imaginary submerged reefs that only I could see so that he would have to stay up there to be careful so as to miss them? What about whales? Could I spot water spouts and announce them just too late for him to see but keep him watching for more of them? I didn't think he would want to run into a whale and be capsized. Would such a thing even be possible? Wouldn't the whale veer away? Wasn't this boat too big and low to be capsized? What about my seeing a huge rogue wave way out that could swamp us if it were nearer and announce it too late for anyone to have seen it? Would I have him so worried he would have to stay up on deck in case another one came and was closer to us? Just what could I dream up? My creativity was running dry. None of these ideas seemed very plausible.

As we sailed on relentlessly, I was getting more desperate for a gimmick to keep Pirrone topside. Then I lucked out, for sailboats started appearing, lots of sailboats. We seemed to have gotten into the middle of a race. After skirting this group, we ran into another covey of sails, this time on larger boats. It was indeed my lucky day. I said to myself there must be a big regatta going on. Pirrone could hardly afford to go below now.

Fortunately it took us a long time to get past the myriad of sailboats. I hoped Erica had completed her relocation of the heroin by the time we finally passed a very large boat. That had to be the committee boat, which would have been anchored near the start and the finish of the races. We would probably not encounter any more sailboats unless one had strayed severely off course, which was unlikely. I thought I had better get down to see if Erica had finished.

"I need to go to the head," I said to Pirrone.

"What, again? What's the matter with you?"

"I don't feel too well. I must be getting what Serena has."

"Well, you can lie down here," he answered me.

"No, you don't understand. I think I have busy bowels."

"You know what I think: you have diarrhea of the mouth."

"Well if you're going to keep me here, you may be sorry." I could be as crude as he if I had to.

He finally let me go. Erica had just barely finished. She said, "I am really beat. I hurried as fast as I could. There was an awful lot of the stuff. That was a horrible job—prying up the bottoms, getting everything out, then putting the bottoms back in and the fruit in the crates so that it looks as though nothing has been touched."

"You did a super job. Nobody could ever tell. You're the best accomplice a spy ever had."

"You mean a drug buster. We really have taken on the job of federal agents busting vice lords. This is pretty heavy and dangerous. Are you sure we want to get rid of the heroin? I was getting more and more scared while I was moving the plastic bags. What is going to happen to us when Pirrone discovers it's missing? You know if he doesn't kill us, Joe Viscantino will."

"Don't worry," I said bravely and foolishly, "they'll never find out it's gone until we're long gone."

"How do you expect to accomplish that?"

"I don't know, but I'll figure something out. We can't stop now." With that I thought I had better get up on deck, although with everything back in order in the galley I didn't have that worry anymore. But I had to keep Pirrone placated and unsuspicious. I would just have to be very relaxed and compliant. I would follow his every command quickly and to the letter.

But getting rid of the stuff was a problem that I was going to have to solve soon. I would have to work out a plan by nighttime. I had to be ready to seize whatever opportunity arose. The solution—getting the bags out from under Erica's, Brian's and my mattresses and tossing them overboard—would be very difficult if not impossible if Pirrone weren't safely and soundly asleep. Ah, I thought, there's my answer. I have to give him a Mickey Finn. But I had no idea how one concocted such a thing. If I could figure that out I would have to be able to slip it into his Pernod. Then if he decided to take all the night watches, which I felt he might, he would be knocked out and wouldn't be able to do it.

I had to somehow consult with Erica about my plan. She could ask Brian, who seemed to know everything, how to make a knock-out drink. It began to get quite dark. Serena was still out of commission, which gave me a chance to help with dinner. I said to Pirrone, "I think everyone must be getting hungry; I know I am. Maybe I should help Erica with fixing something to eat."

He said, "All right, you can help, but please don't do any of the cooking. I don't want to be poisoned."

"Pirrone, how can you say such a thing?" I said sweetly. "Why in the world would I want to do anything like that?"

He answered me rather nastily, "You know what I meant. Your cooking is so bad that it is poisonous."

Ha, little did he know. I wasn't exactly going to try poisoning him, although I would have liked to. But I was going to try to put him out of the way for the night.

Erica and I went down to the galley together. When we got there I told her my idea. She said, "I don't need to ask Brian. I think I have what you need. I have some phenobarbital."

"What in the world is that?" I asked.

"It's a barbiturate, a sedative."

"Why do you have that?" I was thankful she had it, but why would she?

"Sometimes I have a problem sleeping," she answered. It was hard to imagine that anyone as calm as Erica had insomnia, but at this moment I was awfully glad she did.

"How will we crush the tablets and what will they taste like in a drink?"

"Well, they're not tablets, they're capsules, which we could open and put in a drink. But I have no idea how it tastes. I would imagine it is fairly tasteless. Anyway, alcohol increases its sedative effect, which is what we want. One is really not supposed to drink alcohol when taking it because of that. Maybe it really will be a knockout drink."

We proceeded with trying to make dinner, finally opening a bunch of cans of chili and serving it with crackers. First, however, we announced cocktail hour and laid out sliced cheese and lots of peanuts. We poured the Pernod ahead of time, carefully putting all of Erica's capsules in a drink for Pirrone. She did not have a lot of them. We hoped it would be enough to knock him out cold. She had been able to cue Brian in on what we were doing when he had come down to get a sweater to put under his windbreaker.

Pirrone said, "What's this? This is like some kind of business banquet with pre-poured drinks." We each quickly grabbed ours, hoping we had gotten the right ones, leaving only the one with the capsules for Pirrone. He said, "Well, I don't feel like a drink." I could see my plan floating away on the tide.

Brian, trying to be funny, said, "You don't look like one, either."

Pirrone said, "You must be really tired. Can't you thing of something better than that old, tired line?"

"I think we're all exhausted. It's been a long day. We all need this drink."

"Well, you can all relax and I'll relieve you of any watches. I will see us through the night. I need to be alert. So you all can have my drink."

"Don't be a party pooper. I don't want to be the only man drinking. You should just have this short one," Brian said.

"I can decide for myself whether I want a drink or not."

With that Erica said, "Finish your drink, everyone, I think we better eat; the chili is hot." Pirrone's drink was left sitting where we had put it.

Pirrone said sarcastically, "You two are very inventive cooks. It must have taken a lot of preparation and cooking ability to come up with this dinner. Where did you buy this canned junk?" He turned to Serena, who had joined us, and said, "I am glad you're feeling better. Another meal like this and we'll all be starving or poisoned."

He got up and left the table. He said he needed something to get rid of the bad taste as he went to the counter and picked up the glass of Pernod that he had not drunk before and drained it in one long swallow.

Erica and I almost heaved a sigh of relief as we glanced at each other. I was glad the dinner had turned out so badly. I wondered how long it would be before Pirrone would fall on his face, totally passed out. I hoped there had been enough phenobarbital to do the job.

Pirrone went up on deck, while we finished dinner and cleaned up. Serena, of course, knew nothing about what we had done, nor did we want her to, so we could not discuss it. But I was terribly anxious to know if it were going to work or if Pirrone had such an iron constitution that it would not even faze him. And then, of course, he might really be the devil incarnate or at least his messenger come back to take care of his unfinished business at Dañada. If so, he might be immune to any drugs.

I wanted to ask Brian if he knew how long it would take or what would happen, since he was an authority on practically everything, but Serena lingered on. Soon Brian said he was going up to help Pirrone. I was glad to hear that. If the sleeping capsules had already taken effect our boat was without a helmsman.

Serena complained that she was beginning to feel much worse and that she had better go lie down again. When she left I said to Erica, "You know, we completely forgot about Serena. She doesn't want the stuff dumped overboard. We should have saved some capsules for her."

"How can she stop us?"

"Well, she could. She's completely amoral. If she could get a gun—and there are plenty on board and she probably knows about those in the hold—she wouldn't mind killing us to save her own skin. You heard her say she thinks her life will be threatened if Pirrone doesn't deliver the dope to Joe Viscantino. So she'll probably do anything to stop us.

She only cares about herself. She wouldn't even have bothered with us on the boat if she hadn't thought she needed our help with her plan to disembark in Ensenada."

Logical Erica replied, "When it comes down to it, it's only natural. Everyone has a survival instinct to protect one's own life. Where would the race be without it?"

"Well, civilized, moral people do think of others," I answered.

"Are we thinking of her if we throw it all in the ocean?"

"Forget her," I said. "She would never think of us or all the people whose lives could be ruined by the heroin."

Erica said, "None of this solves what we are going to do."

"Did Pirrone drink all the Pernod? Of course he did. Too bad, we could have given her what was left," I said.

"You're not tackling the problem."

"Give me time, I'll think of something. What could we do to make her really sick?" I asked.

"Give her some more dinner."

"I guess we must be tired," I said. "We're getting really silly."

Brian popped his head down the companionway. "Where's Serena?"

"She didn't feel well. She went to lie down again."

"Pirrone is lying in the pilot house, stiffer than the proverbial board, and I'm not feeling so hot myself. What did you give me?"

"Maybe you're catching what Serena has. We only wish she would get a lot sicker."

"Well, I think you've got your wish. I saw her heaving up her dinner over the side of the boat."

"Good," we both chorused.

"What's the matter with you heartless witches?" he asked as he turned and left.

"I think he meant 'bitches' but was too nice to say it," Erica said.

"What's nice about calling us witches? I think that's disparaging, too," I replied. I continued, "Let's take Serena some aspirin. No, that won't do anything. What could we give her that would really put her out?"

"God, I don't know. Let's look through the first aid kit."

We sorted through it. Erica said, "What do you know! Here's some Valium."

"What's that?" I asked.

"It's a tranquilizer. How do you think we can get her to take it?"

"Erica, you go see her and tell her how bad you feel that she's sick and that you're sorry you don't have any chicken soup but that you just happen to have something even better that will really settle her stomach."

Erica soon came back. "I don't think we have a thing to worry about. She's really gotten sick. She told me to go away and leave her alone. But she did take the Valium. I think she was ready to do anything to feel better."

Erica and I went to our bunks, knowing that the rest of our crew was taken care of. It would be a cinch getting rid of the dope now. We decided we should start right away because we had to get it accomplished before our two erstwhile friends felt better or woke up.

Brian came down to check on us, but he was going to have to run the boat so he couldn't help us. However, he said he wished there were some port we could head into for the night. As it turned out we weren't far from Morro Bay. We decided to wait for an anchored boat and calmer water before making our sorties to pitch the drugs, even though we were taking a chance that either of our two incommunicado crew members might come to.

As soon as we were safely moored, we started carrying those miserable plastic bags up to the deck. We felt if we just threw them in the water the way they were that they might float or be recoverable in some way. They might also leave a telltale trail, which could seal our fate. Thus, we decided we had to empty each one separately into the sea, which would be laborious and would leave us with the problem of what to do with the empty bags. We decided to just put them back under our mattresses, thinking no one would ever look there.

On one of our sorties, as we were emptying the bags, I said to Erica, "Do you think the fish here will get hooked on heroin?"

She retorted, "That's better than getting hooked on a hook."

"Touché," I responded. We were getting silly again.

Erica said, "Seriously, how would we have ever been able to do this if Pirrone weren't out cold?"

At that moment I heard someone come up behind us. I instantly became immobilized with fear. It flashed in my mind that being caught *in flagrante* so to speak would be our total finish. Erica also seemed rooted to the spot. A disheveled Serena came up between us and leaned over the rail as she went into a violent spasm.

When she recovered, she asked, "Are you two sick, too?" She looked out as she was saying this. "What is all that white stuff on the water? That's strange looking foam." Neither of us seemed to be able to speak; even cool Erica who always had so much aplomb said nothing. Then Serena started to retch again. After that she just left, clutching herself, sicker than ever. We let out a whoop; we were so relieved that the encounter had gone no further.

We went on with our work, carrying up more armloads of black bags. As we were pouring the latest batch out of their containers, the wind came up and started to blow it back at us. I yelled at Erica, "Don't breathe. We better go below and let it blow away." She was way ahead of me. She had pulled the bandanna she was wearing over her face and was heading back down, also yelling at me.

"How do you feel?" I asked her. "Do you think you got any of it?"

"I feel great. Maybe that's because I did. But I got the scarf over my face immediately. What about you?"

"I'm feeling rather euphoric. But that may be only because we are finally getting this thing done and with so little trouble. Next time we better stay away from the windward side." We went back up with another load, this time being careful to check the wind and go on the lee side of the boat.

Brian came to help us now that he had everything secured for the night and had shut down the engines. We asked how Pirrone was doing. "Don't worry, he's out cold. I don't think we'll hear from him soon."

But that proved to be premature. Back on deck as we were pouring more junk overboard we heard Pirrone stumble out of the pilothouse and yell, "What's going on?" in a slurred voice. We were paralyzed. He lurched toward us. He kept stumbling on as my heart went into gyrations and cold fear gripped me like a huge magnet, holding me transfixed. I prayed that he was in such a dazed condition he wouldn't realize what we had been doing. As we three stood there not making a move, he stopped and swayed unsteadily.

Then the ultimate terror happened: he pulled out a gun and started waving it as he yelled crazily, "Stop whatever you're doing." With that he pitched forward on the deck and the gun went off, the bullet tearing into the deck in front of us.

We hadn't made a move. I was completely numb and I guess Erica and Brian were, too. As we remained motionless, Serena rushed up on deck, shouting, "I heard gunfire. What happened?"

Brian spoke up, "Pirrone must have what you have. He's so sick that after throwing up over the side, he just collapsed here on the deck. His gun went off accidentally when he went down."

Serena started to go over to Pirrone, but then she had to make a detour to the railing. Brian calmly walked up behind her and tripped her. She fell to the deck with a loud thud. Then he bent down as if to help her but instead shook her and at the same time banged her head on the deck. That seemed to put her away, too.

We continued our work without further incident but we had grave fears about how we were going to explain away everything when our corpses came to in the morning. Brian tried to dispose of one of them by carrying her back to her bed. We hoped that the Valium had made her so groggy she wouldn't remember how she fell or how Brian finished her off, also that she wasn't badly damaged with scrapes and bruises for which we would have to think up a reason.

The next morning Brian, Erica, and I were having breakfast when Pirrone staggered down. He looked awful and his mood was way beyond rotten. He glowered at Brian as he accused him in a very menacing way, "What did I ever do to you? Why did you slug me? You're going to pay for this." He grabbed Brian by the throat, then seemed uncertain of his accusation. Letting go of Brian he asked, "You did slug me didn't you? It couldn't have been one of these puny girls. Or just what did happen? And why are we anchored here? Who the hell thought of that?"

Brian spoke up. "Calm down, Pirrone. When I came up to the pilot-house after dinner, you were lying there with that big gash you have on your forehead. You must have slipped and hit your head when the boat was rolling and pitching so badly. It knocked me off my feet when I was starting to come up to the deck, I am just lucky I didn't hit anything."

I said to myself, bravo, Brian. You're getting to be as good a liar as I am.

Pirrone said in an irritated, snarly way, "You don't expect me to believe that. I don't remember the boat pitching. By the way, what was in that drink? I feel awful. I doubt that horrible dinner alone could have poisoned me this much."

Brian said, "I know what you mean; I feel lousy, too. I thought there was something wrong with the Pernod. I threw out what was left so no one would drink any more of it. Besides, I think I am getting whatever Serena has. That's probably your problem, as well."

"You knew we had to get right back to Dañada. Why did you put in here?"

Brian answered, "I told you I felt awful. I knew I wouldn't be able to run the boat all night by myself. We were just lucky there was a harbor here."

"Well, get off your ass, we're leaving this minute."

Brian followed Pirrone up to the deck. I said to Erica, "You have done a good job at training Brian in the art of deceit. I am sure it didn't come naturally to him."

She said, "It's amazing what one will do to save one's skin when it comes right down to it. He had to think quickly with an answer because we all know now that Pirrone will use a gun if he's crossed."

"What are we going to tell Serena when she shows up?" I was running low on invention.

Erica said, "I think we'll be able to handle it. We're getting lots of practice in making up lies. Maybe we can use Brian's story about the ship tossing and pitching. We'll just have to wait and see what she says. We could say that Brian saved her from going overboard when she slipped and fell. Let's hope she was too out of it to know what really happened."

As it turned out, we didn't need to worry. She never did get up that morning. She just moaned and groaned a few times.

Pirrone got us underway very fast. The water was calm, almost like a lake. By that afternoon we were back in Fanshell Bay. It was such an incredibly clear day that each tile on the roofs of Dañada way above us seemed to stand out in distinct outline.

As we motored through the passage that had been blasted in the reef of rocks just outside the bay I felt a sharp jolt. Brian evidently felt it also, because he said to Pirrone, "I think you cut it a little too close."

Pirrone, who never admitted to having made a mistake, said in a surly way, "Bullshit, we came in just right."

As we pulled into the pier, I heard a car horn honking. "It's Tom,"

Pirrone said as if he had been expecting him. He must have reached him on the ship-to-shore. Then he said, "I want you all to bring up that beautiful fruit. We've got to get it to the house and into the fridge before it rots. Tom can help."

Tom came aboard. He was distraught. He didn't even speak to me. (It was just as well, because I didn't want to speak to him.) He handed a newspaper to Pirrone. After reading it with rising anger—as if his anger could rise any higher than it already was—he threw the paper at Erica and me. A large headline proclaimed: "HEIRESS MISSING." The story went on to say, "Detectives reported today that Mrs. Elizabeth Rivelli, 27, of El Mirador, has been missing from her mountaintop estate for three days. Mrs. Rivelli, member of a prominent ranching family, has been gone since the departure of her husband on a yachting excursion. It is yet to be determined whether her disappearance has anything to do with the band of communists, smugglers, and gangsters who were reported to have been associated with the Rivellis."

"Shit!" exclaimed Pirrone. "Who wrote this trash?"

"Don't worry too much, nobody believes the stuff they write in the papers." Tom seemed to be doing his bit to bring Pirrone down out of his rage.

"Where is Liz and who decided she's missing anyway?" Pirrone asked Tom.

"That friend of Liz—what's her name? Lucia something—came over to see her. When I said she wasn't here, she asked me where she was. I said I didn't know. She told the police that Liz had disappeared and she suspected foul play."

"That bitch," Pirrone muttered. "She's a meddling busy-body. By the way why isn't Liz here? Where is she?"

"I really don't know…in answer to both your questions."

Pirrone, Brian, and Tom loaded the fruit crates into the limousine. As a consequence there wasn't room for everybody. Pirrone told me to come with Tom and him. I really didn't want to, but I still feared him so I did as he said.

We headed toward Dañada at full speed. Tom raced up the driveway practically ripping out the cypress along the side. As we got out of the car we could hear camera shutters clicking and could see photographers popping out from behind trees and buildings.

A reporter accosted Pirrone, saying, "Mr. Rivelli, can you give us a statement about your wife?"

"She went to the City for a couple of days to do some shopping. Excuse me, I have important matters to take care of." With that Pirrone led the way down the portico to the library, quickly closing the door behind us.

Pirrone was mirthless. "Where did all those reporters come from? They're like vultures! Tom, we've got to find Liz. I'm going to call a private detective. Do you have any ideas?"

"No," Tom answered, "she took all her clothes and jewelry and didn't leave a note."

Pirrone looked at the papers and letters on the desk, and then made a couple of phone calls. He turned to Tom and said, "Liz took all the money out of our bank account. Here's an overdue light bill. They are shutting it off. She didn't even leave any money to pay it." He seemed very, very angry as he turned and left the library.

Tom said to me, "That was inexcusable of Liz. It wasn't right for her to go without leaving any money for Pirrone to live on."

I said disgustedly, "How can you say that? He's lived off her too long already. And he doesn't really care that she's gone. All he's upset over is that the money's gone."

"That's not true. He really cares about her and he has to put up with a lot because she's crazy."

There was absolutely no point in talking to Tom. He only thought what Pirrone thought. Little Sir Echo, I said to myself, he's been totally indoctrinated by Pirrone.

Tom said, "Well, I guess I better go down to the boat and bring the rest back."

"I guess so. They're stuck there with no way to get back."

I was anxious for them to come because I was beginning to worry about what was going to happen when it was discovered that the heroin was missing. I needed to work out some plan with them to take care of that huge, scary problem.

As I pondered this problem, I walked into the living room, which felt as if it had lain empty through many musty years. Chill, damp air pervaded it, making me pull my jacket tighter around me. Only a few days ago it had echoed with noisy chaos as a cheery fire gave a warming glow. Now an ominous feeling came over me as I looked around. Things were out of place—not in the room's normal disarray but rather as though there had been a struggle and things had been hastily shoved back to cover it up.

Did Pirrone have an accomplice who had gotten rid of Liz while he was at sea, thus providing him with a watertight alibi? Was Pirrone under a master spirit even more sinister than he? Pirrone was probably only a lowly lieutenant in the hierarchy of evil; perhaps the great power had taken over and Pirrone was no longer in control. I had always been fascinated by an Edgar Allan Poe sort of literary evil, but this grim reality was too close, too real. It had been fun while it remained an idea, an unproved, merely hinted-at aura surrounding Dañada. But "murder most foul" was another matter.

I had been sitting there in the icy cold for some time, filled with fearful apprehensions of a gruesome vision of Liz's fate, when Brian and Erica walked in. I said, "Welcome home, but I have unhappy news. I think someone did away with Liz. Or do you suppose the evil spirit induced her to do away with herself? I think the day she talked about dancing to her death on the edge of the cliff, some supernatural, satanic force was working on her."

Erica shook her head. "Alice, you do get more loony all the time. You really do believe in the occult. You know that's superstitious and stupid, don't you? I would laugh at you and say you shouldn't try to be funny but I can tell you are very serious. You're trying to find an explanation for something you can't accept and can't understand. There is probably a simple and logical answer. First of all, her clothes would be here if she had done something like that."

"Well, if not that, then something else could have happened." I was not going to be talked out of my dire forebodings by sensible Erica. "An underworld character could have tried to make a delivery of drugs Pirrone had ordered that she refused to pay for. Because of that they could have kidnapped her with the intent to do away with her. I've seen it happen in the movies. Look at this room. It looks different, doesn't it? As though there was a struggle."

Erica asked, "So what does that prove?"

"Nothing, I guess."

"Alice, you have a wild imagination. She wouldn't have taken all the money out of the bank if that had happened. I think she took the opportunity to escape. Just a few days before we left she told me she would have left Pirrone long ago, but she was sure he'd kill her if she did. I imagine when we were leaving she saw her chance to get far away and go into hiding. Brian told me that when Liz gave him the letter for us just before we left, she told him that she and Pirrone had had an argument about her not going with us and that he tried to force her to come but since we had to leave right away he gave up on it. That's probably what happened. They had a big struggle here in the living room."

I hoped she was right and that Liz was alive someplace. Good, sweet people are often victims while the vicious and evil prosper. Thus, I still worried that she had met an untimely end. There was something in the room that was giving me an eerie feeling.

"But now," I said, "we have to figure out how to cover up for the missing heroin so that we won't meet the same fate that I still fear happened to Liz. And we need to find out what really did happen to her or where she is if she's all right. Things are getting pretty overwhelming again. By the way, where is Serena? Did she ever recover and did she figure out what happened to her?"

"Well," Erica said, "we don't need to worry about her anymore. Rick seemed to know we were back. He came to the boat and gathered up Serena and her belongings. She still seemed ill but she said to me that they were getting out of there immediately, before Pirrone got back, and that they were going to put a lot of distance between them and Dañada in a hurry."

Pirrone appeared at the living room entrance. He immediately started giving us orders as though we were still on the boat. "I want you all to get the fruit out of the limousine, put it away, and then stack the crates in the garage so I can take them to the dump." Of course, he would be taking them straight to Joe Viscantino. We would somehow have to prevent that.

At that moment Tom walked in. He pulled some soggy cigarette packages out of his pocket. "Something's wrong with the boat, Pirrone. The hold is full of water. The bilge pumps don't seem to be working. Thousands of dollars worth of cigarettes are already drowned. The boat is sinking fast. We've got to get back there right away."

I wondered about all those guns and ammo in all that water. Would they be ruined, too? I had always heard that one must keep those things from getting wet—keep your powder dry was the way the saying went.

Pirrone must have been thinking the same thing, because after looking at the wet packages, he said, "Shit, we might as well help it sink and finish the job. I can at least collect the insurance." He probably thought it was a good chance to get rid of the illegal cache of ruined arms since the trip to South America had already sunk.

We heard a helicopter circling the house overhead. Pirrone remarked bitterly, "Newsmen! They're trying to make a big deal out of nothing. They'll blow this up into some kind of conspiracy against the government."

Then Pirrone said, "Before Tom and I go down to the boat, we had better get that fruit out of the limo. All of you guys bring it in, pronto." Still fearful of him, we quickly followed his order and carried the crates into the kitchen.

After they left, Erica said that while they were waiting on the pier for Tom to come back and pick them up, they were talking to a reporter who was hanging around hoping to get a story. The reporter told them that Federal Agents (narcs, as she called them) had been to Dañada and searched it, looking for narcotics, but when they found nothing they left. How lucky that they got there too early. But it didn't really matter because we had disposed of everything, as far as we knew. But they certainly would have given Tom and Pirrone the jitters and they probably would have questioned us all, which would have been uncomfortable.

We tried for quite awhile to brainstorm how we were going to handle the missing heroin, but no one came up with a good solution. We decided the reason was that we were not only tired but also hungry. We went to the kitchen to scavenge up something to eat. Brian said, "If you can't find anything else we can feast on fruit." Which is what we finally ate, and it was a good thing we did because it was getting beyond ripe.

We went outside to enjoy the sunset. Tom and Pirrone were back. Pirrone seemed despondent over the loss of the boat but he brightened as he said, "I hope I have enough insurance." Then his mood changed as he decided he didn't have. He probably was thinking of all the arms that were lost. Of course, they weren't insured. Gloomily he kicked at gravel in the courtyard, hardly his old charming self. (For that matter, his old self had been very uncharming for quite some time now.)

Tom said nothing as he stood near Pirrone. Tom was probably waiting for some signal from him but Pirrone's spirit seemed to have sunk with the boat.

Suddenly Pirrone was infused with new life. "Tom, remember that old army half-track!"

"Yeah." Tom looked more cheerful already.

"I know how we can have some fun. Let's get that baby moving. Those old cars up there need to be moved and the half-track can knock over standing trees. Why not try a few cars."

"Great!" Tom agreed.

They started up to get it and Brian, just like a child finding a new toy, seemed excited as he followed them.

I asked Erica why he was going. "Men are just boys at heart. Brian is just like the rest when it comes to adventure," she said.

As he left, Pirrone ordered us to break out some Pernod so they could celebrate when they got back. We stood there for a minute waiting, then curiosity got the better of us and we followed them. I guess we were just little girls at heart; we wanted to see what was going on.

We watched as they dug the half-track out from under the debris that covered it. Pirrone stood on the hood, sweeping off some of the accumulated leaves and dirt. As we watched, the sun slid into the silent sea far below as if to cool its blast-furnace red-orange heat.

With the help of the battery they took out of Tom's car, which he had brought up there, the engine finally turned over. They told us to come aboard. I guess we had reverted back to childhood, too, because we wanted to join in the fun, even though it was with those two terrible villains. Erica and I clambered over the side of the vehicle and were soon riding toward the top of the property. The black velvet curtain of night was already falling from the proscenium arch of the sky—a backdrop for the dark drama to follow.

Pirrone pushed over the only two lemon trees on the place. Not bothering to open a pair of gates to the enclosure around the old cars, he just drove through them. Brian seemed impressed. As the first car crumpled in our path, I could not feel a thing because the half-track weighed, as Brian informed us, twenty-two thousand pounds and was made of quarter-inch steel armor plate. We pushed three or four cars into smashed scrap metal with horrible clankings and clashings, sounds that could have come from the machine shop of a fiendish sculptor stamping out a metal happening.

The truck roared on while Pirrone tried to destroy everything. He drove on and on, scarring trees and damaging anything in his way. It seemed as though the engine and the crunching tracks were unstoppable. Pirrone was like some possessed madman. He seemed to have become an integral part of the violence. Inseparable from it, he was the personification of witless abandonment.

Pirrone pushed one of the crushed cars, now only about a foot tall, across the road, so that it would look as if it had been in a terrible wreck. "The cops will wonder what kind of accident that was," he shouted, delighted at the thought of throwing an unsolvable case to the police.

Brian, now entirely in the spirit of this mindless adventure, exclaimed, "And they'll really wonder what happened to the other car and how it got away."

"Or," Tom added, "what kind of car it was that could do this much damage."

And even I had fallen into the mad fun, for I yelled, "And what about the people?" But no one seemed to care.

As we drove over a once elegant old limousine, the glass shattered and the steel crunched beneath us. Tom looked back at the squashed heap and said, "Do you think it's dead?"

Pirrone stood up to see the wreck, "I think we kilt it." He was being gay, but he looked insane.

At first I had thought our ride in this crashing monster was fun. There was an awful fascination in driving over something as substantial as an automobile and watching it break apart. But soon the reality of shoving around that deformed material became too horrifying. I wanted to jump off the half-track and run away, yet I was transfixed like a person watching a disastrous fire. Brian's hands were bleeding from handling the cable and Pirrone's eyes had an inhuman look, at that moment I was totally convinced he was the incarnation of an underworld deity.

Finally one of the tracks got stuck on a car and the big truck would no longer move. That seemed to be the end, since no one made the effort to free it. Drained of emotion, we silently made our way back to the house as though returning from a war, the blurred shapes of the scattered wreckage, lit by the young moon, made the hillside look like a battlefield. The wild violence had worked its awful therapy—an instant catharsis of all our assorted feelings of loss.

Back in the living room we were all prostrated but after a couple (or more for some) of glasses of Pernod we became silly and lightheaded. Pirrone, once more his urbane self, looked back humorously at the wild episode. "What kind of accident causes a car to be less than twelve inches high?"

Tom solved the riddle, laughing, "A twenty-two thousand-pound half-track." Then Tom said, "Seriously, Pirrone, how did you manage to get the *Calypso* to sink?"

Pirrone was indignant that Tom thought he had anything to do with the sinking. "The hell you say, it was an act of God!" I thought that was a funny thing for a devil to say, but I believed him in a way. Even though Pirrone had planned to do some pretty terrible things, I could tell by his tone that sinking the boat was one thing he had not planned.

Brian spoke up, "Well, then God must have been in the reef when you scraped it. I am certain that the *Calypso* was gashed by that encounter."

Pirrone was even more indignant. "What reef? I didn't hit the damn reef."

Brian did not reply. I am sure he knew there was only one side to an argument with Pirrone. Brian gave a look of who-the-hell-cares, as if it were good riddance to that boat, which had been, one might say, a ship of fools.

I wondered though, as we sat there drinking, what Erica, Brian, and I were doing socializing with these two awful, no-good creeps. However, I guess there was nothing else we could do until we solved the problem of how to cover up for the missing heroin, unless the three of us rode off into the night on Brian's motorcycle. But once they discovered what we had done they would be after us in hot pursuit.

Finally, exhausted after the long eventful day, we all went off to bed, Tom and I to separate rooms. I told Tom I did not want to be with him ever again. But he didn't seem to believe me, saying, "You'll feel better in the morning."

The next morning Tom and Pirrone went off to view the sunken boat and to decide what to tell the insurance company. As he left, Pirrone, still the captain whether by land or by sea, gave us an order. "You guys get off your asses and haul those fruit crates up to the garage. Tom and I are taking them to the dump when we get back." We knew, of course, that was not their destination.

The deadline was upon us and we still had not figured out what to do to get us out of trouble. Then, born of the pressure of impending doom, the solution came to me. We could say we had saved them the bother of going to the dump because we had burned the crates in the fireplaces. A super idea, because with the utilities turned off we were freezingly cold and thus we had good reason for the fires. I said we had better get out of Pirrone's way in a hurry when he found out what we had done; his anger would be beyond belief.

Erica and I started filling the fireplaces with the pieces of the pine boxes Brian was breaking up. We put lots of newspapers under the wood to get it burning fast, as well as anything else we could find like cardboard cartons and branches that had fallen off trees. We were not careful how we laid the fires; we just threw everything in any old way. Soon we had roaring blazes snapping and crackling, shooting out embers with flames not only racing up the chimneys but licking at the edges of the mantles as well. We had not taken the time to replace the fire screens in front of our badly built fires; nor did we even bother to take the pokers and push back the pieces that popped out.

Feeling very smug, we settled down in the living room to enjoy the cozy warmth that emanated from the glowing hearth. We were ready to make our hasty exit as soon as Pirrone learned the fate of his crates, supposedly still lined with heroin. We knew that at that moment we had to flee the scene instantly, for our lives would be in imminent danger. He would probably kill us all in a screaming rage.

Very shortly, Pirrone and Tom walked in. The three of us jumped up and rushed toward them at the door as if to greet them. Pirrone remarked, "This is nice. I'm glad you thought of making a fire. This place was freezing. Where did you find the wood?"

Brian and Erica had already edged out the door as I said, "Oh, we couldn't find any, then we had a great idea. We decided to burn those old crates. Now you don't have to take them to the dump."

A look of terror seized Pirrone as he rushed to the fireplace, tearing out pieces of burning wood, with Tom right behind him ready to help. I slipped out the door, not waiting to see any more.

Brian had parked his motorcycle right outside for our speedy departure. Like the Three Musketeers, we took off on a wild ride, going south down the Coast Highway. We didn't stop until we came to a small inn set back from the highway, tucked in a grove of tall trees. We checked into rooms there, to hole up until we could decide what our next plan of action would be, waiting for the coast to be clear—in more ways than one. Brian parked his motorcycle deep in the trees where it was well hidden, even though we thought it unlikely that anyone would be looking for us in this out-of-the-way place.

When it was very dark, Brian poked his head outside. After looking around he spotted a bar partially connected to the inn. He asked us, "Do you think we dare venture over there and have a little drink?"

Erica answered, "Why not? I wouldn't think anyone would be looking for us here. Anyway, why would anyone be looking for us at all, unless it was for revenge? As far as Tom and Pirrone know, we wouldn't have the heroin. They would just think it went up in smoke with the containers. And of course, they are probably trying to escape from Joe Viscantino or his henchmen themselves. They are the targets, not us."

I said, "Erica, you are as logical as ever. But I still think if we were found, we would be in danger just because of what we have done to their precious heroin."

In spite of my fears, our hunger and thirst won over and we went to the little bar. The few people there were local to the immediate area. They were discussing the big fire near El Mirador. We asked, almost in unison, "What fire?" sensing immediately that we must have started a conflagration with our cozy, hastily built fireplace-fires. That was only a short time ago. Bad news travels very fast indeed, although it was more like good news for us.

One of the people at the bar spoke up, "Yeah, that old Spanish adobe ranch house on that big estate near El Mirador went up in flames a few hours ago. There is a county rural fire department near here. By the time they got there it was a smoldering ruin. They thought the people who lived there were away. I guess there is going to be an investigation about how it started. Arson maybe, who knows. It's rather strange that it would just burn down with no one there."

That didn't really solve our problem. Where were Tom and Pirrone? Were they out looking for us? What about Joe? He must have heard about the fire already. We drank our drinks silently, not daring to discuss the fire in public. Erica said, "I think we ought to go wash up before we eat." Brian and I both agreed. We needed to get back to our rooms to decide what we should do.

The next morning Brian went out to get a newspaper. The fire was big news in the local paper. The article stated that an investigation was under way. But the really upsetting part was contained in a couple of sentences. One badly charred body was found near one of the chimneys; near another, a man's diamond ring plus a stainless steel watch were found. Everything else had been completely consumed. All that was standing were the chimneys.

The body had to be Tom. I had terribly mixed feelings. Poor Tom. He was really good at heart. He had just been badly corrupted by that evil Pirrone. (Of course, I too, had been corrupted, as had everyone who was enmeshed by his charm.) An intense feeling of loss came over me. I had been so fond of Tom and so close to him. And the jewelry that was found. The article had gone on to say that the back of the watch was inscribed, "Pirrone love Liz." (Which sounded as if Liz had ordered him to love her when she gave him the watch—which he never did. But I guess it was shorthand for "To Pirrone with love from Liz.") Pirrone must have escaped. He had always worn the ring and the watch. I don't think he ever took them off, even to shower, as the chronometer was waterproof. But Pirrone himself had to have been fireproof, too; where he came from it was necessary to survive. Going back down there he would leave his worldly things behind. I didn't dare voice this to Erica and Brian. They would have just laughed at me. Instead I said, "I guess Pirrone got away."

Brian replied, "I don't know what to think about Pirrone. Maybe his body is there too; they just haven't found it. Or maybe the fire was so hot where he was, he just turned completely into ashes. That's assuming the body they found was Tom. But it does seem as though it must be."

"I can't help but feel sad for them, as terrible as they were. And we will miss them. It was always fun when they were around," Erica added.

I had no such good thoughts for Pirrone. I was once afire with desire for him, and now he had fittingly been consumed by a fire.

But Brian said, "We don't know anything for sure. All we know is that a body was found plus Pirrone's ring and watch. Joe could have killed Pirrone and then put his ring and watch in the ashes to throw the scent away from the murder. We'll just have to wait for more news after they have investigated further—such as positive identification of the body. It might not even be Tom's. It could be that someone went in during the fire to swipe something out of the burning house. Who knows?"

Brian, the brain, I thought, what an apt name, switch the middle letters and they're the same. But he was being too circumspect about this. I thought it was all self-evident. However, Brian prevailed on us to stay where we were until it was certain that the charred body was Tom's and until they either found Pirrone's body or found out what had happened to him.

The news in the paper the next day was that Liz had been located at the Fairmont Hotel in San Francisco. She said she knew nothing about the whereabouts of her husband. She stated she was afraid he must have perished in the fire. But the article went on to say no other remains had been found in the ashes except for those of Thomas Rhodes, formerly of Los Angeles. It seemed that this fact had been determined for certain.

We all gave a cheer that Liz was safe and had not been done away with by the gangsters. And I thought, the curse of Dañada would now be broken with the demise of the house along with the end of Satan's agent, Pirrone, who was part and parcel of the curse. Liz would finally be free.

Brian said, "Good riddance to that awful Pirrone. He even gave sex a bad name."

Erica said, "But poor Tom, he was really a good egg. Too bad he hooked up with such an evil character as Pirrone. Alice, we should have a farewell ceremony for Tom."

"Yes," I said, "I feel terrible for him and for me, too. He meant a lot to me. He really was a sweet guy at heart. Let's light some candles for him and wish him well on his next journey somewhere out there."

Brian went to the inn office and managed to get a couple of candles from the manager. We lit them and said our goodbyes and prayers for a good afterlife for him.

Brain came up with a daring plan. Since Tom was definitely gone, he would hitch a ride up to El Mirador and get Tom's car. Then we could drive to Los Angeles immediately. He would risk running into Joe Viscantino or one of his henchmen but that did seem unlikely. Besides, there was no reason for Joe to know that we had disposed of the heroin, and even if he did know, killing Brian wouldn't achieve anything.

After a few tries Brian managed a connection with a beer truck driver who was going up the coast to Monterey. Erica and I waited nervously, hoping he would not be stopped by a gangster or an authority or be thwarted in some way or other.

After several hours Brian arrived back at our lodging. He had seen no one but he told us that it was very depressing to see the dreadful fire-ravaged remains of Dañada that once had been such an enchanting structure.

We left immediately for Los Angeles, driving in silence, each absorbed in our private thoughts of loss. As Brian drove Erica and me back to our beginnings, the thought occurred to me that we all had been living on the edge —literally on the edge of the mountain, of course, but also figuratively as we pushed beyond society's limits, some of us going all the way over the edge.

Above Tom's topless car the tall trees flew by, reminding me of my first trip to Dañada, when I had felt exhilarated as my inhibitions started to blow away in the wind I caught in my hands. Now all I felt was emptiness, a caved-in feeling like being in a void. Yet along with it was a yearning for the excitement and lovely indolence that had been Dañada. But the pleasure dome had vanished—if in fact it had ever existed, for wandering through my thoughts was a sense that the last few months had been a time out of my mind, as if it had all been one of my fantasies. Then, putting my hand in my jacket pocket, I felt something roundish and hard. I pulled it out. The tiny, loose diamond Liz had given me lay glittering in my hand.